W9-BTO-005

PRAISE FOR CAROLYN BROWN

Miss Janie's Girls

"[A] heartfelt tale of familial love and self-acceptance."

—*Publishers Weekly*

"Nobody does characters like Carolyn Brown! Her characters are a little eccentric, unique, and always filled with warmth and love."

—Goodreads review

The Banty House

"Brown throws together a colorful cast of characters to excellent effect and maximum charm in this small-town contemporary romance . . . this first-rate romance will delight readers young and old."

—*Publishers Weekly*

"Mrs. Brown's descriptions of the town and all her characters put you right there as the proverbial 'fly on the wall.' These sisters are more fun than *The Golden Girls*!"

—Amazon review

The Family Journal

HOLT MEDALLION FINALIST

"Brown takes a snapshot of the heart at its most vulnerable and then puts it in our hands for safekeeping. *The Family Journal* dares to expose every emotion we're too afraid to face but determined to conquer anyway."

—Amazon review

"Reading a Carolyn Brown book is like coming home again."

—*Harlequin Junkie* (top pick)

The Empty Nesters

"A delightful journey of hope and healing."

—*Woman's World*

"The story is full of emotion . . . and the joy of friendship and family. Carolyn Brown is known for her strong, loving characters, and this book is full of them."

—*Harlequin Junkie*

"Carolyn Brown takes us back to small-town Texas with a story about women, friendships, love, loss, and hope for the future."

—*Storeybook Reviews*

"Ms. Brown has fast become one of my favorite authors!"

—*Romance Junkies*

"A road trip full of laughs, tears, and deep friendships that prove that heart is truly what makes a family."

—*Em and M Books*

"Carolyn Brown delivers another heaping dose of comfort reading with her latest book . . . all about supportive friendships and overcoming grief and loss. Girl power for the win!"

—*Rainy Day Ramblings*

"Sometimes if you are lucky, you pick up a book at just the right time in your life that every emotion written by the author resonates and you cannot put it down. *The Empty Nesters* by Carolyn Brown is that book for me."

—Goodreads review

The Perfect Dress

"Fans of Brown will swoon for this sweet contemporary, which skillfully pairs a shy small-town bridal shop owner and a softhearted car dealership owner . . . The expected but welcomed happily ever after for all involved will make readers of all ages sigh with satisfaction."

—*Publishers Weekly*

"Carolyn Brown writes the best comfort-for-the-soul, heartwarming stories, and she never disappoints . . . You won't go wrong with *The Perfect Dress!*"

—*Harlequin Junkie*

The Magnolia Inn

"The author does a first-rate job of depicting the devastating stages of grief, provides a simple but appealing plot with a sympathetic hero and heroine and a cast of lovable supporting characters, and wraps it all up with a happily ever after to cheer for."

—*Publishers Weekly*

"*The Magnolia Inn* by Carolyn Brown is a feel-good story about friendship, fighting your demons, and finding love, and maybe, just a little bit of magic."

—*Harlequin Junkie*

"Chock-full of Carolyn Brown's signature country charm, *The Magnolia Inn* is a sweet and heartwarming story of two people trying to make the most of their lives, even when they have no idea what exactly is at stake."

—Fresh Fiction

Small Town Rumors

"Carolyn Brown is a master at writing warm, complex characters who find their way into your heart."

—*Harlequin Junkie*

"Carolyn Brown's *Small Town Rumors* takes that hotbed and with it spins a delightful tale of starting over, coming into your own, and living your life, out loud and unafraid."

—*Words We Love By*

"*Small Town Rumors* by Carolyn Brown is a contemporary romance perfect for a summer read in the shade of a big old tree with a glass of lemonade or sweet tea. It is a sweet romance with wonderful characters and a small-town setting."

—*Avonna Loves Genres*

The Sometimes Sisters

"Carolyn Brown continues her streak of winning, heartfelt novels with *The Sometimes Sisters*, a story of estranged sisters and frustrated romance."

—*All About Romance*

"This is an amazing feel-good story that will make you wish you were a part of this amazing family."

—*Harlequin Junkie* (top pick)

"*The Sometimes Sisters* is a delightful and touching story that explores the bonds of family. I loved the characters, the story lines, and the focus on the importance of familial bonds, whether they be blood relations or those you choose with your heart."

—*Rainy Day Ramblings*

The Strawberry Hearts Diner

"Sweet and satisfying romance from the Queen of Texas Romance."
—Fresh Fiction

"A heartwarming cast of characters brings laughter and tears to the mix, and readers will find themselves rooting for more than one romance on the menu. From the first page to the last, Brown perfectly captures the mood as well as the atmosphere and creates a charming story that appeals to a wide range of readers."

—*RT Book Reviews*

"A sweet romance surrounded by wonderful, caring characters."

—*TBQ's Book Palace*

"Deeply satisfying contemporary small-town western story . . ."

—*Delighted Reader*

The Barefoot Summer

"Prolific romance author Brown shows she can also write women's fiction in this charming story, which uses humor and vivid characters to show the value of building an unconventional chosen family."

—*Publishers Weekly*

"This story takes you and carries you along for a wonderful ride full of laughter, tears, and three amazing HEAs. I feel like these characters are not just people in a book, but they are truly family, and I feel so invested in their journey. Another amazing HIT for Carolyn Brown."

—*Harlequin Junkie* (top pick)

The Lullaby Sky

"I really loved and enjoyed this story. Definitely a good comfort read, when you're in a reading funk or just don't know what to read. The secondary characters bring much love and laughter into this book. Your cheeks will definitely hurt from smiling so hard while reading. Carolyn is one of my favorite authors. I know that without a doubt no matter what book of hers I read, I can just get lost in it and know it will be a good story. Better than the last. Can't wait to read more from her."

—*The Bookworm's Obsession*

The Lilac Bouquet

"Brown pulls readers along for an enjoyable ride. It's impossible not to be touched by Brown's protagonists, particularly Seth, and a cast of strong supporting characters underpins the charming tale."

—*Publishers Weekly*

"If a reader is looking for a book more geared toward family and long-held secrets, this would be a good fit."

—*RT Book Reviews*

"Carolyn Brown absolutely blew me away with this epically beautiful story. I cried, I giggled, I sobbed, and I guffawed; this book had it all. I've come to expect great things from this author, and she more than lived up to anything I could have hoped for. Emmy Jo Massey and her great-granny Tandy are absolute masterpieces not because they are perfect but because they are perfectly painted. They are so alive, so full of flaws and spunk and determination. I cannot recommend this book highly enough."

—*Night Owl Reviews* (5 stars and top pick)

The Wedding Pearls

"*The Wedding Pearls* by Carolyn Brown is an amazing story about family, life, love, and finding out who you are and where you came from. This book is a lot like *The Golden Girls* meets *Thelma and Louise*."

—*Harlequin Junkie*

"*The Wedding Pearls* is an absolute must read. I cannot recommend this one enough. Grab a copy for yourself, and one for a best friend or even your mother or both. This is a book that you need to read. It will make you laugh and cry. It is so sweet and wonderful and packed full of humor. I hope that when I grow up, I can be just like Ivy and Frankie."

—*Rainy Day Ramblings*

The Yellow Rose Beauty Shop

"*The Yellow Rose Beauty Shop* was hilarious, and so much fun to read. But sweet romances, strong female friendships, and family bonds make this more than just a humorous read."

—*The Readers Den*

"If you like books about small towns and how the people's lives intertwine, you will *love* this book. I think it's probably my favorite book this year. The relationships of the three main characters, girls who have grown up together, will make you feel like you just pulled up a chair in their beauty shop with a bunch of old friends. As you meet the other people in the town, you will wish you could move there. There are some genuine laugh-out-loud moments and then more that will just make you smile. These are real people, not the oh-so-thin-and-so-very-rich that are often the main characters in novels. This book will warm your heart and you'll remember it after you finish the last page. That's the highest praise I can give a book."

—Reader quote

Long, Hot Texas Summer

"This is one of those lighthearted, feel-good, make-me-happy kind of stories. But, at the same time, the essence of this story is family and love with a big ole dose of laughter and country living thrown in the mix. This is the first installment in what promises to be another fascinating series from Brown. Find a comfortable chair, sit back, and relax, because once you start reading *Long, Hot Texas Summer*, you won't be able to put it down. This is a super fun and sassy romance."

—*Thoughts in Progress*

Daisies in the Canyon

"I just loved the symbolism in *Daisies in the Canyon*. As I mentioned before, Carolyn Brown has a way with character development, with few if any contemporaries. I am sure there are more stories to tell in this series. Brown just touched the surface first with *Long, Hot Texas Summer* and is now continuing on with *Daisies in the Canyon*."

—Fresh Fiction

the Daydream Cabin

ALSO BY CAROLYN BROWN

CONTEMPORARY ROMANCES

Miss Janie's Girls
The Banty House
The Family Journal
The Empty Nesters
The Perfect Dress
The Magnolia Inn
Small Town Rumors
The Sometimes Sisters
The Strawberry Hearts Diner
The Lilac Bouquet
The Barefoot Summer
The Lullaby Sky
The Wedding Pearls
The Yellow Rose Beauty Shop
The Ladies' Room
Hidden Secrets
Long, Hot Texas Summer
Daisies in the Canyon
Trouble in Paradise

CONTEMPORARY SERIES

THE BROKEN ROAD SERIES

To Trust
To Commit
To Believe
To Dream
To Hope

THREE MAGIC WORDS TRILOGY

A Forever Thing
In Shining Whatever
Life After Wife

HISTORICAL ROMANCE

THE BLACK SWAN TRILOGY

Pushin' Up Daisies
From Thin Air
Come High Water

THE DRIFTERS AND DREAMERS TRILOGY

Morning Glory
Sweet Tilly
Evening Star

THE LOVE'S VALLEY SERIES

Choices
Absolution
Chances
Redemption
Promises

3 1526 05472933 7

the Daydream Cabin

CAROLYN BROWN

 Montlake

This is a work of fiction. Names, characters, organizations, places, events, and incidents are either products of the author's imagination or are used fictitiously.

Text copyright © 2020 by Carolyn Brown
All rights reserved.

No part of this book may be reproduced, or stored in a retrieval system, or transmitted in any form or by any means, electronic, mechanical, photocopying, recording, or otherwise, without express written permission of the publisher.

Published by Montlake, Seattle

www.apub.com

Amazon, the Amazon logo, and Montlake are trademarks of Amazon.com, Inc., or its affiliates.

ISBN-13: 9781542025584
ISBN-10: 1542025583

Cover design by Laura Klynstra

Printed in the United States of America

To my son, Lemar Brown,
with much love for all your support!

Chapter One

S ome school years were just flat-out tougher than others.

"And this is one of them," Jayden said to herself as she dropped her briefcase and tote bag inside her apartment door, laid her cell phone on the end table, and collapsed on the sofa. She threw a hand over her eyes to block the afternoon sun and dozed off for a well-deserved nap.

She was awakened a few minutes later to her phone ringing right by her ear. Vowing that she might shoot whoever was on the other end, she answered it on the third ring without even checking to see who was calling. If it was a telemarketer, their earwax was about to boil.

"Hello," she groaned.

"Hello, this is Mary Wilson from the Piney Wood Academy in Alpine, Texas," a soft voice on the other end said.

Jayden held the phone out from her ear. Her finger was on the way to hit the end button when she remembered that place was where her sister, Skyler, had worked the past couple of years as a counselor for girls who were on probation. She put the phone back to her ear and sat up straight.

"Is this about Skyler?" she asked.

"Yes, in a way, I suppose it is," Mary answered.

"Is she sick?" Jayden hadn't talked to her sister since Christmas. They'd exchanged small gifts and had a lunch together like always, and she hadn't thought she would even hear from Skyler until the next year.

"No, but she was supposed to be here at the end of this week, and she offered your name as an alternative counselor. Our summer session starts next Monday, June first, and she called this morning to say that she was going to Europe with her school's music group," Mary said. "We're a pretty small outfit, so we always ask our team if they know anyone else who might work. We are hoping that you might consider filling in for her this summer."

Wasn't that just like her sister to put her down as next of kin and as a person who would take her place without even asking if it was all right? Jayden shouldn't be surprised. After all, Skyler was the queen of the Bennett family, and Jayden was barely worthy to wipe the mud from her shoes.

"How soon would you have to know?" Jayden wasn't sure where the words came from. She had thought to respectfully decline the offer from the second the woman told her about it.

"The sooner the better. We'd need to do a little vetting for the county beyond the clearance you get for a school, so we'll get started. We pay well and give you room and board for eight weeks. Of course, you will share a cabin with three girls, but it doesn't cost you a dime." Mary gave her an amount.

She was stunned speechless. So that was why Skyler worked at the camp in the summer—not because she was helping the girls who needed her counseling but for the money. And that was why she could afford so many fancy clothes and shoes. "Can I think about it until tomorrow, and would you email me some material to study about the camp?"

"I'll be glad to do that, along with the contract, your responsibilities if you take the job, and our website link," Mary answered. "I'll be looking forward to your call."

"Yes, ma'am, and thanks for the offer," Jayden said. "Bye, now."

"Have a great day," Mary said.

The call ended and Jayden fell back on the sofa again, but this time wide awake and ready to strangle her petite, beautiful sister. She jumped up and paced around her small living room floor. At her height and with her long stride, she could make the round in a short time.

And you thought nothing Skyler did could ever surprise you, the pesky voice in her head said, and it was so right.

Skyler had been three years old when Jayden was born, and from day one, she figured her younger sister had come into the world to wait on her. And that was pretty much exactly what Jayden did—most of the time to keep peace in the family, because Skyler could be a real stinker when she didn't get her way.

Go get my shoes. Get out of my room. Don't touch my makeup ever again—you'll never be as pretty as I am. Knock before you come in my door. Don't you say a word to me unless I ask you a question.

All those barbs came back to haunt her as she continued to pace. Why should she do anything so that Skyler could go to Europe for the summer? She stopped dead in her tracks. Skyler *was* going. She must already have tickets.

Jayden was still trying to decide what to do when her doorbell rang.

"Dammit!" she swore as she headed that way. "No rest for the wicked, I guess." She slung the door open to find her sister only a few feet in front of her. Dressed in cute little lace shorty-shorts and a skintight pink tank top with matching wedge-heeled sandals, she smiled at Jayden.

Skyler never wasted smiles. She used those and tears when she wanted something.

"Aren't you going to invite me in?" Skyler's sugar-sweet tone didn't fool Jayden one bit.

"Of course." Jayden stepped to the side. "Come right in. Don't mind the mess. I just finished up my school year and haven't gotten my things put away. Would you like a bottle of water or a beer?"

"Beer is too fattening for me." Skyler let her blue eyes travel from Jayden's toes to the top of her sister's head. "Have you put on a few pounds since Christmas?"

"Maybe," Jayden said. "I don't worry about that. Water, then?"

Skyler brushed the sofa cushion before she sat down. "Nothing for me. I just had a diet soda."

You will not intimidate me. Jayden repeated the phrase half a dozen times as she took a seat on her recliner and popped up the footrest.

"I'm going to Europe with my school's music group," Skyler said.

"When are you leaving?" Jayden decided on the spur of the moment to play dumb.

"Monday morning. It's the opportunity of a lifetime, and I just can't give it up. We plan on seeing the Vatican and traveling through England, France, Germany, and Italy. Our group will be singing in several churches while we're there, and of course I'll be helping them," she said.

In addition to her birdlike figure, Skyler had been blessed with the ability to sing like a bird, too. Jayden could carry a tune, but she had never been as musically inclined as her sister.

"So, are you still a guidance counselor?" Skyler asked, tucking her blonde hair behind her ear.

"Why wouldn't I be? I've been one for ten years," Jayden answered. "And I've lived right here for every one of those years. You've never been here before. Why now?"

"We always saw each other at Mama's house before she died, and . . ." Skyler shrugged. "I have my own life. You have yours. Our circles don't . . ." She hesitated.

Mine doesn't include fancy enough folks for you, Jayden thought.

"We each have our own worlds." Skyler sighed. "I didn't want to ask you to do something for me on the phone. You know that I've been working at the Piney Wood Academy every summer. Well, I kind of signed a contract for this year, and if I don't have a replacement . . ." She let the sentence dangle.

Well, well, well, Mary didn't mention that part, Jayden thought.

"Please," Skyler begged with tears in her eyes. "I've already talked to Henry and Mary, the caretakers of the camp, and they're fine with you stepping into my place. I put you down as an alternative counselor when I took the job. They might already have vetted you and everything. They do that sometimes."

Jayden Bennett was tough as nails, but just like always the tough side of Jayden melted when Skyler turned on the tears.

The pesky little voice inside Jayden's head said that if she did this for her sister, it might go a long way in mending the fences that had been torn down five years ago when their mother died. But she wasn't quite ready to say that she would do it.

For the first time in Jayden's thirty-one years, Skyler wanted something from her. Jayden could make her squirm for a little while, but that wouldn't be right. Gramps always told her to do what she knew was right and not worry about those folks around her who were doing wrong.

"Tell me what I have to do if I agree." Jayden sighed.

"Mary does the cooking, so you'll have three meals a day, and Henry takes care of the grounds. You'll be given the rule booklet when you get there," Skyler answered. "Going to Europe has been a dream of mine forever and this might be my only chance." She pulled a tissue from one of those tiny packages that she always carried in her purse and delicately blew her nose.

Skyler was always ladylike and prepared for anything. If Jayden were to have a crying jag—even a fake one—she'd have to go to the bathroom and blow her nose on a fistful of toilet paper. The walls wouldn't be able to contain the elephantine noise.

"What's the name of this place again? Where is it? And when do I have to show up?" Jayden continued to not know anything at all, and then added, "*If* I decide to do this for you, then I'd like to know a little more than just 'Mary cooks and Henry takes care of the yards.' Did you already tell the people at your school that you would go?"

Skyler squirmed in her place on the sofa just a little. "Well, I had to tell them one way or the other so they could get the plane tickets bought and travel arrangements taken care of."

"And you're waiting until now to ask me to take your place?" Jayden asked. "Why would you do that?"

"What else are you going to do all summer? Lay around and drink that fattening beer?" Like always, Skyler's mean streak came out when she didn't get her way.

"Drinking beer and reading romance novels actually sounds pretty good to me after the semesters I've had. I've had to play catch-up all year for the time we lost last spring with the virus," Jayden told her.

"So have I," Skyler whined. "I *need* this vacation. Glory Bound School has already bought my plane ticket, and they need me to help with the music, as well as be a counselor to the girls on the trip."

"And the boys?" Jayden asked.

"David, the official music teacher, will serve in that place," Skyler answered. "Are you going to do this or not?"

"Tell me more about who I'll be working with if I do." Jayden covered a yawn with her hand.

"Counselors are Novalene Kemper and Diana Jackson. Novalene is a retired school counselor and Diana is still working as one. Then there's Mary and her husband, Henry. The camp itself is located northwest of Alpine, Texas. You don't even have to worry about travel arrangements— just show up at the Grand Prairie Municipal Airport by ten o'clock on Sunday morning. The girls arrive on Monday. Elijah has a little six-person plane, and he'll pick all three counselors up at the same time and fly y'all down there."

"And who is Elijah?" Jayden asked.

"He's kind of like the drill sergeant at the camp. He's a good guy. He was in the air force before he came to work for Henry and Mary," Skyler said. "If you do this for me, sister, I will owe you, big-time."

Skyler must really want to go to Europe with a bunch of kids to pull out the *sister* card and to actually tell Jayden that she would owe her. Jayden wondered if there was more to this trip than her sister was admitting. Was this David fellow her new boyfriend?

"Yes, you will, and I *will* collect," Jayden said. "Tell me again when you are leaving, and when do you plan to be back home?"

"I'm leaving on Monday, and we'll be gone four weeks." Skyler smiled.

"What if I take over until you get back and then you step into my place for the final four weeks?" Jayden asked.

Skyler shook her head and her big blue eyes floated in tears again. "That won't work. The girls in your cabin need to bond with you. You have to go for the whole eight weeks, or I'll have to step down and let someone else go to Europe as a sponsor for the Glory Bound kids." A few more sniffles emerged, and she pulled another tissue from the little container to dab at her eyes. Mustn't ruin the makeup job that took her an hour to do every morning.

"There are only three girls to each cabin—nine in all. They come from wealthy families who can afford to send them to Piney Wood. It's not cheap by any means, but it keeps them out of juvie. You've taught in Dallas schools for years, so I know you can handle them."

A compliment from Skyler. Maybe Jayden should check the sky to see if there was going to be a snowstorm in Dallas, Texas, right there at the end of May.

"Well?" Skyler's one-word question needed an answer.

Jayden popped the footrest down. "Oh, all right. I only need to pack jeans and T-shirts, right?"

Skyler jumped up, crossed the room, and hugged Jayden tightly. "Thank you so much. I really do owe you."

Yes, you do, Jayden thought.

"When you get home in August, we'll have lunch and I'll tell you all about my trip to Europe," Skyler promised.

Jayden wrapped her arms around her petite sister and gave her another hug. There was something so hopeful about hugging Skyler— she knew they could build a relationship—that it almost brought tears to Jayden's eyes. "We could text and send pictures back and forth."

"Probably not." Skyler picked up her purse. "Maybe if the reception is good in Europe, I'll try to send a selfie when I can. Oh, and pack a pair of good walking shoes, but you won't need a hat. They provide a cap for all the girls and the counselors."

"Why would I need good walking shoes?" Jayden followed her sister outside. "Don't the girls go to counseling sessions and have classes?"

"You'll have group therapy scheduled, and they'll do one-on-one therapy once a week with Karen . . ." She drew her brows down. "I can't remember her last name, but she's really good with the girls," she said with her hand on the doorknob. "You'll need the good boots or shoes because you'll be doing some hiking. The cap they issue to you will keep you from getting sunburned and adding more freckles to your nose." Skyler closed the door behind her.

Leave it to Skyler to ruin the moment by reminding Jayden that she wasn't the pretty sister. Jayden stepped out on the landing and watched her sister drive away in a little low-slung sports car. She leaned against the railing and looked down at her green vintage 1958 GMC pickup truck, so very different from Skyler's fancy little car. Jayden had inherited it from her grandfather when she turned sixteen and had driven it for the past fifteen years.

It seemed fitting that each sister was like the vehicle they drove. Skyler was cute and fancy. Jayden was like her truck—sturdy, dependable, and gullible enough to let her sister talk her into giving up her summer to counsel little rich girls whose folks could afford to send them to a fancy boot camp. *But then*, Jayden wondered, *how would Skyler survive without that extra money?* She couldn't imagine her sister gearing down her lifestyle.

"We haven't been all that close since Mama died," Jayden whispered to herself as she went back into her apartment and picked up her purse. "But if there's more going on, you could have been honest with me. But then, I wasn't up-front with you, either."

She locked the door behind her, crossed the lawn, and got into her truck. Before she left for the summer, she had to go visit her mother's grave and talk to her.

She drove through Boyd, where she and Skyler had been raised. Her mother's house had sold two months after she'd died, and Jayden noticed as she drove by that the yard needed mowing, the rosebushes hadn't been trimmed, and one of the shutters was hanging askew. She and her mother, and then her grandfather when he moved in with them, had spent such wonderful hours together, taking care of the yard and flower beds.

"I'm glad y'all can't see this, but why didn't you leave the house to me instead of Skyler? I wouldn't have sold it. I would have taken good care of it." She wiped a tear from her cheek.

From there, she took a farm road back to Hog Branch Cemetery, where her mother had been buried five years before. She parked her truck under a big pecan tree and wandered back to the tombstone marked WANDA SKYLER BENNETT.

"We were so close, Mama." She laid her hand on the top of the tombstone. "Why didn't you give me power of attorney? I would have never pulled the plug and let you die. People have come out of a coma after years of being asleep."

"Mama, Skyler is holding out on me," she tattled as she dropped down on her knees and pulled a few dandelions from the front of the tombstone. "She's talked me into going to some sort of roughin'-it camp and doing her job so she can traipse off to Europe. I know what you're thinkin'. If we'd kill the elephant that's been in the room since you left us, we could get along better. I'll never understand why you put all the power in her hands, and you didn't even tell me about it. We shared everything, and she just came and went sporadically. Since then she's acted even more high and mighty. I'm not going to agree with her about pulling the plug or the way she handled your funeral. She's too self-righteous and full of herself to say I'm right, so the elephant remains."

Jayden pulled a few more dandelion weeds from around the tombstone, went back to her truck, and looked over her shoulder at the grave site. "I'll miss coming by to see you next month, but I'll be back the first of August." She opened the door and slid behind the wheel, shifted into gear, and started home. With midday traffic, the thirty-minute trip back to her apartment took more than an hour.

Jayden had not dipped strongly into her grandfather Jay Denton Grant's gene pool when it came to patience. Gramps had the patience of Job, even with Skyler's tantrums. "Dammit! Do you have to count to twenty after the light turns green?" she fumed when the fifth person in a row took their own good, lazy time moving forward.

You're showing off your Bennett temper, her mother's voice rang clear as a bell in her head.

"If people don't know how to drive, they should keep their butts at home," she argued, "and if a little road rage is all I got from Daddy, that's a good thing."

When she finally got home, she flopped down on the overstuffed sofa. Thank God she didn't have to explain to anyone why she was leaving for eight weeks. She didn't have a boyfriend, not for lack of wanting one. But relationships weren't easy—neither was trust after being right in the middle of her parents' messy divorce. Her mother and grandparents had passed away, and she'd already been to the cemetery to talk to her mother. Her dad was off with wife number two. Skyler had never blamed him for the divorce and had always kept up with him better than Jayden had, which was another bone of contention between them.

"No one cares whether I'm here or not," she muttered. "Just set the thermostat, call an Uber to take me to the airport, and I'm off to live in a cabin with three unruly girls for eight weeks. Skyler, you owe me big-time, and I've got two months to think of a way to make you pay me back."

Chapter Two

E lijah didn't enjoy flying anymore, but sometimes it was necessary. Every time he got into the small plane owned by Piney Wood, he remembered the missions he'd flown in a helicopter during his years in the air force. His eyes misted over at the memory of the three coffins that he and his teammates had accompanied home. His enlistment had been up, and he only needed one more hitch to get his twenty years for retirement. Yet when it came time for him to sign on the dotted line a couple of weeks after all their memorial services, he couldn't force himself to do it, and neither could Buddy, Chuck, or Tim. His friends went home after the funerals, but Elijah had spent a month and a half of his savings right there in San Antonio, trying to figure out what to do with his life.

"I've always been bad luck. Anyone I get really close to dies," he said out loud.

Bullcrap! Uncle Henry's gravelly old voice was clear in his head.

That brought back the day that Uncle Henry had shown up on his monthly rental motel doorstep in San Antonio and told him to pack his bags.

"You're going to work for me, and once you get yourself straightened out, you'll be taking over my job when I retire," he'd said.

"What makes you think I want to work with a bunch of rich, bitchy little girls?" Elijah had asked as he twisted the top off a beer.

"You've got to do something, and you might like it. Taxi is waiting—put that beer down. You'll be flying us home to Alpine. I brought the plane down here, but it's time for you to stop moping around and get on with your life." Uncle Henry had left no room for argument.

Most of the fight had gone out of Elijah by then anyway. He'd shoved what clothing he had into a duffel bag, left the six-pack of beer in the refrigerator, and checked out of the motel. Looking back two years later, he didn't regret his decision. There had definitely been something therapeutic about putting teenage girls back on the right track.

That first time he settled into the little company airplane, he'd sweat buckets. Nausea had come in waves, and he could swear that he smelled the blood of his buddies. Uncle Henry had laid a hand on his shoulder and said, "You can do this, Elijah. Not only can you do it, you need to fly again."

He worried about being close to his aunt and uncle. Would being around him bring them bad luck, like it had his only brother, his parents, and now three of his best friends?

"So far, so good," he muttered. But he wasn't ready to think about any kind of relationship.

He landed his plane and climbed out to stretch his legs. He crossed the tarmac in long, easy strides and opened the door to the office to find his three passengers waiting with their suitcases beside them. Thank God they had only brought one piece of luggage each. His plane wouldn't hold much more than that.

"Mornin', ladies." He nodded toward them.

"Good mornin'," Diana and Novalene said in unison.

The third woman stood up and extended her hand. "I'm Jayden Bennett."

"Elijah Thomas," he said, looking her in the eyes, which his six-foot frame ordinarily prevented. She was almost as tall as Elijah. Her steely blue eyes held his gaze. Brunette hair floated on her shoulders. She sure didn't look like someone who would be trying to help a group of girls work through their problems.

"You're Skyler's sister, right?" he asked.

"That's right." She smiled. "Kind of hard to believe."

"It sure is," Elijah said, "but thank you for taking your sister's place." He let go of her hand and turned to focus on the other counselors. "How'd your school year go, Diana?"

Diana had told him last year she only had about five more years until she could hang up her school cap and retire. The short woman had gray hair and brown eyes. She blamed her gray hair on more than thirty years of working with kids. She could be compassionate with her girls at the camp, but her voice could cut like steel when a girl needed correction.

He noticed that Jayden had sat back down and crossed one long leg over the other. How on earth could that striking woman be Skyler's sister? Skyler was cute after a fashion, but Jayden would make any man turn and take a second glance.

He glanced over at Novalene. "I'm sure glad you didn't retire like you said you were going to do when the session ended last year."

"Retirement ain't all it's cracked up to be." She settled a floppy hat onto her head. "I need some drama in my life." She was around Diana's height, but forty pounds lighter, and she kept her hair dyed stovepipe black. Her blue eyes could bore holes into a misbehaving kid, but by the end of the summer the year before, all three of her charges had cried when they had to say goodbye. "Jayden was just telling us that Skyler is going on a trip to Europe with her students from Glory Bound, but I guess you already knew that."

Elijah nodded. "Yes, I did. Did y'all welcome Jayden to eight of the toughest and most rewarding weeks of her life?"

Jayden stood up again. "They've been telling me all kinds of stories. I can take tough if there's a reward at the end of the line."

"She sure doesn't look anything like Skyler, does she?" Novalene said.

"Nope," Elijah said.

"We get that a lot." Jayden's voice had a lot of gravel in it, like a long-term smoker, but her eyes looked sad at the mention of Skyler's name. "She looks like our mother. I'm tall like my grandmother, and I'm a lot tougher than my sister."

"That's a good thing to be." Elijah chuckled. "I'm going to make a bathroom run, grab a cup of coffee, and then we'll be on our way. It's about an hour and a half to Alpine, so get ready to settle in . . ."

"And listen to some country music, right?" Novalene grinned.

"You got it." Elijah gave her a thumbs-up and disappeared down a hallway.

He gave Jayden a sideways look one more time as he left the room. He hadn't seen a woman who would make him want to throw his own set of camp rules—number one was never get involved with a counselor—in the fire before then, and he sure wished he'd met Jayden in a bar or even a church social instead.

And then what? the annoying voice in his head asked. *So you can bring bad luck into her life?*

He washed his hands and dried them, then went back out to the office to pour himself a cup of what passed for coffee but tasted more like road tar. He took a few sips and then poured the rest down the sink. "Okay, ladies, let's load it up and get on the way. Mary is planning on us being back by lunchtime, and since she's the cook, I try to never make her mad."

Jayden pulled her black suitcase out to the plane and parked it beside a red one and one that looked like it had been dragged through a flower garden. If a person could be judged by their suitcases, Jayden was as solid as a rock. Once everyone was buckled in, he took his place in the pilot's seat.

"So, are you excited about this?" Novalene asked Jayden as Elijah taxied out to the runway.

"Not particularly," Jayden answered as the plane started ascending.

"Then why are you doing it?" Novalene asked.

"Because my sister cried, and because she's always wanted to go to Europe, and if I didn't take her place, that would be just one more thing she'll hold over my head the rest of my life," Jayden replied.

Elijah could hear aggravation in her voice. She and Skyler weren't only different in looks—evidently they didn't get along. He had never cared about the counselors' lives outside of camp, but he found himself wondering about the sisters.

"I can see where she would do that," Diana said. "Skyler could get pretty emotional, but that's the way she controlled her girls. Sometimes tears work better than a tongue-lashing. I didn't even know she had a sister until you showed up. I knew her mama was gone and her father lived back east, but she never mentioned a sibling. Do you have more brothers and sisters?"

The other counselors were good people—that was what Skyler had said. She forgot to mention that they were nosy as well, but Jayden was adept at deflecting questions.

"Just me and Skyler," Jayden answered. "How about you, Diana? Do you have brothers and sisters?"

"Three brothers," Diana replied.

Novalene chimed in about her siblings without being asked, and soon both of the other ladies were telling family stories. Jayden listened with one ear as she stared out the window. Elijah chuckled, and Jayden wondered if something in the lyrics of one of the songs filling the small plane brought him a good memory. She began to listen, and soon her head was bobbing in time with the music as Travis Tritt sang "It's a Great Day to Be Alive."

"We're coming in for a landing, and sometimes it's a little rough," Elijah yelled back over his shoulder.

Jayden had been so lost in the music and the memories that each song stirred up that she didn't realize they'd been in the air for more than an hour. The landing was rough enough that her head touched the ceiling of the plane at one time, but then they were on the tarmac and coming to a rolling stop. Elijah was the first one out and waited at the bottom of the stairs to help each of the ladies.

Jayden was the last one out of the plane, and when she stepped into the scorching hot day, blistering wind blew her dark hair across her face. She squinted against the blazing sun, but there wasn't much to see between her and the mountains out there in the distance other than yucca plants and cow's tongue cacti. *Holy smokin' hell!* What had she gotten herself into? She fumbled around in her purse for her sunglasses and put them on. That helped a little, but it didn't stop the heat from trying to cook her skin.

Elijah unloaded the suitcases as if each of them weighed less than a bag of marshmallows. His ham-size arms and broad chest stretched the knit shirt that was monogrammed with the PWA logo above his heart.

"Welcome to Alpine," a deep voice said to her left. "I'm Henry, and this is my wife, Mary. You sure don't look like Skyler's sister." A short man in bib overalls and a bright-green T-shirt with PWA embroidered on the sleeve, Henry was tanned to a light brown with dark-brown eyes and a big smile. He turned his green cap around backward over his ring of gray hair and hurried over to help Elijah unload the baggage.

Not looking like Skyler was something that dug deep into Jayden's heart. One pretty sister, one plain one was the message that she got every time.

"I'm Mary." A lady even shorter than Henry stepped away from the other two women. "I'm right glad you are here with us. Your principal

16

at the Dallas school spoke highly of you, and I'm sure you're going to fit right in with all of us."

"Thank you," Jayden said. "I'll do my best, but I'm very different from my sister."

"That might be a good thing in some ways." Novalene looped her arm through Jayden's and pulled her toward the white van waiting a few feet away. "Not to say ill of someone who isn't here, or your sister, for sure, but sometimes Skyler's heart was too soft for this job."

Skyler with a soft heart? These women didn't know Jayden's sister at all.

Chapter Three

*H*enry loaded all the luggage into an old van whose air-conditioning worked just fine. He drove north from the small airport for a few miles, then turned down a dirt road toward the mountains. "We'll be home pretty soon. The camp is only a few miles from here. Mary's done got dinner all planned out for y'all, and like always, we'll go over the rule book. It'll be a refresher course for you two," he told Diana and Novalene, "but Jayden will need to know how we run things. We've got two girls with shoplifting problems and one who's had three DUIs that I'm going to put in Daydream Cabin. Novalene, you'll get the ones with drug issues, and Diana is going to take care of the girls who have struggled with physical violence this time around."

Jayden had dealt with all the above in her counseling job, but she wasn't arguing with Henry. If they wanted her to take on shoplifting and driving under the influence, she wouldn't complain.

"Sounds fair to me," Novalene said.

"Between y'all and us, we're hoping to turn these girls' lives around. Once a week Karen Daily will come in from town and have a one-on-one session with each of them. She's our certified therapist, Jayden, and has done wonders with the girls in the past. She'll be giving y'all guidance on how to handle your group sessions. You'll have those with your girls an hour each day, as usual," Mary said.

Skyler must have had contact with Karen if the woman visited with her girls every single week, so she should have remembered her last name, but then that was her sister—if it didn't pertain to her, then it couldn't be important.

Mary and Novalene chatted in the seat right behind Henry. Diana joined in from across the aisle. Elijah and Jayden each had a seat to themselves with the aisle separating them. He didn't seem interested in talking, so she just kept silent and watched the van kick up a dust storm on the dirt road. Every now and then she chanced a sideways look at Elijah and wondered what his story was, how old he might be, and why he'd chosen to work in a camp like this.

The farther Henry drove, the more her heart dropped. She hadn't known what to expect, but as they passed occasional trailer houses and adobe or stucco dwellings in the desolate beauty, she figured she wouldn't be finding a cute little cabin with lace curtains in the windows at the end of the journey.

The whole place was so very different from the small farm her grandfather had, and even the landscape around Boyd, Texas, where she grew up. In those places the grass was green, and from spring until midsummer folks would be out mowing at least once a week. Here, she recognized several varieties of cacti putting on a show with their yellow and purple flowers. Yucca plants had huge white blooms standing straight and tall, and wild daisies dotted the flat countryside with spots of yellow. She wouldn't want to give up her green grass, but this place was beautiful in its own right.

Henry drove through a gap between two mountains, and she noticed a slight change. There were more orange and red flowers that looked like they'd been stuck down in cactus plants to make the plants less ugly.

She saw a lone cactus towering above the others. *It stands out in this country, kind of like I do in a crowd.*

Henry made a left-hand turn, crossed a cattle guard with a sign above it that read PINEY WOOD ACADEMY, and headed down a long lane toward a cluster of buildings, most of which were the same color as the earth, speckled only by the brightly colored Adirondack chairs on the porches of a few. The front of each of the three cabins was covered with clapboard siding. The other three sides were stucco like everything else, other than a big red barn out in the distance. The cabins didn't have lace curtains, but they did look a little more inviting than the other places around the compound.

"We're home," Henry announced as he parked the van. "We'll unload y'all's stuff after we have something to eat and visit a little."

Elijah and Jayden were the last ones out of the van. Everyone else hurried inside, probably to get out of the heat, but Jayden took a moment to look around at all the various buildings. Each one had a sign hanging between two of its porch posts, and the noise of them swinging back and forth reminded her of the squeaky swing on the front porch of the house that Skyler sold.

DINING HALL was written on the stucco building where Elijah had headed. She squinted across the dusty yard at the three brightly colored cabins. She could just make out their names on the swinging signs. The first one read DAYDREAM CABIN and was painted a light green with pretty red chairs on the porch. The second, MOONBEAM CABIN, was pale blue with hot-pink chairs. The third one in the row was SUNSHINE CABIN, appropriately painted yellow with orange chairs. Each cabin had a flower bed full of petunias, lantana, and marigolds.

"You comin' in or are you about to steal the van and go back home?" Elijah had a deep Texas drawl that, evidently, he hadn't gotten away from in the air force.

"The jury is still out," she told him. "But I am hungry, so I think I'll eat before I decide."

The aroma of something spicy wafted out to greet her when Elijah held the door open. "Mary's cookin' makes all the work worthwhile."

"Something sure smells good. What else is on the agenda?" she asked.

"We'll go over that in the briefing," he answered.

"Is this the only one of these eight-week classes you have a year?" she asked as she entered the building. A buffet bar divided the room in half—kitchen to the left, dining area on the right. The walls were painted seafoam green. Three tables' name cards were already arranged on them. A fourth table for six was set a few feet away.

"Nope," Elijah answered. "We have four a year. One during each season, but the summer one is the only one when the girls don't actually have school classes in addition to everything else. During the other three, they have to keep up with their schoolwork as well as get their lives back on track."

"So, you do these thirty-two weeks out of the year?" She frowned.

Henry was standing right inside the door and evidently had heard her question. "Yes, there's a camp in January and February, one in March and April, and then we close down in May. We reopen for one in June and July, and then close down in August and have one in September and October," he explained. "We don't have anything during November and December. There's just too many holidays during that time. Mary and I are planning a couple of long cruises this year in November and December to celebrate our retirement, and then we're going to settle down in one of those old folks' villages."

"*What?*" Novalene threw a hand over her heart. "You're retiring? Are you going to close down the academy?"

"No, Elijah is taking over," Mary told them. "Don't worry, we're leaving the place in good hands. Now, if Henry will say grace, we will dish up all the fixin's for tacos and enchiladas and have sopaipillas for dessert."

Jayden had been running late that morning, and she hadn't taken time to eat breakfast. Besides, she hadn't wanted to leave dirty dishes in the sink or take the time to wash them. Now it was noon, and she didn't have a bashful bone in her body. As soon as Henry finished saying grace, she was the first in the buffet line. She loaded up her plate with rice, beans, and enchiladas, and then poured herself a glass of sweet tea.

"Why are the cabins so bright, and everything else kind of dull looking?" she asked Mary when she reached the end of the line.

"These girls need to learn how to behave, but they also need a bright spot in their lives. Once they get here, they'll be given jobs, a schedule, and a regimen that they'll hate, but they'll like going home to their cabins, to that one bright spot, at the end of every day. Henry has been working hard to make the flowers grow, but tomorrow the girls will take over. Their flower beds will become a matter of pride for them. We hope their other jobs will, too. The girls tend to get competitive in their jobs after they get settled in. None of them will want to listen to the girls in the other cabins razz them if they can't even grow a petunia," Mary answered, following behind her.

"We are a private camp, and their parents' money will buy them eight weeks here, but it is their last chance before juvenile detention. For most of them, it's their third strike at anything from car theft to shoplifting, drug problems, abuse issues, hot checks, cyberbullying, driving under the influence, or anything else you can name short of murder. We do our best to put them on the right track in the eight weeks they are here, through schedule, physical training, discipline, and counseling. They hate us at first, but by the end of their time, we usually turn out a batch of happier, healthier girls. We don't depend on state financing, but we do have guidelines."

"How long have you been doing this?" Jayden sat down.

"Twenty years," Mary answered. "When Henry retired from the army, we wanted to do something to help others. Henry's father left us this property. Back fifty years ago, it was a little hideaway for the snowbirds, but we decided to put it to better use. We could never have children of our own, and Henry had seen the service turn many a young person around. So, we put our heads together and came up with this place."

"Why just girls?" Jayden bit into an enchilada and rolled her eyes. "This is delicious. You should have a restaurant."

Mary laughed down deep in her chest. "Honey, no one would drive out here for tacos, not when they can drive up to a window in just about any town and pick some up. To answer your question, we thought about having camps for boys, too, but we just don't have the time and space. It's really sad how little support some of these girls have gotten with their struggles."

By then everyone had filled their trays and taken places at the table. "In that twenty years, have you ever had less than a full house?" Jayden asked between bites.

"Nope," Elijah answered for Mary. "We're a pretty exclusive private camp, and our success record is well known. Therapists and judges alike recommend us."

Novalene joined in the conversation. "These girls know when they get here that this isn't a party."

"If they don't, it doesn't take them long to figure it out," Diana added.

"Yep." Mary nodded. "It's tougher on the ones who think that they're coming to a summer camp to lay out in the sun and work on their tans."

Henry passed out booklets from the end of the table. "They change every year according to state regulations, so y'all will all need to go over them."

Jayden opened the small notebook to the first page and almost groaned when she read that every single day, Sunday included, everyone would be up and ready for exercise at five thirty in the morning. If she could have gotten her hands around her sister's throat right then, there would have been one fewer person on that airplane leaving for Europe on Monday. She was used to getting up early and going to the gym, even in the summertime, but not on weekends.

"When your girls arrive, you will give them each a handbook," Henry said. "And then you will take some time to go over the rules with them. Y'all would do well to highlight each and every one of these rules and the disciplinary action that will be taken if they break one of them. We don't take kindly to the I-didn't-know excuse, and you can put money on it that one of them will use it before the first week is out."

"Why would they do that if this is their last chance?" Jayden asked. "Forget I said that. We deal with all kinds of problems in my school, too . . . and just as many excuses for why they did what they did."

"Honey, that's in all schools now," Novalene said. "Family structures and the constantly changing world around us make it tough to navigate. Teachers, and especially us counselors, feel the burden of having to deal with the effect all this has on the kids."

"Amen!" Jayden agreed, and drizzled honey over her sopaipilla.

"Why do you think that is?" Henry asked.

"Because in all the fussin' about what should be done, each of those adults wants their way. They spend more time fighting among themselves about who is right than they do paying attention to the kid," Jayden answered.

When they finished eating, Mary passed around sheets of paper. "These are the specifics on your summer-session girls. Y'all need to know all of them. We'll start with the Daydream Cabin that belongs to Jayden. Tiffany Jordan struggles with bulimia and was caught shoplifting. She also has two priors for cyberbullying—taking pictures of overweight girls and posting them on the internet with hateful messages. Carmella Ruiz has been before the judge three times for shoplifting. Ashlyn Causey was caught for the third time driving while under the influence."

Ashlyn, Tiffany, and Carmella, Jayden repeated the names silently.

"Novalene, you have Moonbeam Cabin as usual, and your girls are Lauren Fielding, who has anger issues combined with drug issues. She's been in rehab more than once. Bailey Morse, who's been caught cooking meth for distribution for the third time. And last is Keelan Johnson, who sells cocaine to her fellow high school students and also to the vo-tech kids she went to classes with there."

Sounds like a Tuesday in my school, Jayden thought.

"Diana, you get Rita Standish. She was beaten so many times by her stepfather that she acted out by trying to burn down the house. Next is Quinley McAdams. She's had assault charges brought against her for fighting with other girls. And last is Violet O'Hare. Her boyfriend got her on drugs and then abused her. She got tired of it and put him in the hospital. He filed assault charges on her."

"Looks like we've all got our work cut out for us," Diana said.

Jayden felt a little better now that she knew what she was dealing with. She enjoyed counseling the kids in her school, and she felt confident that she could be a help to these girls.

These girls will be with you twenty-four hours every day, seven days a week, for two months. You don't get to counsel with them an hour or two and then go home at the end of the day. Her mother's voice was in her head and Jayden couldn't argue with her.

"Dammit!" she muttered under her breath.

"You just realized what you bit off, didn't you?" Novalene asked.

"I'm afraid I did," she said.

Elijah started for the door.

"Where are you going?" Henry asked.

"To get the keys out of the van. We might have a runner," Elijah teased.

Novalene laid a hand on Jayden's shoulder. "I've been doin' this for ten years, honey. You just give them my little speech when they first arrive, and that will set the mood for the whole time."

Jayden was warming up to Novalene. "And what speech is that?"

Novalene pushed back her chair and slowly stood up, squared her shoulders, and narrowed her eyes. Her expression sent chills down Jayden's back. "Listen up, girls, because I only intend to say this once. You may think you are going to drive me up the walls, and you might do just that. Remember this, though. I can only climb up that wall so far"—she turned around and pointed behind her—"and then I'm going to fall, and when I do, it will be right on top of you." She whipped around and pointed her finger right at Jayden.

Elijah chuckled and came back to the table. "That's a pretty good speech."

"It sets the mood very well. We have to be tough at first and lighten up as they earn it." Novalene smiled and sat back down in her chair. "I'm going to go over the book, and then take a nap. Today will be the last time I get to have one for the next eight weeks."

"And now for the crowning glory." Elijah brought out three baseball caps in different colors and explained the reasoning behind each as he passed them out. "Dark blue for Novalene with a moon on the front for the Moonbeam Cabin. Yellow with a bright sun for Diana for the Sunshine Cabin. Clouds on a pink hat for Jayden."

"Why do I get clouds when my cabin is called *Daydream*?" she asked.

"Daydreams are like clouds, ever changing and bringing much-needed rain to the parched earth," Mary answered. "When you read the handbook, you will find that your girls are not allowed to be outside without their caps that go with their cabins. That way we'll be able to locate and know which one belongs to which counselor."

"Amen to that." Jayden crammed the cap down on her head and stood up. "I'm going to help Mary clean up this kitchen and then go unpack and wander around the place so I know where everything is located."

"See you at suppertime," Diana said.

"Thanks for the offer, Jayden, but me and Henry got this," Mary said. "Elijah, you should go show Jayden where everything is located, and you might tell her a little about each place and why we do things the way we do." Mary shooed them out with the flick of her wrist. "Now get going, and help these ladies get their suitcases into their cabins."

"Yes, ma'am." Elijah snapped to attention and saluted.

Mary shook a fork at him. "Don't you go all smart-ass on me. You'll own this place in a few months, but right now I'm still your boss as well as your aunt."

Elijah chuckled and tipped the brim of his cap toward her. "You know I love you, Aunt Mary."

"Aunt Mary?" Jayden asked.

"I claim him most days." She smiled. "When he's being a bad boy, then he's Henry's kin, not mine."

"Henry is my mother's brother," Elijah explained. "Let's get out of here before *Aunt Mary*"—he put emphasis on the last two words—"decides to kick me out and not sell this place to me after all."

"Thanks again for the offer to help clean up, Jayden. I might just take you up on it sometime," Mary said.

"Anytime," Jayden threw over her shoulder as she followed Elijah outside.

Diana and Novalene were halfway across what must be considered a lawn, since it had some sparse green grass on it. But it sure didn't look like the gorgeous lawn her mother and grandfather had kept. Jayden glanced at the Daydream Cabin and sighed as she headed toward the van.

Elijah beat her to it, opened the door, and jerked the keys from the ignition. "Just takin' the necessary precaution. If you run, then I'll have to step in and be the counselor for the Daydream girls, and I don't think it would go over too good to have a man living with them."

"I gave my word, and I never go back on that." She grabbed her suitcase and headed toward her new home. Elijah jogged across the yard and opened the door for her.

"Thank you," she said as she walked into the living room and stopped in her tracks. "The inside is so different from the front of the cabin. Whew!" She wiped sweat from her brow. "It's almost as hot in here as it is outside."

"Yep." Elijah grinned. "We just faced the front with wood siding so it would look a little more inviting. There is a small window air conditioner in the girls' bedroom and in yours, but we advise against using them in the day, because they freeze up so badly in this climate. Save the cool for the night so you can sleep better."

Sweet Jesus! she thought as she parked her suitcase in the middle of the floor and looked around at the stark furnishings. Two worn but soft-looking leather sofas faced each other with a scarred and beat-up coffee table between them. The only inviting thing in the room was a bookcase on the far wall, filled with all kinds of reading material and baskets of craft supplies. She noticed there were no knitting needles or scissors.

"Your room is in here." Elijah opened a door to the right. "The girls will bunk over here." He crossed the room and pointed into another that held a footlocker at the end of each of three cots and a metal rack for clothing beside each one.

"Bathroom?" Jayden asked.

"The bathhouse is out back beside the laundry room," he answered. "I'll show it to you right now."

I hope you have a miserable trip to Europe, Skyler Jane Bennett, she fumed as she followed him out of the cabin. *You could've told me that I'd have to go outside with the lizards and coyotes just to take a shower or use the bathroom.*

"I bet these girls just love this," she muttered as she kept in step with Elijah.

"They hate it, but it's good for them." He stopped at a building with BATHHOUSE painted on the swinging sign above the door. "This is for ladies only. I'll wait for you out here."

"And do you have a bathroom in whatever building you live in?" She crossed her arms over her chest and wished she could cross her legs, but she refused to let him see her do a fancy little bladder dance into the place.

"See that little building beyond the clotheslines? That's my house, and the one on down from there is where Henry and Mary live. We have bathrooms and we also have central heat and air in our places." He grinned.

"Now you're just showing off," she said as she stepped inside the hot building. Maybe they should repaint the sign to say SAUNA AND BATHHOUSE. She counted six showers with plastic curtains and as many toilet stalls, but there were only three sinks, and they did not have mirrors above them. When she finished in one of the stalls, she washed her hands, dried them on a brown paper towel, and went back outside.

Elijah waited with his back against the stucco and arms folded over his chest. Did the man not realize that was a true sign that he was blocking everyone out of his life?

"No mirrors?" She raised an eyebrow. "And I didn't see any in the cabin, either."

"They each have what they need, including a hand mirror in their footlockers," he answered. "We'll walk this way so you can see the stables."

"Horses?" She asked another one-word question.

"Not for riding. We don't even own a saddle. Henry adopted three horses and two donkeys that were going to be sent to the slaughterhouse. Grooming and walking them make for excellent therapy for the girls, plus someone has to muck out the stables daily, so that's another good job." His stride was long, and he walked fast.

She lengthened her step only a little to keep up with him. "My DUI girl can do that. How often does it need done?"

"Every day the horses need exercise. I usually have whoever has that job walk them on the trail out to the half-mile marker and back. Why do you think your DUI girl should take over that job?"

"Seems like a good thing since she's been driving recklessly while drinking. She can see what she'd have to depend on if she lost her license," Jayden replied.

"Sounds reasonable to me." Elijah grinned again. "You're tougher than your sister."

"I do my best." Jayden had worked hard over the years to develop a tough skin and took pride in her resilience. That Elijah noticed put a smile on her face. "Now let's go see these rescued animals."

"We're a working farm. Not only do we have horses and donkeys, we have hogs and chickens, and those ugly critters you see wandering around out there are guineas. They keep the tick population down to a minimum. Mary also has a garden out back of the dining room that provides us with fresh vegetables, and Henry keeps two milk cows and about twenty head of cattle. The girls will learn how to milk, haul hay, and maybe, if we're lucky, we'll even have a calf born out of season so they can experience that," he explained as they walked side by side.

"Oh, I can tell you right now that they're going to love all that," she said. "I haven't had teenagers in my school who think they're entitled. What do I need to expect?"

"Kids are kids whether they have money or not," he answered. "Like we said before, this is a private boot camp, not a state-run one. We do have an agreement with the state through the judges that lets the parents send their girls here. If the girls get three demerits, we can take them to the jail in Alpine and they will go to juvie or back home to visit with the judge who sent them here. Most of the time they hate everything about the camp at first, but by the end of their stay, they hate to leave."

Chapter Four

"Thank God I listened to Henry when he showed up at my motel room," Elijah said to his reflection in the bathroom mirror after he'd shaved and splashed lotion on his face.

He'd thought Henry was downright crazy that summer day two years ago when he'd shown up in San Antonio and told him—didn't ask him or give him a choice—that Elijah was going to work with him at the camp.

He'd been to the camp when he had leave, but never when it was in session, and working with nine smart-ass rich girls wasn't his idea of something to do with the rest of his life, but he didn't argue. Henry and Mary were his only living relatives, and he loved them dearly. He could give them a couple of months, since he didn't have anything else to do.

"Family," he muttered as he turned away from the mirror. "I've learned that they can be taken away in the blink of an eye."

The air force had given him a family with a bond that most people would have difficulty understanding. He had purpose in his life, a reason to feel good about the job he did, and then three of his team members were gone—killed. He and the other three kept in touch, but it wasn't the same as working with them.

Just like that. He snapped his fingers and left the bathroom to get dressed.

Even after more than two years, the memory of helping carry those flag-draped caskets off the plane brought tears to Elijah's eyes. He'd lost three members of his family, and he mourned for them even yet.

He wiped his eyes and reminded himself that today began a new session. He'd settled into the routine fairly quickly from the beginning, when Henry had brought him to the camp the day before the summer session began, sobered him up with coffee and good food, and told him exactly what his job was. For the first couple of days, Henry helped him get acclimated to the regimen, and then he stepped back and turned it over to him.

By the end of July, he could see progress in the nine girls who had been sent to the camp, and he'd felt a sense of pride in what he had accomplished. He decided to give himself a year before reenlisting. More than seven sessions later, he couldn't imagine being anywhere else.

A glance at the clock brought him back to the present. He pulled on a pair of camouflage pants, tucked his shirt in, and buckled his belt. Then he sat down in a straight-backed chair and put on his combat boots. They were the only thing that he still had from his air force days. He'd long since worn out those camo pants, but they'd been so comfortable that he had decided to order more. Besides, dressing that way gave Piney Wood a little bit more of a boot camp feel to it.

He walked out onto his porch and sucked in a lungful of fresh morning air, and then started for the dining hall. The first day of camp was really his favorite time. The girls arrived with their problems all wound up tight around them like chains. It reminded him of those first days of air force boot camp in San Antonio.

He and the other recruits had to learn a whole new world just like these girls did. A couple of guys who started boot camp with him had washed out. During the two years he had been at Piney Wood, he had had to take three girls to the jail in Alpine. They were either shipped on to juvie, or else their parents pulled some strings to get them in private rehab centers, but he wondered about them, just like he did about those guys who didn't make it to the end of boot camp.

Elijah had felt a sense of failure every time he had to drive one of the girls to the jail—just like he did when he couldn't save those three buddies who had died. "Matty, Tommy, and Derrick." He whispered their names. Sometimes he had trouble seeing their faces and had to look at the picture of the seven members of his team to get everything back into focus. When that happened, he felt guilty and oftentimes apologized to the picture even though it seemed silly to talk to a photograph.

"Hey! Wait up," Henry called out from behind him.

Elijah stopped. When Henry caught up, Elijah shortened his stride so his uncle wouldn't have to rush. "You ready for this?"

"Oh, yeah," Henry said. "I can't wait to see how Jayden does. She seems a lot tougher than her sister. Skyler got the job done all right, but just between me and you, I think Jayden might do better."

"Why's that?" Elijah had felt something stirring down deep when he shook hands with her, and every time she was close by, the same thing happened all over again. Nothing could come of it, not when they worked together. Still, it was the first time he had had any type of feelings for a woman in the past two years. Could his bad luck be changing?

"She's worked in a pretty tough school. Skyler came to us from a private religious school that was . . ." Henry frowned.

"That was kind of protected compared to a public school in a big city?" Elijah finished for him.

"Yep, that's it," Henry said. "What did you think of her? We couldn't see a lot from the headshot we got. I figured she'd be a little woman like her sister."

Elijah told him what Jayden had said about one of her girls exercising the horses. "Sounds to me like she's going to be a good addition to the summer session."

Henry laughed and nodded. "If she continues to think like that, she's going to work out just fine. Let's go get some breakfast to get ready for this time around."

"Yes, sir." Elijah grinned.

Jayden and the other two counselors waited on the dining hall porch benches that morning for the girls to arrive. Parents, drivers, pilots, or whatever means the parents sent the girls to Alpine by would bring the girls to the airport. Henry and Elijah had driven the two vans to bring them to the camp.

"Have you got your agenda lined out?" Novalene asked.

"Yep, and extra copies printed so that each member of my team gets one in their hands, plus I taped one to the top of each of their footlockers, since I assigned them different individual jobs like y'all suggested at supper last night," Jayden answered.

"May I look at it?" Novalene asked.

Jayden passed three papers over to her. "Teamwork in the morning, individual work in the afternoons, an hour of counseling before supper, and one hour of free time before bedtime. They can use the hour to catch up on their journals or read a book or visit with the girls from the other two cabins. Think that will keep them busy?"

"Oh, they'll find time to get into trouble," Novalene told her. "They always do, but after a couple of times doing something they hate for whatever rule they break, they won't want to do it again. When I started teaching, my old mentor used to say that I should make the punishment hard enough that they remembered it every time they wanted to do something wrong. I followed her advice, and it worked."

In some measure, Jayden had figured that out from her years in the classroom and then as a guidance counselor. As they waited on the porch of the dining room that morning for the girls to arrive, she gave some thought to what she'd read in the handbook. Smoking in any form was against the rules. What would she do to promote leadership and bring down trouble on the heads of her girls if she caught one with a cigarette, a vape pen, or even a joint?

She was thinking about that when the two company vans pulled up, not far from the dining hall. A group of girls got out of each vehicle, and it was plain from their expressions and their body language that they would rather be shoveling coal in hell than be in this desolate place.

"Drop all of your baggage and line up," Elijah yelled.

Some of them set their fancy suitcases down. Others stared at him like he was something between a lizard and a bumblebee. Jayden could see disgust written on their faces at the very idea of putting their monogrammed leather luggage on the ground in the dirt.

"I said drop your baggage and line up. Anyone who still has a hand on a suitcase, purse, or backpack in the next five seconds can get back in the van they arrived in. You will be taken straight to the Brewster County Jail, in Alpine, to wait for a ride back to talk to the judge that gave you permission to come here rather than go to juvie." Elijah raised his voice. "Your choice, ladies. You've got until I count to three to make it. One, two . . ."

Purses, backpacks, and suitcases all hit the ground so hard and fast that it sounded a little like distant thunder. The girls lined up in something that roughly resembled a line, but most of them had their arms crossed and shot extrasharp daggers at Elijah.

"I want six inches between each of your shoulders, and your toes touching the edge of the sidewalk in front of you," Elijah said. "This is the way you will line up each day before mealtimes for inspection."

"God!" one girl muttered. "We're not in the military."

Elijah took a step forward until his nose was inches from hers, looked her in the eyes, and yelled so they could all hear him loud and clear. "No, you are not. This is going to be tougher than any military boot camp out there, and when you leave here, you won't ever even think of shoplifting, cyberbullying, driving under the influence, grand theft auto, assault, drug dealing, or any other way to break the law." His voice had gotten louder with each word—now it dropped to barely a whisper. "Young lady, since you have not read the handbook, you get a pass on that smart-ass remark, but next time you speak while in formation without being asked a question, you will get a demerit. Three of those will get you kicked out of this program that your parents have paid big bucks for. Now, toes touching the line, arms to your sides, eyes forward, and six inches between shoulders, and then we'll march inside."

Jayden could tell by their attitudes that they didn't like to submit to that kind of authority, but not one of them even batted an eye, so evidently Elijah had gotten through to them on some level. Either that or they had a touch of fear for what the judge would do.

"This line is not perfect, but it will be by the end of eight weeks," Elijah said. "Now follow me single file into the dining room, where you will each meet your counselor and learn which cabin you will call home for the next eight weeks."

As they passed by Jayden, every one of them looked like they could chew up scrub oak trees and spit out toothpicks. They were all wearing jeans—some that probably cost more than a hundred bucks a pair and others with a Wrangler or Levi's brand on the pocket. Most of them had pierced ears and wore other jewelry, and a few had a tattoo or two peeking out from around their bra straps and their expensive tank tops. Poor little darlings, their worlds were about to be turned upside down and inside out.

Jayden could sympathize with them. Her own world had crumbled the day that she found out Skyler was in charge of everything after their mother's death, including the house where they'd both grown up.

"Good morning, ladies," Mary said. "Welcome to Piney Wood Academy."

Elijah and Henry both stepped out of the dining hall and closed the door behind them. The girls relaxed and began to look around the room, and then their eyes came to rest on the tables.

"I see that you've noticed you each have a name card on one of the tables for three." Mary made a sweeping motion with her hand. "This is where you will sit for every meal while you are here." Her tone held as much authority as Elijah's had. "Right now, beside that card, you will find a set of clothing and a brown paper bag with your name on it. You will put everything you are wearing into the bag. That includes jewelry and underwear, and if you are still holding your cell phones, then they go in the bag also. We will see to it all your things are put into your luggage. That will go in storage and be returned to you when you leave."

Several of the girls gasped, and Jayden could tell that they were weighing the idea of pleading with the judge or even their parents about having to stay in this horrible place with no phones for eight whole weeks. They'd just gotten the first shock of their stay at Piney Wood. Every one of them looked like they were about to bolt.

"All of your new clothing is marked with your name and cabin. You have one set on your table, and the other two are in the footlocker at the end of your cot in your bedroom. For the next eight weeks, this is what you will wear, and if you are caught outside without your cap on, it will be one demerit," Mary said. "Now get dressed, ladies, so we can have some lunch, and then your counselors will go over the handbook this afternoon."

When she was fifteen or sixteen, Jayden sure wouldn't have wanted to strip down to her bare skin in front of complete strangers, even if some of them were also teens. Looking back, she was glad that her folks and the police never knew about that pair of sunglasses she shoplifted when she was thirteen, or that drunken weekend binge she'd had in college. She had felt so guilty, she took the sunglasses back the next day and put them back on the rack. Then there was the time she went joyriding with her two best friends in a car one of them boosted from a parking lot. She had lived in fear for weeks that Skyler would find out and tattle on her.

Not a single girl said a word, but their groans left no doubt that they hated the white cotton granny panties and the generic white bras. When they picked up the tan elastic-waist pants with wide legs and the matching shirts that buttoned down the front, Jayden almost felt sorry for them. A few wiped away tears as they traded expensive sandals for lace-up boots and white tube socks that came halfway to their knees.

Jayden was glad she could wear her own clothing, and she appreciated Skyler a little for telling her to take along hiking boots. She'd read a list of her responsibilities and, although she didn't have to join them in a mile-long walk before breakfast, she planned to do so. She would have been miserable in sandals or flip-flops.

The last thing they did was put their caps on. When they did that, Novalene nodded at Jayden and Diana and they all three removed theirs from their hip pockets and crammed them down on their heads. Jayden scanned the room for the Daydream Cabin girls and found Carmella, Tiffany, and Ashlyn—wearing hats embroidered with clouds above the words *Daydream Cabin*. Ashlyn was about five and a half feet tall, had platinum hair with a pink streak on one side, and green eyes outlined with heavy black liner. Carmella looked to be the toughest of the three. Her jet-black ponytail stuck out the back of her cap, and her jaw worked like she was chewing bubblegum. Jayden knew that gesture well. If she could spew out what was on her mind, it would blister the paint right off the stucco. Tiffany dropped gold and diamond earrings and a sparkling diamond pendant into the sack like they were nothing more than dime-store jewelry. She was almost as tall as Jayden, with red hair that flowed to her shoulders and big blue eyes. Freckles shone across her nose in the places where she'd already sweated off a ton of makeup.

Mary crossed the room, opened the door, and motioned for Elijah and Henry to come back into the dining room. "Elijah will take all your belongings to storage. Henry will help me serve dinner. That is what we call the noon meal here. Get a tray and line up. You have an hour to eat, and then you will report to your cabin, where your counselor will explain the rules in your handbook and assign your individual work schedules."

No matter how Jayden played out the scenarios in her head, she could not imagine Skyler, in all her prissiness, tackling this job. Maybe they made a habit of giving her the girls who weren't as tough as Jayden expected Carmella, Ashlyn, and Tiffany to be.

Elijah took his place at the end of the buffet and dished up the salad and spaghetti that Mary had made for dinner. Henry worked the far end and gave them each a couple of hot yeast rolls and a glass of either sweet tea or water, whichever they preferred. When the girls had all been served, then the counselors came through the line.

"So, what do y'all think of your girls?" Henry asked when the adults were all seated at the table set to the side for them.

"Looks like I've got a couple of tough ones," Jayden answered, "but not one of the three can compare to some of the kids I've had in class. I didn't see any of them pulling guns or knives from their pockets and putting those into their paper bags."

"No, but it's a good thing that looks don't kill," Novalene said.

"If they did, we'd all be dead," Diana chuckled. "I doubt they'd even bury us. They'd probably just throw our dead carcasses out for the coyotes to feast upon."

"They don't seem any better or worse than what we've started with before," Novalene said as she bit into her bread. "It's not what we get today that matters anyway. It's what we send home in eight weeks that tells the tale of our success or failure."

"Amen." Mary nodded.

Elijah leaned over slightly and asked Jayden, "Do I need to keep the keys to the vans under lock and key?"

"Not for me, but you should keep them in a fireproof safe for a while. If two of mine were to team up and talk the platinum blonde with the pink streak into making a break for it, you might lose a van," she said.

"The pink streak has to go. I've got some color remover to take care of it, or she can cut it off," Mary said. "That kind of thing is against the rules."

"She's a natural brunette. You can tell by her eyebrows and that tiny little bit of root beginning to show in her part," Novalene said. "She's going to have a hissy fit when she looks like a reverse skunk."

"Will she cut it or dye it? I'm taking bets." Jayden grinned.

"My money is on cutting it," Elijah said. "She'll do it with fire in her eyes just to show how tough she is."

"Don't y'all feel just a little bit sorry for them?" Henry asked. "They're all just craving attention and walls."

"Walls?" Jayden asked.

"They've been acting out, most likely to get some kind of attention," Henry answered. "All kids need walls that let them know where their boundaries are. If they go too far, they hit the wall, get into trouble, and readjust their thinking. Chances are these girls haven't had any walls in their lives, so now they have to be taught responsibility, respect, and teamwork all in a crash course."

"Boot camp taught me," Elijah said. "And when I began to forget it, Henry came to teach me all over again."

"You needed it just as bad as these girls do." Henry chuckled.

"Yep, I did." Elijah grinned. "I just hope these girls come out with a different attitude at the end of their stay, like I did after my first session here at the camp." He nodded toward the first girl to stand up and walk away from the table. "I get to say *I told you so*, Mary."

"What for?" Mary asked.

"I told you to just use those frozen lasagnas today rather than making spaghetti from scratch. I knew this first day that they would all test us," he said. "That girl is about to create a mess. I can see it in her eyes."

Jayden looked up to see Tiffany, one of her girls, give the adults at the table a go-to-hell look. Jayden pushed her chair back, stood, and caught up to Tiffany about halfway across the floor. "You won't get a demerit since I haven't gone over the rules with you yet, but you will bus your own spot. You don't have to eat what you are served, but you do have to scrape it into the trash can to feed to the hogs later. So, turn around, go back, and take care of your tray."

"The hired help takes care of that at our house," Tiffany said in a loud voice.

"You are not at *your house*, young lady, and when I tell you something, the answer is 'yes, ma'am.' If Henry or Elijah gives you instructions, it is 'yes, sir.' Is that understood?"

"Whatever." Tiffany shrugged and started back toward the table. She glared at Jayden, picked up her tray, and dropped it on the floor. Food scattered all the way to the door and splashed up on her pant legs. "Whoops," she said with a cocky little tilt to her head.

Jayden picked up a metal chair and carried it to the back of the dining room. "You will sit, facing the wall, until everyone else finishes their meal."

"Yes, ma'am," she said with a head wiggle.

"You are part of a team here, so your teammates will clean up the mess you made. When everyone gets finished eating, you will pick up the slop bucket, and I will show you where to carry it to feed the hogs. And every meal for the rest of this week, your responsibility, in addition to the ones that are on your list, will be to take that bucket to the hog pen. Do you have another *whatever* or *whoops* to say to me?"

"No, ma'am." Tiffany plopped down in the chair and crossed her arms over her chest.

"Also, you will wear those pants until bedtime. You only get one uniform a day, so if you mess it up, that's too bad," Jayden told her.

Tiffany set her mouth in a firm line and stared at the wall.

"I'm waiting," Jayden said.

"For?" Tiffany hissed.

"Think about it," Jayden answered. "You've got five seconds."

"Yes, ma'am," Tiffany finally whispered as she looked down at the legs of her pants. "Are you really going to make me wear these pants all day?"

"I am, and you can deal with your teammates when they get done cleaning up your mess." Jayden turned around to find the other two members of her team giving Tiffany the stink eye. "The three of you are responsible for each other's actions as well as your own. You are a team for the next eight weeks. If you don't want to clean up after each other, I suggest you make sure that your teammates don't make messes."

If Elijah had ever had a doubt in his mind about Jayden, he didn't anymore. He'd seen female drill sergeants who didn't have that kind of spunk. When she sat back down, he leaned over and said, "Good job, there. You want my job?"

"No, thank you." She nodded and went back to eating as if nothing had happened, but when the other two Daydream girls started trying to clean up the mess, she tapped her metal tray with a fork. "No!" she yelled across the room. "I said when everyone else has finished eating, you may clean that up. It will lay right there, leaving greasy spots and red stains until the dining room is cleared out. Then you may begin your job, and there will not be even the slightest sign of a stain when you are finished. Mary will give you some cleaning supplies, and when Tiffany and I finish feeding the hogs and washing out the bucket, she will drop down on her knees and help you."

Carmella and Ashlyn sat back down.

"I'm waiting," Jayden said.

"Yes, ma'am," they said in unison.

Novalene chuckled under her breath. "Thank you. That set the precedent for all of us. I bet there's not a girl in the place who doesn't know to say *yes, ma'am* now."

"Good job, Jayden," Elijah whispered.

"Respect is the first thing they should learn, and they'll be glad they did," Jayden said out of the side of her mouth.

"I agree wholeheartedly." Elijah finished off his dinner, picked up his tray, and made a wide sweep around all the food on the floor. He went outside and leaned against the porch post, like he always did on the first day of camp.

When Diana brought her girls out, she stopped and nodded to them. "Would you please introduce yourselves to Elijah, our drill instructor, so he can put faces with names?"

"Quinley McAdams." A short girl took a step forward. She had dark curly hair that lay in ringlets to her shoulders and a tattoo on her shoulder of a sword with a rose on the end of the blade. According to what Elijah had read in the report, she was half-black. Her eyes were green with yellow flecks in them.

"Rita Standish." She looked like she might be part Latina with dark-brown hair and dark-brown eyes that were nearly black. Too bad she couldn't use that cold tone to cool the cabin she would be living in.

"Violet O'Hare," the last one said. A skinny little white girl with stringy strawberry blonde hair and hazel eyes, she was the one who had been abused by her boyfriend and who had put him in the hospital when she got tired of it.

They were halfway across the lawn when Novalene brought her girls outside. She stopped on the porch just like Diana and said, "Step up here one at a time, and tell Elijah your name."

"Bailey Morse." She was almost as tall as Jayden. She tilted her chin up and looked down her nose at Elijah. The striking things about her were blue eyes the color of the summer sky and a round face full of freckles. Elijah would guess she had some Irish in her DNA. He also would put her at about twenty pounds overweight, which probably meant that she was cooking meth to sell, not use.

"Keelan Johnson." Her pert little nose twitched like she really didn't like what she smelled. Her dark hair was cut short. Like Bailey, she was multiracial, but in her case, she was half-Latina and half-black.

Elijah had studied the girls' names and their crimes. Keelan also peddled drugs, but like with Bailey, he doubted that she used them.

"Lauren Fielding, and I already hate this place." Her brown eyes locked with Elijah's and a cold chill chased up his spine. He'd never seen such hate in any of the girls who had come through Piney Wood. Her skin was so pale that it looked like it hadn't seen the sun in weeks.

"Okay, now we're going to Moonbeam Cabin and study the rules," Novalene said and then led the way across the yard.

Jayden was the next one to come out of the dining hall, with Tiffany right beside her, carrying the hog-feed bucket.

"So, you are Tiffany Jordan?" Elijah said.

Tiffany had a hard look about her, one of those don't-mess-with-me glares that said she wouldn't mind plowing right into another girl. Since she was as tall as Jayden, Elijah was doubly glad that Skyler wasn't there that session. Jayden was going to have her hands full with this group, but even after only knowing her a short while, Elijah felt like she could handle the job.

"Yes, sir," she almost hissed.

"Carry on with your duties. I just like to meet the girls one at a time on the first day so I can put faces with names and cabins." He headed back inside the dining hall just in case the other two from Daydream Cabin thought they could give Mary a hard time.

He pulled up a chair and sat down at the adult table. Carmella gagged when she had to rake the spaghetti, salad, and bread all into a dustpan with a paper towel. Ashlyn flinched as Mary handed her a bucket of water and scrub brush. Elijah bet that they would give Tiffany a hard enough time that she'd think twice before she did something stupid again.

Chapter Five

y the time Jayden had wrangled Tiffany back into the dining room, Tiffany's two teammates had cleaned up the spilled food and were now on their knees with scrub brushes. Jayden pulled up a chair beside Elijah, sat down, and pointed to the third scrub brush. "I believe that belongs to you. In case the three of you haven't been formally introduced, this is Tiffany Jordan." Jayden pointed at the red-headed girl.

"If you ever do something like this again, I'm going to shove your face into the food you throw on the floor," Ashlyn growled.

"And I'll hold you down while she does it," Carmella added.

"That's between you three," Jayden said. "Tiffany is here for shop-lifting and for cyberbullying. She posted a picture of a classmate wear-ing only a bra and panties that included a nasty comment about only ugly girls wearing granny panties. Tiffany, this girl right here with the pink in her hair that will either be cut off or dyed to match the rest of her hair is Ashlyn Causey. She's here for a third DUI in the past two months. And the other one is Carmella Ruiz, who was caught shop-lifting. Now, y'all feel free to visit while you get the stains up off Miss Mary's floor, and then we'll go to our cabin and talk about rules."

"Yes, ma'am," Carmella and Ashlyn said with so much venom that Jayden should have been nothing but bones and hair on the floor.

A full ten seconds later, Tiffany dropped to her knees and muttered, "Yes, ma'am."

Elijah motioned for Jayden to follow him outside. She hoped that she hadn't gone too far with her discipline on her first day. He could always fire her if she had, she thought as she pulled a paper napkin from the dispenser in the middle of the table, wiped sweat from her forehead, and stepped around the three girls. "I'll be back in a few minutes to check on your progress."

Elijah was sitting on the park bench when she arrived, and he patted the place beside him.

She sat down and wiped even more sweat from her forehead. "It's hotter'n hell out here. Do you think I was too rough on them?"

He shook his head. "Not one bit. I wanted to tell you that, but not in front of the girls. It's a lot harder to tighten the reins later than it is to let up on them once the girls begin to figure things out. Did you ever have to deal with a kid throwing their food on the floor before today, and did you make someone else help clean it up?"

"Oh, yeah," she answered. "I doubt that these kids can do much of anything I haven't seen or dealt with before, but I seldom have the backing of an administration. If I'd told a kid that she had to take the slop bucket to the hogs, I would have had six or eight sets of parents and grandparents filing a lawsuit against me personally, the school, and the school board. Making the teammates help clean it up will make them all responsible for each other. It's a good lesson to learn."

"How did Tiffany do with feeding the hogs?" Elijah didn't really want to talk about hogs, but he couldn't figure out a way to start a conversation about Jayden.

"She dry-heaved when she caught a whiff of their perfume. I'm glad you've got all kinds of animals here. The girls are going to love gathering eggs and baling hay for the cows. Which reminds me, who does all this work when you don't have little lawbreakers around?"

"Henry and I do pretty good during those times," Elijah answered. "Why? Are you looking for a full-time job?"

"No, sir!" Jayden threw up both hands. "There's not enough money in the world to keep me here or to bring me back after the first of August."

"I said that once upon a time, too." Elijah flashed a bright smile toward her. "But the place kind of grows on you."

"It can't grow that much." Jayden got up and headed back inside.

"Oh, but, darlin', it can," Elijah muttered as he headed toward the barn.

Jayden helped Mary spray the trays with hot water and then load them into a commercial dishwasher. "I'd tell all my secrets to have a dishwasher like this in my apartment. I wouldn't have to do dishes for a week at a time." She lowered her voice so only Mary could hear. "Do you think I'm being too rough on them?"

Mary shook her head. "Honey, here at first, you've got to put up those walls that Henry told you about. Later, you can be their friend, but not this first week. I don't think any of us would have handled that as slick as you did. Now, it's time to give them the good cleaner so they can finish that job." She nodded toward a bottle that said "Stain Remover" on the label.

Jayden took it off the shelf and carried it over to where the girls were still on their knees. "See if this works any better." She sat down in a chair at the next table and watched them.

"How do we use it?" Tiffany asked.

"For cryin' out loud." Carmella jerked it out of her hand. "Are you too dumb to read the label?"

"Don't get all high-and-mighty on me. We've both been caught shoplifting, so you aren't a bit better than me, and Ashlyn is a drunk so she's damn sure not any better than I am," Tiffany shot back at her.

Carmella looked down her nose at Tiffany. "Let me show you how this is done. First you read the directions. If the words are too big for you to understand, then you ask someone for help."

"You are a bitch," Tiffany hissed.

Carmella ignored her, sprayed the stain remover on the floor, and ran the scrub brush over it. "Pay attention to how I'm doing this, and you do the same thing." She handed the spray bottle back to Tiffany. "And, honey, you better not call me that again. A demerit would be a small price to pay to get to wipe up this floor with your red hair."

Virtual flames shot out of Tiffany's eyes when she sprayed a section of the floor and began to run the scrub brush over it. "I need rubber gloves."

"Did you have gloves when you dumped the tray?" Carmella asked.

"My hands are going to be ruined," Tiffany whined without answering the question.

"Well, duh!" Ashlyn held up her hands. "I've already broken three nails and chipped the polish that I just had done yesterday on the rest of them. And it's your fault, so don't bitch about your hands."

Carmella groaned as she looked at her own ruined manicure. "I wouldn't do this for my best friend."

"Neither would I," Tiffany agreed, "but they'd do it for me without bitchin' all the time about it."

"Why?" Ashlyn asked. "Because you probably took the fall for them. Well, I'll be willing to bet a hundred dollars that when you get home, all those friends will have deserted you. They won't want to be around someone who spent time in boot camp instead of going to parties."

"I've got friends. I just didn't rat them out," Tiffany declared.

"I'm so sure they appreciate that a hell of a lot," Ashlyn said. "What are they doing right now? Huh? No answer? I'll tell you what your friends are doing. They're out having a wonderful summer while you're in here, and when you go home, they won't even know your name."

"They will, too," Tiffany argued and then glanced over at Jayden. "Aren't you going to give them demerits for their smart-ass remarks?"

"Y'all can work out your own problems as long as there's no blood or broken bones. From what I see, the whole bunch of you are all wind anyway. You've got about ten minutes to finish up this job, or I'm giving you all a demerit whether you've been spoon-fed what's in the handbook or not," Jayden said in a matter-of-fact tone.

"What's that mean? All wind?" Tiffany asked.

"That you don't do nothing but talk." Ashlyn's tone was icy cold.

"I'll knock the wind right out of you so hard that it'll sober you up enough to drive right," Tiffany sneered.

Ashlyn came up on her knees and glared at Tiffany. "I may like my whiskey, but I could whip your skinny ass with a blindfold tied around my eyes and one hand tied behind my back."

Tiffany took a deep breath and let it out slowly. "Let's get this cleaned up so we can get out of here."

"All wind, just like I thought," Ashlyn said as she wiped up the last of the stain.

Jayden could have sworn it would be Carmella who was the tough one, not Miss Pink Streak. Jayden tensed and got ready to break up a fight, but evidently Tiffany saw that Ashlyn wasn't taking any lip off her.

"Mary, would you come over here and see if this job is satisfactory?" Jayden raised her voice over the noise of the dishwasher.

Mary rounded the end of the buffet bar, pushed the table back, and took a long look at the floor. Then she took a few steps back and pointed toward the door. "There's a couple of spots over there, and the door needs cleaning."

"Tiffany, you can take care of that." Jayden pointed as she spoke so they'd really hear her words. "Carmella, you and Ashlyn may each grab a broom and sweep the dining room for Miss Mary."

Carmella sighed. "I'm Cami, not Carmella."

"You are Carmella while you are here. We do not use nicknames at Piney Wood, and that was not the right response when you are told to do something," Jayden reminded her.

She closed her eyes, pursed her lips tightly, and then said, "Yes, ma'am."

"My friends call me Tiff. I hate Tiffany," Tiffany declared as she cleaned the last few spots from the floor and the door.

"It seems that you hate a lot of things," Jayden told her. "Hopefully by the time you leave here, you'll figure out that hate consumes the heart and leaves no room for love. When you finish cleaning, you can hold the dustpan for these two girls."

Are you preachin' to them or to yourself? Jayden's mother's voice whispered so real that she glanced over her shoulder to be sure a ghost wasn't behind her.

I'm doing my best to forgive Skyler, but it's not easy.

Hate was too strong of a word to use for the feelings Jayden had for her sister, but it was difficult to love someone like a sister when Jayden had walked in Skyler's shadow her whole life. These girls were stirring up emotions that Jayden had buried and tried to forget.

Mary stood to the side, and when Tiffany had cleaned the last of the spots off the door, she nodded. "Good job. Now, take the bucket and scrub brushes to the sink and clean them good. I'll show you where they belong, and where you can find the dustpan."

"Yes, ma'am," Tiffany said.

Jayden hoped that, in the days to come, her girls would learn to say that without so much anger. None of them realized that charm would take them further in life than money or power, but they would—or should—before the end of July.

That's what I told you your whole life. Her mother's voice was back in her head. *Why can't you apply that to your own life?*

Because I'm still mad at you for what you did, Jayden answered silently.

"You look like you could chew up nails," Mary said.

"I was fighting with my mother in my head," Jayden admitted.

"We've all done that." Mary smiled.

When the kitchen was put to rights, Jayden led her girls across the barren yard to the Daydream Cabin. "See these lovely flowers that have been planted here in front of the cabin? I expect the dead blossoms to be picked off daily, for the plants to be watered each morning and evening unless it rains, and, when we leave at the end of July, for this flower bed to look as pretty or maybe to be even more beautiful than it is right now. Is that understood? It would be a shame if the girls from the other two cabins did better at such a simple gardening job."

"Yes, ma'am." They all sighed.

"I will not remind you every day about the flower bed. You will take time to do that without me saying a word. The first time I come out here and find wilted flowers, I will give every one of you a demerit." Jayden opened the old-fashioned screen door and then turned the knob on the wooden one leading inside the cabin.

The girls' sighs could have been heard halfway to heaven. Apparently, they had expected it to be as cool as the dining room, but what they got was a stark little place that was almost as hot as it was outside.

"We have air conditioners." Jayden hoped to catch an afternoon breeze through the screen by leaving the door open. "We will save them for night, since they freeze up if we use them too much. Besides, we won't be in the cabin very much in the daytime. Now, sit down, pick up the handbook with your name on it, and let's go over the rules. You each have a highlighter, so I suggest you mark the basics so you don't forget. This is the only time I'm going to spoon-feed you the dos and don'ts in this book. Two of you are fifteen, and the other is sixteen. You are old enough to be held accountable if you break the rules. If being here at Piney Wood isn't proof of that, then you've got more to learn than what's written in this book."

Carmella opened the book and groaned. "No smoking?"

"That's what it says. If you've been a smoker, you'll be quitting cold turkey," Jayden answered. "If you break that rule, not only will you get one of those demerits that you do not want or need, you will be picking up the yard every evening for a week on your hour of free time."

Tiffany read the next one and turned pale. "No phones or calls for the next eight weeks? That's cruel and unusual punishment. Even a prisoner gets a phone call home."

"You can't be trusted with a phone, so quit whinin'," Ashlyn said. "I damn sure don't want my picture taken in these ugly granny panties and shown to the world."

"Oh, hush. Giving up my phone won't be as hard as you giving up your booze." Tiffany pointed at the next rule. "No liquor or beer. How are *you* ever going to survive?"

"I can't drink. You can't take pictures of me and Carmella in our granny panties, and there's nothing for Carmella or you to shoplift. It's going to be a long two months, isn't it?" Ashlyn did a head wiggle that would have made any smart-ass teenage girl proud.

If groans and grunts were candy and nuts, the cabin would have looked like a sweetshop by the time they finished going through the handbook. While they were still reeling from what they could and couldn't do during their residence at Piney Wood Academy, Jayden handed each of them a sheet of paper with their names on the top.

"The handbook is your Piney Wood Bible. This paper is the Book of Revelation, or what will come to pass right here in Daydream Cabin," Jayden said. "This outlines what you will be doing as a team, what you'll be doing individually, and the schedule as to when you will be allowed your turn for showers in the bathhouse. You will have an hour, which will be your free hour this afternoon, to acquaint yourselves with what's written there. Now you may go into your bedroom, which is through that open door."

Tiffany's eyes got as big as saucers. "What do you mean, bathhouse? Don't we, at least, have an individual bathroom in the cabin?"

"No, ma'am," Jayden answered. "The bathroom is located behind the cabins. It has showers and stalls. No mirrors, and when you read your papers there, you will see that every fourth day is your day as a team to clean it thoroughly."

All the color left Ashlyn's face. "You've got to be shittin' me."

"Honey, that won't be nearly as bad as the day you muck out the horse stalls in the barn," Jayden said. "Lay those papers on your cots, and we'll go out to the bathroom as a group. That way you'll know where it is." She led the way outside with all three girls behind her. "The laundry is right beside it, and every other day one of you will be responsible for doing the washing for the group. If you get the bright idea to ruin one of your teammates' uniforms or a piece of their underwear, then I'll take the same from your stash. That means you'll be wearing the same underbritches for more than one day."

"Good God." Carmella laid a hand across her forehead in a dramatic gesture. "I've died and gone straight to hell with the worst people in the whole world."

"Last time I checked, God was very good." Jayden crossed her fingers behind her back. She still hadn't forgiven God for taking her mother from her. "He's given all of you a second chance to straighten up your lives. Here it is." She entered the bathhouse ahead of them to find Novalene already in there with her charges.

"Whinin' yet?" Novalene looped her arm into Jayden's and led her outside.

"Oh, yeah," Jayden answered.

"Mine, too. Is that plate dumper going to be your ringleader when they become friends?" Novalene asked.

"I think my platinum blonde is going to be the hard-ass in the group," Jayden replied. "How about your girls?"

"The most vocal right now is Lauren. She's the one who's been in and out of rehab several times for drugs," Novalene answered. "I've seen worse on the first day, and then I've seen miracles by the end."

"Let's hope it happens that way this time around," Jayden said.

Tiffany was the first one out of the bathroom. "That rough old brown paper is going to ruin my hands."

"And the soap is going to dry my skin." Ashlyn followed her. "Can't we at least get our own toiletries out of our suitcases? I use a special lotion, and I need my makeup kit."

"Sorry, darlin'," Jayden answered. "Your new cosmetics will consist of a bar of soap and a stick of deodorant, both of a generic brand; a disposable razor if you've a mind to shave your legs; and a bottle of generic two-in-one shampoo. They are located in a plastic bag in your footlocker back in Daydream Cabin."

"Holy shit!" Ashlyn paled again beneath her perfectly tanned skin.

"And one more thing, the only tanning bed comes from up there." Jayden pointed to the hot sun. "You will definitely have a farmer's tan by the time you go back home."

"No makeup?" Tears welled up in Tiffany's eyes.

"Not even a little bit of lip gloss, but you do have a tube of generic dollar-store lip balm in your footlocker," Jayden told them. "And for your information, I will be using the same products that you do, so we're all in the same boat."

"You get to wear jeans and your own shirts," Carmella argued.

"You all might remember this when you go home and want to drink and drive, shoplift, or bully other girls," Jayden reminded them. "We have a few minutes left to go over tomorrow's schedule or we can go to the barn, and you can see where your first job will be in the morning after you do your exercise routine with Elijah at five fifteen and walk a mile before breakfast."

"Can we go back to the cabin now?" Tiffany looked like she was fighting tears. "I've never been up that early in my life or walked any farther than to the end of the driveway."

"Except when you're putting ugly pictures on the internet so early in the morning that no one else is up, right?" Ashlyn asked.

"Or sneaking in past curfew?" Carmella added.

"Neither of you have room to judge me." Tiffany marched toward the cabin, leaving them behind. Reluctantly, her two cabinmates followed along behind her, with heavy sighs floating out into the hot wind blowing across the yard.

Jayden wondered if her sister gave up her makeup while she was at the camp. If she did, what did she look like? Jayden hadn't seen her without a full, hour-long makeup job since she was twelve years old and Skyler was fifteen. That was the year that Skyler got strep throat and the world came to an end until she got well. That whole week, Skyler went without makeup.

"Penny for your thoughts." Novalene caught up to her.

"Is this par for the course?" Jayden asked. "Are they always this prickly on the first day?"

"Yep," the older woman answered. "Today has opened their little eyes. Tomorrow, more than just your tray dropper will be crying by bedtime, and then things will begin to get better."

"One baby step at a time?" Jayden asked.

"Oh, honey, one-half a baby step if we're lucky." Novalene waved as she followed her crew back to the Moonbeam Cabin.

Jayden didn't go inside the hot cabin when she got back but sat down in one of the double Adirondack chairs on the porch. Skyler should have told her more, but if her sister had, then she would be at home in her apartment instead of at Piney Wood. That was a guaran-damn-teed fact. Yet now that she could look ahead with hope of helping these girls, she was glad she'd come.

Elijah rounded the end of the cabin and sat down beside her. "How's it going?"

"About as expected. Strip any teenage girl of her makeup, fancy jeans, and phone, and they think the world has come to an end. Right now, they don't even know if the sun will come up tomorrow," she answered.

"By the time it does, they'll have done thirty minutes' worth of exercise and walked a mile." He chuckled. "Are you going to walk with them? You aren't required to join them. The other counselors just wait until I bring them all back for breakfast."

"I'll be right there with them," Jayden answered.

"Skyler didn't—" he started.

Jayden held up a palm and butted in before he could say another word. "I'm not my sister."

"I can already see that." Elijah grinned. "What's this thing between the two of you anyway? She never even mentioned having a sibling."

"She had trouble even acknowledging that I was her sister to her friends. I was the ugly duckling." Jayden didn't know why she was telling him such personal things and wished immediately that she'd just brushed off the comment. "Most of the time, I imagine both of us wish we were only children. What about you? Brothers? Sisters?"

"Brother, but he died of a brain tumor when he was sixteen. I was three years older and had just reached my duty station near Atlanta when I got the news. We didn't even know he was sick, and then six weeks later he was gone. Then a couple of years after that, my folks were both killed when a drunk driver hit them, so Uncle Henry and Aunt Mary are the only family I've got left," he said. "And you realize ugly ducklings grow up to be swans, right?"

"I'm so sorry about your brother." Jayden swallowed a lump in her throat at the idea of losing another loved one, almost not noticing the sweet comment he'd made about a swan. She and Skyler had never gotten along, but she'd never wished that Skyler were dead. Her father had always favored Skyler and still did. She seldom saw him these days, but again, she hoped there'd be more time in the future to maybe mend fences with both her sister and her dad.

"I still miss them, but I'm grateful that I've got Henry and Mary," he said. "At least you've still got your dad."

"We don't get along so well," she admitted and then wondered again why she was talking to a complete stranger about her personal life.

"Why? You don't have to answer that. It's way too personal." Elijah stood up.

"My folks divorced when I was in high school. He moved to Virginia with his girlfriend, who later became his wife. Skyler was in her sophomore year of college, so she didn't have to choose where to live, but I did, and I chose Mama and my grandfather, who had come to live with us when Granny died. He never quite forgave me for that." She wasn't willing to tell Elijah that she'd never felt like her father really loved her like he did Skyler.

"Did you go to the same college as Skyler?" he asked.

"Nope, I went to a juco only a mile or two away and lived at home. Then I went to the university that was only five miles away and still lived at home," she answered.

And I'd be living in that same house now if Skyler hadn't sold it right out from under me, she thought.

"So y'all kind of grew apart?" Elijah suggested.

"You could say that," Jayden agreed and changed the subject. "Why did you leave the air force? You were pretty close to putting in twenty, weren't you?"

"After we lost the other three members of our team, I and a few friends all decided that we didn't want to enlist again. It seemed like a big voice was yelling at me that if I didn't get out, I'd be next," he told her.

"I'm sorry," she said.

"Hard work right here at Piney Wood has helped me move on. Maybe it'll be your salvation, even if it wasn't Skyler's. I always got the feeling she was just here for the money," Elijah said.

"What makes you think that?" Jayden looked up at him.

"Just the way she acted, I guess."

"She's always been materialistic, but hopefully she did help the girls she worked with to be better people," Jayden said.

"We'll hope." Elijah rolled his neck to get the kinks out. "See you in about ten minutes in the dining room. I've spent the last couple of hours up under Henry's house, helping him redo some plumbing." He waved over his shoulder as he headed toward the dining building.

That he'd been in the service was evident in the way he squared his shoulders and walked out across the yard. She drew her brow down as she tried to remember what Skyler had said about him—maybe something about him being a drill sergeant?

"Is it time to go eat?" Tiffany slumped down into one of the other chairs.

Jayden checked her watch. "Five more minutes until y'all line up."

"How come I have to sit with those other girls? Why can't I sit with my own team?" she asked.

"That's so you can get acquainted with the members of the other teams. There are cabin teammates and dining teammates, and then there's a combined team effort when y'all are all together for exercises and the morning walk. I understand that you'll gradually build that up to a two-mile jog by the time you leave," Jayden answered.

"The news just gets better and better," Tiffany pouted.

"Don't ask the question if you don't want to know the answer. I won't lie to you or sugarcoat the truth, either. Do you think you'll eat what's put before you tonight?" Jayden hoped that Tiffany could find the strength to get over the eating disorder.

"Yes, ma'am," she answered without hesitation.

One small victory at a time, Jayden thought as she got up and stepped off the porch. Something akin to a fire siren blew and startled her so badly that she almost dropped to the ground and covered her ears. All the girls poured out of the cabins to see what was happening.

Elijah yelled across the yard when the noise stopped. "That's your call to eat three times a day, and you will also hear it in the morning. It means you have two minutes to line up and be ready."

The girls ran across the yard and put their toes on the edge of the sidewalk, then looked to each side to see if there was six inches between their shoulders.

Elijah smiled at Jayden as she passed him. "They're learning fast."

"Looks like it." She went on inside and tried to ignore the little shiver that danced down her spine when she was near him. She'd been attracted to tall, dark, and handsome men before, but in the end it all came down to trust and her lack of it. According to her own self-therapy, her issues came from the fact that her father had proved untrustworthy when he cheated on her mother.

There was no way she'd encourage anything with Elijah Thomas. She had only eight weeks to spend out here in the wilderness, and then she was going back to her city life. Jayden Bennett did not belong in a barren place like this, even if it was beautiful in an eerie way, so why start something she could never finish? And besides, why would she trust Elijah? She hardly knew him.

"What are you thinking about so strongly?" Novalene handed her a glass of sweet tea when she came into the dining room.

"They've lined up pretty well out there." Jayden took a long sip of the ice-cold tea. "I'm hoping that's a good sign."

"The best sign will be if your girl doesn't dump her food on the floor again. Right now, they're all probably trying to decide if juvie would be worse than this," Diana said from the adult table.

"If she does dump her food, Carmella and Ashlyn might smother her to death in her sleep tonight." Jayden smiled.

Diana shook her head. "If she or any of the other girls at her table pull a stunt like that, we've all decided that the tablemates, not the teammates, will clean it up."

"Sounds good to me," Jayden said. "What's that delicious aroma coming from the kitchen?"

"Pot roast, and Mary made a big chocolate sheet cake," Diana answered. "I always gain ten pounds when I'm here. If I had a lick of sense, I'd walk with the kids every morning, but I'm too lazy for that."

"I'm too old for it." Novalene giggled.

"Besides, I don't care if I gain ten pounds. I figure I'll run it off when I get home and go back to school," Diana added. "What about you, Jayden? Are you going to get up and do the walk?"

"Yep, and I'm going to eat what I want," Jayden answered. "I always go to the gym before school, anyway, so I'm used to getting up early. This won't be any big thing, except on weekends. Those are my days to sleep in, but I don't figure two months of giving them up will kill me."

"Just remember, the gym is air-conditioned and has a roof, so if it rains, you don't get wet. Unless there's lightning, the girls will be walking every morning, rain or shine," Novalene said. "Here they come. Let's see what happens."

Jayden wasn't a bit surprised when Tiffany dug right into her supper and even went back for a second hot roll. When the girl got finished eating, her tray was so clean that it looked like it wouldn't even need rinsing. She crossed the room and asked, "Is it all right if I go to the bathroom before I take the hogs their supper?"

"That will be fine," Jayden agreed. "I'm going with you."

When they reached the bathroom, Tiffany went into a stall and closed the door.

Jayden heard a gagging sound and slung the door open.

Tiffany whipped around to glare at her.

"Why are you doing this?" Jayden asked. "You are a beautiful young lady. What can I do to help you overcome this problem?"

"My friends hate fat girls, and I'm not going to gain weight. I don't want any of your help," Tiffany hissed. "You can't be with me twenty-four hours a day, woman."

"No, I can't, but I can do something even better," Jayden said. "Get back to the dining room."

Tiffany crossed her arms over her chest. "What if I refuse?"

"You can go talk to the judge." Jayden felt so sorry for the girl that she wanted to cry. She'd felt ugly most of her life, so she could relate to Tiffany, but she'd be damned if she let the girl see pity in her face. "If you don't beat me to the porch, then Elijah will be taking you to the Brewster County Jail tonight."

Tiffany waited until Jayden started to jog, and then she ran full-out to the door. When Jayden got there, the girl had bent over at the waist and was trying to get her breath. Carmella and Ashlyn pushed their way out onto the porch, and Jayden motioned for them to sit down on a bench.

"Tiffany is having some trouble with bulimia—we all need to join forces and help her overcome it," Jayden said.

"You're crazy. That's unhealthy," Ashlyn said.

"And drinking isn't?" Tiffany found enough breath to shoot back.

"So"—Jayden shifted her focus from one girl to the other—"from now on, one of you will stay with Tiffany at all times. If she goes to the bathroom, one of you will be with her, and the stall door will be open. If she takes the slop bucket out to the hogs, one of you will go with her. If she tries to throw up, you will tell me. If you don't, you can go with Tiffany to Alpine to the jail to await whatever your folks want to do with you."

"What about when we do our individual jobs in the afternoons?" Carmella asked.

"Then I'll be with her. She needs to learn to love herself and not care what other people think of her. We all need to help each other work through whatever problems we have," Jayden said. "You two can figure out who is going with her tonight to the hog lot. I'm going inside for another glass of tea."

"I've only been doing this for a few months. I can quit anytime I want," Tiffany declared. "I don't need any help."

As Jayden went into the dining room, she heard Carmella say, "I hate you, girl, but I'll take the first shift, and if I catch you even biting one of your fingernails, I will kick your sorry ass all the way to the jail myself."

Chapter Six

Elijah picked up a framed picture on the bookcase in his small living room and stared at the seven guys in it. He could almost feel the sweat running down their faces in big drops, the heat pouring down upon them, the sand that stuck to everything—boots, hair, bedsheets. They had been playing football, shirts and skins, and his team—the skins—had won, but they were all smiling and posturing for the picture.

Now three of them were gone—Matty, Tommy, and Derrick. In the blink of an eye one hot summer day in the sandbox, they were dead, and he felt like he was the cause. If he hadn't had to put fuel in the helicopter, he could have gotten there in time to save Matty. His younger brother was the smart one, the one who was going to be a doctor someday, so Elijah should have been the one to die young. If he had been home, maybe his mother and dad wouldn't have died in that auto accident. He was like a bad luck penny that kept turning up. He wiped the dust from the top of the picture frame and set it back on the bookcase. He crammed his ball cap on his head, got a bottle of beer from the refrigerator, and went out into the darkness for a walk.

The temperature hadn't dropped much that evening and the wind stirred up little dust tornadoes in the places where vegetation was sparse. As he headed toward the barn in long strides, some of the dirt flew up into his face, reminding him again of the day of that football game.

They were thirty-year-old men, young and invincible. They'd cheated death on so many occasions that they figured they'd live forever.

The air inside the barn was cooler and smelled of horses and hay. From the day he first arrived at Piney Wood, the barn had been his haven. When the past closed in on him, talking to Dynamite helped him work through his problems. The horse was a damn fine listener and knew more of his secrets than anyone on earth, including Henry and Mary.

He had that antsy feeling that said he wasn't alone long before he saw Jayden leaning on the railing of Dynamite's horse stall. Without a word, he crossed the barn and joined her, keeping a distance between them. He had mixed emotions about finding her there. Part of him wanted to be angry that she'd invaded his space, but when he mentally flipped the coin, the other side wondered why she'd chosen to come to the barn at that particular time.

"So, you couldn't sleep, either?" she asked.

"Nope," he answered.

"My girls are all asleep," she said. "I wouldn't have left them if they weren't."

"You don't owe me an explanation," he said. "Counselors don't get demerits."

"I'm worried about Tiffany. I've dealt with girls like her who think that skinny is beautiful. Hell, I've had the same feelings. I was never bulimic, but I can sure relate to what she's going through," Jayden said.

"You come off as self-assured and . . ." He couldn't find the right word. *Beautiful* was on his mind, but that sounded lame.

"That's the exterior," she said. "I can feel Tiffany's pain."

"That's exactly what will make you the perfect person to help her get through her troubles." He took a drink from the longneck bottle of Coors. "If I'd known you were here, I would have brought an extra beer."

"Is it against the rules for us to have a beer when the girls can't even have their cigarettes?" she asked.

"We're the adults, and we didn't break the law so often that we have to be here." He handed her the beer. "I'll share if you're not afraid to drink after me."

"Not one bit." She took the bottle from his hands, took a drink, and handed it back. "Lord have mercy, but this tastes good."

"I don't reckon God cares one way or the other," Elijah laughed. "But a cold one is pretty good at the end of a day like we just had. I saw Carmella going with Tiffany to the hog lot after supper."

"One of her teammates or I will be with her no matter where she goes. She can't even shut the bathroom stall door when she goes in there," Jayden answered. "Have you had girls with eating disorders here at the camp before?"

"A few times, but by the end of the session, they're usually over that. They need the food to have enough energy to keep up, and they're mostly competitive enough that they don't want some of the other kids to get ahead of them." He took another drink and then handed the bottle back to her. "You finish it off. I understand these girls, too. Not in the girl way you do, but in an emotional way."

"Want to talk about it?" she asked.

Jayden was a counselor, but she could and probably would talk back. In his eyes, Dynamite did a better job. "Not tonight," he answered.

"Skyler says that whatever I'm thinkin' is written on my face." Jayden took the last sip of the beer and handed the empty bottle back to him. "Thanks for sharing."

"Evidently, you like the beer if what Skyler says is true." He chuckled.

"I'm wondering if the girls, especially Tiffany, can see too much sympathy in my expressions," she said. "And the beer was wonderful."

He tucked the empty bottle in his hip pocket. "Think about the smell of the hog lot when you start to feel sorry for one of them."

"That's really some pretty good advice." She smiled.

"Works for me," he said.

"I should be getting back to the cabin. I just needed a little walk to clear my head. I'm glad that you came out tonight, too." She turned around and headed back to the cabin.

"I'll walk with you," he said.

They walked side by side without saying another word all the way to the Daydream Cabin. He stopped at the bottom of the stairs and said, "Have a good night. See you at five fifteen out in the yard. The siren goes off at five ten. Just sayin' so it doesn't scare you and make you fall out of that narrow bed."

"How do the other counselors sleep through that kind of noise?" she asked.

"They probably didn't their first year here. Some of them have gotten up and walked or jogged with us through the years, but Novalene and Diana have never chosen to do that. Good night, Jayden."

"Hey, if I'm going to eat all of Mary's good food, then I need to do some exercise," she said, "and to be truthful, I'm up at five thirty most mornings for a workout in the apartment gym before I go to school. I do take the weekends off, but I'll do the whole seven days while I'm here to be able to eat what I want."

"Good way to think." He nodded and headed back to his house.

Jayden crawled into her bed, set her alarm for five o'clock, and fell right to sleep. She dreamed that Skyler was standing before a judge in a courthouse with a red-haired guy beside her. Skyler was wearing a pretty white dress and holding a bouquet of daylilies that looked like they'd been picked right out of their mother's flower bed. The next morning, when Jayden awoke at a few seconds before her alarm went off, she tried to make sense of the crazy dream. To begin with, Skyler would never go to the courthouse to get married. She'd want the biggest, most flamboyant event in all Texas. Next, she'd never be satisfied with a bouquet that wasn't professionally made, and to end with, Skyler Bennett went for the trophy boyfriends—tall, dark, and handsome. A pallid redhead would never, ever do.

"That was a stupid dream," she said as she slung her legs over the side of the narrow bed and jerked on her jeans and shirt. She hurried with her hiking boots so she'd have time to rush through the bathroom, and she met Ashlyn and Tiffany coming back across the yard.

"I hate Tiffany more than Carmella does," Ashlyn declared.

"Turn that hate upside down and learn to love each other." Jayden jogged past them, glad to see that one of the stalls was vacated. She was leaving the bathhouse when the siren blew, and the noise really did startle her badly enough that she went from a jog to a full-out run to the yard, where Elijah waited.

"All right, ladies, get in a line and stretch your arms out to the sides. That's how much distance I want to see between each of you." He stopped in front of a girl with dark hair and a tattoo. "Where is your cap, young lady? I don't know what cabin you belong to without it, and that's an automatic demerit. You've got exactly one minute to find it and get it on your head, and I will be putting a note in your file in addition to the demerit that you now have. What is your name?"

"Yes, sir, and my name is Quinley," she mumbled as she ran back toward her cabin. She had to hustle to get back in a minute, but when she did, she gave her other two team members a look meant to fry them on the spot.

"Miss Jayden, you can stand beside me and you girls can follow her movements. I'll go easy on you ladies for the rest of this week, but next Monday, I'll get out the jump ropes and stretching bands, and we will add more strenuous exercises to our regimen," Elijah said. "We'll begin with toe touches."

Jayden bent forward but raised her eyes to see how her girls were doing. They had each followed her lead that morning and put their hair up in ponytails, then pulled them through the holes in the back of their caps. Not only would it keep their hair off their sweaty necks, but it would also keep their hats from falling off like other teams' hats had already done. Even though Tiffany was the tallest and thinnest of the three, her fingertips only reached her knees. Carmella managed to touch her ankles on the first try. Ashlyn palmed the ground in front of her. Apparently, that girl didn't only have a daily appointment with the tanning bed, but with the gym as well.

Elijah went through basic stretching exercises with them for the next fifteen minutes and then said, "Now that you're all awake, I want you to look to your right at that mountain back there. Our goal on the final week you are here is to hike all the way over there. It's about a five-mile trip there, and then that far back to the camp. We're going to walk a mile today. By walk, I mean a good steady pace, not a slow walk like you are moseying through a rose garden. I'll take the lead, and Miz Jayden will bring up the rear. Take a deep breath, let it out slowly, and follow me."

Ashlyn had no trouble keeping up with Elijah, but some of the stragglers, including Tiffany at the very tail end of the group, were panting before they'd even walked the equivalent of a city block. Jayden lengthened her stride until she was right beside the girl. If her bulimia was advanced, she might faint dead away, and someone needed to be there to catch her when she fell.

"I would have thought that you'd fight for first place rather than being satisfied with the tail end," Jayden said.

"You don't know me," Tiffany panted.

"I know that you'll poke your finger down your throat just to please your friends, so that tells me you'll do anything to win. You need to be in control, don't you?" Jayden would have rather jogged than kept up such a slow pace with Tiffany.

"I don't care if these people are ever my friends. I just want to get through this stupid camp and out of this hellhole. And if I'm in control, then no one can hurt me." Tiffany picked up the pace until she was a good twenty yards ahead of Jayden.

The girl was right about one thing. By being in control of her own life, heart, and time, she was less likely to get hurt—emotionally or physically. She didn't want to think about that, so she shifted her thoughts to the plant life around her. A few sprigs of grass had sprung up here and there, and yucca plants were scattered about.

Elijah stopped and pointed to a green plant at his toes. "The common name for this is sotol. It doesn't require much water, so it grows well here in this desert scrubland. Most years, we only get seven to twelve inches of rain, so the plants that survive have to be able to hold water in their leaves. This plant is edible, but it takes preparation, and it's bitter, so you don't want to put it in your mouth."

"Yes, sir!" all nine girls sounded off in unison.

"Remember some of the plants we've talked about. The different kinds of cacti and the others," Elijah was saying when Jayden started listening again. "Tomorrow I will ask you about them. We're about halfway to our turnaround point, so let's pick up the speed just a little."

He didn't stop again until they reached a stake that had been driven into the hard earth. A piece of yellow fabric tacked to the top flapped in the hot morning breeze. "This is it, ladies. Now Miz Jayden will lead the way back to camp, and I'll bring up the rear. Let's get some speed now that y'all are warmed up. Mary will have breakfast ready when we get home."

Home my butt, Jayden thought as she started a fast walk back toward the camp. As if God knew the land was barren and stark, and they needed something bright and pretty in their lives that morning, He gave them a beautiful sunrise. Streaks of pink, blue, and lavender lit up the sky out ahead. An orange ball peeked over the top of the mountain range to the east of them, but it didn't seem to be in a hurry. When they reached the camp, it still wasn't full light yet.

"Water!" Carmella groaned.

"I need my morning latte," Ashlyn, the most fit one in the group, said.

"Sorry, but we don't do fancy coffee here," Elijah said just a split second before the siren sounded. "We do have some creamer and sugar if you can't take it black. Line up, girls. Toes on the sidewalk and six inches between your shoulders."

Jayden went on inside, headed straight for the coffeepot, and poured a mugful. "Smells good in here. What can I do to help?"

"You can take my place," Henry said. "My old hip is giving me fits. I'm glad that we're leaving this in Elijah's hands pretty soon. Another year, and I wouldn't be able to enjoy traveling with my pretty bride."

"You've always been a charmer." A brilliant smile covered Mary's face. "Thanks for the offer, Jayden. You can help the girls with their trays. I'll pour orange juice and coffee or milk for those who want it. I have help from the girls from each cabin for dinner and supper, but since the exercise regimen is important, I choose to do breakfast by myself."

Carmella was the first one through the line that morning. She held her tray out for Jayden to put scrambled eggs onto it and kept it there for a double portion. "I'm starving. Give me two of those hash browns, and two biscuits with gravy. Do we get midmorning snacks?"

"No, ma'am. You get three meals a day," Jayden answered as she finished dipping up gravy.

"This isn't a country club." Tiffany came up right behind Carmella. "You should know that by now."

"Amen," Quinley said. "I'm here to tell you that I would've sold my soul for a bag of potato chips and a good cold root beer last night."

"Amen!" Violet said.

"Not me," Rita said. "If my soul was up for sale, I'd have wanted a chocolate cake."

"I could have said no to the chips, but not a double shot of Jameson," Ashlyn muttered as she went through the line.

Jayden remembered the beer that Elijah had shared and felt a little guilty, but not enough that she wouldn't gladly take another one if he offered it again in a few days. A pang of sadness struck her—she hoped that the girls would all be more secure within themselves when they left the camp.

When the girls were seated, Elijah held out his tray. "Just eggs, bacon, and a couple of those biscuits."

"Yes, sir." Jayden's hand brushed against his as she put the food onto his tray. There was that little spark again. She chalked it up to the fact that she hadn't had a date in a year, hadn't been in a relationship in two years—and Elijah was a sexy guy who would stir any woman's hormones. When she got home, she really should think about going out more.

Chapter Seven

Jayden thought about her grandparents that morning as she crossed the distance to the barn with her girls. When she was a little girl, her mother would let her spend weeks with them during the summer. That could have well been when she fell into the habit of getting up early so she could go help Gramps do the morning chores while Granny cooked breakfast. She remembered thinking that the morning dew was what made the air smell so fresh and clean. Gramps would tell her stories or else teach her some small lesson about farm life in those precious times she spent with him.

Will I be able to pass on anything that these three girls will remember? she wondered as she followed behind them. They weren't talking, but she wanted them to bond together and become friends. There was a far better chance of them doing just that if she let them have time together without her being right there.

They stopped at the barn door and waited for her to catch up to them. "Go on inside. You can't do your job this morning standing out here," she said.

"I'm afraid of horses," Carmella whispered.

Jayden could feel her pain. One of her earliest memories was going out to the farm with Skyler for Sunday dinner at their grandparents'. Skyler wanted Gramps to let her ride the old mule that he sometimes used to plow up the garden. Jayden had been terrified of that huge animal and had cried when Gramps wanted to sit her up on Molly's back.

"You're a big sissy," Skyler told her. "You're bigger than me, and I'm not afraid."

At four years old Jayden had grown taller and weighed more than Skyler did at seven, so it was the truth. But from that day forth, Jayden was constantly measuring herself by Skyler.

Ashlyn slipped through the door first. "Back in the real world, I had riding lessons twice a week when I was a kid, and when I go to my dad's in the summer, I ride every day. Horses are fantastic animals."

Jayden wondered how the girl had time between the tanning bed, the trips to the beauty shop to keep her dark roots from showing through that platinum hair, the gym, and school to chalk up three DUIs when she had had her driver's license for only six months.

Henry met them just inside the barn door and nodded at the girls. "Come right in, and I'll introduce you to the three horses and two mules. We don't ride them, but we do give them a good place to live out the rest of their lives. You will take them out to the corral, clean their stables, and put down fresh hay this morning. I understand that Ashlyn will be responsible for walking each one of them every afternoon. They should be taken out to the half-mile post and brought back. It takes about thirty minutes to take each animal out there, and that long to bring him back. Do you know anything about putting a halter on and dealing with horses?"

"I know how to ride a horse, but my trainer gets the saddle on him for me," Ashlyn told him. "Thirty minutes each way means nearly all afternoon every day."

"That's right. You'll be ready for supper by the time you get done. You should be able to walk each one out and back and then spend some time brushing the critter when you get back," Henry told her.

Ashlyn whipped around to stare at Jayden. Her green eyes bulged, and her palms went up in a defensive gesture. "Are you serious?"

"Yes, I am. Unless we're hauling hay as a group or doing something else where all nine of you are concerned, this is *your* afternoon job," Jayden answered.

"Why would you do that to me? I'll sunburn, and you won't even let me have my good lotion to prevent ashy skin," she moaned.

"You got three DUIs. Horses and donkeys might be your mode of transportation for the next five years if you get another citation. Do you want your mommy or daddy to drive you to college each morning? Think of walking the animals as your trip to the gym each day," Jayden answered.

Carmella giggled. "Ashy skin for Ashlyn. Seems appropriate."

Jayden turned her focus to Carmella. "Did y'all even read your individual jobs for each afternoon?"

Tiffany raised one shoulder. "I didn't have time to read all that crap."

"Me either. I figured we'd be doing crafts or talking to therapists about our bad habits," Carmella answered.

"This is a *working* farm," Henry said. "You will be working at one chore or another every day you are here. You are not at a country club."

"Daddy paid good money for me to come here rather than going to juvie. Believe me, I know how much it costs for us to be here. Daddy told me in a loud voice about a gazillion times. He even said if I get sent home that I have to get a job and pay every cent back to him. Y'all should treat us better than this. We should have counseling lessons in air-conditioned rooms and not have to work like we're in prison." Tiffany yawned.

"Honey, we don't run a fancy spa. We teach responsibility and accountability through hard work and counseling. Ashlyn, since you know a little about horses, you can show these other two how to lead old Dynamite here out to the corral. It's right through that door over there."

"Why's he called Dynamite?" Tiffany asked.

"Because he was a rodeo bronc before he was retired from that business," Henry answered. "We've tamed him down and he's not nearly as feisty as he was back in his prime. The paint is Thunder. He was runner-up in a lot of quarter horse races and used for stud services when he was young, but when he got old, he had to be put out to pasture. Demon is the roan over there. That old boy was a lady's riding horse. When she died, her children didn't want him, and he was on the way to the glue factory when we adopted him. The donkeys are Elvis and Sam, but they will be going back to the pasture this morning. I wanted y'all to meet them before we took them out of the barn. Since this will be your job a day or two each week, you'll get to know all of the horses better."

Ashlyn cautiously opened the stall door and frowned. "What do I lead him with?"

"All you have to do is snap the lead rope to his bridle." Henry took the rope from a nail on the top rail and showed her how to get the job done. "Pay attention, girls, because I'm leaving, and I won't be here when you do this next time around." He handed the rope to Ashlyn, who tugged on it, but Dynamite didn't budge.

"What am I doing wrong?" she asked.

"Make friends with him. He likes to be asked to leave his stall every morning, not just yanked around," Henry answered. "Don't you ever pet your horse or talk to him before or after you ride?"

"No . . ." She paused and then said, "No, sir."

That's what I did wrong with Gramps's old mule, Molly, Jayden thought. *I should have made friends with her instead of being scared out of my four-year-old mind.*

"Well, you best learn. Dynamite likes a little love, and after you walk him, he'll need to be brushed before he goes back in the stall. You other girls can get the lead ropes on your horses and get them all out in the pasture so they can have a little sunshine this morning. Be sure to take the ropes off before you come back inside to shovel out their stalls and put fresh straw down. Scoop shovels are over there by the wheelbarrows. Elijah needs me to bring him gas for the tractor, so y'all are on your own."

Jayden found an old metal folding chair, popped it open, and sat down at the end of the stalls to keep an eye on the girls. Carmella squared her shoulders, opened a door, and picked up a lead rope.

"Ashlyn, please help me. I'm scared," she admitted.

"Why would I help you? You made fun of me, remember?" Ashlyn stepped up close to Dynamite and rubbed his neck and then cautiously ran her hands over his back. "You're a pretty boy, yes, you are. Did you buck a lot of cowboys off into the dirt? I wish you could tell me stories about your rodeos."

Carmella took a deep breath and fastened the lead rope to Demon. Her hands shook as she reached out to touch the horse on the nose.

Tiffany lowered her head and stared at Thunder for a long time before she snapped the rope to his halter. "I'll talk to you, but I'm not going to be your friend."

"So, you're going to let one of the girls in another cabin be his favorite friend?" Jayden asked her. "I wonder if any of them will be as scared as y'all are. When they talk about doing this job at mealtimes, are y'all going to let them get ahead of you? Do you think they'll do a better job of cleaning the stalls?"

Ashlyn gave her the old stink eye. "Our team can outdo any of those other cabins in anything we do."

"Talk is cheap," Jayden said. "Prove it."

Ashlyn didn't even have to tug on the lead rope a second time. When she started forward, Dynamite followed her like a puppy. "Good boy," she said. "We'll show those other girls who you love. I'll bring you apples or carrots if you'll be my friend."

Jayden bit back a smile. A little friendly competition was good for the soul. She looked over at Carmella to find her leading Demon out of the stall, and then Tiffany followed right behind her.

"We did it!" Ashlyn announced when they returned.

"Did you remember to bring their lead ropes back?" Jayden asked.

All three held them up for her to see, then hung them on the appropriate nails.

"Good for you," Jayden said. "Now the donkeys."

"There's only two of them and three of us," Tiffany said. "Can I start shoveling shi—I mean crap . . . instead of taking one of the donkeys to the corral?"

"Something tells me that it'll take more than a little sweet-talking to get those critters to the corral," Jayden answered. "Try the first one before you make plans to grab those shovels."

Tiffany popped her hands on her hips. "What makes you a donkey expert?"

"My grandfather was a farmer. He kept a donkey in the pasture to keep the coyotes away from his calves," Jayden answered.

"What's coyotes got to do with baby cows?" Carmella asked.

"They kill and eat them, but donkeys are their enemies, so it's wise to have one around. They're a little more temperamental than horses, though," Jayden answered, "and they kick, so I wouldn't get behind one."

"You're shi—" Carmella stopped short of saying a word that would get her in trouble. "You're jokin', right? Did you ever see a coyote eat a baby calf?"

"No, but I saw a miniature donkey that Gramps called Waylon stomp the crap out of a coyote, and then Gramps hung its dead carcass on the barbed wire fence," Jayden answered.

"That's gross," Tiffany said. "Why would he do that?"

"To show the other coyotes what they'd get if they went after one of his calves," Jayden replied. She had forgotten all about that experience until that moment. She had been so angry with that coyote for trying to kill a calf that she didn't care if Waylon killed it. When she told Skyler about it later that day, her sister had put her hands over her ears and made la-la-la noises to keep from hearing any more. That was one of the few times that she felt like she could do something that Skyler couldn't.

"Will you help us, Ashlyn?" Tiffany's voice quivered a little.

"I barely got my horse out to the corral. I don't know jack crap about donkeys," Ashlyn whispered. "This is going to have to be a joint effort. Jayden, do we pet them or just snap the lead rope on and hope they follow?"

"Trial and error would be my guess," Jayden answered.

"Okay, Tiffany, you open the gate. Carmella, you grab the lead rope and snap it on, and then hand it to me," Ashlyn said.

At least they were working as a team, even if it was just getting a rope on a spotted donkey named Elvis. In one fell swoop they each did their job, and the donkey had a rope on his halter. He took a step out of the stall, nudged her with his head, and when Ashlyn reached up to pet him, he licked her hand.

"Looks like you made one friend here," Jayden laughed.

Elvis shook his head and started for the door, dragging his lead rope the whole way. Ashlyn ran ahead of him and quickly unhooked the rope about the time that Henry came back into the barn.

"I came to get the donkeys and put them back out in the pasture," he said. "Elijah just saw a pack of coyotes roaming, so it's time for Elvis and Sam to earn their living." He opened Sam's stall and the donkey came right out. Henry removed the bridle and the animal followed him to the stock trailer and climbed inside. He gave a shrill whistle that would rival the siren that went off several times a day, and Elvis bolted through the door and got into the trailer, too.

"They ain't nothing but a couple of pets," Henry chuckled. "Y'all have fun with the cleaning now. See you at dinnertime."

"I guess that means I only have to walk the three horses this afternoon, then?" Ashlyn asked.

"Looks like it," Jayden told her. "Things change by the minute on a farm, but every single day you aren't needed somewhere else, that's your job."

"What's mine?" Carmella eyed one of the three wheelbarrows. "Where do we put the stuff that we scoop up out of the stalls?"

"You'll probably find a big pile at the end of the barn," Jayden answered. "And it won't smell good, so get ready for it."

"Are you going to help us?" Tiffany asked.

"I'm supervising," Jayden answered.

"What's my job after dinner?" Carmella reached for the handles of the wheelbarrow and then jumped backward so fast that she almost fell. "There's a spider in that thing. I hate spiders."

"Seems like y'all hate lots of things," Jayden said. "You loved picking up things that didn't belong to you, so this afternoon you will begin a collection of bugs, insects, lizards, or whatever else you can find out here in this desert place."

"I can't do that," Carmella argued. "Ashlyn is going to be walking horses, and that just leaves me to make sure Tiffany don't puke up her dinner."

"She's going with you," Jayden told her. "Since she likes taking pictures that she shouldn't, she will be drawing a picture each day of a weed, a bug, or even the mountains off in the distance. Y'all can go with Ashlyn when she walks the horses and look for bugs, cactus plants, or anything else you can pick up, and Tiffany can draw. And no stick figures. All of your pictures will be displayed in the dining room so everyone can see them, so think about that when you're drawing the spiders or butterflies."

"What do I draw with?" Tiffany asked. "And do I really have to walk that mile again in the hot sun?"

"Looks like it," Jayden told her. "You will find a sketch pad in the cabin. Be sure to sharpen several pencils before you leave. And there's a box to use for your critters, Carmella, along with a book on insects for this area so you don't pick up a poisonous one."

"I'm not touching a spider," Carmella declared.

"Then don't forget to take a pair of disposable plastic gloves with you. They're in the kitchen," Jayden told her.

Tiffany picked up a shovel and killed the spider. "I hate mice. You owe me now. If there's a mouse in here or in our cabin, you have to get rid of it."

"Snakes are what give me the willies," Ashlyn admitted as she checked around the second wheelbarrow before she rolled it down the center aisle and into the last stall. "Y'all take care of those things, and I'll help with the spiders and mice."

Carmella threw all three shovels into her wheelbarrow and rolled them toward the stalls. "Is this going to be like hypnosis? Every time I see something that I want to shoplift, will I think of the smell of crap and urine?"

"Probably so," Tiffany answered.

Jayden felt like giving herself a gold star. Her girls might still fuss and argue, but, by golly, they were at least going to kill spiders, snakes, and mice for each other. That was another step in the right direction. She couldn't keep the smile off her face when she realized that she'd thought of them as *her girls*, and this was just the first official day of camp. They might not be lifelong friends at the end of eight weeks, but maybe they would at least learn the value of teamwork.

Like you never did with your sister, her mother's voice popped into her head.

That's not all on me, Jayden argued.

There was something about Jayden's steely blue eyes that Elijah couldn't get away from, no matter what. For the first time since he'd left the air force, he had thought about telling her how it felt when he had to fly the helicopter out to get his buddies' dead bodies after the explosion—how he had felt so guilty because he had to fuel the chopper before he left.

He pulled out his chair and took a seat beside her at the dinner table at noon. "I've been checkin' on all the girls this morning. They've all done a good job considering this is their first day. The stalls look good. Think Ashlyn will be able to walk the horses this afternoon without supervision?"

"I intend to go with them today," Jayden said. "Would you pass the butter? I'm wishing there were days when we had kitchen duty with the girls. I like to cook and have a whole collection of cookbooks, but it's no fun to make food for just one person."

Elijah handed her the bowl with the individual containers of butter. "That's another difference between you and Skyler. I remember her saying that she hated to cook, and the reason the girls don't have kitchen duty is that Mary is selfish with her kitchen, and she's afraid they might do something stupid to get even with the other girls."

"I told you before, Skyler and I are as different as daylight and dark." Jayden slathered butter on her hot roll and bit into it, and then changed the subject away from her sister. "I love good bread, and this rates right up there at number one in my book, Miz Mary."

"That's quite a compliment from someone who likes to cook." Mary smiled across the table at her. "When we retire, Elijah is going to be hiring someone to man the kitchen. You should put in your résumé."

Jayden shook her head while she chewed. When she'd swallowed the bite, she said, "Thanks, but no, thanks."

"This desert way of life ain't for me, either." Novalene reached for the butter bowl. "I love coming here for eight weeks, but then I'm ready to go home to Nocona, up in North Texas, where there's green trees and lots of grass."

"Those pretty lawns have to be mowed." Henry chuckled.

"I live in an apartment complex, so I don't have to mow," Jayden said.

Her voice was like a good, smooth Kentucky bourbon with just a touch of honey and was so soothing to Elijah's ears that he could have listened to her read the dictionary.

"Have you always lived in an apartment?" He focused on Jayden's eyes. He could imagine those thick lashes fluttering shut just before he kissed her. He jerked his head away and stared at his food. The woman was leaving in a few weeks. No use wanting something that wasn't available.

"Ever since I got out of college," she finally answered. "How about you? Did you live in the barracks or did you have a place off base?"

"Barracks until I moved in here," he answered, "but we sure had to do our share of keeping the lawns all groomed and looking nice, at least when we were stateside. When we were out there in the sandbox, we didn't have the luxury of grass." He paused and chuckled. "But that's not entirely true."

Henry pushed his plate back with a grin. "Elijah had been over there six months. We asked him what he wanted for Christmas. We figured he'd ask for Mary's fudge or her famous gingerbread, but oh, no, he wanted dirt from home and grass seed."

Elijah could feel the three women staring at him, but he just smiled and finished off his lemonade.

Henry went on. "So that's what we sent him. He bought a plastic container long enough and wide enough to put his feet in and then dumped all that dirt we had sent him from out near Mary's garden into the container, sowed that grass seed, and kept it watered. When it was about three inches tall, he sunk his feet down into that green grass and wiggled his toes in it."

"As Paul Harvey used to say, 'And now you know the rest of the story,'" Elijah said. "I didn't buy a beer for the rest of my tour. Anyone who wanted to feel my grass on their feet paid me with a beer or a candy bar. I had lots and lots of takers."

"I didn't know they let y'all have beer over there," Novalene said.

"Nonalcoholic might taste like crap, but it beats no beer at all," Elijah told her.

Jayden leaned over and nudged him on the shoulder. "But not by much."

He cut his eyes around at her. "Honey, that desert over there makes this place seem like a five-star resort, so even an icy-cold, watered-down beer with no alcohol will wash the sand grit out from between your teeth."

"Sweet tea or lemonade will do the same," Novalene argued.

"I'll tell y'all a story about the desert," Jayden said. "Mama and I drove to California once in the middle of July. Skyler had decided she wanted to be an actress. We couldn't afford for all of us to fly out there, so Skyler got the plane ticket, and Mama and I drove to Hollywood to help her get set up in a new apartment. By midsummer Skyler had changed her mind when the producers or whatever powers that be didn't roll out the red carpet for her. But anyway, we knew we couldn't drink and drive, so we bought a case of beer with no alcohol and put it down in a cooler full of ice. Y'all ever made that drive?"

The other counselors shook their heads.

"Well, it's miles and miles of desert with no services, so you'd better have a full tank of gas. What I remember most about that trip is that we drank that ice-cold nonalcoholic beer, sang Creedence Clearwater Revival songs because Mama loved them, and told jokes . . . and crossed our legs because there wasn't even a bush to squat behind after all those beers were gone. When we finally got to a town with a service station, the line for the ladies' room was longer than the one to buy gas. The bathroom only had one toilet, and you had to put a quarter in the door to even get inside."

"Are you kiddin' us?" Novalene asked.

"Nope," Jayden answered. "And let me tell you, folks, that was the best quarter I ever spent."

"Did you drink any more beer on the rest of the trip?" Elijah mentally kicked himself for asking such an awkward question.

"No, sir, we did not," Jayden answered, "and we sure enough had our quarters ready when we reached that station," she said.

"That's a hoot, but I like Henry's story about Elijah, too," Diana said. "We should all do that for our service guys. I bet they'd love some green grass from home more than about anything."

"Probably so." Elijah wiggled his toes and could almost feel that cool grass on his feet again.

"I see my girls are done eating," Jayden said. "Soon as Tiffany gets finished with her hog lot duties, Ashlyn has to exercise the horses, so I'd better finish up the last two bites of dessert."

"I usually read a book while my girls do their individual afternoon jobs, and just check on them a few times," Novalene said.

"Tiffany is the one struggling with bulimia, so she has to have a chaperone to keep her from throwing up in the restroom. I suspect the therapist will have more tips for us about that when she arrives. Tiffany will be drawing plants, insects, and lizards. Carmella will be making a bug collection. Looks like they're headed out now to the hog lot, so I'll see y'all at supper," Jayden answered.

Elijah couldn't take his eyes off her as she walked across the room and out the door. He had seen tight jeans and good-looking women before, but Jayden had the whole package. He got up from the table and took his empty tray to the cart, then followed her outside. A stinging hot breeze bringing bits of sand and dead grass with it hit him in the face when he left the building. He suddenly had a yearning for a beer, but there was no way he could have one in the middle of the day—not with nine girls watching his every move.

He rounded the end of the cabin in time to see Tiffany and Carmella coming back from the hog lot. Two girls from the Moonbeam Cabin were busy picking trash or stray sticks up from the yard and putting whatever they found in a paper bag. That was a disciplinary move. No doubt about it, Novalene had taken what was in the trash cans from the bathroom, as well as what was in her cabin, and strewed it on the yard before she told them to clean it up.

"Oh, look, Tiffany, the Moonbeams are on trash duty," Carmella said.

"That's better than slop duty." Lauren giggled and pointed at their caps. "Fly away, fly away, you old daydreaming clouds!" She motioned with both hands and then dropped them to her side and glared at Carmella. "Or us Moonbeams will make you disappear."

Carmella bowed up to her. "Bring it on, smart-ass."

Lauren knotted her hands into fists. "I'm not afraid of you."

Tiffany set the bucket down and cocked her head to one side. "Darlin', you'd better be afraid of me. I don't give a tiny rat's heinie if I go to juvie, and I'll mop up this whole farm with you and your little sidekick over there. Don't you ever make fun of our cabin again, or any one of the three of us who live there, or . . ." She shrugged and picked up the bucket.

"Or what?" Lauren taunted.

"Or I will throw your skinny ass over my shoulder and drop it in the hog wallow," Tiffany told her. "We only get one uniform a day, so think about that while I go wash out this bucket. When I get back, if you still want to do battle, we will. It's your choice. I'll take my demerit for putting you in with the hogs."

Elijah heard a soft giggle behind him and whipped around to see Jayden standing back even farther in the shadows.

"Looks like you got some scrappers in your cabin," he said in a low voice.

"Looks that way," she agreed. "Do all of them ever learn to get along?"

"Not always, but it's pretty common to see the three in each cabin bawl their heads off on the last day because they have to leave their friends," he answered.

"Hey, Miz Jayden, I'm ready to go walk Dynamite." Ashlyn came out of the barn with the horse on the lead rope. "Where are Tiffany and Carmella?"

"Wait right there for them," Jayden told her. "We will be along in just a few minutes. They have to get their supplies."

"Hey, cloud girl," Lauren yelled across the yard. "I'll trade jobs with you. I'll exercise that horse if you'll pick up trash."

"No, thank you. You go on and get your hands dirty," Ashlyn yelled back at her.

"Fly away, fly away, cloud girls. Or is it chicken girls? Those clouds on your hats look like fat chickens to me." Bailey made a flapping motion with her arms.

Tiffany and Carmella came out of the dining room about then, and Tiffany wasted no time jogging across the yard. She got right up in Lauren's face and popped her hands on her hips.

"What did I tell you about making fun of us?" she said through clenched teeth.

"Wasn't me," Lauren whispered. "It was Bailey."

Tiffany shifted her focus to the girl. "That's one."

"One what?" Keelan, the third member of the Moonbeams, asked.

"On three, all three of us Daydreamers will roll you in the hog lot. We'll take our punishment like adults, but you'll stink like hog crap all day. Think about that before you test me again." Tiffany turned around and headed toward the cabin, with Carmella right behind her.

"Guess I'd better go smooth some ruffled feathers," Jayden laughed.

"You really think Carmella and Ashlyn would help Tiffany out?" Elijah asked.

"Mean don't come in size, and they're all itching for a vent for their anger right now," she answered.

"What does mean come in, if not size?" Elijah asked.

"It comes in attitude, and if Tiffany was mad enough, she could roll all three of them in the hog wallow by herself and with one hand tied behind her back." Jayden took a couple of steps toward the cabin and turned around. "This isn't a whole lot different than a prison yard, is it?"

"Not at first." Elijah tipped his cap toward her and went on inside the barn. He turned around after a couple of steps and watched Jayden walk away for the second time.

Chapter Eight

Dynamite simply plodded along beside Ashlyn as if she were his best friend. Jayden had been talking to the horse the night before when she'd heard someone coming into the barn. Now she wondered if that slow-moving old rodeo horse was Elijah's confidant, too.

"If that bit . . . witch"—Carmella stumbled over the words—"thought she was going to intimidate Tiffany, she can dam . . . dang well think again. Man, it's hard to talk without using cuss words."

"Don't I know it," Tiffany said. "I've almost had to grow a new tongue for the times I bit mine off to keep from saying the f-word."

"Me too," Ashlyn admitted. "Would you have really rolled her in the hog lot? Or were you just dissin' her?"

"I would have sure tried, even if y'all didn't help me," Tiffany answered. "Seeing that smart aleck covered in hog sh—" She clamped a hand over her mouth. "Crap and mud would have been something worthy of drawing."

"Be still," Carmella whispered.

Ashlyn stopped in her tracks. "Is it a snake?"

Dynamite ran out of rope and came to a halt beside her.

"No, it's a big old fly right on Dynamite's butt, and I intend to catch him for my first insect of the day." Carmella eased up toward the horse and the fly took flight about the same time that the horse lifted his tail and dropped a pile right at her feet.

The fly settled right on the warm crap.

Tiffany dropped to her knees and began to sketch. "Don't move. Don't even breathe until I get this roughed out on paper."

Ashlyn stood perfectly still until Tiffany nodded, giving Carmella the go-ahead to try to trap the fly.

"Well, shi . . . crap!" Carmella swore when it flew away to light on a nearby cactus. She tiptoed across the distance and trapped it in her box on the second try. "Got it!" she shouted.

At first, Jayden thought Carmella's loud voice had spooked Dynamite. The horse reared up on his hind feet, jerked free of the lead rope, and seemed to turn around midair. Then he took off in a fast run back toward the barn.

Ashlyn pointed toward the half-mile post. "Snake," she whispered.

"Go take care of your horse," Jayden said. "Fly like a fast-moving cloud."

"I hate being a cloud," Tiffany said.

Ashlyn took off in a dead run. About fifty yards back along the trail, Dynamite had stopped and had his head down, nibbling on a rare sprig of green grass. Jayden couldn't hear what she was whispering to the horse, but she could only guess that it had something to do with the big black snake that had slithered off toward the far mountain range.

Jayden turned her attention back to Tiffany. "Clouds are beautiful. They can bring rain, or they can just float around in the sky like big old fluffy cotton balls. They mind their own business whether they bring a storm or a peaceful day. We could all take a lesson from them."

"Why did they give us clouds anyway?" Carmella's nose twitched, and she held the box out at an arm's distance. "I think I got something more than the fly in here from the way it smells."

"Daydreams are like clouds. Ever shifting, but still they bring hope to us when we need rain," Jayden explained.

"That's right, and that makes us better than moonbeams and sun-shine." Tiffany straightened up. She tucked her sketchbook into the tote bag and slung it over her shoulder.

"Of course it does." Carmella touched the post with a hand and turned around.

Tiffany put her hand on her hip. "Moonbeams are gone when the daylight comes around. Sunshine is hot, but darkness can put it in its place. Those girls aren't a bit tougher or better than us."

Pretty smart for a teenage girl. Maybe she should be counseling you, so you won't feel like your sister is smarter and prettier than you, the niggling voice in Jayden's head said.

"I'm glad that you believe that," Jayden agreed. "I'm going back now. I think y'all have got this down."

"You're trusting me not to puke, and Carmella to pick up bugs?" Tiffany asked.

"Yep, and for you to finish that sketch of a horsefly on a pile of crap. Just don't let one of those things bite you. It hurts like hell when they do," Jayden told them. "See y'all at the supper table."

"I wish I had a horsefly on my cap. That way those other girls would know that when I bite, it hurts," Tiffany said.

"You want to fly around a horse's butt and sit on piles of crap?" Ashlyn asked.

"Wouldn't be much different than what we're having to do, would it?" Tiffany shot back at her.

Jayden kept the laughter bottled up until she was almost to the barn. Then she giggled out loud. Too bad their cabin didn't have a different name, but she had a feeling that when push came to shove, they would figure out a way to make the other girls wish they were in Daydream Cabin.

She was right.

At suppertime, she was getting a second helping of blackberry cob-bler when she heard Carmella talking to the girls at her table. "It's like this. We're the lucky cloud girls and you're just something that fades away. Moonbeams disappear with the light of day, and there ain't a thing you can do about it. Darkness can wipe out sunshine, and again, not a thing you can do to stop it. A daydream is something that will become real forever with just a little work."

"Bullshit!" Lauren, from the Moonbeam Cabin, said. "Whatever"—she did a head wiggle—"about daydreams, but clouds aren't dependable. They're like y'all. Just floatin' around from one thing to another."

"Watch your language. The rules say no cussin' or ugly language," Novalene called out from the adult table.

"Honey, without clouds there's no water. Try flushing the toilet with no water or taking a shower. We have the power." Carmella's smile was pure saccharine.

"Is that a threat?" Lauren asked.

"Nope, just a fact. I'm goin' to get another piece of garlic bread. Any of y'all want me to get one for you?" Carmella asked.

One hand went up.

Jayden was proud of her for the second time that day. She'd stated her position and then offered to help. Not bad—as a matter of fact, it was damn good.

That evening, her girls had first shower privileges, so they all traipsed out across the lawn as soon as they got back to the cabin after supper. When they returned to the cabin, Ashlyn walked up to Jayden and handed her the lock of pink hair.

"How did you do this?" Jayden asked.

"I used the razor in my kit for shaving my legs," she answered. "My hair is going to look like crap anyway when it starts growing out."

Jayden handed each of them a journal. "This is the only thing, other than your memories, that you will take home with you. Write whatever you want in it or never pick up a pen to scribble the first word. I won't be taking them from you, and you don't get a grade on it. Hopefully, you will take notes or even write stories in it. I think you should write about threatening to roll Lauren in the hog lot, Tiffany. Carmella, you should write about the smell of that box when you brought your horse-fly home. Ashlyn, you had the courage to cut off your hair, and you know it's going to look bad, so write about that. Hopefully, you'll look back through the pages when you get home and see how much things changed from this day to the last hours you spend here."

"I'll write about how my horsefly felt when he was freezing to death." Carmella smiled.

"Freezing?" Jayden asked.

"Yep." Carmella nodded. "Tiffany had to do an insect collection for school, so she told me to put the box in the freezer—then I can pin the frozen bug to a piece of foam. Miz Mary let us use the freezer and gave me a piece of Styrofoam that she was going to throw away."

"That's great." Jayden started out of the room.

"You going to write in one?" Ashlyn asked.

"Yep, and my first entry tonight is going to be titled 'Horses and Horseflies,'" Jayden replied.

"Make that 'Hair, Horses, and Horseflies,'" Ashlyn said. "I loved that pink streak, and I've been tucking it up under my cap so no one could see it. I've been afraid it was going to fall, and I'd get a demerit. But I'm going to look like a skunk anyway. My natural hair color is dark brown. If anyone makes fun of me, they'll pay dearly. I am a loud and proud Daydream girl and we're a tough bunch."

Jayden slipped out of the room with the pink hair in her hand. She took it straight to her bedroom and used a pair of manicure scissors to cut a swatch from it. Then she taped the lock to the first page of her journal. She smiled as she wrote *Hair, Horses, and Horseflies*.

Dear Mother,

If my girls have to write in their journals, then I should
do so, too, and tonight I'm writing to you. Maybe if

I put my feelings on paper, I can get past this terrible pain that I still feel for what happened when you went to the hospital. You knew how much that house meant to me, and if anything, it should have been given to both of us girls, not just to Skyler. She only let me take my personal items out of the house before she had a private sale. She didn't even let me know what she was doing until it was over, and all the sentimental things I wanted had sold. Your precious collection of teapots went for only a few dollars, and the porch swing where Gramps and I sat so many evenings sold for five bucks. All of my memories were nothing more than dollar bills to her. Was your brain already affected by the aneurism, or did you love her more than me, even after the way she treated us during the divorce?

I have no answers, and you can't give me any. I should be writing about horses, hair, and horseflies. Horses because they're part of our camp here and that's what we've dealt with so far. Ashlyn has to exercise the horses because she has three DUIs and she whacked the pink streak out of her hair tonight. Carmella has to pick up bugs because she was caught shoplifting one too many times. And Tiffany has to sketch the bugs because she posted ugly pictures of her classmates. I just know you would have handled things like this. I miss you, Mama, even though I still can't understand why you did things the way you did.

Until later, Jayden

Clouds shifted across the moon that evening, and everything remained dark in all the cabins. Jayden and her team had had a pretty big day, so Elijah wasn't surprised when he didn't find her on the porch, but he was more than a little disappointed. He was about to round the end of the cabin when he saw a movement in his peripheral vision and saw Jayden coming back from the bathhouse.

"Hey, don't run away." Her tone sounded light.

He turned around and headed back. "Thought you had already turned in for the night. Mind if I sit down?"

"Not a bit if one of those beers is for me." She slid back in the deep-red chair and patted the table connecting it to the other one.

He set a beer on the table, twisted the top off the other, and handed it to her. Then he sat down and did the same with the second bottle. "Tell me about your day."

She took a long sip of the cold beer, wiped her mouth with the back of her hand, and said, "Horses, horseflies, and hair."

He chuckled. "Want to give me a few details about that?"

He took a couple of deep breaths and then reminded himself how improper it was for him to even be sitting on the porch with her. If one of the girls came outside, or if Novalene or Diana decided to come over for a late-evening chat, his being there could be misconstrued as something more than just sharing a beer with a fellow employee. But right then he didn't really care.

Jayden started with the story about taking Dynamite for his afternoon walk and then went right into the bit about the horsefly. "I tell you, that Tiffany has surprised me. She's tougher than I thought she would be, and she's got real talent with her drawing. I could almost smell that pile of crap when she sketched it with a horsefly flittering around the top of it. When we got home, they got into the insect book on the shelf in there, and the giggling started."

"Why?" Elijah enjoyed listening to her spin on the stories.

"The female horseflies are the ones that bite, and they don't care if it's humans or animals. They need the blood to produce eggs. The males don't bite," Jayden answered.

"I knew that, but why would the girls laugh about it?" Elijah asked.

"They said it had to be a boy horsefly. A girl one would be more interested in making eggs for babies than playing around in a warm pile of stinky crap. Then they likened the horse crap to sports," she said, "and it went from there. I was sitting in the living room listening with one ear, but I found out that they are all three sexually active, and we took their birth control pills from them when we took away their purses. They were moaning about their boyfriends having to use condoms for a whole month when they got back home."

"They're not old enough to . . . ," Elijah stammered.

"Evidently they are, but Carmella said that none of them would have a boyfriend when they got home because boys didn't wait two months to get laid," Jayden told him.

Elijah was a seasoned veteran, so he didn't blush, but he felt heat rising from his neck. His mind went back to his first sexual experience. He'd been seventeen and his girlfriend was a year younger. He'd taken her to a party on the beach down around Texas City.

"Thinkin' about your first time?" Jayden asked.

"Busted!" He turned up his bottle of beer and took a long gulp, then set it back down. "But being the gentleman that I am, I don't kiss and tell."

"Well, I'll just put a hand grenade in whatever thoughts you might be harboring about that first time." She laughed. "According to my girls, most boys don't know how to make a girl feel all warm and gooey—their words, not mine—inside. They're slam, bam, thank you, ma'am, and on to the next girl, kind of like the old male horsefly does when he flits from one pile of horse crap to the next."

Elijah couldn't do anything but shake his head. "So, who is the horse crap?"

"According to them, it's whoever their boyfriends are home screwing around with right now," Jayden answered.

"But it's not them, right?"

"Oh, no, they are all"—Jayden giggled—"glasses of five-hundred-dollar champagne that the boy horsefly has left behind for the skanky old crap piles." She dissolved in laughter.

"I'm not sure I want to hear about the horses and the hair after this." Elijah laughed with her.

"The rest is a little anticlimactic after all that." Jayden finished off her beer. "A snake spooked Dynamite, and Ashlyn had to chase him down. She did fairly well with him, but when she was taking Thunder back from the half-mile marker, he got away from her, and it took all three of them to chase him down. They cussed and ranted about it the whole time they were in the shower. Ashlyn says that it's a good thing she didn't have a gun, or he would be coyote food tonight. They were all so tired that they didn't even argue with me about the bedtime curfew."

"And the hair story?"

Jayden told him about Ashlyn whacking off her pink streak. "Ashlyn was told she had to cut the pink or dye it. She had been tucking it up under her cap, but tonight she sawed it off with her razor and gave it to me. I'm tellin' you, I've got some tough girls."

"From what I can see, they've got a tough counselor," Elijah told her.

"Thank you for that," she said. "Now tell me about your day."

"Well, it sure wasn't as exciting as yours. I didn't play dodge the horse apples or horseflies, either, but I . . ." He paused and took a deep breath.

She laid a hand on his arm. "Are you all right?"

Her gentle touch made him think of all the times Mary had patted him on the back. He probably shouldn't say a thing, since it might spook Jayden, but he needed to talk to someone. "It's about Mary and Henry. I'm worried about them both, but more about her. They've looked forward to retiring all year, and it seems like Mary is going downhill lately. I've noticed her grabbing her chest a few times, and I'm scared that she's got heart trouble."

He took a deep breath and let it out slowly. "I don't know what he'd do without her. They've only had each other all these years and Henry wouldn't last six months if he lost Mary. She works too hard during the sessions . . ."

"Have you talked to Henry about it, or suggested she see a doctor?" Jayden asked.

"I have, but Henry is in denial, and Mary won't do anything to jeopardize this retirement trip they've planned. It starts with a European cruise and ends with them settling into a pretty little village down on the coast near Beaumont." Elijah covered her hand with his and squeezed gently, and then quickly moved his hand away when he realized what he'd done. "After all the girls they've helped, they deserve a few years together. I want them to have nothing to do but enjoy time together and play dominoes with their new neighbors."

"Is there anything I can do to help?" Jayden asked, concern in her voice.

"Just listening to me put it all into words helps," he said.

She moved her hand away, stood up, and began to pace back and forth across the floor. "Starting tomorrow morning, instead of exercising with you and the girls, I'll go help make breakfast. The girls don't need supervising on their jobs, so I can be there for the other two meals, too. I like to cook."

Elijah shook his head. "I can't ask you to take on all that, plus take care of your girls."

"You're not asking." She sat back down. "I'm volunteering."

A picture of Skyler flashed through his mind. She would never offer to do so much work—not without getting paid double, and probably not even then.

"Then I'll pay you more money," he said.

"Nope," Jayden told him. "I'm not doing it for money."

Elijah wanted to hug her, as a friend, to show his gratitude, but he thought of the implications of such a thing and just nodded. "I can't thank you enough."

"Mary reminds me of my granny. I'd do this for her in a heartbeat," Jayden told him.

He got to his feet and picked up both empty bottles. "You'll let me know if you think she needs a doctor. We may have to take her to the emergency room kicking and screaming, but it would be worth being on her bad side if it means keeping her with us."

"Of course. I will, and I'll be honest." She smiled up at him. "Good night, Elijah."

"Sleep tight, and don't let the horseflies bite," he said.

"That's funny," she said.

The last person who had said Elijah was funny was Matty, the morning that they all went out on the mission. Elijah had told them a joke about a couple of country boys and a mule, and Matty said that he'd be laughing about that all day. "You're funny," he'd said as he grabbed up his gear and walked out the door.

Elijah still wasn't sleepy, so he sat down on the porch of his cabin and watched the clouds play hide-and-seek with the moon. Sometime around midnight he awoke with a start with a kink in his neck from falling asleep with his head propped against the back of the wooden Adirondack chair.

He groaned when he got to his feet, went inside, and saw how late it was. He'd have to be up in less than five hours and Jayden wouldn't even be there. A part of him wished that he had kept his mouth shut concerning his fears about Mary.

"Stop it!" he scolded himself as he climbed into bed. "You're being selfish."

❖ ❖ ❖

"Oh. My. Goodness. Do you already have coffee brewing?" Mary asked. "What are you doing up so early, Jayden? The siren hasn't even blown for the girls to line up for exercises."

"My girls are showing me that they can be trusted. I'm used to getting up early, and I need something to do. Can I help?" Jayden asked.

"Only a foolish person turns down help." Mary tossed Jayden a bibbed apron. "Henry usually helps me get things going before he milks the cows, but he's not feeling too well this morning. I told him to sleep in another half hour and then get up and around. Tell the truth, I'm a little worried about him."

"Oh?" Jayden slipped the apron over her head and tied the waist strings. Elijah was worried about Mary, and she was worried about Henry. Poor darlings, that had to be stressful for all of them.

"It's probably just fear that something will happen before we retire. My daddy retired on a Friday. He and Mama had planned a little trip back to Maryland to see her sister the very next week, but Daddy died on Saturday morning. I've been worried that something like that will happen to one of us. We're so close, and . . ." She wiped a tear away with the tail of her apron. "Listen to me acting like I've got a say-so in the day I take my last breath. Let's talk about something else. Can you make good biscuits?"

"You bet I can," Jayden answered. "After that happening to your dad, I can understand why you'd be worried. Does Henry need to see a doctor?"

"I don't think so. I think he's just needin' to see Joe. That's the last one of his Vietnam buddies. Ever since we bought this place, the guys all came and stayed for a week in our off-season after Christmas. There's just Joe and Henry left now, but there used to be six of them, and their wives, if they were married, came with them. Henry's been talking about him a lot lately and wishing he could see him more often." Mary took a big bowl of eggs from the refrigerator. "I reckon that at seventy-five, our old bodies are just gettin' tired of early mornings and all-day work."

"Good Lord!" Jayden gasped. "I had no idea that you were that age. I thought you were both coming up on normal retirement age—sixty-five."

Gramps died when he was younger than Mary, and that was only two years after they had buried Granny. Jayden's mama said that he died of a broken heart—she'd been surprised it hadn't happened even sooner than it did. Just thinking about the day they buried her grandfather brought a sharp pang to Jayden's heart. She hadn't known Mary and Henry very long, but she could see that they had the same kind of love that her grandparents had had. Like Elijah, she wanted them to have some time to enjoy life before the end.

"Thank you for that." Mary set the eggs down and went up on tiptoe to give Jayden a hug. "And thanks for helping out. Do you think you could do this every morning? That way Henry can get on about his jobs. Even though he don't say as much, he's as worried about me as I am him."

"I sure can. How about for dinner and supper, too?" Jayden asked. "I can dart in and out between meals to check on my girls."

"That would be wonderful. We could even pay you a little extra," Mary offered.

"That's not a bit necessary," Jayden said. "To me, this will be more like a vacation than a job."

"Well, if you change your mind . . ." Mary laid a hand on her chest and took a couple of deep breaths.

"You okay?" Jayden asked.

"I'm fine. Just a little heartburn." Mary started cracking eggs into a bowl.

Jayden could full well understand why Elijah was worried. The whole time she made biscuits, she wondered if she should tell him about Mary's fears for Henry's health as well. Maybe both of them should retire after this eight-week session instead of going straight into another two months with another set of girls.

"Hey, what are you doing in here?" Novalene asked as she came inside and headed toward the coffeepot. "I figured you'd be out there with Elijah and the girls."

"I'm going to give the ladies a little rope and help Mary in the kitchen," Jayden said.

"I'd offer to help, but I can't boil water without the neighbors calling the fire truck." Novalene laughed at her own joke. "Truth is that my idea of cooking is calling one of the two dozen numbers I have beside my phone and getting them to deliver my food. When I was teaching, I ate breakfast and lunch at school, and I picked up takeout on the way home. No wonder I've never been married."

"There's men out there who wouldn't mind eating takeout." Mary stuck a whisk into the bowl of eggs and began to whip them into a froth.

"Not when I was interested in marriage." Novalene sat down in a chair and propped her feet up in a second one. "Speaking of guys, I saw Elijah on your porch last night."

"Yep, he stopped by." Jayden used a glass to cut the rolled-out dough into perfect circles. "We each had a beer, but don't tattle on us." She'd learned years ago to own up to whatever she did, even if it made the devil blush, as her grandfather used to say.

"Wouldn't dream of it," Novalene said. "So how did yesterday go for you? My girls were tattling about yours threatening to throw them in the hog lot."

"Horseflies, horses, and hair," Jayden told her, and then explained briefly what she meant by the statement. She told Novalene and Mary about the lock of pink hair and all the rest, including the part about the girls being sexually active.

"Sometimes I wish I'd lived in this era." Novalene sighed. "In my day if we did it, we damn sure didn't talk about it. I like that journal idea. Next time Elijah goes into town, I'm going to ask him to pick up some for me. Do you mind if I see if Diana wants to do the same? After all, it is your idea."

"Not a bit," Jayden said. "I just thought it would be good for them, and it is something they can take home. Sometimes if I've got a kid who needs help but can't seem to tell me the problem, I have them write it down in a journal. I've started keeping one while I'm here, too. How about your day?"

"Let's see if I can be as clever as you." Novalene took a sip of coffee. "Cigarettes and . . ." She frowned. "Oh, hell, I can't think of anything to go with that. I caught Lauren smoking. She's got another demerit."

"How did she get cigarettes past us?" Mary asked.

"Slipped a pack out of her bra and right into the new one without us catching her. She's a sneaky little thing," Novalene answered. "I took a page out of your playbook, Jayden. If it's all right with you, she will be taking the slop out to the hogs every day for a week when Tiffany's time is up."

Jayden slid a big pan of biscuits into the commercial-size oven. "Maybe that should be the ultimate punishment for anyone who gets a demerit. Seems like they hate it worse than anything, except maybe catching horseflies right off the top of a pile of crap."

Diana yawned as she came into the dining hall and headed straight for the coffeepot. She poured herself a cup and carried it to the table where Novalene was seated. "Good mornin' to all y'all. I'm not fit to be around until I have my first sip, but now I can talk. How are things going in your cabins?"

"Our girls are fighting," Novalene said.

"That may be a good thing if it makes them bond together and work as a team." Diana blew on the top of her mug and then took a sip. "Ahhh, nothing better than the first cup in the morning."

"So, who's your alpha girl this year?" Novalene asked.

"Rita," Diana answered. "She's the one who set fire to her house because her stepfather beat on her."

"Mine is Lauren," Novalene said. "Hands down. But I do believe that she's a little afraid of Tiffany over in Jayden's Daydream cabin. She wouldn't say a word in group counseling. Keelan admitted to having a drug business, and even bragged that she probably made more money in a week than I did in a month teaching school. Bailey is following Lauren's example and refusing to talk about the meth business she had going."

"All of mine," Jayden answered, "have bossy personalities, so I think it'll depend on the day."

"Bless your heart," Diana said. "And I mean that in a good way. You're going to have your hands full if they're all smart-asses."

"Maybe they'll have *their* hands full." Jayden cocked her head to one side. "There's only three of them. At my regular job, I have twenty-five to thirty just like them in each class every day. I've just seen it all—from assault to drugs—and abuse and stealing are as common as breathing."

"Touché." Diana raised her cup to Jayden.

Chapter Nine

A ping on Jayden's phone woke her before the alarm went off that Sunday morning. She sat up in bed so fast that it made her dizzy. She grabbed the phone, punched in her code, and saw that it was a text from Skyler, complete with a selfie of Skyler with Big Ben in the background. The message said that the group was on the way to the airport to fly to Rome.

Jayden's heart stopped pounding after a couple of minutes. "Dammit, Skyler," she muttered. "It's too early for your bragging."

She turned off the alarm, got out of bed, and padded across the floor to turn on the overhead light. Then she sat down on the bed and enlarged Skyler's picture on the phone. She looked happy, but then she always did when she got what she wanted. Jayden remembered the shoebox full of photographs she'd brought to her apartment after her mother died. They could be divided into two categories. The first one was when Skyler was posing with a smile on her face. The other stack would be those that were taken when she had to have her picture taken with Jayden, and she glared at the camera.

"Family is a complicated thing," she said as she laid the phone to the side. She wished she could snap her fingers and go back to the days when she lived with her mother and grandfather in the house on Elm Street in Boyd. Even with Skyler's vanity, things were simpler then.

She dressed in a pair of jeans and a T-shirt, then went straight to the dining hall. The aroma of freshly brewed coffee met her at the door, but she bypassed that and headed to the small half bath. One perk of helping cook was that she didn't have to traipse out across the yard to the bathhouse.

"Good mornin'," Mary singsonged.

"Mornin'," Jayden called out.

When she finished, she washed her hands, poured a cup of coffee, and carried it to the kitchen. "I had a text and a picture from Skyler this morning. They've been in London."

"Are you jealous?" Mary stirred up a batch of buttercream frosting.

"No, ma'am." Jayden flipped a bibbed apron over her head and tied the strings. "I'm just surprised that she even thought about sending me a picture. I usually don't hear from her except at Christmas."

"Maybe it's her way of saying thank you for taking her place here," Mary said.

"Maybe so." Jayden nodded, but she didn't believe a word of it.

They put together oven omelets and biscuits for breakfast that morning and baked three pans of cinnamon rolls that had been rising in the refrigerator all night. Mary spread the buttercream frosting on top of the rolls while they were still hot and set them out at the end of the buffet line.

"That's my Sunday treat for the girls." She smiled.

A vision of her grandmother, who also liked bibbed aprons, flashed through Jayden's mind. "Chocolate chip pancakes are my Sunday treat for your grandpa. He's got a sweet tooth, and he does love chocolate," Granny had told her. Jayden turned away from Mary and wiped a tear from her cheek. Granny and Gramps had accepted her just like she was—tall, gangly, awkward—and never compared her to her sister. But then after she was a teenager and got her own car, Skyler only came around them when she wanted something.

Daylight was pushing away the darkness when the girls came in from their morning exercise and walk. Tiffany, the first in line, held out her tray for a bigger helping of casserole. "I'm starving this morning." She managed a smile that didn't even look like a grimace. "Carmella found an ant the size of a buzzard."

"Everything is bigger in Texas," Carmella said from the second place in line.

Lauren came next and her whole body seemed to hum with pent-up energy. Her eyes were glazed over, and her hands shook when she held out her tray. "I want more," she said with a wicked grin. Jayden gave her a double portion and kept an eye on her when she carried her tray to the table. Jayden took a deep breath and let it out slowly, hoping that everything went well once Lauren had eaten. Jayden had had students with low blood sugar who looked like Lauren, so maybe that was her problem.

"Are you all right?" Mary asked.

"Just fine," Jayden answered. "Lauren seems to be stressed this morning."

"She's been belligerent all morning," Elijah whispered as he came through the line. "She always stops right at the edge of being given a demerit for bullying the other girls, especially Tiffany."

Jayden caught a movement out of her peripheral vision and turned in time to see Lauren push her chair back so hard that it fell backward, clanging on the floor. Everything went quiet, and all the girls seemed to freeze in their chairs. Then she picked up her tray and threw it at the wall, scattering food all over the floor and into the girls' hair. Jayden dropped the serving spoon in her hand and started toward the table.

"I hate this miserable place," Lauren jumped up and yelled at the top of her lungs. "I hate everyone here, and I hate Tiffany Jordan more than anyone else." She took a few steps to the next table, drew back her fist, and knocked Tiffany out of her chair onto the floor.

Tiffany bounced up to her feet, hands clenched in fists, and glared at Lauren. "That was a big mistake." In seconds there were legs and arms flailing about—and screams from both girls filling the dining hall.

Novalene, Diana, and Henry all jumped up, too, but Elijah had been closest to the table, so he beat everyone to the fight. Jayden got there in time to pull Tiffany away, as Elijah was trying to corral Lauren, but she was all flailing arms and kicking legs.

Lauren got free from him and drew back to hit Tiffany again, missed the mark, and landed a right hook on Jayden. Jayden instinctively let go of Tiffany to grab her aching eye, and Tiffany went right back at Lauren.

"I'm going to tear you into pieces and feed you to the hogs for hitting Jayden," Tiffany yelled. The other seven girls stayed in their chairs, but they began to argue—some taking up for Lauren, others for Tiffany. Carmella and Ashlyn finally broke the rules. Carmella rushed over to Jayden and helped her get ahold of Tiffany again, and Ashlyn bowed up to Lauren.

Novalene and Diana waded into the melee.

"Get out of my way," Lauren screamed. "I hate you as much as I do that bitch."

Henry had the good sense to cross the room and hit the button to blow the siren. The noise made every one of them stop and stand at attention. Novalene grabbed Lauren by the arm and marched her toward the door. "We're going to the cabin. You've racked up so many demerits that it'll be a wonder if you get to stay here another day."

"When I get to that miserable cabin, I'm going to get my razor out of my footlocker and slit my wrists, and if you try to stop me, I'll cut you, too. I'd rather die and go to hell as spend another night here," Lauren hissed.

"I'll get her things and the van," Elijah said. "You keep her on the porch until I get here. Jayden, will you help watch her?"

"Of course." Jayden nodded.

"Put me in jail. My folks will get me out and send me off to a fancy center, and even that will be better than this place. I'll be out before you losers finish serving your time in this slum." Lauren broke free of Novalene's grasp on her arm, ran around the end of the buffet line, and slapped Mary across the face. "And I hate your cooking, so add that to my demerits."

All the color rushed from Henry's face as he ran across the room and wrapped his arms around his wife. Jayden grabbed Lauren and held both her hands behind her back with one hand, whipped off her apron with the other, and tied the girl's wrists together with the strings.

"You can't do this to me," the girl screamed.

"I just did." Jayden's heart raced and her breath came out in short gasps.

Lauren struggled against the restraints and screamed. "My daddy will sue this place."

"Bring it on, sweetheart," Jayden said. "I'm going to take you outside now. You got any last words for your teammates?"

"Go to hell, the whole bunch of you," Lauren said.

Henry's hands knotted into fists and he took a step away from Mary. She reached out and got his arm. "I'm all right, darlin'. Let it go. I just wish we could have helped her."

"Some people can't be helped." Henry hugged Mary tightly. "She's not the first one to be sent away, and she won't be the last."

Jayden felt like a police officer as she grabbed Lauren's collar with one hand and the makeshift handcuffs with the other. She and Novalene together took Lauren outside, but the girl fought them every step of the way.

Elijah pulled the van up and parked it. Jayden and Novalene got Lauren into the back seat, but it was no easy feat. She tried to fall down on the ground, then braced a leg on each side of the van door and used every cuss word in her vocabulary. Jayden finally got the girl into the back seat and was fastening her seat belt when Lauren slammed her head against Jayden's. Everything went dark for a second, and Jayden felt the earth coming up to meet her—then strong arms bore her up. She shook off the dizziness and looked up into Elijah's eyes.

"Are you okay?" he asked.

"I'm fine," Jayden answered. "I don't think I'm hurt. More shocked than anything. Should I ride along in the back seat with her? You have to drive, and Novalene might need my help corralling her."

"No, you need to get some ice on that eye and your forehead," Elijah answered. "When I get back, we'll take you into the emergency room and have you checked out."

"That's not necessary." Jayden took a step back. "I've had this bad and worse from my students at the school where I teach, but you could order a couple of sets of handcuffs in case this ever happens again."

Tiffany seemed to appear out of nowhere. "Take those strings off her and give me five minutes of her time. I'll show her that she can't treat people like that."

"You just see to it that Jayden gets some ice on her eye," Elijah said as he got behind the wheel and closed the door.

"Yes, sir," Tiffany said.

Tiffany threw an arm around Jayden's shoulders and led her inside the dining hall. Somehow the mess had been cleaned up, and the rest of the girls had continued eating breakfast. The difference was in the buzz of conversation in the room. Where things had gone quiet as a tomb when the siren blew, it now sounded like a beehive.

Tiffany went to the kitchen, got a bag of frozen peas from the refrigerator, and handed it to Jayden. Jayden held the peas against her eye and crossed the room to sit with the adults. Her heart had settled down to a slow, steady beat, but the pain in her eye and head would take a while to disappear. It wasn't her first black eye, and she'd had a minor concussion before, so she knew this wasn't one of those, but it still hurt like hell.

Mary leaned across Elijah's empty chair and laid a hand on her arm. "Are you all right? Did they get her into the van without too much trouble?"

"I'm fine and she's on her way to Alpine," Jayden answered with a reassuring smile. "And this casserole is good enough to eat cold. I earned *two* of those cinnamon rolls after this. Are you and Henry all right?"

"We're fine, but I got to admit that's the first time I've had a girl hit me," Mary said.

"Hopefully, it will be the last," Henry added.

"While you were outside—" Diana began, but then drew in a short breath. "Good Lord, girl, your hands are shaking. Are you sure you're all right?"

"Just a little shook up." Jayden made a conscious effort to still her nerves. "What happened when I was outside?"

"Rita told me that Lauren said she wasn't going to stay here no matter what she had to do. She was so mad when she stepped in horse crap this morning on their walk that she declared this was her last day here. Rita also said that Lauren told her she had some pills that she'd hidden with her cigarettes and managed to hang on to them even when Novalene confiscated the smokes," Diana answered. "I've dealt with kids that were high in my school before, but I've never seen anyone as wild as that girl."

"Me either." Jayden willed her hands to stop shaking so she could finish her breakfast.

"Diana, would you drive the second van to church this morning?" Henry asked. "Mary and I like to steal away for an hour and go to *our* church on Sunday morning. After what's happened, it'll be good for both of us to go sit quietly before the Lord for a little while."

Jayden's three girls finished their meal and came over to form a circle around her.

"What can we do to help you?" Tiffany asked.

"You can help me and Mary out in the kitchen." Jayden could see that they needed something to do, and Mary was covering it well, but her hands were trembling.

"Yes, ma'am," Tiffany said. "I'll start rinsing trays."

"It's a good thing Lauren is gone, or I might have done something stupid and gotten sent away with her. If I get a demerit for not staying in my seat, it'll be worth it."

Carmella led the way to the kitchen. "Me too, but let's go get started."

"That Tiffany is a tough cookie," Henry whispered.

"She'll have bruises," Jayden said, "but she's showing all the other girls that she's meaner than Lauren was."

"I admire her and hope my girls take a lesson from what happened this morning." Diana picked up her tray and headed toward the kitchen with it. "Since Lauren isn't here for slop duty next week, that's going to be Rita's job. She stole my cell phone last night and was attempting to call her boyfriend when I caught her."

Jayden just nodded and joined her girls in the kitchen.

"I hate this job." Ashlyn sighed. "I'd rather clean horse stalls any day of the week than wash nasty old trays. We've got an amazing chef at home who makes whatever each of us wants, and she does the cleanup."

"Stop griping," Tiffany said. "We're here to help Jayden."

Jayden turned away so they couldn't see her smile. She was proud of them for stepping up to the plate and taking on extra work.

"You mean you don't have to eat whatever is fixed?" Carmella asked.

"Nope, we get to tell Martha what we want in the morning, and it's ready for dinner." Ashlyn rinsed trays and stacked them in the dishwasher. "I've never had to work like this before. I don't like therapy, but I'll take it over this."

"Therapy ain't so bad," Tiffany said. "And I like Karen. I wasn't going to talk to her when it was my hour, but she's so sweet and she really listened when I said something."

Jayden appreciated the meeting the counselors had with Karen. She addressed several of the girls' problems and gave the counselors positive ways to help with them. Hearing that Tiffany liked Karen was a plus and gave Jayden hope that the girl would truly leave with a better self-image.

"I like to cook," Carmella said. "Our cook lets me help in the kitchen all the time, but Mama decides what the menu is, and I can eat what's put on the table or have a peanut butter sandwich."

"What about you, Tiffany?" Jayden asked.

"My folks are gone all the time. They don't give a crap what I eat or even *if* I eat. The housekeeper will fix food some of the time, but mostly I just live on takeout," Tiffany answered.

No wonder the girls got into so much trouble, Jayden thought. Seemed to Jayden like their parents were much more taken up with careers and their own lives than seeing to it their daughters had the right kind of positive attention, but then she was used to seeing similar in her own school.

Elijah would have much rather been back at camp making sure that Jayden and Mary were really all right than taking a petulant girl to the county jail. His thoughts were all over the place. What if Mary had a heart attack over this incident? What if Jayden's eye swelled shut? Would that affect her ability to help Mary or to take care of the girls in her cabin?

At first Lauren didn't cry, but when Novalene and Elijah wouldn't argue with her, the waterworks started. She cussed, long and loudly. She tried to kick the side window out, but then she got sick and threw up in the barf bag that Novalene had the good sense to bring along.

"Daddy is going to hate me. He loves my brother, but then Joseph is perfect and never does anything wrong. I wish he would die so Daddy would love me."

"That's your problem." Elijah didn't care right then if she hadn't been loved enough or potty-trained right, or if her brother had wings and a halo.

"If you would take advantage of group sessions and your counseling, you might get over that feeling," Novalene told her.

"Counselors are stupid," Lauren said and stared out the window. "Take me back. I'll be good."

"Can't do that," Elijah said as he eased into a parking space behind the jail. Two deputies waited beside a patrol car and started walking toward them. "Looks like your dad has already arranged something."

"I hope someone sets fire to Piney Wood and you all die," Lauren hissed.

Elijah rolled down the window and said, "We're delivering Lauren Fielding into your care."

A deputy slid open the side door and held out a pair of cuffs. "Young lady, your father has instructed us to take you back to the airport, where he will have a private plane waiting to take you to a rehab center."

Elijah got out of the van and walked around the front of it.

"Is Daddy going to be on the plane?" Lauren asked as she slid out of the seat.

"Fancy ties you got there," the deputy chuckled as he fastened the cuffs around Lauren's wrists before he untied the apron and tossed it in the back seat.

"No, ma'am," the other deputy answered. "He's sending your brother to accompany you. Are you going to go quietly?"

"Yes, I'll be a good girl." Lauren almost sounded like a sweet little mistreated child. "Just don't make me go back to Piney Wood. They abuse all us girls at that place."

The deputy winked at Elijah as he escorted Lauren to their unit. "That's a shame. Deputy Jones will get your bag, and hopefully this next place will be nicer to you."

"Well, that's that," Elijah said as he got back into the vehicle with Novalene. To his surprise, his hands trembled when he put the van in gear and drove out of the parking lot. Elijah didn't handle failure well, and he felt as if he'd failed Lauren. As he drove north, he thought back to the time when he'd flown out to get his teammates. He didn't know at that point how many were hurt, if any were dead, or exactly what he was going to find. The only information he had was that there had been an explosion and Matty, their corpsman, was hurt too badly to render help to the others. The picture of Buddy and Tim running across the ground between those two mountains was forever burned into his brain. Elijah had smelled fresh blood many times, but anytime he thought of that day when three of his teammates were killed, the metallic smell that filled his nostrils always came back to his mind.

"Where's Tim and Matty?" Elijah had yelled over the whirring noise of the blades.

"They're right behind us. Their Humvee got hit. Matty's hurt bad," Buddy answered. "But he's alive."

Tim was a huge man, six foot four and weighing in at 280 pounds, but there wasn't a spare bit of fat on his body. He carried Matty like a baby across the desolate field that day and held him all the way back to base. Elijah could still hear his deep southern voice telling Matty to hang on.

"Elijah's going to get us back to safety. You're going to be fine. Open your eyes. Look at me," Tim kept repeating.

But Elijah didn't make it in time, and Matty was declared dead on arrival at the base. And Elijah had always wondered if those few extra minutes without refueling the chopper might have made the difference.

"I feel like a complete failure." Novalene's voice brought him out of the past and back to the present. "This is my first time ever to lose a girl, and she slapped Mary. I'm sick to my stomach over that. I keep asking myself if something I did or didn't do caused her to flip out like that. Should I have gone easier on her over the cigarettes?"

"Don't beat yourself up. Like Henry said, some folks can't be helped. Maybe Lauren will get some good professional help at this new place." Elijah made the last turn and parked the van in front of the dining hall.

"Well," Novalene sighed, "it's a good day for church after all that."

"Amen," Elijah agreed.

Novalene's two remaining girls had been on milking duty with Henry that morning and had evidently finished their job, because they were sitting on the Moonbeam porch. Jayden's crew was on the dining hall porch. The remaining three were coming across the grounds with Diana behind them.

"We've got about an hour." Novalene unfastened her seat belt and got out of the van. "I'm going to use the time to talk to the two I've got left. Do you think this will shake the whole camp up?"

Elijah held up his forefinger in a gesture that said he would answer her in a minute, and then followed her to the porch where Jayden waited.

"Hey, everyone, gather up here," Elijah yelled.

When the rest of the girls had come close enough, he said, "Lauren won't be coming back, but we'll continue on with our lives just like before. We will be attending church and then coming back here for Sunday dinner. Any questions?"

No hands went up, and not a single one of them opened their mouth.

"Okay, then go on to your cabins and get ready for church," he told them.

When they were out of hearing distance, he turned to the counselors. "Novalene asked me if I thought this incident would shake the whole camp up. It usually does when we have to take one away. The rest of the girls realize what they're up against if they don't finish the course," Elijah said. "Let me know if you have any problems."

"If we have any, they'll probably come from my cabin. Keelan and Lauren were pretty close," Novalene said. "Hopefully, going to church as a group will help them."

"Let's hope so, and we will be attending the first church on the list this morning."

"If I remember right, that would be the small one with the nice red chairs rather than long pews, right?" Novalene asked.

"Yep," Elijah answered. "Henry and Mary still think it's best if we go to a different one every week."

"If we do what?" Jayden asked.

"We attend a different church each Sunday," Elijah explained. "We know that the girls don't all have the same religious affiliations, so that makes it fair. When we have girls that usually attend a temple or a mosque, we make arrangements for that, too, but this time around we don't need to include those."

"Makes sense to me." Jayden started to get up and follow them, but Elijah reached out and grabbed her hand. "Just a word before you go." He dropped her hand and asked, "Are you all right? How's Mary?"

"I'm just fine," Jayden assured him. "Mary and Henry have already left for their services. She seemed fine when they drove away."

He tucked his hand under her chin and turned her face toward him. "You're going to have a shiner."

This just proved that people who got too close to Elijah had bad luck. First his brother died, then his parents, and then almost half his team. Jayden would do well to steer clear of him.

She put her hand on his and gave it a gentle squeeze. "I've had black eyes before, and from a person a whole lot smaller than Lauren. My first one was from a seventh grader who was throwing a tantrum over not being able to eat candy in the classroom. He decked me harder than she did."

Elijah dropped his hand. "I'm so sorry this happened. I'd still feel better if you would let me take you to the emergency room."

"I'll be ugly for a few days, but we've got to take these girls to church this morning. That's more important than a bruised eye," she told him.

He walked across the lawn with her. All three girls were sitting on the porch, their young faces filled with questions.

"We want to know more about what happened to Lauren," Tiffany said. "Did she settle down or do something stupid like kick the windows out of the van?"

"We took her to the police station, where they were waiting. Her father sent his private plane to take her to a rehab center," Elijah answered.

"What if her father pays for her to come back?" Carmella asked.

"Three-strike rule applies here, and there's no coming back, ever. If her father didn't have the means and connections, she'd be on her way to talk to the judge about spending some time in juvie. What do you think would happen to you if you got two more strikes?" Elijah locked eyes with Tiffany.

"My daddy might have pity on me, but Mama wouldn't. She says I'm an embarrassment to her. Last time she wouldn't even let me talk to the judge. I'd go straight to jail if she had her way." Tiffany stood up and headed toward the cabin. "Do we get a siren when it's time to go to church? And what place do we go to? At home, Mama takes me to mass on Christmas and Easter."

"And do me and Carmella get a demerit for not staying in our seats this morning?" Ashlyn asked.

"No to your question, Ashlyn. You were trying to help, not hinder, the situation. And to answer your question, Tiffany, we go to a different one every single week," Elijah said. "You've each got a list of the churches. This is the first Sunday you are here, so we start with the one at the top. It's a small church, not far from here."

"I looked at the list this morning. That's the kind of church where Mama's housekeeper goes," Ashlyn said. "I went with her a couple of times. I like their singing. Can we please at least have our own jeans and shirts for Sunday services?"

"Sorry, girls," Jayden said. "Rules are rules, like you just heard. You will attend services in what you are wearing. You can brush your hair and your teeth, but don't forget to put your caps back on."

Carmella wiped sweat from her brow. "Thank God we go to a different place every week."

"Why?" Jayden asked.

"Because if there's any sexy boys there, they'll only see us lookin' like this one time," Carmella answered and then went inside the Daydream Cabin.

"All of the girls expected you to bring Lauren back and give her another chance, and that concerned me," Jayden said. "I'm glad you didn't. She seemed way too violent to have around the other kids. What if she really did decide to go on a rampage?"

"Part of why she didn't come back. She's got problems way beyond what we can do to help her. Had Henry settled down when he and Mary left? His blood pressure was probably out of sight," Elijah asked.

"He seemed to be fine," Jayden answered. "How's Novalene?"

"Feeling like a failure. You and the other ladies might want to visit with her this afternoon. I'm going to get a softball game going with the girls so they'll keep busy." Elijah turned to walk away and then stopped and looked over his shoulder.

"Thanks for all you're doing in the kitchen, and for having the foresight to use an apron for handcuffs. Henry appreciates it and so do I."

"I enjoy working with Mary, and I love to cook, so it's a win-win there. And working in an underfunded school district has taught me to use whatever is at hand," she said. "But you might invest in some real restraints for next season."

"You sure I can't take you away from your job at the school? I'll pay you better and you'll get more time off. Since you'd be a full-time cook, you wouldn't even have to take care of a cabin. I'll give you my house, and I'll move over into Henry and Mary's place when they retire," he offered.

"I'm not staying here, Elijah, but again, thanks for the offer."

Jayden sat down on her porch and wished she had a good cold beer in her hands. She'd lied about her first black eye. That had come at the hands of Skyler when she was twelve and her sister caught her using her lipstick. Skyler had picked up a silver-plated hand mirror and smacked her in the eye with it. She'd cried after she'd done the deed, but not because she was sorry for hitting Jayden. Her little hissy fit was because she'd broken her mirror, and she said that Jayden had caused her to have seven years of bad luck.

Jayden put that memory out of her mind and was trying to figure out if she could have helped Lauren in some way when "I Saw the Light" came over the loudspeaker that usually sent out the sound of a siren.

"Nice touch," she muttered. Then she opened the door and yelled, "Church time!"

She hadn't set foot in a church since her mother's funeral. God was supposed to be merciful and kind, right? Well, He had failed Jayden when He didn't answer her prayers, so she had turned her back on Him. He could have woken her mother up from the coma that she'd fallen into after the aneurism.

Jayden's three girls came out of the cabin and got into the van with Diana and a couple of her girls. The rest of the camp members rode with Elijah and Jayden. Turned out that it was on the north side of town, and it was a very small place, with only five or six rows of chairs on two sides of a center aisle. As luck would have it, when they all walked in the door, the back rows were filled. Apparently, the back two rows on the right-hand side were where the cute boys sat, and all eight girls put a little extra swing in their walk when they passed by them to sit on the front pew.

Elijah was the last one in the door, and since the only chair left was right beside Jayden, his broad shoulder touched hers all during the service. Cool air flowed down from a vent right above her, but her hands were still sweaty, and her pulse jacked up another notch or two every time he leaned a little more her way.

If he was getting the same vibes she was, there was no way they could ever work together every day like Mary and Henry did. No, sir. No way. With the chemistry she felt, she'd be dragging him off to her cabin instead of cooking meals.

A lady wearing a purple dress took her place behind the lectern and said, "Special welcome today to the girls and their sponsors from out at Piney Wood. We're always glad to see y'all when it's our turn for you to visit us. If everyone will turn to page three eighty in the hymnals that are under your chairs, we'll begin our services with congregational singing," she announced, and then continued to the sound of pages flipping. "Everyone likes to sing, so we just let the whole church be our choir."

You can't sing in the choir. They wouldn't have a robe long enough for you, and besides, your voice sounds like you're a boy. Maybe you should *have been a guy. God knows you're tall enough to be one.* Skyler's voice came back to Jayden's mind.

Jayden must have been about fourteen at the time, and that was the last time she ever asked her mother if she might start going to choir practice with Skyler on Friday nights.

The pianist played a short prelude and then the lady led them in "Abide with Me," with an upbeat version of the song that bore little resemblance to the music notes in the hymnal. The boys on the back rows kept time by clapping their hands. Jayden mumbled through the first verse, but by the second one, she had it down.

Skyler had chosen this very hymn to be played at their mother's graveside service, but Jayden had been too angry that she and her sister were the only ones there that day to even pay attention to the lyrics. Now as she sang the words, it seemed fitting. The last verse talked about pointing me to the skies, and heaven's morning breaking. It asked that, in life or death, the Lord abide with me—whoever *me* happened to be.

When they had finished the hymn, the song leader and pianist took a seat over on the wall behind the piano, and the preacher stepped up behind the lectern. "I'll add my welcome to the ladies and to Elijah from out at Piney Wood. This morning's reading is from John 15. 'Abide in Me, and I in you. As the branch cannot bear fruit of itself unless it abides in the vine, so neither can you unless you abide in Me. I am the vine, you are the branches; he who abides in Me and I in him, he bears much fruit, for apart from Me you can do nothing.' Now, I ask you all, each and every one of you, what does it mean to abide in Him? Well, that's what I'm going to tell you this morning."

That word *abide* stuck in Jayden's mind. Was someone—she looked up at the ceiling—bringing back memories of her mother's death and burial so that she would talk to Skyler about it? Or was the fact that Elijah was sitting so close supposed to be an omen telling her to think about abiding right there at Piney Wood? *Would* God speak to her after she had cut all ties with Him? Until that moment, she hadn't even considered such an idea, but suddenly she found herself wondering what it would be like to do something with her life other than be a counselor at school.

Chapter Ten

One of the red chairs on her front porch was the perfect place to watch that afternoon's softball game.

"*My* front porch," Jayden muttered. "This place isn't mine by any means." She took a sip of her cold root beer.

Ashlyn was doing a fine job of pitching. Tiffany was on first, Carmella in outfield, and Rita had two strikes, and then she hit the ball.

"She's got a home run if Carmella don't catch it." Diana sat down in a chair at the other end of the line. "They seem to be having a good time."

The ball went high and landed right in Carmella's glove, giving Rita a third out and sending that team back to the sidelines.

"I'm glad they're doing something fun." Novalene came up the steps and sat down in the chair right next to Jayden. "They need it after this morning."

"I love these chairs," Diana said. "I keep saying I'm going to have one of these connected ones built for my front porch at home, but then I don't get around to it. How are you holding up, Novalene?"

"Church helped," Novalene said. "I don't know if it was the message I was supposed to get, but what I heard was that we should just leave it in God's hands and abide with Him."

"Did you talk to your other girls?" Jayden asked.

"Yes, before and after church," Novalene answered. "They verified that Lauren had managed to sneak some pills past us when they arrived.

They told me she got so angry with them over not taking some of them with her that they were actually a little afraid of her. Rita said that she was glad to see her leave, but Keelan told me she felt sorry for her. I've never lost a girl before. I got to admit that even leaving it in God's hands, I still feel like a failure."

"One of my favorite sayings is that a change in behavior begins with a change in the heart," Diana said. "You can't expect fourteen, fifteen, or sixteen years of behavior to change in just a week, especially when that kid's heart didn't want to change."

"I kind of got that impression when she started ranting and raving about her brother being perfect," Novalene said. "Seems to me like she wants everyone around her to change and make her world better, but she doesn't want to do what she can to make herself a better person in her world."

"That's the way we get 'em, and then if we're lucky, they leave us with a different heart," Diana said.

"What do you think, Jayden?" Novalene asked.

"I think that I may be learning more than the girls are," she replied.

"That's the way of it sometimes," Novalene said. "Want to talk about it?"

"Before my mother died, she gave my sister the job of executor over her estate and then gave her power of attorney. When my folks divorced, I stayed with Mama. Skyler was in college, but she seldom came home until that last year. Mama gave Skyler the house where we were both raised, and she sold it without even giving me the option to buy it. I've had trouble forgiving either of them," Jayden began. "I didn't even know about the decision to put Skyler in charge until our mother went into a coma because of a brain aneurism, and Skyler held everything in her hands. All she would tell me was that Mama had a dream that her time was up, and she made final arrangements in case it came true. Even as children we were never close like sisters should be.

She was the pretty and smart one, and I was . . . I have always been a 'you get what you see' girl."

"Why do you think your mother did that?" Novalene asked. "Maybe the brain problem had already affected her mind, and she made the wrong decision."

"Maybe so, but I intend to nail Skyler down when I go home and find out if she knows why," Jayden answered. That word *home* stuck in her mind. After the thoughts she'd had that morning about Elijah's offer, she had begun to wonder exactly where *home* was.

"You girls definitely should talk about it," Novalene said. "Skyler is a good person, a little religious, and, in my opinion, always coming close to preaching to her girls when she was here, but she's your sister. I would give anything to have my sister back to talk to her. We had our differences, but we were best friends as we got older. I lost her last summer, and my first thought this morning when all that went down with Lauren was that I wished I could call Dora Lou and talk to her about it."

"I never had a sister, but I've got three brothers. I've told folks that's why I went into teaching—so I could be the boss for a little while," Diana said. "But one of my sisters-in-law has been my best friend since first grade, so it's almost the same thing. She and my brother live up in central Oklahoma. We talk on the phone at least three times a week, and we can't wait for the family gatherings when we get to see each other. I don't know what I'd do without her."

Everyone has their own stories, Jayden thought as she watched Tiffany hit the ball way out into left field and make it to third base. She'd had a best friend from kindergarten to eleventh grade. Lee Anna had long red hair and was as tall as Tiffany, and she and Jayden were inseparable. Then Lee Anna slept with Jayden's boyfriend right before the junior-senior prom. Jayden had already bought a dress and was so excited about going to the prom with Kyle. Then overnight he called to break up with her and say that he was taking Lee Anna to the event. That was only a few months after her parents' divorce, when Jayden's trust meter was at an all-time low. After the trust issues that came with that, and the way that Skyler treated her, she had learned to keep everyone at arm's length.

Can you trust Elijah? the voice in her head asked.

"If either of you hadn't chosen a job working with kids, what would you have wanted to be?" she asked to get her mind away from the past and from Elijah.

"I would have been a race car driver," Novalene answered first. "I love to drive fast with rock music playing as loud as I can get it."

"You're joking, right?" Jayden's eyes felt like they might pop right out of her head, roll down the steps, and land out there in the dirt.

"Nope, not in the least, and Elvis Presley is my favorite. Lord, that boy could sing, and he looked like sex on a stick." Novalene fanned herself with the back of her hand. "I saw him once in concert out in Vegas."

"Did you throw your panties at him?" Jayden asked.

"Damn straight I did. My sister and I both did. Mine were black lace and hers were red satin." Novalene laughed. "I can see that I've shocked the sin right out of y'all. Now it's your turn to answer that question, too."

Diana raised her hand. "I'll go next. There were times when I got tired of Mama telling me that my brothers got to stay out later and do more than I did because they were boys. So, if I could be something other than a teacher, which Mama thought was a good, safe route for me to take, I would have gone into the army and trained to be a sniper. I go to the shooting range every month. I've earned my expert marksman status."

"Do you really think you could shoot someone?" Jayden asked.

"I could have this morning." Diana smiled. "But we'll never know whether I really could or not, because that ship sailed a long time ago. My folks would have dropped graveyard dead if I would have even mentioned joining the army. Your turn, Jayden."

"Is this a therapy session?" Jayden asked.

"Could be," Novalene answered. "I sure never told anyone that I drive ninety in a seventy-five-mile zone and listen to Elvis so loud that it shakes my car. They'd send the boys in the white jackets after me."

"Before I tell y'all what I might have been, what do you think the answer will be?" Jayden wondered how folks—other than her sister—might see her.

"I think you're stalling and that you are playing the role of the therapist," Novalene said, "but I'll go first. You would have been a chef in a big fancy restaurant."

"No, she would have been a baseball player," Diana disagreed. "She's been watching the game out there pretty close. She would have been like Geena Davis in *A League of Their Own*. Matter of fact, she looks like Geena. She even has the same smile as Geena. But Jayden has freckles and Geena doesn't."

"Geena probably did, too, but the makeup covered them," Novalene argued.

"Maybe so," Diana agreed. "But I also think she would have been a writer, maybe of romance novels. She's watching the game, but her eyes are also on Elijah. What was your major in college? Did you teach before you became a school counselor?"

"I majored in English, and I taught three years before I got offered the job of counselor," she answered.

"Then I'm right about her being an author. She's had heartache in her life, so she could touch a reader's emotions."

"Bingo! Give Diana a prize." Jayden grinned. "She got pretty close. I'm not sure I could tell a story good enough for someone to read. I always thought I'd like to be an editor, but I'm a counselor and that's probably what I'll be until I retire."

"Diana, how old are you?" Novalene asked.

"I turned gray before I was thirty, so you might think I'm older than I am. I don't mind tellin' you that fifty is in the rearview mirror for me—way too old to join the army now. But don't ask me about my weight. Only me, my doctor, and God know that number. I threatened to make the nurse that weighs me once a year sign an affidavit in blood—hers not mine—that she would never utter that bit of information out loud, write it on any piece of paper other than the doctor's notes, or even think it after I left the office," Diana said.

"If you want to be a sniper, you should teach shooting classes instead of counseling kids," Novalene told Diana.

"Another thing I wish I'd done was get married and have kids," Diana said.

"It's not too late for that," Novalene told her. "Don't wait until you're sixty like me and too old to have kids. I regret that most about my life. Kids and grandkids would have been nice right about now. Maybe that's why I love these mean little girls so damn much. They're surrogates for what I don't have."

Diana shrugged. "I've thought about both of those, but . . ."

"But what? Have you looked into it?" Jayden asked when she paused.

"This really is group therapy." Diana chuckled. "It's your turn, Jayden. How old are you?"

"I was thirty-one last month," Jayden admitted. "Thanks for thinking I look like a young Geena Davis, too. I always felt like an ugly duckling because I was tall and gangly, and there wasn't a delicate thing about me."

"Ugly ducklings often turn into beautiful swans," Novalene declared. "You have a good heart, woman. You are strong. I saw a quote once that said something about us all needing to surrender to the beauty of revealing ourselves to ourselves, to realize that our beauty comes from within, not from without."

"I saw that same one. The whole thing hangs on the wall in my office. Doing that is a daily battle for all of us, but most of all for these girls. Looks like our session is over." Jayden pointed to eight girls and one handsome fellow walking away from the makeshift baseball field. "I bet they're starving tonight, and speaking of that, I'd better hustle on over to the dining room and help Mary get the pizzas ready to serve."

Everyone has a story, a daydream, or even a regret, she thought as she stood up. "Thanks for the visit. Novalene, I don't think you should drive the second van to church next Sunday."

The older woman chuckled as she got to her feet and headed over to the Moonbeam Cabin. "I doubt any of these girls would love Elvis like I do, anyway, and even as tough as they think they are, they'd be cryin' their little eyes out for me to slow down once I got into my zone, as the kids these days say. Maybe that's where I went wrong with Lauren. I should have taken her for a ride, and then she would have thought this place was right up there next to heaven. I'll see y'all at supper in a few minutes."

"Pizza, pasta, and pie with ice cream tonight," Jayden said as she hurried across the yard, making it to the dining building in time for Elijah to open the door for her.

"Don't get downwind from me or the girls," he said. "All of us will be glad for showers tonight."

"Looks like you had a good time, though." Jayden went into the kitchen and grabbed an apron. "Do you do this every Sunday?"

"Nope," Mary answered for him. "Sometimes he gets them into a horseshoe competition or some other game. It teaches them sportsmanship."

"And teamwork," he said. "Can I help with anything? It's five minutes before the siren goes and I have to see that their toes are on the edge of the sidewalk."

"What does that teach?" Jayden asked.

"Obedience, which helps them learn to listen to rules, and *that* helps them hopefully grow up and live long enough to be productive citizens. When their boss tells them to do something, they do it, and in turn, it teaches them to like themselves for doing a good job," Elijah answered.

"Or when the law says that they don't drink and drive, they obey and maybe don't wind up killing someone and themselves," Mary added. "So, everyone wins, but most important, the girls do."

Jayden nodded in agreement. She had always preached that going to school wasn't just to learn to read, write, and do math. Getting up and going to class taught them how to be on time for their jobs when they were adults. Listening to lectures taught them to pay attention so they could learn the ins and outs of a job. All of it together made them learn responsibility.

Elijah left the kitchen when the siren echoed out through the land. Jayden covered her ears.

Mary giggled.

"I liked the hymn this morning better than this. Why can't we call them to dinner with a country music song?" Jayden asked.

"We've tried everything from something like bells ringing to an old-fashioned telephone sound, but nothing reaches all the way out to the barn or the bathrooms like the siren. This way they don't have an excuse for not getting lined up," Mary explained.

"That makes sense." Jayden slid two pies out of the oven and put two more into it. "Now that some time has passed, how are you holding up?"

"Fine." Mary took the lids off the pasta dishes and stirred the pot of marinara sauce. "We've had wild ones before, and it's not uncommon to lose one or two in a season."

Jayden thought of all the times she'd had to send a kid to the school nurse because they were too high to even pay attention to their teacher and had been sent to her office. Maybe Skyler was right to teach in a parochial school, where there was more emphasis on God. But she sure wasn't right with God when Mama died, or else she wouldn't have been so mean about things.

Jayden had never seen the girls as dirty or sweaty as they were that evening when they lined up for supper, not even after they'd cleaned horse stalls or when they had gone through the morning exercise regimen.

"Little bit of dirt on your forehead," she whispered to Tiffany when she was the first one through the line.

"Yep, and I earned it when I slid into third base," Tiffany said. "Ashlyn broke two fingernails and Carmella's going to have a bruise on her hip."

Ashlyn held up her hands like trophies. "Worth it because we won by a run. We might get a rematch before we leave here so we can whip them again."

"What about you, Carmella?" Mary asked.

"I hate anything that makes me sweat, but to show up that other team, I'll gladly play another game," Carmella answered. "Can I, please, have another helping of that baked ziti? I'm starving."

"Of course." Mary scooped up another big spoonful, put it on her tray, and whispered to Jayden, "I bet we don't have much to put in the hog's bucket tonight."

"That will make Tiffany happy." Jayden moved on down the line and started pouring sweet tea and water into glasses. "She's only got one more day and then she's done with that job."

Elijah picked up a glass of tea and winked at Jayden. "Too bad Lauren didn't stick around and get to know the hogs."

Did that wink mean that Elijah was flirting with her or was he just being nice?

Jayden's girls were second in line for showers that evening, and more than ready to get all the dirt, sweat, and grime washed away. She wasn't a bit surprised when they headed out the door as soon as they saw the Sunshine girls returning to their cabin. She figured they'd stand under the water as long as their time allowed, but they were out in record time. When they came back, they dropped their shower bags on the porch and sat down in the red chairs.

"I would have thought y'all would have had all the outdoors you wanted for one day." She slid into the last chair and enjoyed what little night breeze blew across her face.

"We want to talk," Ashlyn said.

"About what?" Jayden asked. They had had group therapy right after supper and all three of them had been pretty quiet.

"Lauren got what she had coming, but none of us three have ever not been given another chance," Tiffany answered. "It's kind of scary."

"Learning to be accountable, to stand up and take responsibility for what you've done and not blame it on someone else, is very scary, but those things are what adults do. Little kids blame everything on someone else," Jayden said.

"What does that mean exactly?" Carmella asked.

"You stole a tennis bracelet, which was worth enough to be considered grand larceny and could have gotten you at least a year in juvie. *You* did it. Your *parents* didn't do it. Your *friends* didn't do it, even though you might have been trying to impress them with your badass ways. *You* did. So, you should say that you did and take full responsibility. None of you are children anymore. You're bordering on young adulthood, so own your mistakes and take your punishment."

Tiffany sucked in a lungful of air and let it out slowly before she spoke. "I took the pictures of those girls, and I posted them. It's on me, but my friends were in on it, too. They told me that I couldn't be a part of their group if I didn't do it. It was kind of like an initiation. When I got caught the first time, they said I'd failed and if I really wanted to be included, I had to keep trying until I didn't get caught. When I failed the second time, I had to steal something. They gave me a shopping list of what each one of them wanted. I got a pair of diamond earrings from one store, a two-thousand-dollar purse from another one, and an expensive makeup kit from the third one. I got caught at the last store."

"What does that tell you about your friends?" Jayden asked.

"That they're stupid bi—jerks," Tiffany answered.

"What does it tell you about you?" Jayden asked.

"That I'm more stupid than they are since I listened to them." Tiffany had a wholesome beauty about her when she smiled like she did right then. "But I got to admit, I still want to be in with that crowd. They get invited to all the parties, and they're all going to the same university that I want to attend, and the boys all want to date them."

"No one told me to steal the bracelet or the other things I got caught shoplifting." Carmella gazed out over the yard. "It's all on me, like Tiffany just said."

"Why do you think you did it?" Jayden asked.

"The thrill," Carmella answered.

Jayden thought of Novalene and her love of driving fast with loud music blaring. "Are you sorry that you did it?"

"I wasn't until I had to come here," Carmella replied. "If I could go home now, I would find something else to give me that adrenaline rush."

"Like sex?" Ashlyn asked.

"Nah." Carmella shrugged. "My boyfriend don't give me that kind of rush. He's all about gettin', not givin'."

"He your only one?" Ashlyn asked.

"Yep, and he's probably already with another girl by now." Carmella finally focused on Jayden. "How old were you when you first had sex?"

"Sophomore year in college," Jayden answered honestly.

"For real?" Ashlyn gasped. "That means you were like nineteen?"

"Twenty," Jayden said. She watched the color drain from Ashlyn's face with amusement.

"Well, then I don't feel so bad," Ashlyn whispered. "I been lyin' and sayin' I already did it with my boyfriend, but that's why I was driving drunk the last time I got caught. I drank so I wouldn't be scared to do it, and then I caught him kissin' another girl, so I got in my car and started home. The policeman pulled me over and"—she raised a shoulder in half a shrug—"it was the third time they'd caught me. Lord knows, I'd been driving drunk lots more times than that."

Jayden waited for the next confession or question, but instead Tiffany pointed out into the yard and whispered, "What is that thing? Carmella, you've got to catch that, and I have to draw it."

Just like that, the serious moment was over, and they were all headed out into the yard. Flip-flops that they'd been issued as shower shoes smacked on their feet as they chased down a lightning bug. They'd gone from talking about heavy topics to giggling like a bunch of little girls as they tried to catch the flickering yellow bit of light.

"All this after less than a week. We're finally making progress," Jayden muttered through a smile as she watched them.

Elijah appeared out of the dusky darkness and propped his elbows on the porch rail. "What's going on out here? I figured I'd worn all of the girls out with that ball game."

"They've discovered lightning bugs, or maybe I should say a lightning bug. I only see one," Jayden answered. "Carmella wants to capture it alive, and Tiffany wants to draw it."

"That's strange. If we see fireflies at all in this part of the country, it's usually in the spring, not hot summer," Elijah said. "Look over there between Daydream and Moonbeam." He pointed. "There's two more."

"Maybe it's magic that's happening just for my girls tonight," she said.

"After this morning, you deserve some magic." Elijah nodded.

"We got it," Carmella yelled. "And it's alive and look, Jayden, it's still blinking."

"There's two more over there." Jayden pointed toward Moonbeam Cabin, but by then there was nothing there.

"Guess they fell in love and have gone on their honeymoon," Elijah teased.

All three girls stared at him as if he had an extra eyeball in his forehead.

"Lightning bugs flash their lights to attract mates," Jayden explained.

"My poor little bug is a reject," Carmella said, "and now I'm going to freeze him, so he'll never have a wife or children."

Jayden bit back a smile. "Could be that it's a girl lightning bug and she'll never know true love."

"I don't care if it's a girl or a boy—it'll be fun to sketch the thing," Tiffany said. "Let's get it in the freezer before it flies away. We've only got five minutes before bedtime."

They all three hurried across the yard to the dining hall, and then jogged back together. Right at nine o'clock, the lights went out in the cabin. Jayden patted the table between her chair and the one connected to it. "Come on up here and have a seat."

Elijah sat down in the chair next to her. "What's your take on Novalene? Is she holding up all right? It's always tough on everyone to lose a girl, especially this quick, and Novalene has never lost one of hers."

"She's one tough lady. I want to grow up and be just like her," Jayden answered. "How about Mary?"

"I'm still really worried about her and Henry," Elijah said. "She comes off as bulletproof, but she holds a lot of stress inside and doesn't talk about it. She's going to crumble one of these days. I just hope that she and Henry get a few years of retirement before that happens."

"So do I," Jayden said. "I really have gotten close to her. When I first said I'd come here, I didn't think about making friends. I only came so Skyler would be happy. I planned to do my job and go home. Look!" She pointed out toward the dining building. "Now there's dozens of lightning bugs flitting around."

"And our two eloped before they got to know anyone else," he joked.

"How do you know that?" Jayden cut her eyes over toward him. "Maybe they were hiding out of fear until the girls went inside. After all, none of them want to be frozen and then pinned to a board. When they realized Myrtle was caught, and the girls had quit running around in the yard, they all came back out to put on their show for us."

"Myrtle?" he asked.

"I named her after my aunt Myrtle. My grandmother's sister. She has always been a fireball of energy. She still made a garden and lived by herself when she was a hundred years old. I figured that would be a good name for the firefly," Jayden answered.

"Is she still living?" Elijah asked. "Your aunt, not the firefly."

"Yep, she's a hundred and two and just got married six months ago for the first time. Her groom is ninety. After they went on a honeymoon to Disney World in Orlando, they moved into an assisted living center in Fort Worth," Jayden answered. "She grows tomatoes in pots on their balcony, and he still plays golf twice a week."

"Why don't you want to grow up to be like her instead of Novalene?" Elijah asked.

"Aunt Myrtle has energy and uses it wisely. Novalene likes to drive fast and listen to Elvis blasting on the radio," she answered.

"So, you are a risk-taker?" Elijah pulled a bandanna from his pocket and wiped his forehead.

"Nope. I've never done much in the way of taking risks in my life," Jayden admitted. That was another way she and Skyler were different, even though they had the same specialization. Skyler had worked in several jobs since Jayden got her teaching degree and then her counselor's certification. Jayden was still in the same school she'd started at when she was twenty-two years old. "But I'd like to see how it would feel. That's so unlike me to even say that. Must be this place."

"Maybe it's because you're staying in this particular cabin," Elijah said. "What do you daydream about? A handsome knight on a white horse coming to carry you off to happy ever after?"

"Happy ever after doesn't exist except in romance books, and a sexy knight would have to be a big old boy to carry me anywhere," she giggled.

❖   ❖   ❖

With so much on her mind, Jayden had trouble getting to sleep that night. Finally, she got out her journal and started to write.

Dear Mama,

I went to church this morning for the first time since you left me. I don't know if it's mandatory for me to go or not, but to set an example for my girls, I went. I'm still not over being mad at God for taking you away from me. I didn't have a problem with losing Gramps. He was old, and he was ready to go spend eternity with Granny, but if God can truly perform miracles, then He could have healed you. Skyler sent a selfie from London. You'd tell me, like Mary did, that it was her way of saying thanks to me for taking her place here at the camp. But I know my sister, maybe better than anyone else does, and she was showing off. How could two people as different as we are ever have the same parents?

I've met a guy here at the camp, and there's feelings that I don't know how to deal with. I wish you were here so I could talk to you about Elijah. He's got a good heart, but from what little he's told me, he's dealt with a lot of pain and loss. Maybe he's like me. I have trouble trusting other people. He has trouble trusting himself, from what I can tell.

That's all for tonight. Miss you, Mama.

She put the notebook back in the drawer and turned out the light. When her head hit the pillow that time, she had no trouble going to sleep.

Chapter Eleven

Elijah awoke with a start, his heart pounding and his sheets drenched with sweat. His left hand gripped an imaginary control on the chopper so tightly that his fingernails dug into his palms. He had to get back to base with Matty. He had to save his friend. He wouldn't think of the other two being dead, not now. He would just fly the helicopter through the mountains and get Matty to the hospital tent. Then, suddenly, it was his parents in the back of the chopper, and he was trying to get them to a Texas hospital.

The nightmare in Elijah's head was still running. For a few minutes he couldn't tell the difference in what was real and what was the dream. He blinked several times and suddenly realized that he was awake. He shook his head to erase the images. He'd been thousands of miles away when he got the news his folks had been killed. There was no way he had flown them to a hospital.

"It's a biological family all tangled up with my air force family." He switched off the clock and threw back the damp sheet. "And that's why I don't need to be in a relationship," he muttered as he slung his legs over the side of the bed. "I couldn't save any of them. Lauren could have killed Jayden today with that headbutt or knocked Mary into something sharp when she hit her, and I would have lost even more."

His thoughts ran in fast circles as he got dressed. Henry and Mary were all the family he had left. What would he do without them? He could run the camp—that wouldn't be a problem. But not having anyone was a terrifying thought. He went to the dining hall, turned on the lights, and made a full pot of coffee. He had finished half of the first cup when Mary came in that morning. One look at her face and Elijah knew something was terribly wrong.

"You look like you're about to cry. Is Henry all right?" he asked, dreading the answer.

"He's fine," Mary said. "No, that's a lie. He's not fine. He's downright heartsick, and I'm barely holding it together."

"Is he sick?" A cold chill chased down Elijah's spine.

"No, but his friend is." Mary poured herself a cup of coffee and sat down at the table with Elijah. "Remember Joe? He came here a couple of Christmases ago with Henry's old air force buddies. Joe is dying. He's dying with pancreatic cancer. He's got maybe six weeks to live." Mary sighed.

"I remember two old guys coming to stay a few days. They spent hours around the table playing dominoes and drinking whiskey. I loved listening to their stories, but I don't think I knew which one was Joe." Elijah's remaining three buddies had a conference call at Christmas, but he really should invite them to the camp so they could talk like Henry did with his old Vietnam teammates.

"The short one with a high-pitched voice," she answered. "The other one was Ellis and he died that next spring."

"Where does Joe live?" Elijah asked.

"West Memphis, Arkansas. That's just this side of the Mississippi River. He used to grow rice out there in that flat country, but he retired when his wife died a few years ago. They never had children, so I guess he'll wind up in a home of some kind until he dies." Mary wiped the tears from her cheeks with the bottom of her apron.

"Why don't you and Henry go stay with him? I can run this place. That way Joe can die in his house with Henry beside him," Elijah said.

"Oh, honey, we couldn't ask that of you." Mary almost smiled. "That would be leaving you right in the middle of a session."

"Joe might be gone before the end of July, and Henry will never forgive himself if he doesn't go. Wouldn't Joe do that for him if the roles were reversed?" Elijah was already wondering if he and the three women could manage, but he had to offer. If any of his three friends needed him, he'd be there as fast as that little plane sitting at the Alpine Municipal Airport could get him to them. He was a little surprised at his thoughts, since he and what remained of his team had all drifted apart since coming back to the States.

"He would, but . . ." Mary shook her head slowly back and forth.

"If there's one thing I've learned since you and Henry took me in after the air force, it's there are no *but*s in friendship," Elijah told her. "I'm not saying it will be easy or that I won't miss you, but if we can't handle it with the hands we've got, I'll hire more," he said. "You and Henry need to talk about this. Y'all could either drive and be there in a couple of days, or I can fly you in the plane. Joe should spend his last days with y'all rather than a bunch of strangers."

"I can't believe that you're even offering to do this," Mary said.

Elijah stood up, rounded the table, and hugged his aunt. "I'd do anything in my power for you and Henry. Go and stay as long as you need to. I've got help and we can take care of this place."

"I'll talk to Henry, and thank you," Mary said.

"No thanks necessary." He hugged her again and tried to swallow the lump in his throat. If he could have sat at the bedside of any of his late teammates, he would have never passed up the opportunity. And yet the burden of running the place without Henry and Mary lay on his shoulders like a ton of concrete.

The siren blew and the girls poured out of the cabins, lined up fairly well, and got ready for Elijah to lead them in the morning exercises.

Henry came out of the barn just as they were finishing the drill. He looked like he was carrying the weight of the world on his shoulders and might break into tears at any minute. "I believe I'll walk with y'all this morning. Can we talk?"

"Of course," Elijah agreed and then pointed at Carmella. "You girls from the Daydream Cabin are responsible for leading the way this morning. Henry and I will bring up the rear."

"Mary said she'd talked to you," Henry said as they fell into step behind the eight girls.

"Going to be with Joe is the right thing to do," Elijah said. "Mary doesn't say much and keeps things inside so she doesn't worry me or you, but she needs to get away for a while."

"You're right. I'm a tough old bird, but that girl hitting Mary kind of . . . well, it knocked both of us for a loop."

"Me too," Elijah agreed. "Would we need to do any paperwork?"

"We already did everything six months ago when we decided that this would be our last year. You've already been doing the business end, and we've got a good CPA who will continue to take care of the corporation end of things like payroll," Henry answered. "It's the physical part of things that bothers me. Will Jayden be agreeable to taking over the kitchen? Should we call Skyler and see if she would come back and do Jayden's job in Daydream Cabin?"

"The girls might not like a change," Elijah said, "but that's a good idea. I'll see if she's back from that trip right after breakfast. Does this mean you'll go?"

"Before we make a final decision, we'd like to have a visit with the staff, too. Being down a girl will help a little, but they all need to be willing to do a little more if it comes down to it," Henry answered.

"Fair enough. How about while we're all in the dining room at dinnertime, we talk about it with the staff?" Elijah suggested.

"This is a big decision for us." Henry sighed. "I'm glad you're willin' to take over a little earlier than we planned."

Elijah draped an arm around the shorter man's shoulders. "I'd do anything for you and Mary. I owe you so much."

Elijah talked to each of the counselors that morning, and they were all in agreement with him. Jayden had offered to take over the kitchen duties and said that she'd enlist her girls if she needed help. Novalene and Diana both said they would watch over Jayden's girls when they were needed. Elijah breathed a sigh of relief that things had gone that smooth, and now it was time to have a group visit around the table after dinner.

"We can't tell you how much we appreciate all of you offering to do this for us," Henry said. "We talked ourselves into leaving and then talked ourselves out of it a dozen times since breakfast."

"I'm glad to take over the kitchen," Jayden said. "And there's no need to call in another counselor. I can do both jobs."

"I'll help with Jayden's girls or in the kitchen. Either one," Novalene said.

Diana raised a hand. "Ditto. I'll do whatever needs doing in any place."

Elijah felt such a surge of emotion that he had to swallow three times to get the lump in his throat to disappear. He was nervous about taking over on such short notice, but it wouldn't be all that much different than if he'd done the same thing in December—except by then he would have hired more help.

"We just didn't feel right. What kind of example would it set for the girls for us to leave in the middle of their time here?" Mary asked.

"You know how you get that prick in your heart when you make the wrong decision?" Henry said. "Well, we both got that feeling when we decided we couldn't leave this place in the middle of a season. Then we talked about it and decided that we need to be with Joe, and that

140

brought peace to our hearts. I don't want my friend and brother-in-arms to pass from this earth all alone in a strange facility, so we've decided to retire a few months early. We don't want to miss a single minute with Joe. We'll be leaving in the morning, and Elijah, we thank you for the offer to fly us, but we want to drive so we'll have our own vehicle while we're there."

Jayden got up and rounded the end of the table to give Mary a hug. "The example you'll be setting for these girls is that you stand by your friends—your real friends that have been true to you."

"Thank you all again for your sweet support," Mary said. "If you have questions, we'll have cell phones with us. I wouldn't agree to do this if I didn't think y'all could take care of the girls and this place just fine. Other than Jayden, you are all seasoned camp counselors, and she's proven herself very well in the kitchen as well as in her cabin."

"You don't worry about a thing," Novalene said. "I'm not worth a damn in the kitchen when it comes to cooking, but I'm a whiz when it comes to washing dishes or cleaning up, so if Jayden needs help, I'm here for that, too."

Diana nodded in agreement. "Like I said, I'll do whatever Elijah needs me to do. I know that Henry oversees the girls when it's their turn to milk the cows or gather eggs. I'll be there at anything the girls from Sunshine Cabin, and all of them, are doing."

"Call it semiretirement." Jayden pulled off her cap and wiped sweat from her brow with a paper napkin. "Why don't y'all spend this afternoon packing and let us prove to you that we can do this?"

"I'd like to do just that." Mary dried her wet cheeks on her apron tail. "We thought we'd leave about five in the morning, and we don't want a bunch of fanfare."

"At that time of morning, you might get a yawn or two from the girls out in the yard, but no big send-off." Elijah managed a smile, but the thought of seeing them drive away tightened his throat.

"Maybe a wave from the more energetic ones," Jayden added.

"Have you called Joe and told him?" Elijah asked.

"Yes, I did, and he's so grateful." Henry pulled a red bandanna from his bib pocket and wiped his eyes. He cleared his throat and then draped an arm around Mary's shoulders. "Darlin', before we both get all emotional again, we should go get our SUV packed and ready to go."

Elijah watched them walk out of the dining room, hand-in-hand like they went everywhere, and hoped that someday he would find a woman he could love just like that. His eyes fell on Jayden. *A woman like that,* he thought.

He turned to the three women and said, "I tried to call Skyler to see if she would be interested in coming back for the remainder of the session, but all I got was her voice mail. Just wanted y'all to know that we might have a little more help on the way."

Jayden went over every possible scenario she could think of as she prepped for supper that evening. How would she and Skyler get along if her sister decided to come and finish out the session? Would it be a good thing, or would it drive the wedge between them even deeper? What if Skyler treated her like pond scum as usual? How would she affect the friendships Jayden was building with the other counselors and her girls?

"My girls," she whispered. "I can't leave them in her hands, not when we're just now breaking through some problems."

A tingling feeling on her neck told her that Elijah was close by even before she turned around and saw him pouring himself a glass of sweet tea at the far end of the buffet line. "You snuck up on me." She hoped he hadn't heard her muttering.

"I just need a minute to settle . . ." He took a big drink of his tea, and his expression said something was terribly wrong.

Jayden stopped what she was doing and rounded the end of the bar. "Did one of the girls do something wrong? Was it mine? I can tell that something isn't right."

"Everything is all right, even if it's just hitting me that everything being good and right doesn't mean it's not a little bit scary," Elijah answered. "Your girls are fine. They are all doing their jobs. Henry and Mary just drove away, and now it's up to me to make this place work."

Jayden got herself a bottle of cold water and sat down at a table. "I thought they weren't leaving until morning."

"Henry is in a hurry to see Joe, and there's lots of daylight left in today. They can be halfway to Dallas by dark and have a big jump on tomorrow's leg of the trip." Elijah pulled out a chair and sat down. "I want to thank you again for stepping up to do the cooking. The rest of the counselors are taking on more work, but you're biting off the biggest chunk, so thanks."

"You are welcome. Like I said before, I didn't come here expecting to make friends, but I have, and I'd do about anything for Mary and Henry." Jayden picked up her water and downed a third of it.

"I've known for months that this transition was coming, but I thought I'd have more time to interview help for the cook's job and maybe hire someone to help with the outside work," he said.

"Change is always scary," Jayden said. "Didn't it terrify you to enlist in the air force? I know it scared the bejesus right out of me when I went to college the first day, though I still got to go home when classes were over."

"Yep, but not like this. I always had someone up higher than me in the chain of command to make the decisions. But I'm the boss now," Elijah answered.

Jayden reached over and laid her hand on his. "Just like the air force has protocols to cover whatever might go wrong, or what goes right, for that matter, we have a handbook that pretty much outlines the same thing. You're the boss, but that doesn't mean you're out on the end of a tree branch with someone throwing rocks at you. We're all here to help you enforce what's in the handbook, just like we did with Henry and Mary."

"Thank you for that." He laid his free hand over hers. "Now I've got another favor to ask of you. Would you help me interview some folks to help out around here? If I can't talk you into staying on permanently, then I'll need a cook. And they could step in and learn the ropes while you're still here to help with the transition."

"I'd be glad to help you interview." Jayden wondered how a new mix in staff would affect the girls. A new cook and maybe Skyler back in the Daydream Cabin—would all that change turn their world upside down so much that they would lose the progress they'd made?

"Thanks. That means a lot," Elijah said.

Carmella, Ashlyn, and Tiffany all pushed inside the dining room at the same time. Jayden jerked her hand away from Elijah's and smiled at them to cover her nerves.

"We're all done walking the horses," Ashlyn said. "Carmella found a really ugly bug. We looked it up and it's a fire ant. We're going back to put it in the freezer so that she can pin it to the board tomorrow."

"It's not very big, but the book said that a sting from it can hurt real bad, and since it's called a fire ant, I'm going to sketch it on the end of the devil's tail," Tiffany said.

"How did y'all get done so quick?" Jayden asked.

"We each walked a horse at the same time, and we brushed them for an extra half hour. They looked all pretty when we put them back in the stalls. Dynamite even smiled at us," Carmella answered as they all three made their way to the kitchen. "I can look for bugs and lead a horse, and Tiffany sketches after the thing is frozen anyway."

"So, you worked as a team?" Elijah smiled.

"Yep, but don't expect us to act like sisters or any of that crap," Ashlyn told him. "That ain't about to happen."

"*Isn't* about to happen," Jayden said.

"That's what I said." Ashlyn was the first one back from behind the buffet bar. "They ain't my sisters, and I'm probably not going to use proper grammar. Us kids don't talk like you old people do."

"Ouch!" Elijah laid a hand over his heart.

"Well, we *are* trying to teach them honesty." Jayden smiled.

"Where's Mary?" Carmella grabbed two bottles of water and threw one across the room to Ashlyn.

"She and Henry have officially retired," Elijah said.

Ashlyn caught the water but almost dropped it. "No! You mean they really just left? Who's going to help us milk the two cows when it's our turn? I never can get the hang of it, and Henry's been giving me tips."

"I'll be there and so will Miz Diana," Elijah assured her. "What's your favorite job of all?"

Ashlyn twisted the cap off the water and took a long drink. "Walking Dynamite. I love that horse. You want to sell him? I'll ask Daddy to buy him for my birthday if you'll sell him to me."

"Sorry, I couldn't ever let him go. He's going to live out the rest of his days right here at Piney Wood," Elijah answered.

"If you change your mind, just tell me," Ashlyn said.

"I figured you girls would like kitchen work better since it's cool in here," Elijah said.

Ashlyn shook her head. "I don't like to cook, but me and Dynamite have us some long conversations when I'm walking him. I've whispered things to him that I wouldn't even tell God or Jesus."

Jayden wondered how many other girls during the sessions felt the same way about that big black horse. If they did, poor old Dynamite's brain must be full of secrets, her own included.

"I like cooking best," Carmella answered. "I really don't like collecting bugs, but when I have to deal with them, I just think about not ever shoplifting again."

Elijah glanced over at Tiffany. "What about you?"

"I like drawing best," she answered, "and I don't mind doing the laundry. It's hot as hell in that building, but it kind of reminds me of a spa, and besides, when everything is all clean and folded, there's a sense of accomplishment. Kind of like washing all those ugly things I did out of my past and starting off with a clean future."

"That's pretty deep thinking for a teenager," Elijah said.

Tiffany glared at him. "Isn't the whole reason we're here to make us think about our sins and never do them again? I get that feeling when I'm talking to Karen. She's not bad for a therapist. She doesn't just listen—she makes me think."

Elijah pushed his chair back. "I can't wait to see your next picture. You are really good at art. My favorite one is the millipede on the devil's pitchfork. In my opinion all those stinging bugs belong down there in hell."

"Yep." Tiffany nodded.

Jayden headed back to the kitchen. "Since y'all teamed up and got done with the horses early, then I reckon you can help out in here. Wash your hands, and get your hair tucked up under your caps."

"Yes, ma'am," they said at the same time.

If only I could get my own life in order as fast as they're doing, Jayden thought as she watched Elijah put his glass in the dishwasher and then leave the dining room. *Maybe I will as soon as Skyler gets home or comes here to work, and when I quit daydreaming about working here rather than teaching school. Do I need a few sessions with Karen, too?*

You know giving up the career you worked so hard to have is not a good idea. Her mother's voice was back in her head.

I know, Mama, she agreed, *but it's a sweet little daydream, because I love working here and making a difference in these girls' lives.*

Jayden took out the journal that night after the girls were in bed, opened it up, and wrote:

Dear Mama,

Tonight, I'm happy and sad at the same time, if that's possible. I'm the official cook for the camp now. Mary and Henry have left to spend some time with his old Vietnam war buddy who is dying. I'm sad to see them go because Mary and I've become friends. She reminds me of a mix of you and Granny, and I've enjoyed working with her so very much. But now the kitchen is all mine, and I'm happy about that. I inherited your love of cooking, and getting to do this job makes this seem like a vacation.

Maybe it's a good thing I'm only talking to you about these emotional feelings I have for Elijah. I have no one to talk to here about this, but I need to work through it.

You would like Diana and Novalene, Mama. I don't think I've ever had friends like them. They are restoring my trust in people.

Good night, Mama . . .

She laid the journal aside, got into bed, and watched the patterns that clouds shifting over the moon made on the ceiling for a long time before she fell asleep. She had forgotten to mention in her journal entry that Elijah was a man who could be trusted. She'd have to go into more detail another time about that.

Chapter Twelve

*I*n the middle of the afternoon on Thursday Jayden's phone pinged. She stopped cutting up oranges for a fruit salad and pulled it out of her hip pocket to find a second selfie and text from Skyler. This picture showed her with a red-haired guy in what appeared to be an airport terminal. The man didn't look much taller than Skyler, which was a surprise. Skyler usually went for the tall, dark, and handsome guys—like Ray Don, the bad boy she'd had a crush on in high school. The text said that she would be in Alpine on Friday and she had exciting news.

Jayden took a deep breath and let it out in a whoosh. "I was hoping that Mary was sending me a message," she said out loud.

"Everything all right in here?" Elijah removed his cap and wiped sweat from his forehead as he entered the building. "Summer has arrived with a vengeance. It's ninety-four degrees out there."

"Have you heard from Skyler?" Jayden asked.

"Nope." Elijah picked up a bottle of water and downed half of it. "Have you?"

"I just got a selfie and a text that said she'll be in Alpine tomorrow," she answered.

"That's the first I'm hearing of it," Elijah said. "I wonder if she's coming to accept the offer that I left on her voice mail or just to visit you."

"I guess we can see easily enough." Jayden took another deep breath and called her sister, but she couldn't imagine Skyler visiting the camp. After five rings it went straight to voice mail, and she didn't even bother leaving a message. "I guess we'll know when she shows up."

"Are you okay with her being here? I'm pretty desperate for help right now." Elijah finished off the bottle of water and poured himself a glass of lemonade.

"I'll be fine," she told him, and sincerely hoped she was telling the truth.

"I'm going back to plow another field. Karen is in Moonbeam Cabin now. She said of the six that she's seen so far today, there's some clear progress." Elijah settled his cap back on his head. "See you at suppertime."

"That's good news about the girls." Jayden really didn't like giving up her job with her girls, but hiring more help was up to Elijah, not her.

"Yep," Elijah threw up a hand and waved on his way out the door— then he stopped. "If she is coming to help us out, you can move over to Henry and Mary's house."

"Thank you," Jayden said. "I'd like to still sit in on their counseling hour so that we don't lose any ground. Too bad Skyler hates to cook and never learned how to do much more than open cans and microwave frozen dinners. As much as I like cooking, I'd give her this job so my girls wouldn't be upset."

"Maybe it'll be a smooth transition," Elijah said as the door closed behind him.

"Yeah, right," Jayden said. "It'll be about as smooth as a ride down a dirt road with a flat tire."

"We're here," Keelan yelled as she and Bailey arrived in the kitchen to help with supper duties. "We're finished with our therapy, and Novalene said for us to come out here and help with whatever you say for us to do. I wish I could take Karen home with me so she could be my therapist all the time."

"Make the best of your time here with her and maybe when you go home, you'll be ready to open up to your therapist there a little more," Jayden told her. "You are all making great progress in learning to be comfortable in your own skin, and I'm proud of you."

"Do you think it's because we're all away from our circle of friends?" Bailey asked.

"Could be. Do you think you'll change that group when you leave here?" Jayden asked.

Keelan got two aprons from the hook on the wall and tossed one toward Bailey. "I'm going to change a lot of things when I get back. I don't need drugs or to be around people who use them. I only used the money I got from them to buy stuff—bad stuff like liquor for parties—anyway."

"Me either," Bailey agreed.

Who would have thought they'd figure that out in such a short time? Jayden thought. *But then I'm questioning my own job, my past, my future, and lots of things since I came here, so it shouldn't be any big surprise that these kids picked that up so fast.*

Jayden beat her pillow until there wasn't a lump in it. She counted how many sounds came from crickets and how many from tree frogs until the noise of the air conditioner compressors kicking on blotted out both. Then she closed her eyes and tried to imagine sheep jumping over a white picket fence. When Elijah leaned his elbows on the top rail and smiled at her in the vision, she lost count. Finally, she threw back the sheet, pulled on a pair of jeans and her shoes, and headed for the barn.

When she arrived, she went right to Dynamite's stall and stuck her hand over the top rail to pet him. "Did you sense that I needed to talk tonight? Is that why you're still awake, too?"

The horse whinnied and nudged her hand.

"I thought so," Jayden said. "My sister is coming tomorrow and quite possibly may be staying. I don't want to work with her, but Elijah needs the help and it would be selfish of me to say anything to discourage her. And who knows, she might need the money after that trip to Europe. Living with her fancy ways until she went away to college wasn't easy. Of course, Mama said it was both of our faults that we couldn't get along. Did she think that giving Skyler some responsibility would help us to bond together when Skyler sold the house? Maybe she was right, and us working together will be a good thing. What do you think, Dynamite?"

Jayden could have sworn the horse sighed.

"Yep, that's where I am, too," she said. "I've always wanted her to like me, so maybe this is my opportunity to learn not to give a damn. Thanks for the advice." She gave him a couple more pats and headed back to Daydream Cabin. She got out her journal and started to write in it, but she was way too sleepy, so she put it aside, fell right to sleep, and dreamed about putting up a Christmas tree in the dining hall.

"Like that would ever happen," she said when her alarm went off. She got out of bed, stretched the kinks out of her back, and pulled a pair of faded jeans from the closet.

She stared at them for a moment, then hung them back up and got dressed in one of her nicer shirts and newer jeans. "I'm not really doing this for Elijah," she muttered, but in her heart she knew better.

The aroma of brewing coffee met her when she entered the dining hall. Elijah was sitting at the table with a cup in his hands.

"This is a nice surprise," she said.

Elijah smiled. "I had trouble sleeping last night. Are you going to be all right with Skyler working here? I should have asked you before I called her."

"We don't have much of a relationship." Jayden poured herself a cup of coffee and joined him. "But I'll do what's best for the camp and the girls."

"You two might not have been close as kids or even as adults, but you are blood kin. Like that old song says, 'Love Can Build a Bridge,' and it doesn't have to be talking about between a man and a woman. It can be between sisters," he said.

"I hope so. I really do."

"Mary always says that everything works out for the best, but once y'all talk, if you've got any misgivings, I won't hire her. Nothing has been signed," Elijah said.

"Thank you, but again, we have to think of the girls, not me." Jayden picked up her cup and carried it to the kitchen. "It's not like it's forever. Six more weeks and this session will be over. If I can live with her for fifteen years, I can make it through that short time."

"Thanks go to you for caring more about the kids than yourself." He pushed back his chair and stood up at the same time the siren went off. "See you at breakfast."

"Bring a healthy appetite," she told him.

"Always do." He smiled as he left the building.

Jayden wasn't sure what time to expect Skyler, and every time the dining hall door opened, she jerked her head around, expecting to see her sister toting in suitcases. By midafternoon she'd almost given up on Skyler even showing up and was coming out of the pantry with a bag of sugar in her hands when she saw her sister standing on the other side of the buffet line. Her long blonde hair framed her delicate face, and her makeup was flawless. She wore white capris, a red T-shirt, and matching red sandals.

"Surprise!" Skyler said.

"I've been looking for you all day," Jayden said. "Did you already put your suitcases in the cabin?"

"Don't be ridiculous," Skyler said. "I'm not staying."

"Didn't you get the message from Elijah offering you a job? Henry and Mary have retired. I've taken over the cooking, and Elijah needs some help." Jayden set the sugar down and poured two glasses of sweet tea.

"I didn't even check my messages, and FYI, I definitely do not want a job here for the rest of the summer," Skyler said. "David and I are on our way to Brownsville to spend a few days with his grandmother, and I thought I'd stop by and"—she held out her left hand and wiggled her fingers—"show you this and see Novalene and Diana. Seemed the right thing to do since we're in the area."

Jayden stared at the sparkling diamond—the thing had to be at least three carats—in an antique setting. "It's gorgeous. Is this David you're talking about the lucky guy?"

"Remember? I told you that he's the music director at Glory Bound. I sent you a selfie of us from the trip." Skyler couldn't take her eyes off the ring. "He dropped me off, but he'll be back for me in an hour, unless I call him to come back sooner. Where are Novalene and Diana? I want to show them my ring."

Jayden carried the two glasses of tea to the table and motioned for Skyler to sit down. "David must be rolling in money to afford a ring like that."

"David isn't rich himself. His grandmother has all the money in the family, and he's an only grandson, so it will all go to him someday." Skyler sat in the folding chair, but she pushed the tea back. "I don't drink anything with sugar in it. I'm dieting so I can get into a size two wedding dress." She cut her eyes around at Jayden and drew her perfectly arched brows down. "Have you gained a few pounds since you got here?"

"Maybe," Jayden answered. "If my jeans fit, then I don't worry about that too much. Did you just come by to show me your ring?"

"Pretty much. I want to talk to you about something else while I'm here, but before I do . . . since you're my sister, I should ask you to be part of the wedding party, but"—she pursed her lips and frowned—"you'd be uncomfortable since you're taller than even the groom and his party, and all my bridesmaids are tiny like me. I'm thinking of you."

"Yeah, right," Jayden said.

"Don't get all pissy about it," Skyler said. "I might let you help serve the cake or maybe you can sit at the guest book." She held up her hand and flipped it around so the gem would catch the sunrays pouring in from the window. "David's great-grandfather had this designed for his bride and it was passed down to his grandmother and now she's let David give it to me. I'm such a lucky woman."

"You said you had something to talk to me about?" Jayden prodded. Better to cut this short.

"David and I won't live in Texas this next year. We'll be running our own little private school in Mexico for the children of diplomats and folks who need our services. His grandmother is setting it all in motion, and we'll be very busy with his side of the family and with Daddy when we do get to come back to the States for a short visit."

"Does that mean you won't be wasting your time coming to see me?" Jayden asked.

"Our wedding has to be in late August, so we don't have much time to plan for it, and I sure won't have time to come see you." Skyler sighed. "I'll have to buy a dress off the rack instead of having a designer make it special for me, but"—another long sigh—"at least I can get a nice one. I won't have time to save up the money for my dream wedding, and with all his family's doing for us, I can't possibly let them pay for the wedding." Skyler pulled out her little package of tissues.

"With what you got from the sale of Mama's house, you should have plenty of money to pay for a wedding." Jayden thought again of their childhood home occupied by another family.

A single trained tear dropped from Skyler's eyelash. "That money has been gone for years. It wasn't all that much anyway after I paid off the mortgage she still owed, and I really needed a new car. I know that she left you what she had in savings . . ." Another tear made its way out to the end of her eyelash.

"You took three-fourths of the profit from the house and all of the money from the sale of the contents. You didn't even ask me if I wanted to have some of the smaller things that meant a lot to me, like Mama's old teapots. Are you asking me to give you the little I got after you divided the money?" Jayden asked.

"Yes, I am." Skyler dabbed at her eyes. "I should have the wedding of my dreams—some cheap little thing would be an embarrassment to this gorgeous ring. You don't need that money, and you'll probably never get married anyway."

"No," Jayden said.

"As in no, you do plan to get married?" Skyler asked.

"I'm not giving you my money." Jayden could feel guilt floating out of the sky like a big black cloud and settling in her heart. Refusing her sister was so tough that it put a lump in her throat. Her mother would be disappointed, and her father would hate her even more.

Skyler's chin quivered. "I'll let you go with me to pick out the dress."

Jayden shook her head. "The answer is still no."

"You're being mean and selfish, just like you always have been," Skyler accused.

"Maybe so, but I'm not giving you my savings." Jayden had trouble even saying the words.

"Then I guess this is goodbye." Skyler stood. "I never want to see you again. I will have my dream wedding if I have to borrow the money, and you aren't invited."

"I wish you all the best," Jayden said, "but step back and listen to yourself. You sound like a teenager, not a thirty-four-year-old woman."

Skyler crammed the tissues back in her purse. "I hope you are happy that you've reduced me to taking out a loan. What's family for anyway, if you can't support me? I'm leaving."

Elijah had left the barn when he saw Skyler coming across the yard. He waved and pointed toward the dining hall, but she kept coming toward him. They met about halfway and she held out her hand.

"I'm engaged." She held up her hand for him to see the ring.

"Congratulations," he said. "Did you get my message about working the rest of the summer?"

"No, but Jayden told me. I can't take another job. David and I have so much to do the rest of the summer. We'll have to really rush to get the wedding ready and then we're going to Mexico to begin our exclusive new school at the first of September. It's all so rushed that I simply wouldn't have time to help you out," she answered. "Do you know where I can find Novalene and Diana?"

"They're around here somewhere, probably overseeing a job. You remember how busy we are from daylight to dark most days." He wondered why he'd never noticed how self-absorbed the woman was.

"I do remember, and FYI, darlin', Jayden just broke my heart, so I don't care if I ever see her again." Skyler's tone was full of hate, but then she smiled, and everything changed again. "There's Novalene coming out of the barn. Bye, now," she yelled across the distance and left him standing there without any more explanation.

Holy hell! What had happened that Skyler would say such a thing? His thoughts were spinning like they were on a merry-go-round. He had just realized how much he was counting on the idea of Skyler helping, but after that comment she had made, he was worried about Jayden. He lengthened his stride and hurried to the dining hall. He scanned the whole place, but there was no Jayden. He had turned around to go to the Daydream Cabin when he heard a whimper.

"Jayden?" he called out.

"Right here." Her voice was barely above a whisper.

He rushed into the kitchen to find her sitting against the back side of the buffet bar, weeping into her hands. He sat down beside her and wrapped his arms around her. "Are you all right? Are you hurt? What's happened?"

"I told Skyler no and now she'll have to take out a loan for her wedding, and I feel so guilty, I probably should just write her a check," she said between sobs.

Elijah could barely make out the words. Something about taking out a loan.

"You did what?" He massaged her back and drew her even closer.

"I said no," she told him.

That was what Skyler was talking about when she said Jayden had broken her heart. Why would the woman need money? That rock on her hand had to cost thousands, so evidently she was marrying into wealth. He could have wrung her skinny neck for making Jayden feel guilty.

"I'm here," he whispered. "Talk to me."

Between sobs she blurted out what Skyler had told her. "She's used all the money she got from the sale of Mama's house and now she wants my savings so she can have a beautiful wedding. She said that I'd never get married anyway, and she meant that I was too big and ugly for anyone to ever fall in love with . . . I'm sorry that I'm acting like a big baby."

He kissed her on top of her head. "Shhhh, don't cry. You're just sad that she's been hateful, but you did the right thing."

She leaned back and wiped her eyes on the tail of her apron. "I need to suck it up and get back to work."

"Work can wait. You need a few more minutes, and *I* need to hold you for a little while longer. I'm so sorry things worked out like this," Elijah said.

"Why do you need to hold me?" she asked.

"Because you are my friend, and that's all I know to do for you right now, other than listen. It's not much to offer . . ."

She reached up and laid a finger across his lips and then snuggled down even closer to him. "Thank you. That means the world to me."

Elijah had liked the tough Jayden a lot, but he could so easily fall in love with the vulnerable Jayden. His pulse raced at the thought of the L-word. Maybe he was confusing that word with feeling bad for her. After all, her only living relative had just treated her like dirt.

It's about damn time you woke up and saw what's right in front of your face. Don't make excuses. You have had feelings for her ever since she got here. The voice in his head sounded an awful lot like Mary.

Jayden didn't hear the dining hall door open and wasn't even aware that Novalene was standing in front of them until the woman spoke.

"Is she hurt?" Novalene whispered.

"Yes, but not physically," Elijah answered. "Is Skyler still here?"

"Nope, we just waved goodbye to her and that little red-haired feller. He's not more than an inch or two taller than she is. But what happened in here?" Novalene asked.

Jayden remembered her dream about her sister carrying flowers picked from their mother's flower beds when she got married at the courthouse. She had been with a red-haired guy in that dream. Skyler might be an annoying, narcissistic woman, but she deserved a better wedding than that. Maybe she should call her and offer to give her half her savings.

Don't you dare, Gramps's voice was scolding her. *She's made her bed. Let her lay in it.*

Jayden didn't want to move away from Elijah. She was safe in his arms. As long as she didn't move, nothing could hurt her ever again, but Novalene deserved an answer.

"That's Jayden's story to tell," Elijah said.

Jayden took a deep breath and let it out slowly. "Let's all have a glass of sweet tea, and then I really have to get back to work."

"Hey, Jayden, what did you think of Skyler's ring?" Diana called out as she headed across the room to the coffeepot. "Did she ask you to be maid of honor?"

"Of course she did," Novalene said. "How can you drink that hot stuff when it's a hundred degrees outside? I need iced tea to cool me down."

Jayden untangled herself from Elijah. He stood up and offered her a helping hand. She took it, and, strangely enough, just his touch gave her strength.

"I'm leaving now so you can visit with these ladies. If you need me or just want someone to be close by, call me." He squeezed her hand gently and then let go.

"Thank you." She managed a weak smile and then turned around to look at Diana and Novalene. "I'm not invited to the wedding because I won't give her my savings for her wedding."

"Good God!" Diana gasped. "Are you all right? No wonder you were crying. Doesn't she have her own savings?"

"She probably went through that within a month," Jayden answered.

Diana poured two glasses of iced tea. "Come on over here and sit down."

With his hand on the small of her back, Elijah guided her to the table and pulled out a chair for her to sit in. "See y'all later."

Novalene and Diana both waved him away.

"Now talk," Novalene said as she sat down right beside Jayden.

"Hey, Jayden, we got done with the bathrooms and wondered if you need some help in the kitchen," Tiffany yelled from the door.

All three Daydream Cabin girls headed over to the end of the bar to get bottles of water, and then, as if on cue, noticed Jayden in a collective double take. Tiffany's eyes went big and she ran across the floor to hug her.

"Did somebody die?" Carmella came right behind her.

"You don't have to leave, do you?" Ashlyn asked.

"No, I'll be right here until the last day." Jayden could feel the love surrounding her even though these people didn't share a bit of DNA with her. She had to be honest with her girls, but she only told them the bare bones and didn't mention the cruel things Skyler had said.

"Holy crap on a cracker!" Novalene whispered. "I knew she was a little on the vain side, but that's downright mean."

"Is that the blonde that we saw talking to you out by the laundry room?" Carmella asked.

Diana nodded. "She was showing me her engagement ring, and she asked me to walk back to the yard with her to meet her fiancé, David. He didn't even get out of the car. She sure didn't tell me about all this, or I would have given her a talkin'-to."

"I don't think it would have done a bit of good," Novalene said. "Skyler is who she is, and until she sees a need to think of other folks more than herself, you'd be wasting your time and breath."

"You can't change a leopard's spots," Diana added.

"I would take a demerit to get to knock her on her butt," Tiffany said through clenched teeth. "That's no way to treat your sister. My older sister and I argue all the time, but I'd never be that ugly to her."

"Thank you for your support and love," Jayden said, "but right now we need to get dinner going, so yes, I'll be glad for your help. Just because I got my feelings hurt doesn't mean we won't have a bunch of hungry girls coming in here pretty soon. I'd planned on making meatloaf for supper, and it can be done in an hour, so we'll get it in the oven."

"I'll peel potatoes for loaded mashed potatoes," Carmella offered.

"And I'm real good at opening a can of green beans and making a salad." Tiffany grinned. "What's all those pie shells for?"

"Chocolate pies, but I still need to make the meringue." Jayden said.

Whoever said you had to share DNA with a person for them to be family had rocks for brains, Jayden thought.

"I hate meringue," Ashlyn said. "I'll put the pudding in the shells, set them in the fridge to cool, and just before we serve them, I'll put whipped cream on the tops. That's a lot better than calf slobbers and you won't even have to make meringue."

"Where did you hear that? I haven't heard egg whites referred to like that in years." Novalene took all the dirty glasses to the kitchen and put them in the dishwasher.

"From my daddy," Ashlyn said. "He doesn't like meringue, either."

Jayden finally giggled and looked around at her new little family—folks that wouldn't ask her to give them her savings, who were there to support her. "My gramps used to say the same thing."

Compartmentalize, Jayden kept telling herself through the day when her mind would wander back to the revelation her sister had sprung on her. *Put it in a box and close the lid.*

Finally, everything was finished and she turned the lights out, carried a bottle of orange juice across the yard, and slumped down into a chair. Her girls came out of the cabin, and soon, one by one, all eight of the girls at Piney Wood Academy had gathered around her on the Daydream Cabin porch, and all of them wanted to talk about Skyler. Drama was a teenage girl's lifeblood, and this was big news.

"With a sister like that I bet you wish you were adopted," Tiffany said. "I've thought I might be sometimes. My parents are such beautiful people, and my sister is, too, and I'm so plain."

Carmella threw up a palm. "That's enough of that kind of talk. Every one of us are beautiful."

"That's right," Jayden said. "Beauty is the light within you that shines out, not the jewelry you hang on your body, the fancy clothes you wear, or the makeup you use. A person can be gorgeous on the outside, but the evil inside them ruins every bit of the prettiness." She wasn't sure if she was preaching to herself or to the girls—maybe they all needed to hear it.

"Why not be both? Pretty on the outside and inside?" Ashlyn asked.

"Yes, but the inside one is the most important," Jayden said.

"I've wished a bunch of times that I was adopted," Keelan said, "and that I'd find my real parents, and my mama would be a stay-at-home mother, and my dad would have time to spend with me."

"I'm so sorry." Ashlyn got up from the porch step and gave her a hug. "I'll be your sister if you'll let me. I always wanted a big sister to talk to. I'm an only child."

"If you'll be my big sister, Jayden, I'll come stay a week with you in the summer and spend Christmas with you," Tiffany offered.

"Are we puttin' up a tree at your house?" Carmella asked. "If we are, then don't decorate it until I get there."

Violet shook a finger at them. "Hey, just because y'all are Daydream Cabin girls don't mean you get to be her only little sisters. I vote that we all adopt her as our big sister."

"Lose one, gain eight." Jayden smiled. "Seems like I'm like that man Job that we heard about last week in church. I lost everything, but in the end, I've got more than I had in the beginning."

"So have we," Tiffany whispered. "But you didn't answer us. Will you be our big sister?"

"Of course I will." Jayden smiled through the pain.

The girls had been playing a card game while they visited. Jayden realized it was close to their bedtime and raised her voice a little. "Okay, ladies, as the old song says, 'Turn out the lights, the party's over.' Thank you all for coming to cheer me up, and for adopting me. I love all of you."

"Love you!" they chorused as Bailey gathered up the deck of cards and they all left her porch.

"But we love you the most," Tiffany said as she and the other two Daydream girls started inside. "Bet you never thought you'd hear me say that after I dumped my food on the floor that first day."

"I had high hopes." Jayden smiled.

"Can we really call you when we need help, and come see you?" She held the door open and waited for an answer.

"Yes, you can," Jayden told her. "I'll always be there for you just like I am here, and I'd love for any or all of you to come visit me anytime you can manage it."

They went on inside, and in a few minutes the lights went out. She could hear them whispering for a little while and then all the noise stopped. Gramps and her mother both had often said that hindsight was twenty-twenty, and Jayden fully understood that old adage that evening. Now that the dust had settled, she felt even more like she'd handled the situation wrong. She would still have told Skyler no about giving her the money, but she wouldn't have fallen to pieces and felt sorry for her sister afterward. Her sister had made her own bed.

She was still too wound up to sleep, so she went out to the barn and visited with Dynamite for a while. When she started back to the cabin, she saw Elijah heading across the yard, going toward the dining hall.

"Hey," she yelled out as she got closer.

"What are you doing out here?" he asked.

"I might ask you the same thing, but to answer your question, I went out to the barn to talk to Dynamite. He's an excellent listener," she said. "Need a midnight snack?"

"I can always use a snack." He grinned and held up a thick catalog. "But my real purpose is that I brought these out for you to take a look at. This is our uniform book, and we always get the girls one new one midway through the session to replace the worst one they have. They get stains and rips and tears and, besides, it makes them feel good to have a new one after four weeks. I'm hoping you can figure out sizes for me."

"Be glad to," she said.

"After what happened today, would you like a little nightcap?" Elijah asked.

"You got a beer hiding inside that catalog?" She raised an eyebrow.

"Nope, but I know where Henry hides a little bottle of whiskey for special occasions." He grinned. "How are you holding up now that you've had time to think about things?" He held the door to the dining hall open.

"Then bring it out." She smiled.

He went to the kitchen and got a bottle from the freezer. "Henry hides things very well, and he likes his whiskey cold."

"I'd love a nightcap." She nodded.

He poured two fingers in a couple of glasses they used for sweet tea and handed her one.

Jayden took a sip of the whiskey and enjoyed the warmth that flowed all the way down to her stomach. "I'm pretty good, actually. I just gained eight little sisters. I guess that's almost as good as one big sister."

"This bunch of girls is finding a lot to bond over, but I'm sorry that your heartache has to be part of it." He touched his cup to hers and then sat down in the chair beside her. "Here's to tomorrow. May it be a better day."

"Amen, but on another note, I couldn't ask for more love and support through it all. I never expected to make friends with Novalene and Diana. I just thought I'd come here, do my job, and go home, but now I've been surrounded by all this love, and I got to tell you, it's pretty damn nice." She took another sip of the whiskey, held it on her tongue for a few seconds, and then swallowed. "And that includes you having a drink with me." She smiled across the table at him.

"You are welcome," he told her.

She'd never been one to take risks, or to do anything without weighing all the odds. Gramps had said that was because her zodiac sign was Libra. Folks born under that sign had a tendency to think things through and put everything on the balance scales. She wanted to tell him that what had been on her mind since Skyler left was making a brand-new start, but she needed to lay out the pros and cons before she made a decision.

She was eager to write in her journal that evening. Maybe by writing to her mother, her decisions would become clear.

Dear Mama and Gramps,

Skyler came to see me. We thought she was coming to accept a job as counselor, but I was so wrong. She's engaged to a guy named David, who comes from a lot of money. Her ring is gorgeous, but then we wouldn't expect anything less. She wanted to show her huge diamond and ask demand that I give her my savings to pay for her wedding. When I said no, she really got ugly—just like always. I felt so guilty when I told her that I wouldn't give in to her that I cried. She needs help, not for a wedding, but psychiatric help, Mama. She's probably needed it her whole life. I'm surprised that she ever worked here with young, troubled girls—she's a school counselor and can't see her own problems.

On another note, I'm in quite a quandary here. I've been offered the job of full-time cook here at Piney Wood, and I'm seriously considering it. I'm not a risk-taker so I keep wondering if I'll have regrets. I can hear you telling me not to throw away my education. I want to make the right decision, but the way my feelings are all jumbled about you, Skyler, this place, and Elijah, I'm not sure that I can. Maybe I should go back to my school job for a year and sort out this thing with you and Skyler before I dive into a new job or a relationship. Until I get rid of that baggage, I won't have much to give to a relationship anyway.

Thank you both for listening. I could always depend on y'all.

She yawned and laid the journal aside, but that night she dreamed again of decorating a Christmas tree in the dining hall. When she awoke, she wondered if perhaps that meant she and Elijah might not say a final goodbye at the end of July. After all, she had dreamed that Skyler would marry a red-haired guy, and that had come true. She just might come back for a minivacation in December. Would the girls all join her? Maybe her returning at Christmas would be for them and not Elijah at all. She was taken aback at the disappointment that she felt at the idea. Seeing her girls and maybe even Novalene and Diana would be great—but Jayden wanted to know there was more.

Chapter Thirteen

"S unday morning must be the day for the demons to come out,"
Jayden muttered as she listened to her girls arguing in their bedroom. By the time the siren blew telling them to line up for exercises,
Jayden was ready to throw up her hands, quit the job, and go back to
Dallas as fast as she could run. No wonder Elijah flew up to Fort Worth
to get them. Bring them in by air and leave their means of transportation behind. That kept them from getting into their vehicles and getting
the hell out of Alpine.

"What's the problem in here?" Jayden leaned against the jamb of
the door into their room.

Ashlyn popped her hands on her hips and said through clenched
teeth, "I want Tiffany to cut my hair and she won't do it. It's growing
out and I look horrible."

"I've got one demerit. I'm not getting another one," Tiffany declared.

"I read that handbook from one end to the other, and I didn't find
a thing about cutting hair or not cutting hair," Carmella said. "What
do you think, Jayden?"

"I can't think that if Ashlyn wants her hair cut it would warrant a
demerit," Jayden answered. "Maybe you should both sign a paper saying
that Ashlyn wouldn't hold Tiffany responsible and that Tiffany would
do the best job she possibly could. We could put it in your files."

"We have a file?" Tiffany asked. "What do you do with it when our time is up here?"

"We send them to the court when you finish this course, and they can see by our recommendations, or by what kind of demerits or merits you earn, whether or not to allow you to go back to your high school or if you'll need to do some time in juvie," Jayden answered.

"Holy sh—" Carmella clamped a hand over her mouth. "I don't want to waste a demerit on a cuss word."

"If it is directed at a counselor or an employee of the camp, it is, and the f-bomb is forbidden," Tiffany answered. "Page fifteen, paragraph six."

"What are you, like a lawyer?" Ashlyn asked.

"Nope, but I read that whole thing, too, after my demerit because I don't ever want to do the hog lot stuff again." Tiffany shuddered. "I hated that job worse than even doing the stalls with all that horse crap and wet straw."

"All right, already," Ashlyn almost snorted. "Can she cut my hair or not, Jayden?"

"Not right now because in one minute it's going to be time for you to hustle outside for exercises," Jayden said. "So, get your hair put up in a ponytail and pull it out the back of your cap."

Carmella reached for her cap that hung on the bedpost and dropped it—then it bounced up under her cot. When she bent to get it, she jumped back and yelled, "Spider."

The siren sounded and both of the other girls took off out of the bedroom in a run. All the color left Carmella's face and she started to whimper like a puppy. "Jayden, the spider is on my cap, and I'm going to be in trouble if I go out there without my cap."

Jayden got down on her hands and knees and peeked under the bed. "That damn thing is as big as King Kong! Here, you take my cap and get on out of here. I'll deal with this monster before I go to the kitchen."

"Thank you." Carmella jerked the hat onto her head and pulled her ponytail out the back as she ran for the door. "If you can catch it, please put it in the box and freeze it," she yelled just before the wooden screen door slammed shut behind her.

A big brown tarantula sat on the top of Carmella's cap like a king on a throne and seemed to glare at her as if it were daring her to approach him without permission. She wasn't afraid of a normal spider, but in her mind this thing was as big as a gorilla and looked twice as vicious.

"Is everything all right in here?" Elijah yelled from outside.

His voice startled Jayden so much that she jumped backward, lost her balance, and sprawled out on the floor on her back. The spider must've heard boots on the wooden floor because it hopped off the hat and became nothing more than a dark blur as it ran right toward Jayden's hair.

"Help!" She jumped back and tried to yell at the same time, but her voice came out more like a cross between the whine of a hungry puppy and the screech of an owl.

She was still scrambling backward when Elijah entered the room. Even though he wasn't riding a white horse, Elijah damn sure looked like a knight in shining armor when he reached down with one hand and let the spider crawl right up on his arm.

"Are you crazy?" Jayden gasped.

He extended his free hand toward her. "Need some help?"

She put her hand in his, but once she was standing, she let it go and took a few steps back away from him. "Doesn't that thing bite?"

"Not unless provoked. This is mating season for them, so they come out of their burrows in the wilds looking for mates. This boy got lost. What do you want me to do with him?" Elijah asked.

"Put him in Carmella's collection box"—she pointed to the shoebox sitting on top of a footlocker—"and then make sure the lid is on it. I'll take it from there. Why aren't you out in the yard with the girls?"

"I left Ashlyn in charge." He managed to get the spider into the box and quickly put the lid on it. "After a couple of weeks, I do that so they can learn even more responsibility. I knew something was wrong when the dining room was still dark, and you didn't come out of the cabin with your girls like you always do."

"Thank you for rescuing me." She grabbed a broom from the corner of the room and swept Carmella's cap out from under the bed.

"You are welcome." He nodded. "But why did you use a broom? You could have reached the cap with no problem."

"You said those things are harmless, but, honey, they could cause me to hurt myself." She settled the cap on her head. "If his new little wife had set up housekeeping under the cot with him, I might have busted up a leg or an arm when I fell this time. Better to be safe than sorry."

"Is that your whole philosophy about life?" Elijah asked.

"Nope, just when it comes to big-ass spiders." She brushed past him, picked up the box, and started for the door, but she did sneak a glance over her shoulder at him on the way.

"What are you going to do with him?" Elijah followed so close behind her that she could feel his warm breath on her bare neck.

"He's about to have an up-close-and-personal cryogenic experience," she answered. "Then Tiffany will figure out a way to sketch him. I'm hoping she draws him on top of a skyscraper with airplanes flying all around him."

Elijah opened the door for her, and they walked side by side across the yard. Ashlyn had finished the morning exercises, and the girls were still in formation.

"All right, girls. We're going to do a fast walk this morning and cut our time by a third. We're up to three miles now, and some of you can do it without groaning. By that last week, you'll all be ready to go all the way to the mountain and camp out for a night."

"What is this *all* you are talking about?" she asked. "You got another tarantula hiding in your pocket. Is it going with us? I love to exercise, but I'd just as soon you leave all spiders at home."

Elijah chuckled. "I don't carry spiders in my pockets, and I mean all of the girls and you counselors. We wouldn't leave you out of the fun—those hot dogs won't cook themselves. See you later."

Jayden went straight to the big freezer in the pantry and carefully put the whole box inside it. She wasn't sure if she shivered because of the cold air, or if it was the idea of that huge critter in the box, or if maybe it was because she could still feel Elijah's breath on her neck.

The calendar on the wall in the kitchen said it was the third week in June, but the weather said something altogether different. For the second Sunday in a row, it rained. Not just a little sprinkle or two to water the cacti between the camp and the far mountains, but a serious downpour. Thank goodness it didn't start until they were in church, but still, when the service was over, all eight girls got soaked running from the church to the vans. They were all moaning about having to stay inside all afternoon when they reached Piney Wood and jogged from the parked vehicles to the dining hall.

"I'm not looking forward to this afternoon," Novalene groaned.

Jayden was the last one to sit down at the table with the adults, and she nodded in agreement. "I have an idea, and it might not be a good one, so I want all y'all to voice your honest opinions."

"I'm all ears," Novalene said.

"Me too," Diana added.

"Ashlyn was throwing a fit this morning about her hair. She wanted Tiffany to cut it, but Tiffany already has one demerit, and she's afraid to do anything against the rules. What if we let them do each other's hair this afternoon, since they have to stay in anyway? I've got a decent pair of scissors in my suitcase if any of them want a haircut," Jayden suggested.

"Man, that would take a lot of trust. Some of them are still pretty wary of the girls who aren't in their cabin. But I'm willing to give it a try, and I've got a curling iron they can use," Diana said. "Who's going to do the cutting, and who'll use the curling iron? What if one of them decides to do a shabby job on the styling or burn someone with the iron?"

"We could have a war," Novalene said, "but if it will keep them from being bitchy all afternoon because they can't play softball, then I'm all for it."

Elijah covered a yawn with his hand. "If y'all are going to primp all afternoon, then I'm going to my cabin for a nap. You don't need me to play beauty shop."

"Oh, come on," Jayden teased. "I thought maybe you'd like a facial."

"In all the years I've been here, I can't remember ever letting the girls do something like this after only three weeks in camp," Diana said.

"No, but it sounds like a good idea." He pushed back his chair and stood up. "They haven't gotten to primp in a while, and they have been pretty good, even with the transition." Elijah took his tray to the counter. "See y'all at supper. My cell phone number is on the front of the fridge if you need me."

"So, how do we get this started or even find out if they're interested?" Jayden asked.

"It's your idea—you tell them," Novalene said.

Jayden tapped a fork on the side of her iced-tea glass, and the room went quiet. "As you all know from your damp uniforms, it is raining, and it doesn't look like it's going to clear up, so . . ." She went on to tell them about her plan, ending with, "Does anyone here have any kind of experience in hairstyling?"

Novalene's two girls raised their hands. "You learn something new every day. Neither of them mentioned having any cosmetology experience until now," Novalene said.

"We have a stylist that comes to the house every week, and she's taught me a little about hair," Keelan said.

Bailey raised her hand. "Sometimes me and my friends all get together and have a makeover. I can do about anything with hair if

I have the right equipment. I can't believe y'all are going to let us do something like this."

"It's a reward for not one of you having a demerit all week," Novalene said. "You might think about that when you want to do something stupid in the coming days."

"Yes, ma'am," Keelan said. "Is there a spray bottle somewhere in the kitchen I can use to wet hair?"

"I know where one is." Tiffany hopped up and started around the end of the bar.

"How about a towel?" Bailey yelled. "We can use it for a cape."

"Will this work?" Tiffany held up a muslin tea towel.

"It will do just fine," Keelan said. "Who's first?"

Ashlyn held up a hand. "Me."

All eight girls who had been used to makeup, hair salons, and the best that money could buy were suddenly in their element, laughing and talking and getting everyone's opinions about how much hair to cut, and what style would look best.

"I betcha if one of them breaks a rule this next week, they'd better sleep with one eye open." Diana laughed.

"Why's that?" Jayden asked.

"Because after all the fun they're having today, if one of them keeps the whole bunch from getting a treat like this next Sunday, the other seven might not take too kindly to it," Novalene explained.

"Hey, Jayden, could I have a word?" Elijah poked his head inside the door and motioned for her.

"Uh-oh!" Diana nudged her on the shoulder. "If you get a demerit and all us counselors have to do something awful, we may banish you from the camp."

"And you'd never see Elijah again," Novalene teased.

Jayden pushed back her chair. "I can outrun every one of you, so I'm not worried."

173

She really wasn't worried about her two friends, but the way her stomach knotted up told a different story when she headed for the door. What had she done that Elijah would single her out in front of all the girls and the other two counselors?

The rain had slowed down to a nice drizzle, but the yard was muddy. Thank goodness the bench on the porch was set back far enough that it was still dry. Elijah motioned for her to have a seat and then sat down beside her.

"I thought you were going to take a nap." The bench was narrow enough that their shoulders touched. She didn't know how that affected him, but ever since he'd held her during that crying jag after Skyler left, every time he was close by her heart threw in an extra beat.

Elijah removed his cap and ran his fingers through his hair. "Rain has slowed down. God knows we never complain about rain in this part of the country. I'm just glad we didn't have the hay cut and drying or we'd be in a mess. According to the weatherman, it's supposed to be sunny the rest of the week, so we should be able to get it cut, baled, and into the barn by next Saturday."

Jayden wondered why Elijah had brought her outside to talk about rain and hay. He could have done that in front of the other three counselors.

"Do the girls help haul hay?" she asked.

"Soon as it's baled, we issue them a pair of gloves, put them in two teams, and have a contest to see who can get it into the barn and stacked first," he answered. "But I didn't really want to talk about that."

Halle-damn-lujah! she thought. Not that she didn't like the delicious little shivers chasing down her spine every time he changed positions and pressed even closer to her side, but she did want to know what was on his mind. Then she realized that the news might be bad and gasped. What if something had happened to Henry or to Mary, and he was building up his courage to tell her?

He cleared his throat to go on, and heaviness filled her chest.

"I just had a long conversation with Mary and Henry," he said.

"Thank God!" she spit out before she even thought.

"What does that mean?" he asked.

"The way you were hemming and hawing around, I thought maybe something had happened to them," she told him.

He flashed a smile that heated up the porch at least another five degrees. "They are both fine, and I didn't mean to be evasive."

"Then why are we talking about rain and hay?" she asked.

"Downright blunt, aren't you?" he chuckled.

"I can be," she answered.

He laid a hand on her shoulder. "I like it, but you're right. I have a favor to ask, and truth is, I like talking to you."

"Ooo . . . kay . . ." Jayden drew the word out. "I miss them, too. I didn't realize how much Mary and I visited while we worked until she was gone."

"I can still call Henry if I've got a question about anything, and I'm fine with the work and taking over this place, especially since you're here to cook for us. But I miss visiting with them. I think I've heard all his old war stories, at least the ones he was willing to tell, a dozen times or more." Elijah sighed. "But back to the favor. I need help in hiring a cook for the next session, and I was hoping you would help me. I don't know where to start."

"To start with, you should call the employment agency and tell them what you're looking for. Do you want a temp that will only work eight weeks at a time, or someone to stay here year-round? Can you have a man or a woman? Or just a woman? You've got a lot to think about." Jayden had a lot to think about, too. She had worried about Skyler taking over Daydream Cabin, but that had worked itself out. Hiring a new cook would mean she'd have to give up the kitchen, and Jayden wasn't ready to do that.

"That's all good advice," Elijah said. "Would you help me do some interviews while you are here? I'll get in touch with some employment agencies, and we can set up a schedule for interested folks to come out here, maybe work a day with you in the kitchen. Are you sure you won't consider my offer to stay on?"

"I went to school four years to earn my certification and took night classes to become a counselor. I've kept up with ongoing summer classes to keep my position. I'm not so sure I'm ready to throw all that away and make a huge change in my life."

"I was once a soldier," he told her. "If you're really, really happy at your job, then you should stay with it. I wasn't happy when we lost part of the team, so it was time for me to make a change."

"I'll be glad to help you find a cook," she said. "Maybe we should sit down this evening and list what you want so the employment agency will know who to send out here."

"Thank you. I'd like that," Elijah said. "That would be great. After supper and your group therapy, could we meet out in the dining room?"

"I'll be there." She nodded.

Elijah gave her shoulder another nudge and then stood up. "Thanks again." With his broad shoulders hunched against the drizzle, he jogged out across the yard toward his cabin.

Jayden mulled over the idea of a new cook again, and it didn't sit well with her, but maybe they'd find a perfect fit when they did the interviews.

Not damn likely! Those were the words her grandfather used when nothing was going to work.

With a sigh, she went back into what had become a beauty parlor. She got herself a bottle of water and sat down with the ladies at the table.

"Personal or business?" Novalene winked.

"Business," Jayden answered.

"That answer was pretty quick. Think she's tellin' the truth?" Diana teased.

"If she's not, I wouldn't play poker with her," Novalene added. "Can you tell us why you got called out, and if we can expect Elijah to invite each of us to the porch?"

Jayden took a long drink from her water bottle. "He wants me to help interview prospects for a new cook. He's already gone back to his cabin, so I think y'all are all safe."

"You should take this job, Jayden, and I'm speaking from the heart now. I'm not kidding," Novalene said.

"Why do you say that?" Jayden asked.

"It pays better." Novalene held up a finger. "You get four months off work, rather than three." Another finger went up. "And you trade a whole building full of problem kids for nine students at a time. And last, you won't have rent or board, so you can save more for retirement. You like cooking, plus you are wonderful with kids." She held up the next two plus her thumb.

"Five good reasons, and then add"—Diana held up a finger and whispered—"Elijah has a big crush on you."

Jayden's hand popped up. "What if"—her forefinger stood straight and tall—"you are right about there being a little spark of chemistry between us, and we got into some kind of relationship and it didn't work. It would sure make working with him and for him pretty damned awkward."

"Don't close the door of opportunity until you see what's behind it." Diana reached over and put Jayden's finger down. "I did, and I have regrets."

"You can stick around here a year, and if it doesn't work, you can always go back to teaching, or you can drive race cars in my honor," Novalene suggested.

"Or else go down to the army recruiters and see if you can get into sniper school."

Jayden crushed her water bottle and tossed it in the recycle bin across the room. "I promise to think about all your advice, but I imagine that I'll be flying back to North Texas with y'all when this session is over."

Chapter Fourteen

he rain finally stopped that evening after supper, and Jayden
called the girls out of their room to see a beautiful double rainbow in the sky.

"Isn't it gorgeous?" she asked.

Carmella shrugged. "It's a rainbow."

"I'd like it better if there was a real pot of gold at the end, and I
could use it to get out of this place." Tiffany's tone was ice cold.

"Stop your bitchin'." Ashlyn glared at her. "I can't even get my hair
up in a ponytail, so I'll have to be careful my cap doesn't fall off."

"What's the problem?" Jayden almost sighed, but then it was
Sunday. The whole bunch of them did much better on the days when
they had a routine and jobs from daylight to dark.

Tiffany shot Ashlyn a dirty look and a middle finger. "I'm going
to write about this in my journal. Y'all can leave me alone and don't
even try to talk to me." She stormed off into the house and slammed
the screen door behind her.

"She and Carmella don't like their haircuts," Ashlyn explained.

"This is the worst styling job I've had since I got high and cut it
myself with my boyfriend's pocketknife," Carmella told them. "Mama
took me to the salon the next day and got our hairdresser to take care

of it. Seems to me like Tiffany has the right idea. I'm going to go bitch about it in my journal."

It was a blessing that they weren't threatening to go over to Moonbeam Cabin and start a fight or, worse yet, shave Keelan's and Bailey's heads for not giving them high-dollar haircuts.

"I hate mine, too," Ashlyn admitted, "but it looks like crap anyway with my dark roots growing out and my pink streak gone, so I really don't care. No one except a few people in church are going to see it anyway, and we go to a different place every Sunday. Speaking of that, I didn't like the service this morning. The sermon was so dry that I fell asleep. I think Tiffany and Carmella just need something to gripe about today. They're homesick, and both of them are wishing for school to start so they can see their friends. Me, I don't give a good hot"—she paused and sucked in air—"darn if I ever see any of mine again. I've decided to never drink again, not even a beer, and I may ask my folks to put me in a private boarding school. They've wanted to for a while, but I thought I'd die without my friends."

"Afraid you'll get drunk and dye your hair pink again?" Jayden asked.

"Nope." Ashlyn shook her head. "I'm afraid I'll get behind the wheel and hurt someone. I'm going to go inside and write about this in my journal. I really, really hate this place tonight, just as much as Tiffany. I want to see green grass and rosebushes. Not even those flowers right there"—she pointed at the petunias and the lantana growing in front of the cabin—"can come close to the gardens at our estate. I want to sleep in a bed that's big enough I can sprawl out and not fall off onto the floor where spiders and bugs crawl around, and I want my clothes back. I will never take my bikini underpants for granted again."

"That's the whole idea of this place. To teach you teamwork and to build your self-esteem so you can be a leader instead of following the wrong influences." Jayden sat down in one of the chairs.

"Well, it's damn . . . I mean *dang* sure working. They should have named this place Nightmare Cabin instead of Daydream," she said. "The only thing I daydream about is going home."

"Maybe that's a good thing," Jayden said.

Ashlyn didn't flip her off, but her expression said that she sure wanted to. She whipped around and went into the cabin, but she didn't slam the door. Evidently, she was serious about wanting to keep her nose clean so she could go home.

Jayden caught a movement out of her peripheral vision, and, thinking it might be Elijah, her heart did one of those crazy flip-flops that it did when he was around. She was more than a little disappointed when Novalene eased down into a chair.

"I thought the beauty shop went well until I got home." She sighed. "I overheard my two girls talking in the bathroom at shower time about deliberately making a mess of your girls' hair. They said it was payback for Tiffany threatening to roll Bailey in the hog wallow when Lauren was still here. I'm going back and forth between giving them each a demerit or giving them a good talking-to. What do you think?"

"That's your call, but because this is their first offence since Lauren left, maybe a talking-to would do," Jayden said. "They were all doing so well a couple of days ago. Is this normal behavior for the halfway mark?"

"Oh, yeah," Novalene sighed. "It happens, but then they're teenage girls, not angels. They have to have a little drama and hatefulness. Have you given any thought to what we talked about?"

"You mean staying here?" Jayden wished that she could go over to Moonbeam Cabin herself and give those two girls a piece of her mind, but that wasn't her place. "The possibility has got a lot of pros, but I'm weighing the cons as well."

"I think you'd be perfect for the job, but you've got to figure this out for yourself." Novalene sucked in a lungful of air and let it out slowly. "I've got a confession. When we learned that Skyler wasn't going to be with us this summer, I almost backed out. I didn't like the idea of working with someone new, maybe even having to train you, but I like you, and I'm glad I came. You've got more spunk and sass than your sister, and you really do have good ideas. I'm just sorry that my two have been little turds today."

"My mother would quote scripture and say the Lord says that vengeance is His, or something like that," Jayden told her just as she saw a flash of what looked like platinum hair behind the screen door. "It's a bit of an oxymoron to me. Looks like He could stop the problem rather than bringing down brimstone and fire on the ones who were evil or just downright mean."

Novalene frowned. "How's that an oxymoron?"

"Seems like if we're going to have trouble, it will happen on Sunday, so that kind of loosely fits, doesn't it?" Jayden answered. "Want a bottle of water or lemonade?"

"No, I'm good," Novalene said. "I get what you're saying. Church seems to bring out the worst in them rather than the best."

"We've got a little more than a month to prove my theory." She suddenly got that antsy feeling that only came about when Elijah was nearby.

"Hello, ladies," Elijah greeted them with a smile. "Mind if I join you?"

"Not a bit," Jayden said.

Novalene stood up with a groan. "I was just leaving. These old bones love to sit in those chairs, but they don't like getting up out of them so well."

"You don't have to rush off," Jayden said.

Novalene shot one of her sly winks toward Jayden. "I'd better get on back and make sure my Moonbeams haven't figured out something eviler to get into. We'll talk later."

Elijah stood to the side and let her pass, then joined Jayden on the porch. He'd shaved and changed from his usual company T-shirt into a snap-front plaid western shirt. The soft evening breeze brought the woodsy, musky scent of his shaving lotion right to Jayden. She inhaled deeply, taking in as much as she could before the wind shifted.

"What evil is going on over in Moonbeam?" Elijah handed her a bottle of root beer and took a drink from the one he had in his other hand.

Jayden lowered her voice and told him about the haircuts that Keelan and Bailey had given her girls. Just as she finished, she could have sworn she saw another flash of platinum hair peeking around the corner of the screen door. Then the air-conditioning unit in the girls' room started rattling and the lights went out, so she couldn't be sure what she'd seen.

"They should've kept their mouths shut." Elijah grinned. "After hearing them talk about it, now Novalene knows to watch them closer. Too bad they've destroyed the trust they had built up with her. Now they'll have to start all over. Have you got that uniform order ready?"

"I've got the order all made out and tucked into the catalog, but it's out in the dining hall. Do you need it tonight or will tomorrow morning do?" she asked.

"Tomorrow's fine. Now about this cooking job? Have you thought about anything else we should list as requirements when I get in touch with the employment office?" He sat down on the top porch step and took a notepad and pen from his shirt pocket.

She couldn't very well say that the last thing she was thinking about was interviewing cooks when he was this close to her. He caught her eye but quickly looked back down at his notepad. Did he get the same feelings when he was close to her as she did when he was nearby?

"I put down that they have to have some experience cooking for a group." He flipped the notebook open. "And next is that they will be provided room and board."

"Pets?" she asked.

"I don't mind if they have outside pets as in dogs or cats, but nothing in the cabin." He wrote that down and locked gazes with her again.

"How about children? Both living here permanently or visiting?" Her voice was an octave higher than normal.

He blinked a couple of times, cleared his throat, and focused on the notepad. "Good questions. No children here all the time, but visiting during the off-seasons would be fine."

"You don't like kids?" Jayden asked.

"Love them," he answered. "Wouldn't mind having a yard full of my own right here in this desert country, but I wouldn't want the headache of other people's children being here permanently. Can't you just see a cook with two or three little school-age kids quitting on the spot because one of our girls cut their hair wrong or upset one of them somehow? Or what if you get a girl in here who has abused her younger siblings?"

"It is going to be a challenge to find the right fit." The tension between them was thick enough that Elijah had to feel it as much as she did. "Male or female?"

"Can't make a preference there or they'll call us out for it, so we'll leave that alone and just refuse to hire someone if, like you say, the fit isn't right." His hand trembled a little when he tucked the pen back into his pocket. "This is way more trouble than I thought it would be. What I'd really like to have is a semiretired couple, kind of like Henry and Mary, only ten or fifteen years younger."

"Write it down and tell whoever you talk to that's your dream couple," Jayden told him.

"Do you think the fact that I'm sitting on Daydream Cabin porch will have some good juju?" He chuckled.

"Never hurts to hope," Jayden answered. "What about a young couple, say about twenty-five, who've just gotten married, and he has ranchin' in his background, and she's been studying to be a chef?"

"Find me that couple, and I'll let them raise as many kids as they want here on this place," he answered. "Do you know someone like that, or are you just teasing me?"

"I'm just throwing out ideas so that you'll be prepared for whoever applies," she said.

"Well, honey, if someone like that sends me a résumé, I'll believe that you have superpowers." He tipped up his root beer and finished it off.

"Just call me a superhero," she teased.

He stood up and said, "I'd call you Daydream Angel if you'd stay. We work well together."

"Let's do some interviews," she said. "Maybe you'll find someone who works even better with you." She didn't want him to go. She wished they could talk about personal things instead of hiring a cook. Evidently, he was only interested in the hiring of someone to work for him—not a woman whose heart had begun to get all warm and soft every time he was near her.

"There ain't a snowball's chance in hell of that happenin'," he said as he disappeared out into the dark.

What's that supposed to mean? Jayden wondered. Could he possibly feel the same vibes she did every time they were together? If so, why didn't he make a move?

Questions upon questions, but not a one had an answer.

Chapter Fifteen

T hirty days hath September, April, June, and November," Jayden recited that morning instead of crossing the kitchen to look at the calendar. That meant the next day was the first day of July, and half of her time at Piney Wood Academy was gone.

Is the glass half-empty or half-full? Her mother's voice was so clear in her head that it startled her.

"I'm not sure," she muttered an answer. "Some days I feel like it's half-empty, Mama."

Then you need to change your attitude.

"What does that mean?" Jayden popped a pan of biscuits in the oven.

Novalene came inside and headed toward the coffeepot. "What does what mean?"

"I was talking to myself," Jayden answered. "What are you doing up and about so early?"

"Moonbeam Cabin had a spider episode this morning, and Bailey is terrified of them," Novalene said. "If this had happened a couple of weeks ago when they had the hair-cutting thing, I would have thought your girls were retaliating."

"I was afraid they might, so I never mentioned it to them." The minute the words were out of her mouth, Jayden remembered platinum hair that had flitted past the screen door the evening that she told Elijah about the incident.

Novalene took her coffee to the table, sat down, and let out a long breath in a whoosh. "It was about three o'clock. I'm surprised it didn't wake everyone up in all of the cabins. Bailey was screaming at the top of her lungs for someone to get the big brown tarantula off her forehead. Keelan was standing four feet back with the broom in her hand like she was going to swat the thing away. I should have gotten my phone and filmed it."

"What happened?" Jayden bit back a giggle. After what those two girls had done, this had to be payback.

"Bailey was flat on her back like she was about to go into rigor. She was afraid to move. She kept whimpering like a dying coyote and rolling her eyes up to catch sight of the thing that seemed to be considering making a nest in her hair," Novalene answered. "I grabbed the broom from Keelan. The way she was swinging it around, she could have put out one of Bailey's eyes, and then I coaxed it into crawling off the girl's head and onto the broom. I started out toward the bathhouse to flush it down the toilet, all the time praying the damn thing didn't clog up the plumbing. When I was about halfway there, it jumped off the broom. I didn't know those things could move so fast. One minute, it had hunkered down and was enjoying the ride across the yard, and the next, it was gone."

"Thank goodness the one we found was hiding under the bed and not on Carmella." Jayden used a wooden spoon to point to the wall where Tiffany's drawing of the tarantula hung. "I bet Bailey appreciates the art in that picture a lot better today than she did when Tiffany put it up there."

"No doubt about that," Novalene agreed.

"God, what a morning," Diana said as she came through the door, likely for coffee if Jayden knew anything. "In all the years I've been here, I've never seen a tarantula. I swear that Tiffany jinxed us by hanging that picture up in here. One showed up on the Sunshine Cabin porch this morning. Remember me tellin' y'all that Rita was my alpha girl when we first got here? Well, when that spider hopped up on her leg, she did some kind of fancy footwork. The other two girls took off in a dead run toward the exercise yard with Rita right behind them, trying to shake the thing off her pants before it made its way up toward her shirt. If I hadn't seen the spider on her, I would have thought she was trying to learn some new steps." Diana poured herself a mugful of coffee.

Had the one pinned to the board in the corner of the living area in Daydream Cabin come back to life? Jayden began to wonder if there was such a thing as zombie spiders. She made a mental note to check that evening to see if Carmella's tarantula was still there.

Diana took a sip of her coffee and went on. "Lord, I hate two things in this old world, and spiders are both of them. The damn thing jumped from Rita's pants right over onto Violet's bare arm once they got to the morning exercise spot. She fainted dead away. Just dropped like a rock with every one of the other girls standing at attention for fear they'd get a demerit if they broke ranks. The spider took off for the bushes while I got her revived. I told her that she didn't have to go on the hike this morning since she had fainted, but she insisted that she was fine. You got a new story about the spiders, Jayden?"

"Nope." Jayden pointed to the picture on the wall. "Our bad boy is still pinned to a board, and the picture up there on the wall is the only thing left to attack us."

"Well, one thing's for sure, I bet every one of these girls remembers that there are tarantulas in these parts, and they think twice about their behavior once they go home," Novalene said.

"Bless their little hearts," Jayden said. "They've lived an entitled and totally sheltered life. Someday they'll look back on this and appreciate the fact that they got the opportunity to turn their lives around."

"But today isn't that day. I bet they check under their beds and in every corner before they go to bed tonight," Novalene said. "Truth is,

I intend to do the same thing in my room. Spiders or anything that crawls, including snakes, give me the heebie-jeebies."

Diana shivered. "Me too. I don't like those things, but a mouse or a rat will put me to running in high gear a lot faster than that. How do those big old things get into a cabin anyway?"

"I think our spider came through that little tear in the spacer where the air conditioner hangs in their bedroom," Novalene answered.

Jayden pulled the biscuits out of the oven and set the pan on the buffet line next to the scrambled eggs, sausage, and blueberry muffins. "Do you think Lauren tore the plastic to let the smoke out when she was there?"

Novalene shook her head. "No, she was cracking the other window for that. I bet Bailey and Keelan talk Elijah out of some duct tape before bedtime tonight, though. They will most likely tape every crack and cranny in the whole cabin, and if they do, I'm not saying a word about it."

"I bet all of them have nightmares for the rest of this week." Diana sighed. "We'll be up at night with them like they're tiny babies."

Not mine, Jayden thought. *If they made that tear in the plastic and shooed that big-ass spider into Moonbeam Cabin, then Bailey and Keelan had it coming.*

The commotion started the second the girls all filed into the dining room. Bailey got right up in Tiffany's face and narrowed her eyes until they were barely slits. "You turned that spider loose in our cabin to pay us back for giving y'all bad haircuts, didn't you?"

Tiffany's smile was so saccharine that Jayden had no doubt her girls definitely had something to do with the whole escapade. "Bad haircuts? We thought y'all did a fine job on our hair, didn't we?" She turned toward Carmella and Ashlyn on down the line.

"Love my new shorter ponytail," Carmella said.

"I was thinkin' of askin' y'all to cut another inch off mine," Ashlyn told them. "But if you deliberately gave us ugly haircuts, then you should be ashamed. We trusted you. I guess what we heard in church last Sunday about vengeance belonging to God went right over your heads."

"God didn't put that spider in our cabin," Keelan argued.

"Maybe the devil did it, just like he made you give us bad haircuts," Carmella said in a sugary-sweet tone. "Y'all should ask God for forgiveness for your evil deed, and maybe He will step in and keep old Lucifer from bringing more fire and brimstone down upon y'all's heads."

"You are related to the devil himself," Bailey hissed. "I saw you put that spider in the box you carry around."

"Why don't you come visit us in our cabin and look at all the bugs pinned to my board?" Carmella smiled. "You'll only see one tarantula there, and unless he's turned into a zombie spider and came to visit you, then I expect that you're confused. I didn't even like the first one, so I surely wouldn't want to deal with a second one."

Jayden couldn't keep the smile off her face. Carmella had given a convincing argument, but not once had she denied doing the dirty little deed.

Bailey took a step back. "What do you mean by fire and brimstone?"

"Talk to God," Tiffany answered as she picked up a tray and slid it down the buffet line. "He's the one who takes care of that, not us."

"Besides, *we* didn't do anything mean to the Daydream girls, and the spider came to visit all of us, too, so don't blame them. I flat out fainted," Violet chimed in as she shoved her way between Tiffany and Bailey and picked up a tray. "Get over yourself, girl, and eat some breakfast. We're in the danged desert. We can expect spiders and lizards. You didn't even faint like I did, so stop your whining."

"It sat on my forehead." Bailey shivered.

"Well, it crawled up my leg," Rita countered.

"At least you had pants on," Violet told her. "I thought for sure it was going to take a bite out of my arm and scar me for life."

189

The girls all completed the line and took their trays to their tables. They were still talking about spiders and the worst thing they'd experienced since being at the camp as Jayden filled her tray and joined the other counselors and Elijah at the adult table. She was sure her girls had something to do with the spider issue, but since she didn't have a single shred of evidence, she decided to take the advice her mother always gave her and keep her suspicions to herself.

Elijah nudged her with his shoulder. "I thought we'd have to leave Violet behind after she fainted, but she made the entire three-mile hike. What a trouper."

Novalene nodded in agreement. "I was surprised that Bailey kept up this morning at all. For a little while there, I thought we might have to call out the EMTs to get Bailey breathing again." She told Elijah what had happened to start off her day that morning.

When she finished, Diana told her part of the morning's incidents. "At least it wasn't a scorpion. If one of those gets loose in a cabin, the girls might burn it to the ground."

"Be hard to burn down a stucco building," Elijah laughed. "I imagine they'll remember this with a shiver when they get home."

"Did I hear *scorpion*?" Carmella stopped by the table on her way back from getting another bottle of orange juice. "What do they look like? Will they kill me if they bite me? Where can I find one for my bug collection?"

"Look it up in the bug book this evening," Jayden said.

Elijah pushed back his chair, stood up, and tapped his coffee mug with a spoon. The room quieted immediately. "Carmella has just asked a good question. July and August are the months when we begin to see scorpions in this part of the country. Could any of you identify one if you saw it?"

Not one hand raised.

"Carmella has a bug book that she's going to go get when I get through talking. You will all look at the picture of scorpions in it so you know exactly what they look like. Bark scorpions are what is most common here. They can climb walls and walk across ceilings," he said.

Several of the girls looked up and scanned the walls in the dining hall.

"They show up in bathtubs, sinks, and even beds because sometimes they fall from the ceiling," Elijah told them. "They can crawl through a crack as small as an eighth of an inch wide, and outdoors they can be found in piles of lumber, bricks, and brush and trash. A sting will not kill you, but it will deliver acute pain for about three days. If you get stung, go to your counselor or come to me immediately, and we'll treat it so you don't have nausea or vomiting."

"We're in hell," Bailey groaned. "I thought that spider was the worst thing we'd have to deal with."

"I don't mean to alarm you, but you need to be sure you recognize the scorpion and don't mess with it in any way. That includes catching and sketching, girls." Elijah's tone left no doubt that he was very serious.

"Have you ever been bitten by one?" Ashlyn asked.

Elijah nodded. "Twice. That's why I'm telling you to be careful. Chances are you won't even see one, since they're nocturnal."

"Sweet Jesus!" Novalene sighed. "Now I'll have to go with them to the bathroom if they need to go at night."

Diana shook her head. "Don't worry. I bet not a one of them will even get out of bed once they check the whole room before they lay down."

"If they're smart, they won't." Elijah crossed the room and poured himself a second cup of coffee. "I was sicker with those scorpion bites than I was with the flu."

Jayden made a mental note to threaten her girls with exile from the camp and a trip straight into juvie if they caught one of those evil critters and turned it loose in a cabin. No ugly haircut was worth that kind of thing.

❖ ❖ ❖

That evening, when supper was over, Jayden put four bottles of water into a plastic bag and carried them across the lawn. After what Elijah had said about scorpions, she kept her eyes on the ground. She saw a few beetles, and a couple of bees flew around her head, but there were none of those critters that looked to her like a cross between a dinosaur and an alien.

She set the water on the tables separating the two sets of chairs, opened the cabin door, and yelled, "Y'all girls come on out here. We need to talk."

"Are we in trouble?" Carmella asked.

Jayden motioned for them to sit down. "Should you be?"

Tiffany's eyes never left the bottles sitting on the tables. "You going to waterboard us?"

"Nope," Jayden answered. "Thought y'all might be thirsty."

They all three sat down, and it didn't take a rocket scientist to see that they were nervous. Probably about that beast of a spider. Jayden picked up her bottle and twisted the lid off. "I'm not going to ask any questions about that spider, but I am going to warn you about scorpions. I'd better not find out that you caused someone to get sick from a sting, or else I'll pile on extra demerits and you'll end up talking to a judge again. Understood?"

"Yes, ma'am," they said in unison and reached for their water at the same time.

Jayden took a long drink from her bottle while they uncapped theirs, and then she changed the subject. Her father and stepmother both belabored a point, especially when they thought that she had done something wrong. Even though they weren't children, she often took the fall for anything that Skyler did wrong when they were both at their father's new home. In his eyes, Skyler did nothing wrong, and since Jayden had decided to live with her mother, she had to be the one who was to blame when the girls argued. That was why she refused to see them after a couple of visits.

"I'm glad we don't have scorpions in El Paso," Carmella said.

"You probably do," Jayden said. "They're pretty much found all over Texas. But we never have talked about where y'all live. Why don't each of y'all tell us about your hometown?"

Carmella raised her hand. "I'll keep goin'. My daddy is a heart surgeon, and he was really angry with me when I got caught shoplifting for the third time. If he'd known how many pieces of jewelry I'd walked out with and given away, he would have sent me straight to juvie himself. I gave a thousand-dollar bracelet to a homeless lady once and told her to go pawn it for money for food, and I can't count how many pieces of jewelry I've given my friends. They probably don't even remember me now."

"What does your mama do?" Jayden asked.

"Daddy got custody of me in the divorce. My stepmother says she's my dad's office assistant, but her main job is to be beautiful. According to her, she can't even hold her head up in front of her friends because of me. Truth is, I kind of like that idea after the way she's put me down for years. My mother moved to Paris to work for a fashion designer, so I only see her a few times a year and then it's usually just for a day."

"I'm from Tyler, Texas," Tiffany said. "My dad owns Jordan Oil Company, and my suite of rooms back home is bigger than this cabin. I have a sitting room, a bedroom, and my own walk-in closet with a huge dressing room and bathroom attached to it. My mama is the company lawyer. My therapist, the one at home, not Karen, said I act out to get their attention. I thought she was full of crap, and I acted the way I do because I want people to like me. But, I see that now, and it's crazy, but neither of my folks have ever had time for me. I feel like they were ashamed of me even before I got into trouble. They're both beautiful people, and they wanted a boy to carry on the family name after they had my beautiful older sister. Instead, they got a tall red-haired throwback to Daddy's grandmother, and then Mama couldn't have any more kids, so it was bye-bye to ever having a boy."

Jayden's eyes stung with unshed tears, and when she tried to say something, her mouth had turned as dry as if she'd been eating a green persimmon. She picked up her water bottle and took a long drink, but the lump in her throat didn't shrink a bit. No wonder these girls had such problems. Jayden wished she could wave a magic wand and fix them all, but she could only be there for positive support. They had to *want* to change, or it would never happen.

"Amarillo," Ashlyn offered without being asked. "My mama inherited a string of hotels that are scattered all over the state of Texas. She and my stepdad travel a lot in connection with that, and I've always known my nanny better than I know them. My daddy's family has a horse ranch in Virginia, and he helps run that. My stepmother trains horses, and I usually have to spend a couple of weeks with them in the summer. They don't get me this year, and I'm glad. As much as I don't like this place, I'd rather be here than there. Spending time there is just trading off one mostly empty house for another, because they're too busy to even pick me up at the airport. My sweet nanny died last year"—she stopped and wiped a tear from her eye—"and"—she sighed—"there's two wet bars in our house. One downstairs in the den and one in the media room on the third floor. No one even missed the bottles of whiskey that I drank to help me get past all the pain of her death."

Listening to them tell their stories was cathartic. Jayden hadn't been the only outcast in the world. She hadn't been the only one who felt unloved by a parent or had been left behind by one. Kids today had the same problems she'd grown up with. This bunch just had more money and access to booze and cars than she had at their age.

"Do y'all ever look at the kids that don't have a lot of money and wish you had their life?" Carmella asked. "A mama who makes cookies for an after-school snack and that tells you that you're pretty and smart, and she's so proud of you?"

"Only every day, but that kind of mama doesn't really exist," Tiffany answered.

"My mama worked the three-to-eleven shifts at the hospital in the emergency admitting office, so she was home during the day," Jayden told them. "We couldn't have an after-school snack together, but she left something for me and my grandpa, who lived with us. Course, at home I always took a back seat to my big sister, so I can feel your pain."

"Are you serious?" Ashlyn frowned.

"Yes, ma'am, very serious." Jayden smiled. "Even though she got home late, she got up and had a hot breakfast with me every morning, and we visited while we ate. My school was only a couple of blocks away, so I went home for lunch and we spent that half hour together, too."

"What about your dad?" Tiffany asked.

"He and my mother divorced when I was sixteen. My grandmother died and Gramps was helpless without her, so Mama moved him into our house. Daddy said that Mama put us kids and then her father before him and that was the cause of the divorce, but the truth was that he was having an affair and married the other woman as soon as he could. They made me come spend time with them one summer after the divorce, but I was miserable and they were, too, so they didn't push the issue anymore," Jayden answered.

"Did that make you mad?" Carmella asked.

"No, I was just glad that I didn't have to go," Jayden replied.

Ashlyn raised her hand. "Testify, sister."

"The bottom line is this," Jayden told them, "you have to learn to love *you* for who you are. Get so comfortable in your own skin that nobody else's opinion matters. One of my favorite sayings is, 'To thine own self be true.' I don't always do a good job of doing it, but I'm trying to do better lately." Immediately Jayden wondered if she should have shown such a vulnerable side to the girls.

"One day at a time, sweet Jesus." Ashlyn giggled.

"Pretty much the truth." Jayden laughed with her. "Now, the bunch of you best get your things together and go to the bathhouse. It's your turn to go first tonight. And just one more reminder: leave the scorpions alone or kill them if you can do that safely."

"Yes, ma'am," they all chimed together.

Jayden got up and walked across the yard to Moonbeam Cabin, where Novalene was sitting on the porch with a glass of tea. She sat down in one of the hot-pink chairs, and Novalene pushed the tea over toward her. "Looks like you could use a drink of this. I've been using the straw, so you can drink out of the side."

Jayden sucked up a mouthful and almost choked when she swallowed it. "You could have warned me," she sputtered.

Novalene chuckled. "Have another sip. I always come prepared to make at least a couple of these while I'm here. I buy two each of those little single bottles of rum, vodka, gin, tequila, and triple sec. Without a doubt, I will need it at least twice. Today, we're celebrating half of the season being gone, and the fact that we lived through the spider episode," Novalene said. "Did you give your girls the 'come to Jesus' talk about scorpions being set loose in anyone's cabin?"

Jayden nodded and took one more drink of the tea. "If I come back next year, I'll remember to bring something to celebrate with and share with you."

Novalene chuckled. "I don't know if I'll return, but if I do, I'll hold you to that."

"What's so funny?" Jayden asked.

"The idea you won't come back next year," Novalene said.

"What makes you think that?" Jayden asked. "Skyler could be here instead."

"Who knows what will happen in a year, but you won't 'come back'"—Novalene put air quotes around the last two words—"because you won't ever leave."

"In your dreams." Jayden laughed out loud. "Tarantulas, scorpions, and God knows what else is hiding in the corners of this place. Not much to keep me here."

"I'll bet you a bottle of Knob Creek Smoked Maple bourbon that you'll find something you don't want to leave behind in the next few weeks," Novalene told her.

Jayden stuck out her hand and said, "Deal!"

They shook hands to seal the deal, and then Jayden pushed up out of the chair. "I hear my girls coming back from the bathhouse. See you at breakfast."

"I'm going to enjoy every drop of that bourbon you're going to have to buy for me," Novalene called out as Jayden jogged across the yard.

"You should be in Daydream Cabin," Jayden hollered, "with that kind of thinking."

She went to her bedroom and got her journal out, picked up a pen, and began to write:

Dear Mama,

I'm not sure if I made a mistake today. I let my tough girls see a vulnerable side of me. Now I worry that they'll think I'm a softie and try my authority. Maybe I should have kept things on a professional level and not gotten into my own personal background. I've disclosed more of my feelings since I've been here—with the counselors, Elijah, and the girls in my cabin. I feel a closeness to all of these people that I haven't had before. Friends and something like peers with Novalene and Diana. Something that sets my emotions into a tailspin with Elijah. And like a big sister to these girls. I just hope I haven't made a misstep tonight by letting them into my own personal world.

Time will tell, I suppose . . .

Chapter Sixteen

*J*ayden wiped her hands on a paper towel, flipped her apron up over her head, and hung it on a nail on the kitchen wall next to several others. She had just finished filling a plastic bag with ice when Elijah arrived at the dining hall. Straw stuck to his chambray shirtsleeves, to his jeans and boots, and even to his cap, which he removed and stuck in his back pocket. Sweat dripped from his square jawline onto his already wet shirt. He yanked a red bandanna from his pocket and wiped his face with it.

Jayden quickly tossed him a bottle of water and poured a glass of tea. "Is the job done?"

He downed the water without coming up for air and then took a long drink of the tea. "Thank you. I was so dry I was spittin' dust," he joked.

Jayden couldn't take her eyes off him. Her chest tightened and her breath came in short gasps. She could spend every day with him if she wanted, and right then she really, really wanted to listen to her heart and say yes. But—there always seemed to be a "but" in her life—she had to be sure that a major move like that was truly best for her.

"Are the girls spittin' dust, too?" She smiled.

"Oh, yeah," he answered. "I've refilled the coolers, but they'll love having some ice to go in their cups."

"I remember hay hauling being hard, sweaty work," Jayden told him. "I used to help Gramps out before Granny died and he sold the farm. Thought I'd ride out with you and see how the girls are doing."

"They're whining, bitching, competing with one another, and sweating." He grinned. "I'd love to have you go with me."

"Be all right if we take a dozen bottles of cold sweet tea as well as water?" she asked. "After all that sweating, something other than water might taste real good to them."

"Hey, until we find another cook, we're pretty much partners in this business," he answered. "You don't even have to ask about little things like that. A bottle of sweet tea might even give them enough energy to get the hay all in before those storm clouds in the southwest blow up some rain."

Sun poured into the kitchen window that faced the north, so it was hard for Jayden to imagine clouds anywhere, but when she carried a paper bag with a dozen bottles of tea out to the truck, she saw big black ones billowing toward them. "That's weird," she said. "If I stand right here and don't look over my shoulder, it's kind of scary looking. If I turn around, all is happiness and sunshine."

"Kind of like life, ain't it?" Elijah opened the truck door for her. "It all depends on what way you're lookin'—backward or forward."

"That's pretty philosophical," she muttered as she watched him round the end of the old work truck and slide under the steering wheel.

"I'm a man of many talents." He put the truck in gear.

"Are Novalene and Diana out in the fields, too?" she asked.

"They're in the barn to supervise the girls who take in the loads and stack them," he answered.

"I've pretty much got supper ready, and if it's twenty minutes late, it's no big deal. I'll drive a truck and that will free up a set of hands."

"I would never turn down help," he agreed. "With you driving, we might get done early and supper won't even be late." He parked the truck in the middle of the field and the girls all came running that way for something to drink.

Jayden hurried around to the back of the truck and lowered the tailgate. Elijah opened a new sleeve of disposable cups and filled each one with ice. "We've got ice, a bottle of sweet tea for each of you, and water."

"I'll take enough ice to cover me up," Violet said.

"Yes!" Ashlyn cheered. "What she said for me, too."

Quinley took a cup and a bottle of tea, sat down on the ground, and leaned back against the truck tire. "I'd settle for a lukewarm shower and my own clothes."

"You can have the shower tonight," Jayden said, "and if you are really good and finish the eight weeks, you can have your own clothes back."

"That's at least something to look forward to. Scoot over and share the tire, Quinley," Tiffany commented as she sank to the ground.

Once all eight girls had their drinks, Jayden propped a hip on the tailgate and pointed out into the field. "Why are you still making small bales instead of big round ones?"

"Girls can't wrestle one of those big ones, and Henry didn't want to invest in the machinery to make them," he answered. "We don't have a huge cattle operation, so the little ones work just fine for us. If you've hauled hay before, then your grandfather must have felt the same way."

"He did." She smiled at the memory of having this same conversation with him. "He said basically the same thing you just did. He only ran about twenty head of cattle on the farm. Just enough to bring in a little calf crop each year. Most of his income came from growing and selling soybeans."

The clouds moving toward them from the southwest produced a semicool breeze that whipped the ponytails of the girls who still had one around like frayed flags as they finished their tea and then gulped down cups of water.

"I've never been this sweaty in my whole life, and we're last in the showers tonight. If it really starts raining, I may go out in the yard and use the rainwater on me like I'm going through a car wash," Tiffany declared as she finished her second cup of water and then tossed her cup into the plastic garbage bag beside the cooler.

"I dare you," Quinley said.

Tiffany narrowed her eyes at her rival. "I will if you will."

"You're on," Quinley declared.

"Elijah, you might want to stay in your cabin if it rains tonight," Tiffany told him, "because I'm daring all these girls from Moonbeam and Sunshine to dance in the rain in their underwear."

Keelan finished off her bottle of sweet tea, put the empty back into the bag, and gave Tiffany a brief nod. "I double-dog dare the Daydream girls right back at y'all."

"Y'all ain't got the nerve to do that," Tiffany taunted them. "Us Daydream girls are so tough, we would do that and enjoy it."

"Bullcrap," Diana said.

"Just watch us. We'll even sing while we dance," Ashlyn said.

Elijah leaned over and whispered for Jayden's ears only, "If I double-dog dare you, will you do the same?"

A slow burn traveled from her neck to her cheeks, turning them bright red. "Not even if we got an ice storm and a foot of snow right behind the rain right here in July."

"All right, girls." Elijah raised his voice. "It looks like the storm is getting serious down south of us. I can see a few streaks of lightning, so let's do some double-dog hay hauling instead of daring each other to get out in the rain. We can probably get all this into the barn in one more trailer load if you hustle. And one more thing: if any of the counselors catch you out playing in the rain when it's lightning, you will be racking up demerits. I don't care if you go out when it's only pouring down rain, but it's dangerous to be out when it's lightning."

"Yes, sir," Tiffany said and then dashed off toward the few bales of hay still on the ground.

The other girls followed her lead. Some of them hopped up on the trailer to stack the bales that the rest of the girls threw up to them.

"They're going to be sore in the morning," Jayden said. "I remember whining with aching muscles after my first day of hauling hay."

Elijah leaned back on the fender of the old truck and crossed his arms over his broad chest. His biceps stretched the knit of his sweaty shirt, and his dark hair hung in wet ringlets at the back of his cap. Jayden's pulse jacked up a notch or two just looking at him—she'd never dated or been in a relationship with a hardworking man before. Most of the men she'd known wore dress slacks to their jobs, not snug-fitting blue jeans, and she couldn't imagine a single one of them hauling hay or doing the kind of manual labor that Elijah did.

"Since we never see the girls after they leave, and only a few of them even stayed in touch with Mary, I often wonder what they feel when they think back on these days," he said.

"Probably relief to be gone, and hopefully a little bit of pride that they accomplished something like this." She headed toward the driver's side of the truck. "I like this old truck. Want to sell it? I could drive it back up to Dallas at the end of the month."

"It's not for sale." Elijah followed her. "If you want to drive it, you have to stay and cook for me, and be my partner in this business."

"Very funny. You realize I've got a truck similar to this, only older, at home," she told him.

"Are you serious?" he asked. "I figured you'd drive something like a fancy sports car."

"Then you don't know me at all." She laughed. "That's Skyler's choice of vehicle. My grandfather gave me his truck when I was sixteen and he came to live with us. It's the only thing I've ever had or wanted."

"What year and make?" Elijah asked.

"Nineteen fifty-eight GMC, painted green with black leather interior that's worn so soft it's like sitting in butter." She sighed. "I miss her a lot."

"Her? Does it have a name?" Elijah asked.

"Gramps named her Betsy the day he brought her home from the dealership." Jayden pushed a strand of hair back up under her cap.

"I'm jealous," he said. "If you were to stay here at Piney Wood, could I drive Betsy?"

"I've never let another soul drive her," Jayden told him.

"Then I'd be real special if you let me get behind the wheel," he teased.

"Anyone who even gets to ride in the passenger seat is special." A picture popped into her head of him driving and her in the passenger seat. She shook the visual out of her mind and pointed out at the field. "Looks like they've got it all loaded and are ready to fill up the back of this one. Who drives the truck up to the barn?"

"Ashlyn." He grinned. "I thought it would be good for her. If she ever decides to drink and drive again, maybe she'll remember how hot and sweaty driving a hay truck is."

"You think of everything, don't you?" she asked.

"I try to," he answered, "but mostly it just comes from past experiences with the same kind of girls. Have you ever thought about the fact that you can tell a lot about a person by the vehicle that they drive?"

"So, I'm old and green?" She cocked her head to one side.

"No, you are a little sentimental and practical," he answered.

"You got that out of a truck?" She frowned.

"Yes, ma'am. You don't need flashy things to make people like you. You appreciate and take care of Betsy because she reminds you of your gramps and you loved him. Practical, because you could trade it in for something new and more modern, but why should you, when it runs good and takes you from point A to point B?"

"Did you ever think about being a therapist?" She opened the truck door, stepped in a gopher hole, and was falling backward when his strong arms caught her.

"Whoa, darlin'," he said. "I can't have my cook breaking a leg."

For just a few seconds the world narrowed, and they were the only two people in it.

Elijah's eyes locked with hers. She licked her lips and her eyes started to flutter shut. Then he blinked and set her down on her feet. "Best look out for those gopher holes. They can be deadly."

"Looks like it," she muttered.

He kept an arm around her waist to steady her as he helped her into the truck and closed the door behind her. "I'll gladly let you fall into my arms, and ride in my old work truck, too."

"Thank you. If you're ever up around Dallas, I just might let you ride in my truck, since you saved me from a broken leg." On one hand, she was mildly embarrassed at her clumsiness. On the other, it felt really good to have Elijah's arms around her.

"Don't tease me, Jayden. I've wanted a truck like that ever since I saw one just like it on the television series *Longmire*. Henry Standing Bear, a character on the show, has a truck just like that."

She held up a palm. "You don't have to explain who Henry is or any of the other characters on that show. I could probably recite the dialogue. I watched every episode, and then I went out and bought all the seasons so I could binge-watch it again, so I know who you are talking about. My truck is a shade darker than his, and I don't have blankets on the seats, but other than that, it's pretty much the same."

"Will you marry me?" Elijah teased.

"Are you proposing to me or my truck?" she asked.

"Busted!" He chuckled. "But what would the answer be?"

"Betsy says to tell you that you're way too young for her," Jayden said.

Jayden shifted the truck into gear and drove it out to the middle of the field where Tiffany, Quinley, and Keelan waited to load it.

By the time it was loaded as high as they could get it, all three girls piled into the cab with her to ride back to the barn. "What has this job taught y'all?"

"That it makes us stink." Tiffany snarled her nose at Keelan.

"You all three smell like sweat and hay," Jayden said. "I'm speaking from experience here—you are never going to enjoy a shower and getting to wash your hair more than you will tonight."

"Amen." Tiffany nodded.

The storm clouds continued to roll in the rest of the afternoon, but the first jagged streaks of lightning didn't strike until they had both the trailer and the truck inside the barn to unload. Novalene and Diana had things under control there, so Jayden started back to the dining hall to finish supper. She had only taken a few steps when Carmella jogged over to her and leaned over to whisper in Jayden's ear.

"Please take Tiffany with you. Say you need some help in the kitchen," she said.

"Why?" Jayden asked.

Carmella's eyes rolled up toward the roof. When Jayden followed her gaze, she saw two rats sitting up there on a rafter, their long, hairless tails dropping down almost close enough to touch Tiffany's head as she caught bales that the other girls were tossing up to her.

"Please," Carmella begged. "She killed spiders for me. I owe her, and if she falls or if the others know she's afraid of mice and rats, they'll never let her live it down."

Jayden cupped her hands over her mouth and yelled, "Hey, Tiffany."

The girl leaned forward and looked out from under the brim of her cap. "Yes, ma'am?"

"Come on down from there. I need someone to help me, and I'm choosing you," Jayden said.

"Why does she get out of stacking?" Bailey whined.

"Because Jayden said so," Elijah answered. "If you want supper to be ready when you get done, then she needs some help, so stop griping and use your energy to get this job finished."

"Yes, sir," Bailey grumbled and wiped sweat from her face with the back of her hand.

"Thank you," Carmella whispered and ran back to the trailer to throw bales up to Ashlyn, who'd taken Tiffany's place.

"Why'd you choose me?" Tiffany asked as she kept pace with Jayden on the way from the barn to the dining hall.

"You can thank Carmella for it later this evening," Jayden answered. "I could have gotten supper ready all by myself, but Carmella remembered that rodents terrify you as much as spiders do her."

Tiffany shivered in spite of the heat. "Was there a mouse in the barn?"

"No, there were two rats right up above your head. Their tails were so close that if you'd have swatted a fly close to your hat, you would have slapped one of them," Jayden explained. "Carmella didn't want you to fall off the top of that stack of hay or for the other girls to make fun of you if they found out about your fear. She was being a good friend."

One tear made its way from Tiffany's eye to her chin, leaving a long, clean streak on her otherwise dirty cheek. "I have never had anyone do something like that for me before."

"That's what teamwork is all about," Jayden told her.

"I wish all three of us lived closer to each other." Tiffany smeared the wet streak across her face. "My other so-called friends sure wouldn't do anything like that for me. They'd be the ones laughing at me."

"You'll have your phones back when you all go back to your homes, so you and the other girls can call each other or FaceTime or even visit once in a while." Jayden opened the dining room door just as the first raindrops fell from the dark clouds. "If I remember right, y'all were never going to be sisters or even friends when you first got here."

"We've been through a lot together and we talk about our problems while we work. They have my back, just like today," Tiffany said. "That don't mean we won't argue again, maybe a lot, before we leave here, but no one else would understand this place, not even if we tried to tell them about it, or how much being here is helping us. I wonder if what we feel is something like the military does when they go out on missions and are away from their homes. It's kind of like a bond that can't be explained."

"Maybe so." Just thinking about the bond she didn't have with her sister made Jayden's chest feel heavy. "Go wash your hands and face in the bathroom, and then you can cut the cake into squares for me. We're having pulled pork sandwiches, slaw, and baked beans tonight. I thought something like strawberry cake and ice cream would be good for dessert after spending a day out in the fields."

"Yes, ma'am." Tiffany nodded.

Jayden removed the lid from a huge slow cooker and used two forks to pull apart the pork roasts that had been cooking all day. While she worked, she thought about what Tiffany had said and wished that she and Skyler could form a bond like her three girls had done. She had no doubt that if her sister had seen a rat right above her head, she would have kept her mouth shut until the damned thing jumped down on Jayden. Then Skyler would have laughed, but not hard enough to ruin her makeup. If these girls could overcome the past, maybe there would be hope for the future for Jayden and Skyler.

"Everything smells so good." Tiffany slipped an apron over her dirty uniform. "I'm wearing this so I don't get bits of hay in the cake. I hate to admit it, but I hate the thought of going home now. I've gotten spoiled having good food three times a day."

"And you are beginning to have a beautiful, healthy glow about you," Jayden said.

"No, because I've worked it off." Tiffany pulled on a pair of latex gloves, picked up a knife, and began cutting the sheet cake into squares. "When I get done, do I get to lick the knife?"

"Just be careful and don't cut your tongue. You're sassy enough without having a split tongue," Jayden joked.

"Just think how much I could cuss Keelan out if I had two tongues going at once." Tiffany giggled. "I really don't like that girl. I bet this camp hasn't done her a bit of good, and it wouldn't surprise me at all if she gets sent home before this month is over. Do you realize that we're half done now?"

"Yes, I already thought of that." Jayden dipped the meat up into a big silver serving pan. "I hear the herd coming. Would you help me serve?"

"Yes, ma'am." Tiffany nodded. "They'd better get what they want, because I'm hungry, and when I get done making my tray, there won't be any leftovers for the hogs."

Novalene came in first, poured glasses of sweet tea, and carried them to the adult table. "The girls are making a run through the bath-house to clean up their faces and hands," she said. "Diana is keeping an eye on them."

"The only thing I really like about kitchen duty is that I don't have to stand with my toes on the edge of the sidewalk," Tiffany told her. "I always feel like I'm going to either fall forward or get off balance and go sideways and knock someone down. If I ever do, I hope I'm standing next to Keelan."

In a few minutes, Elijah came inside. His face had been washed. His shirtsleeves were rolled up above his clean arms. He looked over the top of Tiffany's head and winked at her. Just that small gesture jacked up her pulse a notch or two.

Lightning zigzagged through the sky, crackling every now and then when it hit an old scrub oak tree or bounced across the flat land in a ball of fire. Thunder followed right behind it so low overhead that it sounded like drums being beaten right above the cabin roofs. The black clouds brought on darkness earlier than usual. The first raindrops fell, stirring up dust when they hit the ground. Then it got serious, and the wind blew in hard rain that came down in great waves.

Jayden was doing some prep work for breakfast the next day, and Elijah was waiting for the rain to slack off before he jogged to his own house. He lingered behind, wishing for an excuse to stay, and then realized that he didn't need a reason. It was raining outside. He liked being with Jayden. That was enough.

"I'm glad that there's lightning with the rain." Elijah watched her line up flour, sugar, and baking powder and then set a big bowl beside all of it. "Need some help?"

"No, I've got it under control, but what's that about lightning?" Jayden asked. "I doubt the girls are brave enough to dance in their underwear in this kind of rain, anyway, even after all the double-dog daring."

"I was thinking that if they did, I'd have to go home in this weather, and I'd rather have my shower indoors," he chuckled. "But if you wanted to dance with me in this downpour, I will put some Travis Tritt on the loudspeaker, and we can dodge the lightning bolts."

"Some example we'd be setting when we told the girls they couldn't play in the rain if there was lightning," she told him.

"If we were the only ones here, would you dance in the rain with me?" he flirted.

"Yep, I would, but not in my underwear," she answered.

Heat crawled from Elijah's neck to his face. He couldn't remember the last time he blushed, or even why, but he was damn glad that he was far enough away that Jayden couldn't see his burning cheeks. He had expected her to get red cheeks when he made that statement, but she'd come right back with a saucy comment.

"For real?" His voice sounded a little higher than normal even in his own ears.

"Might be fun." She smiled. "I'm a dancing-in-the-rain virgin. How about you?"

"Never done it before," he answered, "but I'd be willing to give it up for you."

"Well, thank you."

She was flirting back, and he liked it—a lot. "You are very welcome. What are you getting things ready for?"

"Chicken and waffles," she answered. "What else have you never done?" She crossed the room and sat down at the table with him.

"Show me yours, and I might show you mine." Damn, but it felt good to flirt again, to even want to for that matter. Could it be that his luck was changing? Man, that was a thought he never figured would pop into his mind.

"I've never gone skinny-dippin'," she answered.

"I haven't, either," he said. "Would you do that with me if we had a pool, or if we were on a secluded beach?"

"Maybe." She nodded. "Now your turn."

"I'm thirty-four years old. I've been here for two years and was on an extended deployment before that. I haven't dated in more than three years and would probably need a *Dating for Dummies* book to even know where to begin," he answered. "I'd be willing to give up a few hours to read the book, if you'd agree to go out with me." If she could feel the same sparks between them that he did, he would truly feel like his luck had changed.

"I'd probably have to borrow it and read it before I'd agree but, just so I'd know, exactly what would a date with you mean?" she asked.

"You are a special woman, so it would have to be something big." He cupped his chin in his hand and drew his brows down. "Maybe we'd fuel the plane and fly down to Panama City Beach, Florida, for the afternoon and evening. Walk in the warm sand and have seafood at Jimmy Buffett's place."

"So, I'm special"—she smiled—"or is that just a pickup line?"

Might as well go for broke and tell her exactly how he felt. "You, Jayden Bennett, are more special than any woman I've ever dated," he answered. "And on that note, the rain has almost stopped, so I'm going to jog to my house and get a shower. See you at breakfast."

He brought her hand to his lips and kissed her knuckles. "Until then, good night, lovely lady. Sleep tight. I'll see you at breakfast."

"I'll be the one behind the buffet line in a white apron."

She sounded as breathless as he was, and he liked it a lot.

He released her hand and stood up. "You rock that apron," he said as he walked away.

He sucked in lungsful of the night air. Nothing smelled as fresh and clean as the earth after a hard rain, unless it was the scent of whatever lotion Jayden had rubbed into her hands that evening after her shower. He hummed an old Travis Tritt tune, "Love of a Woman," but he couldn't remember all the lyrics, so when he got back to his room, he found it on YouTube and listened to it while he took a shower.

He dreamed about dancing in the rain with Jayden to that very song. He woke himself up at midnight singing the lyrics with Travis about a man being his woman's hero.

"I want to be Jayden's hero," he muttered as he rolled over and went back to sleep.

Chapter Seventeen

July Fourth arrived in a blaze of heat and glory, but not much changed at Piney Wood Academy that Saturday. The sirens sounded before daylight. The girls lined up and did their new routine, which included jumping rope and using stretching bands to strengthen their muscles, and then they were off to walk a mile out to the second marking post and back before breakfast.

As usual, Novalene was the first one in the dining hall that morning. "You do know that since Mary isn't coming back, you can schedule the girls from each cabin to have kitchen duty instead of just whenever you ask them," she told Jayden.

"I kind of like doing it myself." Jayden pulled a pan of blueberry muffins out of the oven. "I've always been selfish with my kitchen. Even as a teenager, when I cooked, I wanted the room to myself."

"Well, anytime you need cleanup or serving help, I'm volunteering myself or my two girls," Novalene told her. "What are we having this morning?"

"Oven omelets, hash browns, biscuits, and these muffins for dessert," Jayden answered.

"Sounds wonderful. You're doing a fine job of taking over for Mary. I'm glad you came instead of Skyler. I can't imagine her stepping in and doing the cooking, but then I damn sure wouldn't want the job, either," Novalene said.

Diana entered the room, poured herself a cup of coffee, and topped off Novalene's before she sat down. "I'll add my thanks to Novalene's. I called about a job that I applied for on the internet. I didn't want to tell y'all before I heard back for fear I'd jinx it. They're sending someone up from Del Rio to interview me next week. Keep your fingers crossed. If I get the job, this will definitely be my last year to come to Piney Wood, but before we all split seven ways to Sunday and leave, I want y'all's contact numbers so we can stay in touch."

"What kind of job is it?" Jayden asked.

"I'd be working at a security firm that hires ex-military to do contract work like protecting famous folks or dignitaries. It pays three times what teaching does. I get to carry a gun, and the benefits are amazing, plus I'll have no paperwork or smart-ass students to deal with. I'll have to undergo a six-week fitness program, but I'm willing to do that to get the job. At my age and with my years of experience, I can freeze my Texas retirement."

"Sounds to me like you've made up your mind," Jayden said.

"I have if they hire me. I'll give my notice as soon as I know, and if everything works out, I'll go to work for the firm on Monday after we leave here on Saturday. I'm really excited." Diana blew on the top of her coffee and then took a sip. "That leaves you and Novalene to teach the newbies the ropes next year, Jayden."

"Oh, no!" Novalene threw up both hands. "Y'all leave me out of this. I'm not teaching anyone jack squat. This is my last year here, too. Everything runs its course, and I'm tired. It's time for me to hang up my Moonbeam Cabin cap and go home, drive fast, and listen to Elvis."

"Y'all are leaving and yet trying to talk me into staying," Jayden said.

"Honey, you belong right here," Novalene said. "You'll wake up and see what we're seeing pretty soon. We're ready to move on, but you should move in."

"Got any proof to back that up?" Jayden asked.

"Just that we can see the chemistry between you and Elijah," Diana said.

"I'm changing the subject." Jayden smiled. "Before y'all throw in the towel, will you tell me if we celebrate July Fourth here?"

"We always have," Diana answered. "We spend the day as usual, but at dark, Elijah will put on a fantastic fireworks display for the girls, and then he brings out the watermelons and slices them into wedges. The girls eat them without forks and have a seed-spitting contest. He'll tell them all about it after breakfast so they can look forward to it, but if even one of them gets a demerit today, all the fun is off. You can bet they'll be on their very best behavior."

"Speak for your own girls," Novalene said. "Keelan and Bailey just might do something stupid so none of them get to have fun."

"Rita will kill them both if they do," Diana said.

The girls filed in and most of them headed straight to the end of the line and got a bottle of water, guzzled it down, and then came back for food. That three-mile hike must have gotten to them. Ashlyn tossed her empty bottle into the trash, slung an apron over her head, and tied it in the back, then put on a pair of gloves. "I'll help dish it up so we can get through the line faster. It's our day to clean the stalls, and we're worried about Dynamite, so we want to hurry up and go see about him."

"What's wrong with Dynamite?" Jayden asked.

"He's been off his feed for a couple of days, and when we walk him, he goes real slow." Ashlyn slipped a hash brown onto Keelan's plate and got one ready for the next girl in line.

"I want two of those," Keelan said. "I'm starving this morning. There's nothing wrong with that horse. I cleaned his stall yesterday and he was fine."

"I walk him every day, and I know more about horses than you do." Ashlyn put another hash brown on her plate and turned to Tiffany, who was in line behind her. "One or two?"

"Two," Tiffany answered.

Keelan shot them both a dirty look and moved her tray on down the line.

"Don't start anything," Jayden whispered to Ashlyn. "This isn't the day for it, believe me. You'll understand when Elijah makes his announcement after breakfast."

"Yes, ma'am," Ashlyn said and then lowered her voice. "There's always tomorrow. I'm savin' my demerits up until the last week, and then I'm going to use two of them on Bailey and Keelan."

"Good mornin'." Elijah caught Jayden's eye and smiled when he started through the line.

"Mornin' to you." She smiled back at him. "Happy Independence Day."

"Is it July Fourth?" Ashlyn asked as she put food on her tray. "Do we get to go to town and watch fireworks?"

"Do you want to do that?" Elijah asked.

"Of course I do," Ashlyn answered. "Can we leave the Moonbeam girls at home?"

"Nope, it's all or none," Elijah answered.

"Well, crap!" Ashlyn carried her tray to her table and sat down.

Jayden was the last one to dish up food onto her tray and take it to the adult table. Elijah waited until she was seated and then tapped a spoon on the edge of his coffee mug. As usual, when he did that, all the noise in the whole dining hall ceased in a split second.

"In the past we have celebrated Independence Day right here at Piney Wood. If not one single girl got a demerit all day, we always had fireworks and then watermelon and a couple of freezers of homemade ice cream. Since all of you have been pretty good kids through the first half of this session, I'm going to change things up a little bit this year.

After supper, we are going to make homemade ice cream and then let it set while we take all y'all into town to the football field and let you watch the show that the fire department puts on each year. Then we'll come home to have our watermelon and ice cream. The rule about the demerits stands, though. If one of you gets out of line today, then we all stay home. I haven't bought fireworks, so there will be none and we won't churn ice cream or cut watermelons, either. So, I recommend that y'all all be on good behavior today."

"Yes, sir!" the girls all chorused.

"What's the chances we'll actually do this tonight?" Diana whispered.

"Good, I hope," Elijah said. "I talked to Henry and Mary on the phone last night, and they thought it might be smart to reward good behavior now. We've only had to send one girl away and it's been a couple of weeks since anyone got a demerit."

"I just hope they all behave today," Novalene said. "If one of them gets out of line and we have to stay here, the others *will* get even, and I don't imagine that it will be a pretty sight."

Jayden thought about Ashlyn's comments and shivered.

"Cold?" Elijah asked.

"Nope, just a little worried," Jayden admitted.

"It pays to be concerned. Listen to them, buzzing like a bunch of bees at the idea of getting to go somewhere other than church on Sunday." Novalene nodded toward the tables where the girls sat. "I plan on spending the rest of this day staying right with my two. It's their day to do laundry and then clean bathrooms. I won't let them out of my sight. Y'all would do well to do the same with your girls."

Jayden wasn't sure how she could do that and cook, too, but at least it was their day to clean the stalls, which would keep them away from the other girls. After they walked the horses, she would make them come to the kitchen and help her with supper even if she would rather have the kitchen to herself.

Elijah nudged her on the shoulder. "What are you thinking about?"

"Sorry, did you say something to me?" she asked.

"No, but you looked like you were a million miles away," he said.

"Ashlyn says that Dynamite isn't doing well. Keelan disagreed with her," Jayden replied.

"It's normal for them to get antsy about this time," Novalene said. "If there's going to be a multiple-girl problem, it usually happens about the halfway mark. I'm glad we're taking them into town tonight. That might help."

"Dynamite is almost forty years old, which is well past the expected life span of a horse," Elijah said. "He's been steadily slowing down this past year, and he *has* been off his feed lately."

"Lord have mercy!" Jayden gasped. "I hope he doesn't die while we're here. Ashlyn would be devastated."

"So would Keelan," Novalene said. "She's taken quite a fancy to the old boy."

"He's Rita's favorite on the days when my girls clean the stalls, and Quinley has really taken a liking to him, also," Diana said. "We'll have a bunch of weeping girls to deal with if he goes over the Rainbow Bridge while we're here."

"Guess we've all got something to pray about in church," Elijah said.

"Better not wait until then, since today is pretty important, too." Diana's tone was dead serious.

"Amen!" Jayden agreed and then called out to her girls, "Hey, Daydream Cabin girls, if you have time after you do the stalls this morning, you should check on our flower beds and then pull weeds from the garden behind the dining hall and then come help me in the kitchen."

Ashlyn chuckled. "Yes, ma'am."

"What's so funny?" Tiffany asked.

"There's always tomorrow," Ashlyn answered.

"What does that mean?" Carmella asked.

"I'll tell you later," Ashlyn promised.

Elijah always moved around among the three groups during the day, but that Saturday he kept special watch on the whole bunch of them. Bailey and Keelan spent most of their time in the laundry and then went over to clean the bathrooms. The Sunshine girls helped Elijah move the cattle from one pasture to another. At noon, they were all ready to eat and get after whatever they had on their lists for that afternoon.

"Things are going smoothly," Elijah told Jayden when the dining hall had cleared out. "They're all wound up about the fireworks show tonight and getting to leave the camp for a little while."

"Have they realized that they'll be going in the same uniforms they've worn to shovel crap, weed a garden, milk cows, and walk horses?" She carried a pot to the deep sink and rinsed it.

Elijah followed her with a chuckle and pointed out the window. "On that first day they were here, did you ever think you'd see them doing that?" He was so close to Jayden that his heart threw in an extra beat. He wanted to do more than flirt or nudge her with his shoulder at the dinner table. He visualized taking her in his arms and kissing her full lips until they looked bee stung, then scooping her up like a bride and . . .

The picture in his mind disappeared when she spoke. "I had my doubts as to whether any one of them would even be here after the first week."

"Not me," Elijah said. "I'm a little surprised that we even lost one out of the bunch. They all looked like little scared first-grade girls when I yelled at them to drop their suitcases. On my first session here, one girl hurled her bags at me like they were rockets. That got her the first demerit, even though she didn't know the rules. She was in the Brewster

County Jail before suppertime. This is a pretty calm bunch compared to that first one."

"Were you a drill sergeant in the service?" she asked.

He shook his head. "Nope, but I used to do a damn good impression of my sergeant. It's a good thing he never caught me, or I'd have spent some time in the brig for sure. Mostly my team and I did classified work—rescue missions, reconnaissance, that kind of thing."

"You could tell me the details, but you'd have to kill me, right?" She turned toward him with a smile.

"Something like that." He grinned. "But enough about me. I'd rather talk about you."

"You know almost everything there is to know about me. You've got my résumé on file. Which reminds me, do you keep a list of potential folks who would like to come here for one of the sessions? Novalene and Diana aren't coming back," she said.

"Of course we do," he answered. "We've got lots of counselors who would like a part-time job in the summer, but we don't have a file for cooks or for folks to help on the grounds when we don't have girls at the camp."

"Guess you'd better start one then." She picked up a tea towel, dried the pot, and put it back where it belonged.

Elijah sure wished Jayden would stay and take the job. Did that mean he was crazy? He couldn't ever remember having that kind of feeling with any other woman. He headed out toward the barn, thinking about Jayden the whole way. He started to call Henry to talk to him about his feelings, but that seemed silly.

"Remember your training, Elijah Thomas," he muttered. "Keep business and pleasure separate. Jayden is your employee. Sure, you've flirted, and she even said she'd go on a date with you, but be sure you're not still bad luck when it comes to folks you care about."

He remembered when Tim teased him about trying to analyze his feelings, but nowadays he realized that just meant he needed time to think. Men, especially guys like him who had done the work he had in the air force, did not worry for hours on end about a woman. They flirted, they either got lucky or they didn't, and then they went home and had a beer or two and forgot all about it. He didn't want that kind of relationship with Jayden. He wanted more, and he needed to think about it.

"Just a little time," he whispered.

I believe that I'm ready to settle down, and that's why I'm questioning why Jayden is twisting me up in knots to the point that I make up excuses to spend a few minutes with her when I can, he thought.

"You talking to yourself?" Jayden startled him when she spoke from a few feet away. "Have we driven you completely bonkers?"

Not y'all, he thought, *just you, Jayden Bennett.*

"Just thinking out loud," he said. "We'll divide up the girls so that Keelan and Ashlyn are riding in different vehicles."

"That's smart thinking," she agreed.

Elijah's heart did a couple of flips at just the sound of her voice. Dammit! He shouldn't let himself get all stirred up over a woman who would be going home to the big city in only three weeks.

The heart wants what the heart wants. Henry's voice couldn't have been any clearer if the man had been standing right behind him.

Elijah could feel the energy coming from all the girls as they made their way up into the bleachers at the football field just as the sun dropped below the horizon. The chamber of commerce president stepped up to a microphone just below the goalpost, introduced himself, and welcomed everyone to the fireworks display. "But first, we'll stand for the Pledge of Allegiance and, in honor of Independence Day, we will remain standing and everyone will sing the national anthem together."

Tiffany tapped Elijah on the shoulder. "Can we take our caps off for this?"

"Yes, we all should." He removed his and motioned for the girls to do the same.

"They look different," Jayden said.

"Yep, and they've got farmer's tans on their foreheads. When they get home, they are going to whine for days about that," he whispered.

"That's where their makeup will come into play." She smiled.

"I pledge allegiance . . . ," the man behind the microphone started, and the crowd joined in. Immediately after that, the high school band started to play and everyone in the stands joined in with the singing. When the last note died away, the first burst of fireworks lit up the sky in red, white, and blue.

The girls put their caps back on, and the ones with ponytails pulled them through the back—then they sat down. The night breezes steamed their faces like a sauna, but none of them seemed to mind. Elijah had deliberately lined them up with the Daydream girls right behind him and Jayden, Diana's three after that, and the Moonbeam ladies on the far end behind Novalene.

If everything went well that evening, he fully planned to do this every year. It saved money, and it came at a good time in the summer program to reward the girls. A buzzing behind him came all the way down the line from one girl to the other.

"Are they playing that old game we used to at parties?" he asked Jayden.

"Which one?"

"The one where one person whispers something, and it goes around the room until the end, and then the first one and the second one . . ."

"Do you mean the telephone game?" Jayden asked.

"Yes, that's it," Elijah answered. "I think the girls are playing that. Keelan whispered something to Bailey and now it's all the way to Tiffany."

Jayden turned around just in time for Tiffany to lean forward and put one hand on Elijah's shoulder and the other on Jayden's. She did not whisper but said right out loud, "See that little posse in short shorts and tank tops behind Keelan? They're laughing at us and calling us convicts."

"Ignore them," Elijah told her.

Tiffany sucked in a lungful of air and let it out in a whoosh. She leaned forward and sent a message down the line to Keelan's attention to ignore the other girls.

Keelan nodded, and Elijah didn't give it another thought. He was enjoying watching Jayden's face as each display lit up the midnight-black sky. She was an extraordinary woman who enjoyed the little things, like lightning bugs and a cold beer after a hard day's work—the kind of woman that Henry would tell him would be the type to ride the river with.

As was normal with all fireworks shows, the best was saved until last. A loud boom lit up half the sky with the American flag in bright sparkling lights. When the oohs and aahs had died down and the flag had disappeared, folks began to stand up and make their way to the end of the bleachers. The Piney Wood girls got to their feet and started moving in that direction.

Things went just fine until Keelan took the final step out onto the grass. Elijah and Jayden were ahead of them, waiting beside the entry gate, when he heard one of the girls that had been picking on the Piney Wood girls say, "Y'all convicts don't belong here."

Ashlyn got right in the girl's face. "Bless your heart, darlin'. I'm going to save this nasty uniform just for you. With your attitude, you'll need it. If you want a piece of any of us, just step right up."

A second girl took the blonde by the arm. "Come on, Justina. We've got a party to go to. We can't stand around listening to these losers all evening."

"We can give you a little tour of Piney Wood if you'd like and even let you slop the hogs, or shovel crap from the horse stalls," Keelan said. "You might change your mind about us being losers if you come out and visit us."

"Go to hell!" The girl reached out to slap Keelan, but Ashlyn stepped between them.

"You go first, and we'll send you some ice-cream sandwiches." Keelan glared at the girl.

The hand was still raised when a police officer stepped up and grabbed it. "That's enough out of all of you. You girls from Alpine go home, or I'll lock the bunch of you up. You Piney Wood girls . . ."

Elijah finally made it to the bottom of the steps and got between both sets of girls. "Girls from Piney Wood, go get in the vans."

"I'd take my demerit and punishment if you'll let me go back and hit her." Keelan stomped all the way to the place where the two vehicles were parked.

"Me too," Ashlyn said.

"I thought you two hated each other." Elijah opened the door to the first van.

"We do," Keelan said, "but nobody is going to diss any one of us, especially a girl who takes up for me in a fight. I've got all y'all's backs, Piney Wood girls," she called out as she got into the van.

"So do I," Ashlyn yelled. "That don't mean I like you any better, either, but us Piney Wood girls have to stick together."

"Amen!" The five girls in his van all did fist pumps.

Elijah got behind the wheel and closed the door.

"Do we get demerits for standing up for each other?" Tiffany asked.

"Are we still going to have ice cream?" Quinley asked.

"Nobody gets demerits tonight, and I appreciate you girls obeying when I told you to get in the van. I know it wasn't easy to keep from hitting those smart alecks, but you did good, and yes, there will be ice cream when we get back to camp."

Chapter Eighteen

All the girls filed into the dining hall with their heads held high. Jayden wasn't sure what would happen next. The girls had almost gotten into a fistfight with those snotty little brats from town, and she wasn't sure what their punishment would be. Truth be told, she wanted to give them a medal for holding back and only throwing barbs at those girls. They took their seats at their usual tables and waited in total silence—all eyes on Elijah.

"Tonight, you can sit wherever you please while you have your Fourth of July treat, and I'm going to be first in line this time. To those of you who weren't riding with me and Novalene, there will be no demerits given, and I'm proud of you for obeying me when I told you to," Elijah said.

Elijah joined Jayden in the kitchen. "I'll help dip up the ice cream. What do you think, partner? Did our girls do pretty good?"

"I'm proud of them, but if I'd been in Keelan's shoes, I might have decked that girl and took my punishment," Jayden whispered.

"Did you feel like knocking Skyler on her butt when she was here?" he asked.

"No, I felt guilty for not handing over my checkbook and credit cards to her, but then that's the way I've always felt when I denied her anything," she answered.

"You shouldn't have felt that way, ever. Skyler must have been able to manipulate you from the time you were a little girl." He removed the lids from both freezers of ice cream and set them on the counter.

"Oh, yeah, she could, but I wasn't the only one. When she wanted something, she would keep it up until Mama and Daddy or Grandpa let her have her way. Believe me, living with her when she wasn't happy was awful," Jayden said.

"What do you want us to do?" Novalene asked.

"There's a pan of brownies over there on the cabinet. Would you cut them into squares? Diana, would you get the watermelon basket out of the refrigerator, and please take that bowl of strawberries over to one of the tables. I thought we would let the girls help themselves to the fruit. Elijah is going to help me serve ice cream," she said.

"Watermelon basket?" Diana questioned as she headed toward the refrigerator. "Well, I'll be danged. You cut the watermelon in the shape of a basket and made little balls so they'd be easier to eat. You really should stay here, Jayden. You're good at what you do."

"I hear you," Elijah agreed.

"No comment." Jayden dipped up the first bowl of ice cream.

"I'm still betting I leave here with a bottle of bourbon," Novalene whispered.

"Still no comment," Jayden said.

The girls started out sitting with the others from their own cabin, but as they went back and forth to get more watermelon or another brownie, they wound up pushing chairs around until they were all gathered around one little table for four.

"Progress for sure," Novalene said as she finished off a second bowl of ice cream.

"It might not last long." Diana went back for another helping of watermelon.

"Probably not, but it sure is nice tonight," Jayden told them. "I never thought I'd see Keelan take up for anyone."

"Me either," Elijah said. "That ruckus back there seemed to be just what they needed to unite and have each other's backs."

"I'm remembering that old song about sisters," Novalene said. "Seems like the lyrics asked for the Lord to help the mister who came between me and my sister. We could change that to 'Lord help the smart-ass who comes between me and my campmate.' It don't rhyme worth crap, but that's what tonight brings to my mind."

"They are all like siblings. Fighting among themselves until someone else tries to step in, and then it's 'Katy, bar the door,'" Diana agreed.

"I wonder where that saying came from," Elijah commented. "I've heard it all my life but have no idea where it originated."

"Me either," Novalene added.

"Who knows, but it sure means trouble is coming these days," Diana said.

"Yep, it sure does," Elijah agreed.

Tiffany walked past and heard what they were saying. "Maybe we should've told that smart aleck girl that we were about to bar the door with her inside the barn with all of us. If that bunch ever messes up and lands here, will you send me a message and tell me, Elijah?"

"That might be against privacy laws," he answered.

"Well, rats!" Tiffany yawned. "Is it all right if I go grab a quick shower and go to bed? It's been a long day."

"That's fine." Jayden nodded. "I need to do a little cleanup, and then I'll be along."

"I'll help get the ice-cream freezers washed and put away." Elijah stood up and started toward the kitchen.

"We can help, too," Diana offered.

"Y'all go on and be sure everyone gets showers in the right order, and we'll do this," Elijah said. "It won't take fifteen minutes."

"Bourbon is looking better all the time," Novalene teased as she passed by Jayden.

"Yes, it is. I'm going to enjoy every drop," Jayden shot back at her.

"What was that about bourbon?" Elijah asked when they were alone in the dining hall.

"Just a little bet that Novalene and I have going," Jayden answered, then changed the subject. "I thought we'd have lots left over, but there's not even a pint in each freezer."

"Fighting off bitches is tough work." Elijah laughed out loud.

"Evidently so." Jayden took the freezer from him and dried it. "How many fights did you get into when you were their age?"

"I'm a lover, not a fighter." He handed her the second freezer. "Truthfully, though, my best friend in high school was a little short guy that wouldn't have weighed a buck twenty soaking wet and with rocks in his pockets. Trouble was, he had that short guys' syndrome and couldn't keep his mouth closed. I used to tell him that the hardest lesson he'd ever learn was when to shut his trap."

"So, you had to step in and take up for him when his motorcycle mouth got ahead of his tricycle butt, right?" Jayden asked.

"Something like that." He handed her a dasher to dry. "How about you? Ever get into a fight?"

"Couple in elementary school when I had enough of being called names, being bullied about my height, and being told that my sister got all the beauty and brains and I got beat with the ugly stick. I was always the tallest and, most of the time, the biggest kid in my class," she explained. "After I put the bullies on the ground, they didn't mess with me anymore. Believe me, I know exactly how hard it was for all our girls to walk away from that fight tonight."

"How did it make you feel when you fought with the bullies?" he asked.

"Glad that they stopped tormenting me, but a little sad that I had stooped to their level," she answered.

"Yep, me too." He dried his hands on a towel and hung it over the edge of the sink. "But when a person gets pushed so far, they can't take any more. Those kids shouldn't have bullied you like that. Skyler doesn't have near the beauty or brains that you do. Ready to turn off the lights?"

"I don't know. Is the party over?" she joked.

Elijah held out his hand as he started singing the old Willie Nelson song "The Party's Over." Jayden took a step forward and put her hand in his. He pulled her close and two-stepped around the kitchen with her as he sang the lyrics.

Even though his broad chest was hard as a rock, she could feel the thump of his heartbeat through his shirt. She wondered if he could tell that hers was doing double time. Did he realize that being so close to him caused a breathlessness in her that had nothing to do with dancing around the kitchen floor? He twirled her when the lyrics said something about tomorrow starting the same old thing again and then held her even closer when he brought her back.

"Do you know every word to this song?" she asked.

"Yep, it's one of Henry's favorites. He and Mary have danced around in this kitchen to it many times through the years," he answered, and then continued to sing the next verse.

"So, you came here to see them before you took this job?" she asked.

"I tried to spend a week or two with them every year when I could get away," he answered, and then he pulled his phone out of his hip pocket, touched the screen, and laid the phone on the buffet counter.

She recognized George Jones's voice right away as he sang "Tennessee Whiskey."

"I don't know this one as well, and I like Chris Stapleton's version, but this one is what I heard first. It's going to be our song." He took her in his arms again and did a slow country waltz around the floor.

"We have a song?" she asked as she paid close attention to the words. She was more than a little startled at the idea. In the few relationships that she'd had, they'd never had a song. This was beginning to sound serious and it hadn't even started.

"We do now, and we're doing our debut dance to it," he answered. "Those kids who bullied you when you were young should see the strong, smart, amazing woman you've become," he whispered in her ear.

This was some serious flirting, and Jayden loved every minute of it. She hadn't danced in years, and his warm breath, so close to the tender spot on her neck, sent warm shivers up and down her spine.

When the music ended, Elijah tipped up her chin with his fist and looked deeply into her eyes. She barely had time to moisten her lips before his eyes closed and his mouth found hers in a steaming hot kiss that came close to fogging the kitchen window. When it ended, she leaned into him for another one, but he took a step back. She had to fight gravity to keep from falling right into his arms. Thank goodness he chose that moment to reach out and give her a tight hug.

"Thank you for closing out the day with me, but it's probably really time to turn out the lights now," he murmured, "even though I'd rather dance until dawn with you." He slipped an arm around her shoulders and they walked side by side all the way to the Daydream Cabin.

When they reached the porch, he dropped his arm and said, "Good night, Jayden."

"Good night," she called after him as he disappeared into the dark.

It was just a dance and a kiss. She eased down into one of the chairs on the porch to catch her breath before she went inside to gather up her things to go take a cool shower. A shuffling noise came from inside the cabin. The lights were out but the girls were definitely still awake, most likely peeking out the window to spy on her and Elijah. She gave them time to get back into their bedroom and pretend to be asleep before she went inside and got her shower kit, a clean pair of underpants, and a nightshirt.

"Nosy little snots," she muttered all the way to the bathhouse. "I could really give them something to gossip about if I stayed in Elijah's cabin tonight." *What am I thinking? That wouldn't be the right example to set for the girls, and I need to make up my mind about the future before I go getting into something that could break my heart.*

Elijah's eyes popped wide open on Sunday morning five minutes before the alarm sounded. He rolled over to find the other side of the bed was empty. That meant he'd only been dreaming about Jayden spending the night with him. With a heavy sigh, he kicked the covers away, turned off the alarm on his phone, and headed to the bathroom for a wake-me-up shower.

His hair was still a little damp when he stuck his cap on his head. He'd hoped to see Jayden on the way across the yard, but the lights in the dining hall told him that she was already out there. The siren sounded just as he reached his normal morning spot for exercises, and the girls poured out of the cabins, most of them in a hard run so they wouldn't be late. The kids had come a long way in the five weeks they'd been at Piney Wood. That meant he and the small staff were doing their jobs. The little boosts of happiness that success with the girls brought him had been chipping away at the pain that losing his fellow airmen had left in his heart.

If they'd been recruits in the air force, their trainer would have been busting his buttons, bragging to the other drill sergeants about his team. He gave Jayden a lot of the credit for the progress. Though brand new, she was tougher than nails, and still had a soft heart. He wished that he had counselors just like her for every session at the camp.

"Okay, ladies, you know the drill. We'll start with stretching exercises, then go into jumping rope for five minutes," he told them that morning.

"Mornin', Elijah," Novalene called out as she made her way across the yard.

He waved and kept leading the girls in their morning routine. "Well, dammit!" he muttered under his breath. He'd meant to tell Jayden that they had two ladies coming that afternoon to interview for the cook's job. The dancing and kissing must've scrambled his brain because he'd forgotten all about it until that moment. He made a mental note to tell her right after breakfast.

His phone rang just as the girls finished up the last of their exercises and started to walk toward the new post he'd set up a mile and a half out toward the mountain. In another three weeks, they would be ready to hike out to the base of the mountain, each carrying a backpack full of what they'd need to camp out for the night.

"Hello," he answered the call as he brought up the rear of the line.

"How're things going?" Henry asked.

"Better than average," Elijah answered. "It's good to hear your voice. How're you and Mary doing?"

"Loving this place more and more. Joe's doing a little better, but the doctor says it won't be long, and that it's because we're here that he hasn't given up and passed away before now. He and I sit on the screened porch most of the day and talk about the old days," Henry answered. "I called to tell you that Joe has signed over his property to me and Mary, and we've canceled our cruises. We like it so well here that we're just going to stick close to home. We've even found a church, and everyone has taken us in and treats us like family. Folks have even been bringing food by a few times a week, stuff they remember Joe liking," Henry said.

"That's great," Elijah said, "but I'd hoped y'all would find a place a little closer to Alpine."

"That's what we had in mind, but we're happy here, and besides, you need the space to run Piney Wood by yourself. If we were very close by, I wouldn't be able to keep away from the place, and Mary would always have an itch to be back in the kitchen. How're things working with Jayden doing the cooking? Did you convince her to stay on?" Henry asked.

"Nope, but I'm trying." Thoughts of dancing with her threw an extra beat in his heart. "She's going to help me interview a couple of prospective cooks this afternoon."

"Are you being smart about that?" Henry chuckled.

"I hope so," Elijah replied. "I like her a lot, Uncle Henry."

"I knew that before we left," Henry said.

"How?" Elijah asked.

"It was all in the way you looked at her from that first day," Henry said. "Don't fight against the best thing that's happened to you in a long time. The hospice nurse is leaving, so I should be getting out to the porch. Mary sends her love."

"Give her a hug for me," Elijah said.

"I sure will," Henry told him.

Elijah felt more than a little bit lost at the idea of Henry and Mary being so far away, but Henry was probably right. If they lived close, they'd both be in and out of Piney Wood, and that wouldn't be a retirement at all.

How are you going to feel when Jayden leaves, too? Mary's voice rang clear in his head. *If you want her to stay, you've got to make her see that her place is right there.*

"Yes, ma'am," he sighed.

"You talkin' to me?" Tiffany asked. "And why are we getting a new cook? Are you firing Jayden? Does she know about this?"

"It's not nice to eavesdrop on conversations." Elijah lengthened his stride to get away from the girl.

She just stepped up her pace and kept in step with him. "Please don't fire Jayden. We like her a lot, and the meals here are five-star restaurant quality. You don't know how lucky you are to have her."

"Who's firing Jayden?" Keelan lingered until they caught up to her. "Are you crazy? Out of your freakin' mind?"

"You should be droppin' down on your knees and beggin' her to never leave," Bailey told him and then cupped her hands over her mouth and yelled. "Hey, all y'all up ahead of us. Elijah is firing Jayden. We're all going to starve or end up eating boxed macaroni and cheese and peanut butter sandwiches for the next three weeks."

Elijah stopped in his tracks and held up his fist as a sign for them to stop. "I'm not firing Jayden." He raised his voice so everyone could hear him. "As a matter of fact, I've offered her the job permanently and she turned me down. I would love for her to stay on here at Piney Wood and help me run the place. If any of you have any pull, then *you* could help me out here."

"Do you like her?" Tiffany asked.

"A gentleman doesn't kiss and tell," he answered. No way was he discussing his love life with eight drama queens.

Love life! He stopped in his tracks. Was he falling in love with Jayden?

"Well, girls, I vote that we band together and see what we can do about this," Keelan said.

Rita raised her hand. "Let's meet in the barn during our hour of free time this evening. Bring your ideas and we'll sort through them."

"All in favor of helping Jayden see that she's too good of a cook and counselor to go back to working at the school raise your hand," Carmella said.

All eight hands shot up into the air. "Okay, then, Elijah, we're all on your side. We'll do what we can, but you got to do your part, too."

"You girls need to take care of your own business and stay out of mine. I can take care of my own love life," he warned them with a stern look.

"Yes, sir," Tiffany said loudly.

But he noticed that she winked at Carmella and nudged Ashlyn with an elbow.

"It wouldn't hurt to pray for some help from"—Ashlyn pointed toward the sky—"while we're in church this morning. If any of y'all have any connections up there, you might pray that Dynamite gets better, too. He's gettin' skinnier by the day and walking slower and slower."

"I'll say a prayer for him and Jayden," Quinley said. "I like that old horse a lot. Yesterday Jayden let me have a carrot to take to him, and he wouldn't even eat it, so I know he's not doing well."

Elijah grinned at the thought of the girls lumping Jayden and a forty-year-old horse into the same prayer, but hey, he wasn't going to argue with them. He'd take all the help he could get.

Something was afoot. Jayden could feel it in her bones. The girls came in for breakfast that morning whispering among themselves. She shouldn't have been surprised. After all, it was Sunday, and so far that had been the day for things to get upside down in a hurry.

"What's going on?" she asked Elijah as he came through the line.

"As in?" he answered as he loaded his tray with three fried eggs, a slab of ham, and a generous helping of hash brown potatoes.

"As in, the girls are being too nice to each other," she said.

"Maybe they're still wound up about last night. Hey, I should have told you earlier, but I forgot. We've got two people coming by at two this afternoon to interview for the cook's job. The other counselors will be in charge of horseshoes and cornhole games out in the yard while we talk to them," he said.

"Two at once, or one at a time?" She picked up a tray and put a piece of ham, two biscuits, and some hash browns on it.

He followed her to the adult table. "Same time will be quicker. These two have the best résumés. Maybe if we like one of them, we won't have to visit with any more."

"Visit with whom?" Novalene asked.

"We're talking to two people interested in taking over the kitchen," Jayden answered.

Elijah set his tray down and crossed the floor to the table with the coffeepot on it. He returned with it in his hand. "Who needs a warm-up?"

Novalene held up her cup.

"Jayden and I will be talking to two prospects for a new cook this afternoon. Would y'all supervise the girls?" Elijah asked. "I've got horseshoes and beanbag-toss games planned for them this afternoon."

A flash of lightning zigzagged across the windows in the dining hall, followed by a clap of thunder that caused several girls to throw their hands over their ears.

"Looks like you better plan something else," Novalene told him. "If it don't rain, it's going to miss a good chance."

Elijah groaned. "Y'all remember the last time the girls had to stay in the dining hall? They got into trouble for bad haircuts, and the time before that, they whined and bitched about playing board games. Anyone got any ideas?"

"How about we give them some free time for naps or let them visit with each other in the cabins?" Diana suggested. "None of my girls have been inside anything but Sunshine Cabin. Seems like they're all atwitter over something that they want to talk about as a group."

"We can wander back and forth among the cabins to be sure they aren't killing each other," Diana offered.

"Keep all the scissors, knives, and even fingernail files out of their sight," Jayden suggested.

"We'll call y'all if there's any blood or broken bones," Novalene laughed. "They definitely have something up their sleeves today, the way they keep whispering and throwing looks toward us. Maybe they're planning to give us a party for being good counselors."

"Or maybe they're joining forces to mutiny," Diana whispered.

"Like on a ship?" Jayden asked. "They can't throw us overboard."

"I doubt they'd take over Piney Wood," Elijah said on a chuckle. "They want to get away from here, not own the place. All joking aside, if you need me or if Jayden's girls need her, just holler and we'll leave the interview."

Oh. My. Sweet. Jesus. And all the angels in heaven, Jayden thought when the two people drove up in the yard that afternoon. Rain had come down in a steady drizzle all morning, soaking into the yard, and the two ladies would have to wade through mud to get from their vehicles to the dining hall. If it was true what Elijah had said about judging a person by their vehicle, then she should just tell those two to get back in their cars and go on home.

When the first one opened the door of her older-model black car, several pieces of trash fell out. Duct tape held the left front headlight in place, and the rest of the vehicle looked like all that was keeping it from falling apart was dried mud. Who went to a job interview in a tank top and denim shorts that had once been jeans?

Jayden would guess her to be no more than twenty-five, but she had that hard look about her that added ten years. She kicked the paper and what looked like a disposable container for a foot-long hot dog under the car. If she knew how to boil water, it would shock the hell right out of Jayden.

The second woman was a little better. Nothing fell out of her car, but sitting in the back seat was a big black dog that looked like maybe its father was an Angus bull. The woman wore sweatpants and a button-up shirt that pulled across her chest. She seemed friendly enough when she waved, but then she let the dog out. It promptly ran over and hiked its leg on the porch post.

"Okay, now, Bruiser, get back in the car so Mommy can get this job. Look at all this space you're going to have to run and play in when we move here." She put the dog back in the car and left the window down far enough that he could get his nose out for a breath of fresh air. "Where do I sign? I'm Madge. Don't suppose it would be all right if I brought Bruiser in with me, would it? Even though the rain cooled things down, he can't be left in the car very long."

"Over my dead body," Jayden whispered.

"This won't take long, and we can't have animals in the dining hall," Elijah said. "You ladies come on inside, and we'll talk. Jayden has a pot of coffee made and there's a plate of fresh cookies put out for y'all."

"That's right sweet," the first lady said. "I'm Ferry, by the way, and I had a late dinner, but I might take a dozen home with me for my boyfriend. He does love sweets. You won't mind if he moves in with me, will you?"

"We'll visit about all that when we get inside," Elijah answered.

Had Elijah lost his mind and gone nuts? Jayden wondered. *Why in all that was good and holy would he even entertain notions of hiring either of these two women?*

"Where does your boyfriend work?" Jayden asked as she led the way into the dining hall. She motioned for the two women to sit down at the adult table. When they were seated, she and Elijah both took their places across from them. Elijah opened a folder and laid out two pieces of paper with very little writing on them.

"He doesn't work. He's on disability," the woman answered, "but the marijuana sure helps the pain in his back. He's got a medical card, so it's all legal, and on his good days, he could help me out here," she answered. "As you can see by the papers I filled out at the employment place, I was the fry cook down at Bob's Burger Barn in Del Rio for three years and I seldom ever missed work. How much does this job pay?"

She batted her lashes at Elijah as if a little flirting might get her more money. Jayden fought the urge to *accidentally* kick her bare shins under the table.

"We can talk about that later. We have several applicants to interview before we make a decision, and the wages will be determined by experience," Jayden answered.

"That's me"—Madge reached for a second cookie and talked with food in her mouth—"right there on that left-hand résumé." She gave Ferry a dirty look. "I worked in a school cafeteria for two years back maybe fifteen years ago. And since then, I've been in home health care, fixin' meals and working for homebound folks. I like this kitchen and this place. My kids are all grown, and only two of the six have moved back in with me."

Jayden thought that she would choke. "Well, ladies, it's been real nice of you to come by so we could put your faces with the names on these résumés. Ferry and Madge. We will give you a call in the next two to three weeks if we need a second interview."

Madge tucked a strand of bleached blonde hair behind her ear. "You mean you ain't hirin' me today? I drove out here for nothing, and even made Bruiser wait in the car."

"Like Jayden said, we've got several more applicants to interview over the next two weeks." Elijah stood up.

Jayden followed his lead, hoping that they would take the hint and leave so she could fumigate the kitchen.

Ferry got up so fast that her chair fell over backward. A clap of thunder hit about the same time, doubling the noise. "I can't believe you'll get anybody to come out here in this godforsaken place that will be more qualified than I am. Didn't you understand that I'm a fry cook, and what does a bunch of outlaw girls want to eat anyway but french fries and burgers with some onion rings every so often, maybe?"

Jayden ushered them to the door. "If we don't call you, then feel free to call us after three weeks. Y'all drive safe now on the way back to town."

The minute they were out of the dining hall and she could hear the rattle of their vehicles starting up and driving away, she turned around and pointed a finger at Elijah. "What in the hell were you thinking? You can't have people like that around the girls."

"Résumés looked pretty good." He shrugged. "They both had experience in cooking."

"From now on, maybe we'd better ask for mug shots." Jayden marched across the kitchen and poured herself a glass of milk. She would have loved a double shot of Jack Daniel's right about then to calm her nerves, but milk would, at least, keep her stomach acid from burning holes through her insides.

"That would be discrimination," Elijah reminded her. "An applicant could come back on us and declare that we were discriminating on the basis of age or race."

She turned up her glass and drank a third of the milk before coming up for air. "You've got to find a big sister or mother figure to work around the girls." She paced all the way around the buffet bar and across the kitchen. "You can't have women who want to move their pot-smoking boyfriend in with them, or one who *only* has two grown kids and a dog the size of an elephant living in your old cabin with her. What if that big monster bit one of our girls, or what if one of those *only two grown kids* is a pervert of some kind? You need to get health records and criminal records right up front before they come out, not after. And maybe a drug test the minute they arrive. They're going to be around young girls, for God's sake." She made a lap around the whole kitchen. "If that's the best in the area, hiring a cook is going to be a nightmare."

"I agree." He nodded. "It sure ain't going to be a daydream, and if you think you can pick better ones to call in for an interview, the résumés are right there."

"Well, I damn sure can't do worse." She picked up the first stack and flipped through half a dozen short job applications. "I don't see a single one that looks acceptable. We need someone that can do something more than fry burgers and make hot dogs."

"I agree, so what's our next step?" he asked.

"We go pick up the paper that Ferry left on the yard, and then we get some disinfectant and wash the dog pee off our porch post," she answered as she tossed the résumés back on the table. "Tomorrow morning, you should call the employment place and tell them none of these will work."

"Yes, ma'am." He grinned. "Did I hear you say *our* porch post and *our* girls?"

"Yes, you did," she huffed as she went to the cabinet and got a bottle of spray cleaner, a roll of paper towels, and two sets of latex gloves. "Here, put these on. You never know what germs are on the porch post, and that litter Ferry left for us could have botulism or salmonella on it."

"There's one good thing about those interviews," he said as he stretched on the gloves. "They didn't take very long. You might even have time to catch a nap before you start supper."

"I'm way too wound up to sleep," she said.

"Do you need a hug and maybe a kiss?" he asked.

"After being around those two women, I'd need a shower before I even thought about something like that," she fumed.

"It's raining, so a shower shouldn't be a problem." He grinned.

"With eight girls and two counselors watching?" she asked. "No, thank you!"

Chapter Nineteen

As Jayden made her way across the yard to the dining hall that Monday morning, she remembered her grandfather saying that "what will be, will be, and what won't be just might be anyway." It had seemed like a riddle to her when she was young, but after interviewing those two women the day before and realizing how much she had come to love Piney Wood—well, that latter part of what Gramps said was beginning to make sense all these years later.

"Is it my calling to stay here?" she asked herself that morning as she turned on the lights in the dining hall and went to work. Was that why she'd gotten so angry at the idea of anyone taking over her kitchen? Or was she angry because that hussy Ferry had flirted with Elijah?

"What are you all spun up about?" Novalene asked as she came in, poured two cups of coffee, carried one back to Jayden, and then took her regular chair.

"Thank you," Jayden said, accepting the coffee, "but what makes you think I'm worried about anything?"

"It's written all over your face," Novalene answered. "You'd make a lousy poker player. Does it have to do with those women who came by yesterday? We haven't had a chance to talk about the interviews."

Jayden cracked eggs into a bowl and whipped them with a whisk. "Well, rest assured that we didn't hire either one of those women, and I don't intend to bring them back for a second interview, either."

Diana, like always, went straight to the coffeepot.

"What'd those eggs do to you?" Diana asked. "Looks to me like you're taking out your frustrations on them."

"Maybe I am," Jayden answered. "If the two prospects we talked to yesterday are the best this area has to offer, then, as my Gramps used to say, the pickin's are going to be mighty slim. I just can't imagine turning Mary's kitchen over to someone . . ." She shivered and kept stirring scrambled eggs.

"That bad, huh?" Novalene asked.

"One had a pot-smoking boyfriend who would be moving in with her, but he has a 'medical card.'" She air quoted the last two words. "The other one had two grown kids and a dog the size of a gorilla that would be living with her. She brought the dog along and let it hike its leg on the porch post. They both left mad at us because we didn't offer either of them the job."

Diana blew on the top of her mug and giggled at the same time. "Mary wouldn't rest easy a single day knowing someone like that was in her kitchen. If they hadn't had so much baggage, would they have worked out?"

"Nope. Not the right kind of experience, either," Jayden answered.

The girls came filing in before anyone could ask another question. Elijah usually followed them and picked up a tray, but that morning he joined her behind the buffet line.

"I'll help you serve this morning," he said.

"Why?" she asked.

"Because if yesterday's two prospects were the best we've got, it might be easier to hire a retired drill sergeant to do my job and take over cooking myself." He scooped up scrambled eggs for Ashlyn, who was first in line that morning.

"Can you make anything other than ice cream?" She spooned up home-fried potatoes cooked with bacon onto Ashlyn's tray and then took a step to her left, added a biscuit, and topped it with gravy.

"Mary left her recipe book, and I can follow instructions," Elijah answered.

"There's a person out there who is perfect for the job." Jayden tried to reassure herself as much as she did him. "We just have to find her."

"I hope you're right," Elijah said, but there was doubt in his tone.

Ashlyn, Tiffany, and Carmella had finished their breakfast and headed out to the barn to clean the stables by the time Jayden and Elijah had taken their trays to the adult table. Jayden had just taken the first bite of her biscuit and gravy when Tiffany came running into the dining hall with tears streaming down her face.

"Come quick, Jayden. It's Ashlyn. We can't do anything with her," Tiffany said between sobs and then whipped around and ran out of the hall.

"Go!" Novalene said. "We'll watch over everything here."

"I better go, too." Elijah followed right behind her. "This sounds serious. You don't think she'd do something stupid, do you?"

"Not for a second." Jayden's breath came out in short gasps.

They followed the sound of weeping from the barn door to Dynamite's stall. Tiffany and Carmella were on their knees, patting Ashlyn's back and trying to console her. She held the horse's head in her lap and kept stroking his nose. Tears flooded her cheeks, and she wept so hard that her breath came out in gasps.

"He's dead, Jayden. Dynamite is gone," she said between sobs.

Jayden sat down in the straw right beside her and wrapped the girl up in her arms. Ashlyn laid her head on Jayden's shoulder and continued to sob. "I loved him, and he's dead."

Jayden remembered crying like that at her grandmother's and then her grandfather's funerals. The last time she had wept that hard was at her mother's service. Tears spilled out of her blue eyes and flowed down her cheeks as the pain she had felt at her loved ones leaving her returned. Human or horse—the ache of losing someone or something was the same.

"Shhh," she soothed Ashlyn. "He's in a better place, darlin'."

Ashlyn raised her head, her delicate chin still quivering. "But I don't want him in a better place. I want him to be here when I leave. I didn't even tell him goodbye."

Tiffany wiped her eyes with the back of her hand. "What do we do with him?"

"We have to bury him," Ashlyn answered.

"And have a funeral," Carmella added.

"We don't usually bury a dead horse," Elijah said. "We call a disposal company to come take them away."

"No!" Ashlyn declared. "He's been better than a therapist for me since I got here. He needs to be put in the ground out by the half-mile marker. He loved his afternoon walks, so he should be buried out there."

"Do you know how big a hole you'd have to dig to bury a horse?" Elijah asked. "It's six feet down even for a small human."

"What's going on in here?" Keelan yelled from the door. "Is everyone all right?"

"No, we're not," Ashlyn wailed in a high-pitched voice.

Keelan didn't even stop at the stall gate but fell on her knees beside the horse and hugged him like a long-lost brother. Pretty soon the other girls had gathered round the dead animal, and all of them were sobbing.

Jayden let go of Ashlyn and carefully made her way out of the stall, leaving the girls to console one another. Elijah laced his fingers in hers and led her back to the main part of the barn. He sat down on a bale of hay and pulled her down beside him.

"Those kids have no idea how much a horse weighs," he whispered.

"Can you use any of the farm equipment to get him up on the hay trailer?" she asked. "They need to bury him and have a funeral.

They'll have closure for something deeper and entirely different than what they're feeling for Dynamite."

What about you? the voice in her head asked. *What would bring you closure for your parents, and for the way your mother treated you at the end of her life? You would have been much happier to have had the home than the small savings account, but Skyler got the house. Nothing was sentimental to her, and now it's all gone.*

"Are you all right?" His voice cracked.

She wiped a tear from her cheek. "No, I'm not. I used to come out here at night when I couldn't sleep and talk to that horse. I don't want to see him taken off to a landfill or wherever dead horses go."

"I've talked to Dynamite pretty regularly for the past two years," Elijah admitted. "The vet came out about a month ago and wanted to put him down, but I couldn't let him. I wanted the old boy to die when he was supposed to."

"From everyone's reactions, I think he must have been a therapist to a lot of us," she whispered.

"Oh, honey, I would have never gotten this far without Dynamite. He helped me so much when I just couldn't get past the idea that if I'd done something better, my friends wouldn't have died," Elijah said. "I flew the helicopter to bring six of them home after they'd been attacked. Three made it; three didn't. I've gone over the whole day so many times that it's burned into my brain, and I keep thinking that if I'd done something different . . . they were my family, my brothers—no, that's not right. They were closer than even a brother, and just like that they were gone. Dynamite listened to me work through some of that."

"I'm so sorry," Jayden said. "I talked to him about this thing between me and Skyler. I stayed with Mama and yet she made Skyler executor over everything. Skyler got the house. I got a small savings account that Mama had inherited after Gramps died. I still feel like it was the wrong decision. I would have kept the house forever."

"Guess Dynamite will take a lot of secrets with him, including mine and yours." Elijah sighed. "And I'm sorry, but we don't have a backhoe around here to dig a hole big enough for a horse." Elijah slipped an arm around her shoulders and drew her closer to his side.

"If you can get him out to the half-mile marker, the girls will take care of the rest," Jayden said. "This will teach them teamwork more than anything they've done yet, and it will help them heal."

Elijah gave her a gentle hug. "All right. I'll trust you to know what you're doing. Thank goodness for the rain yesterday. At least the ground won't be as hard as a rock, like usual."

"Even if it was, they would find a way to dig a grave. I should go check on them," she said, but she didn't want to leave the comfort of his arms.

"I'll go with you." He dropped his arm and stood up.

When she got to her feet, he slipped his arm around her shoulders again. "I'm glad you are here, Jayden. I don't know what I'd do without you."

"Me either, where you're concerned," she told him.

He stopped long enough to brush a soft kiss across her forehead, and then together they headed toward the stall.

All the girls looked up at them with red, swollen eyes. Apparently, those who didn't love Dynamite as much as Keelan and Ashlyn weren't going to let the rest of them mourn alone.

"Do we have to let them take him away?" Ashlyn asked. "Can't we bury him and have a proper funeral? He was our friend."

"Elijah says he'll figure out a way to get his body out to the half-mile marker but that he doesn't have equipment to dig a hole big enough to put him in," Jayden told them.

Ashlyn stood up and squared her shoulders. "Give me a shovel. I'll take care of the grave even if it takes me all week."

"I'll help." Keelan got to her feet and stood beside Ashlyn. "Two of us digging will make the work go faster. Can we start right now?"

One by one the other girls got to their feet.

"How many shovels do we have?" Tiffany asked.

"I could probably rustle up four," Elijah answered.

"Then half of us will dig for thirty minutes and then rest while the others take a turn," Quinley said. "I'll take the first shift with Ashlyn and Keelan."

"Add me to that," Carmella offered.

Elijah pointed to a couple of wheelbarrows. "The shovels are in the tack room. Take the wheelbarrows with you to help move dirt. I'll bring him out there when you're done and, girls, you'll want to wear gloves, or you'll have some mighty big blisters on your hands before the job is done." He handed Ashlyn a tape measure. "You might want to use this to get an idea of how long and wide to make your hole, and I'd suggest piling rocks on top of it when you get him covered with dirt. That will keep the coyotes from trying to dig him up."

"Thank you, Elijah," Ashlyn said. "Tiffany, will you help me?"

Tiffany reached out and took the end of the tape measure, and Ashlyn stretched it from one end of Dynamite to the other.

"I'll remember the numbers for you," Quinley offered as Ashlyn called them out.

When they were finished with that, Keelan picked up the handles of one of the wheelbarrows and led the way out of the barn. Rita followed behind her with the other wheelbarrow, and the other girls carried shovels. All the girls left with their heads hanging low and with tears still dripping onto their shirts.

"I'm going with them," Jayden said.

"Let them go out there alone," Elijah suggested. "It's their little procession. Give them half an hour, and then I'll drive you out there in the truck. That way you can tell the others what's happened and ask them if they'll take shifts watching over the girls. You could stay a couple of hours, and then one of them can relieve you so you can come back in and make dinner. If they're not done with the digging at noon, I'll drive them all back. How does that sound?"

"You're probably right, but I can't stand to see them in so much pain. I want to support them and do something," Jayden said.

"You'll be helping them the most by letting them depend on each other," Elijah told her.

"Okay, but it's not easy," she said on a sigh.

"I know, darlin'." He gave her a sideways hug. "As adults we want to shield them." He wrapped his arms around her and held her even closer to his body. He hadn't cried like the girls had, but his eyes brimmed with unshed tears. "Now all I have to do is figure out how to get a thousand-pound horse onto a hay trailer."

She finally took a step back. "If I can help in any way at all to get him on the trailer, just tell me what to do."

"Thank you," Elijah said. "I'm going to figure out something while you're talking to the others. I'll be down to get you in half an hour."

She nodded his way and headed outside. The sun was a fireball in the eastern sky by then, promising a hot, humid day after the rain the day before. How could the sun shine on such a sad day for the girls? It didn't seem fair, but then Jayden had had the same thoughts the day she and Skyler went to the cemetery—Skyler in her sports car, Jayden in her old green truck. The sun had been shining that day, too. Wildflowers bloomed in the medians, and her mother's roses were thick with blooms. She had picked a huge basket of red, pink, and yellow roses and set them at the end of the casket. Skyler had sneered at the basket, but she hadn't brought a single flower with her.

She'd held the tears back to be strong for the girls, but the dam broke on the way back to the dining room. Tears streamed down her face, dripped off her jaw, and made wet circles on her shirt. When she reached the dining hall, she squared her shoulders, forced herself to stop sobbing, and went inside.

Diana and Novalene had put the kitchen and dining room to rights and made a new pitcher of sweet tea while she was gone.

"What's going on out there?" Novalene rushed to her side. "Are you okay? Is Ashlyn all right? We started to come on out there, but we figured you'd call if it was serious."

"Dynamite died," Jayden answered.

"No!" they chorused.

"Is Keelan all right?" Novalene asked. "She's awfully attached to that horse and has been fussing about Ashlyn thinking he wasn't doing well. I think she knew he was on his last legs but was just in denial."

"They're all taking it hard, and"—Jayden poured herself a tall glass of sweet tea, and slumped down into a chair—"they're going to bury him and have a funeral this afternoon."

"They are going to do what?" Diana's eyes almost popped right out of her head.

Jayden repeated what she'd said. "They're out at the half-mile marker digging a hole right now."

"Those girls have never done anything like that," Diana gasped. "We should go supervise and be there to comfort them."

"Exactly." Jayden laid out her plan. "I'm going to take bottles of water out with me for the first shift."

"Let us take care of that," Novalene suggested. "You need to cook. Elijah can drive us out there. Maybe they'll have the grave done by lunchtime, and they can have their little service right after they eat."

"Are you sure?" Jayden asked. "I don't mind taking the first couple of hours."

"Of course we are." Diana laid a hand on Jayden's shoulder. "We'll get some water and maybe put some of those leftover cookies that you made into a bag. Digging is tough work, and they may need a little snack about midmorning. Poor darlin's, the death of a pet is tough, and Dynamite has been a friend to all of them."

Novalene bent down and slipped an arm around Jayden's shoulders. "How are you holding up? It couldn't have been a party out there with all eight of them, was it?"

"I'm fine," Jayden answered, but she wiped a hand across her wet cheeks. "No, I'm not fine, but I will be. It hurts to see the girls in pain, and to tell the truth, Dynamite was my sounding board, or maybe I should say 'sounding horse.' I used to go out there at night and tell him my troubles."

"I'm so, so sorry," Diana said as she and Novalene gave her a three-way hug.

Family doesn't have to share DNA, her gramps's voice came to her mind. He was so right. These folks—the counselors, girls, and even Elijah—were family even if they didn't share a drop of blood.

"For some of them, it might be their first time to deal with death," Jayden said.

"Poor things." Novalene took a step back. "They'll learn today that their parents' money can't buy a cure for death and the pain of losing something or someone dear to them."

"Ain't it the truth." Diana picked up a tissue and wiped Jayden's cheeks.

Jayden whipped up two applesauce Bundt cakes. While they baked, she made gazpacho and put it in the refrigerator to chill. Cold soup served with chunks of homemade Italian bread, wedges of cheese, and chicken salad sandwiches would be good for hot, sweaty girls who'd used up a lot of energy and emotion that morning.

The whole time she worked, she worried about all the girls, but even more about her three—Ashlyn in particular. They hadn't discussed the death of grandparents or pets, but Ashlyn had said something about her nanny dying, and that was when she turned to alcohol. When the cakes were out of the pans and cooling, she chopped up peppers, onions, and tomatoes to sprinkle on top of the gazpacho and sliced the warm bread when it came out of the oven.

"French fries and hamburgers, my butt," she fumed as she thought about the two women from the day before.

You just need someone to be pissed at, don't you, baby girl? Her grandfather's voice was pretty real in her head.

"Yes, I do," she agreed aloud.

Remember what I told you about arguing with yourself.

"I'm not arguing. I'm agreeing with you." She got down bowls for the soup and then started making chicken salad sandwiches.

If you're fighting with yourself, you're about to mess up.

"I told you, I'm in complete agreement with you," she said again.

Follow your heart, and then you won't be pissed at anyone—most of all yourself.

With dirt smeared on their sweaty faces, the girls filed in at noon. Ashlyn was first in line with Tiffany and Carmella right behind her. She managed a weak smile when she saw the gazpacho. "That looks really good. It's so hot outside that cold soup will go down good."

"I'm glad." Jayden smiled. "Did you get finished, or do you have to do more digging this afternoon?"

"Elijah says it's big enough and deep enough. We had four shovels, and we had a system," Ashlyn said. "He said he'll bring Dynamite out to the grave when we get done eating and then we can have our service."

"There's a poem called 'The Rainbow Bridge.' I've never read it, but Quinley said that her friend gave it to her when she lost her dog. She says it would be perfect for the funeral." Tiffany held out her tray for a sprinkling of peppers, onions, and fresh tomatoes to be put on top of her soup. "Would you be able to find it and print it off so I can read it at the service?"

"I'll do my best," Jayden promised.

"And we all want a song," Carmella said. "Can we borrow your phone and play 'The River' by Garth Brooks? The words kind of fit all of us here, and we're all sorry that Dynamite is gone. We should've told him how much he meant to us. We've decided that for the rest of our lives, it's going to be our theme song from what we've learned while we've been here. It talks about a dreamer, and we're in Daydream Cabin."

"I can make that happen." Jayden tried to remember the words to the song but only something about daring to dance on the tides came to mind.

"Thank you," Carmella said. "We're planning to walk back out there together after we eat. We brought the wheelbarrows back with us to put the rocks in that we'll gather as we go."

"We'll all go with you," Jayden told her.

Elijah arrived as the last girl sat down. He picked up a tray and asked, "What is this?"

"Gazpacho and sandwiches," Jayden answered. "I figured something cold might be good after the morning they've all had."

"Haven't had it in years, but it sure looks good. Is that cinnamon I smell?" He added several spoonfuls of extra vegetables to his soup and picked up two chicken salad sandwiches.

"Applesauce cake with brown sugar and cinnamon in the center, and fresh fruit salad for dessert. How's it going in the barn?" she asked.

"I went ahead and put Dynamite in the hole the girls dug. I covered him with a horse blanket. Everything is ready," he answered. "Y'all want me to drive you out there after we eat?"

"The girls are planning to walk. I'll tag along with them," she said.

"Me too," Diana piped up from the table. "We'll stay back a little way and give the girls some space, but it won't hurt us to walk a mile today."

"Speak for yourself," Novalene said. "I'll ride with Elijah. These old bones have sat out in the sun all morning. Watching those girls work so hard was all the exercise I need for the next six months."

"How did they do?" Jayden asked.

"They cried a lot," Diana said.

"And giggled a little when they remembered something special like the story of Dynamite and the snake," Novalene added.

"But mostly they worked like troupers to get that hole big enough to put a horse in," Elijah said. "They should be emotionally and physically drained by bedtime tonight."

"Same as you, huh?" Jayden nudged him with her shoulder.

"You got that right," he said.

Jayden could tell that Tiffany was nervous about reading the poem. Her hands shook as she took her place at the end of the grave. A relentless, broiling sun beat down on everyone's heads, but the girls didn't even seem to mind. Sweat circles and dirt stained their uniforms as they gathered around the hole with the horse lying in the bottom, covered with a blanket. She pulled a piece of paper from her pocket and read:

> By the edge of a woods, at the foot of a hill,
> Is a lush, green meadow where time stands still.
> Where the friends of man and women do run,
> When their time on earth is over and done.
> For here, between this world and the next,
> Is a place where beloved creatures find rest.
> On this golden land, they wait, and they play,
> Until the Rainbow Bridge they cross over one day.
> They trot through the grass without even a care,
> Until one day they whinny and sniff at the air.

All ears prick forward, eyes sharp and alert.
Then all of a sudden, one breaks from the herd.
For just at that second, there's no room for remorse.
As they see each other . . .

Her voice broke and Ashlyn slipped her arm around Tiffany's shoulders.

So, they run to each other, these friends from long past.
The time of their parting is over at last.
The sadness they felt while they were apart
Has turned to joy once more in each heart.
They nuzzle with a love that will last forever.
And then, side by side, they cross over together.

"Rest in peace, Dynamite. Someday I'll be with you again," Ashlyn said as she picked up a shovel and began to fill in the grave.

Jayden slipped her phone from the hip pocket of her jeans and started the song Carmella had asked for. The girl had been right. The words did fit every one of the kids gathered around the grave that hot, sultry afternoon. The lyrics of the song talked about a dream being like a river, trying to learn from what's in the past, and that they would never reach their destination if they never tried.

They were still shoveling dirt when the song ended, so Jayden hit the "Repeat" button and let it run until there was a long mound of dirt beside the half-mile marker. Then Quinley and Violet pushed the wheelbarrows close to the grave and all the girls piled rocks on top until it was completely covered.

Ashlyn carefully picked a yellow flower from a cactus and laid it in the middle of the rocks. "You were a good friend and you will be missed. Now, we've got stalls to clean before supper, and two horses to exercise. I'm sure all y'all from the other cabins have work to catch up on, too, so let's get it done so we won't be behind tomorrow. I hope all of y'all listened to the words of that song. When any of us think about getting into trouble when we get home, we should play that song again and remember what we've learned here."

"Wow!" Novalene muttered under her breath.

"Amen," Diana agreed. "I believe we're going out on a victory note with this group."

Jayden didn't comment. She was too proud of Ashlyn for words, and besides, she couldn't have gotten them out past the lump in her throat, anyway.

Chapter Twenty

$\mathcal{J}$ayden had just turned off her bedroom light when a soft rap on her door made her sit straight up in bed. "Yes?" she asked.

"Jayden, can we talk?" Ashlyn asked.

"Of course." Jayden reached out and turned on the lamp on the nightstand beside her bed.

She was surprised when all three girls came into her room and sat down on the floor beside her bed. They'd evidently turned their hats around when they were slinging dirt, because they had half-moon-shaped sunburns on their foreheads.

"Have you ever been to a funeral?" Tiffany asked.

"Three that really affected me," Jayden answered honestly. "My grandmother died when I was sixteen, and my grandpa came to live with me and Mama. Then he died a little while after that, and I lost my mother a few years later. How about y'all?"

"My nanny died, but Mama said I couldn't go to the funeral. She said they were depressing, and that I hadn't seen her since I got too old for a nanny, so . . . ," Ashlyn answered.

"I haven't been to a funeral before today," Tiffany said, "but I got to thinking about how hard it would be to lose my mama or my daddy or my sister. They're not perfect, and they don't have much time for me, but to stand there and look at their dead bodies in a casket would break my heart."

"I went to my grandmother's memorial when I was about four or five." Carmella frowned as if she was trying to bring up the memory. "I don't remember much about it, except that I wondered how they got a big woman like her in that gold urn."

Jayden's chest tightened until it was hard for her to breathe. She wished she could shield her girls from the heartaches that lay ahead of them. "Funerals are really more for those of us who are still alive than for the one who has passed away. I'm sorry that you didn't get to go to your nanny's service, Ashlyn. Tiffany, it's good that you are realizing how empty your life would be without your parents. We should use our experiences as guidelines to show us what to do, or maybe to show us what not to do. Carmella, did you ask your parents about your grandmother?" Jayden wasn't sure if she was preaching to the kids or to herself.

"No, ma'am." She shook her head. "I learned early on to keep my mouth shut, to sit up like a lady, and speak when spoken to. I like what you just said about using our experiences to show us what not to do. When I have kids, I'm going to let them ask questions, and I'm going to do my best to give them honest answers."

"Me too," Tiffany added. "We all felt so sad today about Dynamite. It made me wonder if folks will be sad when I die."

Carmella ran her fingers through her hair. "I never thought much about death until today, and now I'm kind of scared."

Jayden wanted to hug all three of them at once. "Don't be afraid of dying. Be afraid that you don't make the most of every single day you are alive. I read about an old lady who said she wanted to slide into heaven with nothing left."

"You mean like money?" Tiffany asked.

Jayden wasn't at all surprised that Tiffany, or any young girl at the camp, would think of that at first. "No," she said, "she wanted to have used every bit of her energy, every second of her time, and have given every drop of her love away so that when she got to heaven, what had been her on this earth was all finished and done with. She wouldn't have anything physical left, and she could be a perfect spiritual being up in heaven."

For several minutes, they just sat there staring at her, then Tiffany grinned. "Like you, huh? At first, I thought you were mean as a snake, but the more I got to know you, the more I realized you're a good person."

"I'm glad you're here." Carmella reached up and patted Jayden's hand. "I'm just sorry that other girls won't get to eat your cooking and break curfew like we're doing right now."

"And that they won't ever get to talk to you about funerals and having sex with boyfriends, and all that stuff," Ashlyn told her. "But I've got another question. How long does it take to get over it when someone close to you dies?"

Jayden thought about that for a while before she answered. "I'm not sure you ever get over it. As time goes by, the pain gets a little less severe. Maybe I can explain it like this: Healing from a broken bone or a bad cut takes a while, and it hurts really bad at first. But then it begins to heal, and the ache kind of goes away. But there's always a reminder in the bone or in the scar tissue where the cut was that lets you know that something isn't quite right." She stopped and frowned as she tried to collect her thoughts. "I'm making a mess of this."

"Nope," Tiffany disagreed. "It makes sense to me. In a year, we'll just remember our walks with Dynamite, and the hurt in our hearts today won't be like it is now."

"I hope so," Ashlyn yawned. "Thanks for listening to us, Jayden. I couldn't sleep before, but now I can't keep my eyes open."

"Good night." Jayden smiled at them. "Five o'clock comes early, so y'all really should get some sleep."

Carmella was the first one to stand up. "See you tomorrow."

Tiffany closed the door behind them, and Jayden propped the pillows up against the wrought iron headboard of her narrow bed. She picked up a romance novel that she'd brought along in case she got bored. That sure hadn't happened in the weeks she'd been there. She looked at the back cover and the blurb looked good. A cowboy with a penchant for red-haired women had met a sassy one.

She read two pages and laid the book aside. The hero in the story already reminded her of Elijah and caused her to think of the comfort she felt when he drew her close to him that morning. She closed her eyes and got a vision of him as he led her away from Dynamite's body and the girls. Then she touched her lips and thought about the electricity his kiss had stirred up. Even though he wasn't really a cowboy like the hero in the book, he did wear cowboy boots most of the time and lived on a small farm—or was it a ranch? She'd never really understood the difference between the two.

"A cowboy isn't necessarily a person, anyway, it's more like an attitude." Her mind flashed back to what her grandfather had said when she once asked him what made a real cowboy. "A man can dress up in a hat, fancy boots, and a pearl-snap shirt and go out dancin' on Saturday night. That doesn't make him a real cowboy."

"Then what does?" Jayden had asked.

"It's respecting women, having a kind heart, working hard, loving the land—all those kinds of things make a cowboy, not a fancy hat and boots," he had answered.

"Elijah is all those things," she said as she laid the book back on her nightstand beside her Bible. She hadn't opened the Bible in years, not since her mother had gotten sick. As far as she was concerned, God had failed her. His word said that if she prayed with her whole heart and believed, then He would answer her prayers. He had not, and her mother had died, so why should she trust anything He had left on record in the Bible?

The black, zippered book seemed to be calling her name, but she ignored it. She had only tucked it into her suitcase because she thought since Skyler had been a counselor at the camp, it'd be the kind of place to have a devotional study every day. Antsy and jittery, she got up and paced around the room several times, then sat on the edge of her bed.

Finally, she reached for the Bible. When she undid the zipper around three sides of its leather binding, a letter fell out onto the floor and slid under her bed. Her brow wrinkled, and she narrowed her eyes so tightly that a pain shot through her head. She couldn't remember ever tucking a letter into her Bible. Bookmarks, yes, but never a letter. She laid the Bible aside and noticed that it had fallen open to Psalm 23, which was one of her mother's favorite passages. Then she got down on her knees and retrieved the envelope.

Still sitting on the floor, she leaned back against the bed and removed the pages from the envelope with her name on it. It was written on lined paper with a ragged edge where it had been ripped from a spiral notebook. "Oh. My. God," she whispered, afraid to blink for fear her mother's handwriting would disappear before she could read what was written.

Just looking at the first line put a lump in Jayden's throat and tears welled up behind her eyes. "My dearest daughter," she whispered, and then began to read silently:

> I know you have stopped reading and praying because you think God has failed to make me all better, but after my funeral, you will seek solace and eventually get back in church. That's why I'm tucking this away in your Bible instead of giving it to the lawyer with Skyler's. I want you to read this after a little time has passed and you are through being angry at God.
>
> First of all, I've always had a sixth sense about things, and I knew something was wrong with me

that couldn't be fixed before I went to the doctor yesterday. The doctor confirmed my suspicions, and I'm choosing not to tell you about the bubble in my brain. It will burst, probably sooner than later, but it's not something that can be treated or cured. I'm choosing to live each day I have to the fullest and not think about it until the very end.

However, I have made some decisions that will affect you and Skyler. Since your father and I divorced, I admit that I've been closer to you. You've been here with me, and together we've faced a lot of emotional upheavals. I cannot burden you with choosing the right time to take me off life support if it comes to that, so Skyler will have to do it. You would always hold out for one more day to see if I got better. I can't bear knowing that each day would just bring you more pain. Skyler will take care of it so that you don't have to. Also, I do not want a big, lavish funeral. I want a simple graveside service with only you girls attending. You would never let that happen, so I'm leaving that to Skyler, also. It's her turn to shoulder some of the responsibility that you've taken on all these years while she's been off at college or working in the summers at her camps.

I'm leaving her the house because you need to move on with your life and not live in the past, which you will do if you have the homeplace to move into. It needs to be sold, and the profits split between you girls. It's just a house and should never be a shrine to me or your grandfather. Please, forgive me for keeping things from you and understand that I've loved you from the day the nurse at the hospital laid you in my arms. You were so much easier to raise than Skyler, but that was my fault. I thought she was the only child I'd ever have so I let her have her way with everything from the beginning. Once it started, it snowballed, and your father didn't help matters.

Don't blame Skyler. She's only done what I've asked her to do in the letter that I've left in the lawyer's hands for her. I'm ready to go. When you are reading this, I will have finished my race here on earth. Don't mourn for me, but rather remember all the good times we've had.

It was signed, *Love you a bushel and a peck and a hug around the neck, Mama.*

Jayden read through it three times, and every time tears fell on the paper, leaving water marks and blurring part of the words. She finally held it to her heart and remembered that her mother had said that thing about bushels and pecks many, many times when she was just a little girl.

When she finally got her emotions under control enough to talk, she picked up the phone and called Skyler. She didn't care if her sister was mad at her—she wanted to hear about the letter her mother wrote to her.

"Hello!" Skyler's voice sounded downright chipper.

"Where are you?" Jayden asked.

"I'm in my apartment looking at bridal magazines. Have you changed your mind about giving me the money for my wedding?" Skyler asked.

"No, I have not," Jayden answered. "Why didn't you tell me that Mama left letters for us?"

"I figured that the lawyer gave yours to you like he did mine. What did yours say?" Skyler asked. "Did it tell you to be nice to me when I need money?"

"What did your letter say?" Jayden asked.

"Lord, I don't remember. That was years ago. She mainly said that we were to sell the house and split the profits. I kept a bigger portion because I was the one who did all the work when it came to selling it, and I had to make the decision to pull the plug on life support. I deserved more of the house money. Oh, and that she loved me." Skyler sighed. "Now, about my wedding?"

"The answer is still no," Jayden said.

"You're a sorry excuse for a sister," Skyler said and then the line went dead.

Jayden was too restless to sleep. The guilt surrounding her for not confronting her sister back when things were happening seemed to smother her. She finally pulled on a pair of shorts because her nightshirt barely covered her underpants and went outside to look at the stars. Going from a nice cool house into the hot night air almost sent her right back inside, but she sat down in a chair and let out a long sigh.

"I heard that." Elijah appeared out of the darkness at the end of her porch steps. "You having trouble sleeping tonight, too?"

She motioned toward the empty chair next to hers. "Come on up and have a seat, and to answer your question, yes, I've got insomnia and guilt all rolled up into one big ball."

"Guilt?" He set a bottle of water on the table between them. "What on earth would you have to be guilty about? I told you a week ago that Dynamite was beginning to feel his age."

"This has nothing to do with a horse and everything to do with another funeral that I've blamed my sister for all these years." She told him about the letter she'd found. "If only I'd opened my Bible years ago . . . but I was so mad at God for not saving my mother or for not giving the doctors the know-how to do it for Him. I should have given

Mama more credit than to think she didn't trust me. She was trying to save me from pain, like I wanted to do with my girls today."

Elijah reached across the table separating them and took her hand in his. "Honey, I believe that everything happens for a reason. You might not know what it is right now, but in a few more years, you'll look back and realize that whatever happened was for the best and led you to this very day. Every decision a body makes has an impact on the future.

"This has been the most emotional session I've ever had here at Piney Wood. I like you, Jayden, and if we didn't have all these girls and this camp to take care of, I would love to begin a relationship with you."

He brought her hand to his lips and kissed each knuckle. "When this session is over, would you consider sticking around for a week or two? That would give us some time to . . ."

"Yes," she said. "I would love to do that."

Chapter Twenty-One

Since that call after she had found the letter, Jayden hadn't heard from Skyler. But then, since their mother had passed away, they seldom talked, so it wasn't something that she missed. That evening the girls joined her in the red chairs, and then one by one the kids from the other two cabins showed up. Some of them sat on the steps, and others parked their butts on the porch, most of them sitting cross-legged.

"We think you should take the job as cook for this place," Keelan said.

"Is this some kind of intervention?" Jayden giggled, relieving some of the pent-up stress of the day.

"Yep, it is." Violet nodded. "You can always find a job teaching in Texas if you don't like it here after a year. If I could stay and help in any way, I would love to. I could go to high school in Alpine and live right here. I've never felt so safe and wanted as I have here in the camp."

"Why don't y'all turn this place into a boarding school for nine girls?" Rita asked. "I'm sure my folks would gladly pay whatever it would cost for me to stay here. That way, they wouldn't have to be bothered with me, and I'd be one freakin' happy kid."

"That's not for me to decide," Jayden said. "That's something you need to talk to Elijah about. I can't imagine any of you wanting to stay here your next two or three years of high school. You all hated this place when you first got here."

"That was then," Keelan said. "This is now. We've kind of found ourselves since way back then, and you need to do the same thing."

"Almost every evening when you leave the dining hall, you are humming a tune or whistling under your breath. You're happy here, whether you know it or not," Ashlyn said.

Jayden smiled at the bunch of them. "Of course I'm happy here. I've seen you girls learn to love yourselves for what's inside you, not for the fancy clothes or jewelry on your bodies or the hundred-dollar haircuts and expensive makeup. And I'm more than just happy that you all have overcome the issues you came here with. That would make any grown-up happy."

"Just think about making other girls feel like us for however many times Elijah has a session out here," Tiffany said. "You don't have to decide right now, but it would make every one of us happy if we could wave goodbye to you on that last day and know that at least one of us was living here at Piney Wood."

"If you did stay," Keelan started, "could we come back and visit you sometimes during the off-seasons? My mama would pay for me to have a vacation here, like over Christmas."

"I don't think that would work. This is just part of your journey on the path of life. Y'all need to go home, face off with the same things that sent you here, and overcome them," Jayden told them. "And now, you should all get going. You've only got about five minutes to get into your beds. I'd hate for you to get demerits because you were having an intervention of sorts for me."

The girls from the other cabins left, and in only a few minutes Novalene and Diana joined her on the Daydream Cabin porch. Novalene handed her a bottle of water and sat down beside her. Diana took one of the other two chairs. Neither was wearing her cap, and their hair looked damp from fresh washing. Novalene's gray roots shone in the moonlight. Diana's hair hung in wet strands.

Jayden twisted the top off the bottle and took a long drink from it. "Don't tell me y'all are here to give me a pep talk about not going back to teaching."

"Is that why the kids were all gathered up over here?" Novalene asked.

"It's like they're on a mission to get me to stay here," Jayden laughed.

"You can make up your own mind about all that," Novalene replied. "We came over to see what's got you all twisted up today. You've been distracted, and you forgot to make sweet tea for dinner and then again for supper until the girls were already lined up. So fess up—are you and Elijah fighting?"

"We're not prying," Diana said. "We're just here to help."

"A few days ago, I found a letter from my mother," Jayden spat out and went on to tell them how angry she'd been at her mother for the decisions she'd made.

"She kept more than her half of the money?" Diana was aghast. "That's downright mean and hateful no matter which way you think about it."

"And she wouldn't let you buy her out?" Novalene asked. "Even if your mama wanted you to move on, it would have been only right for Skyler to offer the place to you first."

"Or at least to give you more than your personal belongings. I would be devastated if I didn't have my grandmother's rolling pin," Diana added.

"It is what it is." Jayden sighed.

"You are so right. All our bitchin' won't undo it, so let's go back to my question," Novalene said. "Are you and Elijah fighting?"

"No, we are *not* fighting," Jayden said.

"Good," Novalene said. "We've had such a pleasant experience this session that . . ."

She hesitated and Diana picked up where she left off. ". . . that we don't want things to get awkward here at the end."

"What's that supposed to mean?" Jayden asked.

"We're not blind, darlin'." Novalene laughed. "We can feel the . . . what do kids call it these days . . . vibes? Whatever it's called—chemistry, attraction, sparks, electricity—we can see it between y'all, and you know better than to mix business and pleasure. It never works, and things would get strange if y'all started up something and then had a falling out."

"Everything is fine between me and Elijah. We would never start something with the girls here, but I have told him I'd stick around a couple of weeks after this session. We feel that tension or whatever it is between us, too, and we'd like some time to see exactly what it is," she admitted.

Novalene smiled. "I'll make sure you have my address so you'll know where to send that bottle of bourbon."

Chapter Twenty-Two

Jayden had made her list of pros and cons and studied it the whole fifth week that she was at the camp. The biggest thing against the whole idea of moving to Alpine was that she had tenure and security with her teaching job and a three-month block of time off in the summer. What lifted her heart and put a smile on her face when she looked at her list was the fact that if she stayed at Piney Wood, she wouldn't have casework or kids and parents to deal with, and she would be doing something that she loved every day. Plus, even though it wasn't in one solid block, she would have four months off through the year. Other than cooking for Elijah and herself and helping him out some around the place, she would be free to actually write that novel she had thought about for years.

By the end of the sixth week, she still hadn't made up her mind, and the need to make a decision was weighing heavy on her heart. She shouldn't wait until the last minute to tender her resignation to her school if she was going to stay in Alpine. Telling them she wasn't coming back at least a month to six weeks before the new school year started would be the right thing to do. That Saturday afternoon, she was busy making peanut butter cookies when Tiffany came into the kitchen and taped a new picture up on the wall.

Jayden glanced at the drawing of a butterfly sitting on the top of a cupcake with pretty white clouds floating in a blue sky in the background. "Well, that's sure different from your other work."

"I'm not the same person that I was when I drew the first pictures, and, besides, we have clouds on our caps to show everyone here that we're from the Daydream Cabin." Tiffany got out a second cookie sheet for Jayden. "I need to talk," she said with bluntness.

"About?" Jayden scooped up cookie dough, rolled it into a ball, and placed it on the cookie sheet.

"I'm afraid to leave." Tiffany sighed. "We all are. It's scary going back to our old environment. What if we mess up again? Every one of us is a three-time loser, and the judge told me if I came up before her again, I'd be in juvie until I'm eighteen. At first, I thought I'd never get in trouble again. All I'd have to do is remember having to take the scrap bucket to the hogs, or shovel out the stalls, and I'd put on a halo and angel wings, but now I feel like I'll be homesick for Piney Wood."

Using a fork, Jayden began making crisscross lines on the four dozen balls of dough that were lined up on the cookie sheet. "What you'll be homesick for is the companionship you've found here. Real friends that don't demand that you bully other girls by taking ugly pictures of them or shoplift to stay in their little club or . . . what did you girls call those other ones at the fireworks show?"

"Posse." Tiffany smiled.

"That's right. You don't need a posse. Find true friends or stay in touch with the ones you've met here. Call one of us, and that includes me, if you feel like you're slipping back into your old ways. Find something to do that keeps you out of trouble. Maybe find a part-time job or volunteer at a nursing home or a hospital."

"Hey, I like that idea about working at a hospital." Tiffany stuck her hand into an oven mitt and pulled the first batch of cookies from the convection oven. "Mama wouldn't mind me doing that, but she'd probably throw a hissy fit if I went to work flipping burgers. That would ruin her image. Will you make a copy of all our phone numbers for each of us to take home so we can stay in touch?"

"I can do that if you'll be in charge of getting them all written down for me," Jayden agreed.

"Yes, ma'am." Tiffany picked up a cookie and bit off a piece. "I love these right out of the oven when they're still warm. Are you ever scared of anything?"

"Wh-what?" Jayden stammered. "Why would you ask that?"

"You took care of that spider under the bed. You weren't afraid to stand up for us and believe that we could dig a hole for Dynamite. Even when your sister was mean to you, you got up and didn't whine around for a week about it. I could go on and on," Tiffany answered.

"I'm terrified of making decisions." Jayden put the second sheet of cookies into the oversize oven. "I'm always afraid I'll make the wrong one and then regret it."

Tiffany flashed a brilliant smile. "Listen to your heart. Seems like those are the words you said once when we were having a talk during group session."

"Did I?" Jayden couldn't remember, but then she'd had a lot on her mind the past couple of weeks. To stay at Piney Wood or to go back to teaching? The decision had to be made without thinking of a relationship with Elijah.

"You might not have said it in those exact words, but that's what's been going through my mind. What if I can't trust my heart? What if it tells me wrong?" Tiffany asked.

"The heart never tells you wrong," Jayden said. "You might not want to do what it says, and you might argue with it, but when you do, that's when you're about to mess up. Think back to when you were doing those mean things. Did you feel any remorse?"

Tiffany looked sheepish. "Yes, but I wanted to be in that circle of friends, so I figured it was worth the price. That was my heart talking to me, and my own selfish pride kicked it out of the way, didn't it?"

"That's right," Jayden told her. "So, from now on, listen to your heart and kick the selfish pride out of the way."

"You are even better than my therapist back home." Tiffany picked up three cookies and headed for the door.

"Hey, that will ruin your dinner," Jayden called out.

"One for me, one for Carmella, and one for Ashlyn," Tiffany threw over her shoulder as she went outside.

What a difference seven weeks had made in all their lives, Jayden thought as she took the second pan of cookies from the oven. Not just the girls, either. Diana was excited about a new job. Novalene was really retiring from the camp, and Jayden had decided in that moment not to be afraid of change or taking a risk. While the cookies cooled, she slipped her phone from her hip pocket and called her school in Dallas.

"Listen to your heart," she muttered as she listened to the phone ring three times. "If it goes to voice mail, then it's a sign I shouldn't stay here."

She recognized the principal's voice the minute she said, "Hello, Jayden. What can I do for you today?"

Jayden inhaled deeply, let it all out, and said, "You can accept my resignation. I'll be sending it by mail tomorrow."

"I'm sorry to hear that," Melanie said. "Did you find another job?"

"Yes, but not in teaching." Jayden told her about Piney Wood Academy.

"That sounds wonderful, and you'll still be helping kids," Melanie told her. "We will sure miss you, but I understand completely and wish you the best. I appreciate you letting me know this far in advance so I can get another teacher lined up. I just got an application today from someone with your last name. Do you know a Skyler Bennett?"

"That . . . would be my sister." Jayden's thoughts went spinning out of control. Had Skyler lied to her about going to Mexico to start a fancy school with her fiancé? "When's the woman's birthday? Dallas is a huge city. There's probably a dozen or more Skyler Bennetts living in or near the place."

"April third, nineteen eighty-six," Melanie answered.

What in the world? "That's probably her, then. I can't imagine another person having the same birthday as she does." Questions still ran around Jayden's head like words on a merry-go-round.

"I told her that we only had an opening in middle school math, but I may call her back and see if she'd be more interested in high school English. Since she's your sister, what do you think she's best qualified to teach?" Melanie asked.

"I'm really not sure how to answer that question. I would think that she could do a good job in whatever she sets her mind to do, and she's been working as a counselor for the past several years," Jayden answered, even though she couldn't imagine Skyler teaching in a rundown public school instead of a prestigious private one.

"Thanks for being honest. Stop by and see me if you have time when you come back up here to move your things."

"I sure will, and you'll have my formal letter of resignation in the next few days." Jayden ended the call and plopped down in a chair. Should she call Skyler, or leave things alone? What could have happened that she would leave Glory Bound? It might be petty, but she hoped that Skyler was getting a little bit of her own medicine.

"Thought I'd run by for a pick-me-up glass of tea," Elijah said as he came through the door, hot air whooshing in behind him.

"I'm hoping that offer to stay on here as the cook still stands. I just quit my teaching job," Jayden spit out all at once before she lost her nerve.

Elijah rushed across the room, picked her up out of the chair, and twirled her around with her feet off the floor until they both started to wobble. Then he set her down and cupped her face in his hands. "Please tell me you're serious."

"Very much so. I can't stand to leave future girls in the hands of someone like those two we interviewed," she teased. "Seriously, I want to be here at the camp with you."

His lips met hers in a fiery kiss that caused the whole world to disappear, leaving only herself and Elijah in a vacuum where no one existed but the two of them. If she had a single thought that she'd made the wrong decision, that kiss and his body pressed so close to hers erased it completely.

Storm clouds brought thunder, lightning, and rain that afternoon. Any outside work came to a halt and the girls spent time in their cabins. Jayden did all the prep work for supper and then made a run for the Daydream Cabin to check on her girls.

She'd just cleared the porch when Novalene yelled over from the Moonbeam Cabin porch. "Hey, your kids are over here. I'll keep them until suppertime. Right now, they're giggling about their first days here."

"Thank you," Jayden hollered above the noise of the rain pounding the rooftops. She caught her breath, wiped the water from her face, and was about to go into the cabin when her sister's little red sports car parked so close that it almost took out the edge of the flower bed.

If the chairs hadn't been wet, Jayden would have fallen backward into one of them out of pure shock. The last person in the world that she thought she'd see that day was Skyler. A loud clap of thunder brought with it a brand-new downpour. Skyler got soaked when she got out of the car. When she tried to run around the vehicle and get in out of the rain, she slipped and fell into a mud puddle.

A giggle bubbled up from inside Jayden that she had no control over. Skyler gave her a dirty look as she fought her way to her feet and made it up the steps and onto the porch. She looked like a drowned rat that had just barely survived a hurricane. Her blonde hair hung down her back in limp strands, and her mascara made long black streaks down her face. Her cute little white shorts and tank top looked like they'd been dragged through the hog wallow.

"I need help," Skyler whined.

"I think you need to take a trip through the bathhouse," Jayden told her.

"Give me one of your old shirts. It'll be miles too big, but it will do until I can get back out to my car and get my suitcase," Skyler said.

"Why would I do that?" Jayden led the way inside and sat down on one of the sofas.

"Because . . . ," Skyler started and then stopped. "Because you'd do it for a stranger. You're that kind of person, and I need more of your help than just a shirt. I need to talk to someone, and I don't have anyone else but you."

Jayden got up, went to her bedroom, and brought back an old T-shirt and a package of wet wipes. Where was Skyler's rich fiancé? Had he figured out that he didn't want to be strapped to a self-centered woman?

"You'll need to go to the bathhouse to clean up, but I have a bottle of water right here. We keep those here in the cabin so we can keep the girls hydrated." She tossed the shirt and wipes on the sofa.

"*I know that,* you realize. These will work fine." Skyler stripped out of her shorts and shirt, kicked off her shoes, and used ten wipes to clean the mud off her arms and legs. "I've applied at your old school, but I simply *cannot* teach in a place like that," Skyler said.

No surprise there, Jayden thought. "I don't see an engagement ring. Are you and David having problems?"

"He broke up with me, and the school took him back because his grandmother is a big, big supporter, but they wouldn't give me back my job. Now my perfect wedding is ruined, and the thousand-dollar deposit I paid the wedding planner is nonrefundable."

No tears. Very little emotion. She could have been talking about what kind of toppings to order on pizza rather than the person she had planned to spend her life with.

"Why did David break up with you?" Jayden asked.

Finally clean, except for a smudge of dirt on her neck, Skyler slipped the T-shirt over her head and sat down on the other sofa. "Because he can't forgive, and he claims to be a Christian. He's not even thinking about the position he put me in. I'm scrambling to find another job before school starts. Do you know how hard it is to find just the right fit for someone like me?"

"I didn't ask you about the school administration," Jayden said. "I asked why David broke up with you."

Skyler tilted her chin up and looked down her delicate little nose at Jayden. "I don't want to talk about that."

"You're *going* to talk about it, or else I'm not listening to anything else you've got to say," Jayden told her.

"I've got an interview at a Catholic school in Brownsville tomorrow morning. I'm on my way down there now, and I'm going to give you as a reference." Skyler scowled. "I need you to back me up."

Jayden cleared her throat, tucked her chin against her chest, and looked up from under her drawn dark brows at her sister. "If I remember right from your last visit, we aren't friends or sisters. That was your choice, not mine, and you still haven't answered my question about you and David."

"I don't appreciate your snide remarks." Skyler jumped up and popped both her hands on her hips. "If you won't agree to help me, then I'll just leave."

"You've always gotten your way about everything," Jayden said. "It must be hard for you right now, but either tell me what happened or there's the door."

"He caused me to lose all my friends at Glory Bound, and he took back my ring." Skyler sniffled.

Tears wouldn't work this time on Jayden. "Keep going. You must want a reference pretty bad to come to me. Am I the last person on your list? You do know that whatever school you apply to will call Glory Bound and ask them why you weren't given your old place back, don't you?"

Skyler's chin quivered and tears rolled down her cheeks. She put her head in her hands and wept worse than she had at any one of the three funerals Jayden had attended with her. "I messed up real bad. If I have to work at a minimum wage job, I'll lose my car and have to move into a ratty apartment."

"Keep talking." Jayden felt so sorry for her that she almost went over and put an arm around her.

"Do you remember Ray Don Wilson?" Skyler raised her head, but the tears kept flowing.

"That bad boy that Mama and Daddy wouldn't let you date back in high school?" Jayden asked. "He was always into something shady or downright illegal."

"He's settled down now and is part owner of a construction company that frames out houses," Skyler defended him.

Suddenly, everything came into focus for Jayden. "You haven't been . . . you didn't . . ."

"We've been friends with benefits since our senior year in school. Every now and then we get together and spend a weekend with one another, or maybe just a couple of hours together. David and I decided not to have sex until we were married, and, well, I do have needs," she stammered. "Ray Don came over to my apartment, and dammit! David was supposed to be at a meeting with his grandmother all morning."

"Good Lord!" Jayden gasped. "He caught you cheating on him."

"We weren't married yet." Skyler's tone went back to the ice stage. "And I told him that it would be the last time."

"So, you think that it's not cheating since you weren't married? For God's sake, Skyler, own up to your mistakes. This is your fault, not David's," Jayden told her.

"Well, you should be happy," Skyler all but hissed at her. "David took back my ring and called off the wedding. Ray Don offered to marry me, but I can't be tied to a man like that."

"Why not? He's a hardworking guy, and he probably makes three times what a teacher or even a guidance counselor does, so he's got more money than David had, if that's what makes a good husband in your eyes," Jayden said.

"I don't love him," Skyler moaned.

"But you loved David?" Jayden frowned.

"No, but he would be an ideal husband. His family has money, and we were going to start our own private school, and the ring . . . Lord, that ring was beautiful," Skyler said. "Now no one at Glory Bound will even talk to me just because David couldn't keep his mouth shut."

"Grow up!" Jayden began to pace around the room. "You've been spoiled your whole life, and it's time you figure out that things aren't as important as other people's feelings and for sure aren't as important as love. I'll give you a recommendation if a private school calls me, but only because I believe you can do any job that you set your head to do. My opinion of you as a person . . . well, that's a different story."

"How can you talk to me like that when I'm scrambling just to survive?" Skyler whined. "I will probably have to borrow money from you just to get by since I spent that thousand dollars on a wedding planner."

"I'm not your bank." For the first time Jayden didn't even feel guilty about telling Skyler no.

"Why are you so mean to me?" Skyler asked.

"I will not loan you money," Jayden said. "I will give you a piece of advice. Learn to live within your means, and if you ever want to have a sister or even a relationship with me as a friend, I'll be right here. I'm not leaving at the end of next week. I'm taking the job of cook for this place and moving into Elijah's cabin. He'll be moving over to Henry and Mary's place."

"Well, well, well." Skyler's grin was downright condescending. "So, you *owe* me. I'll take that payment in cash."

"I don't think so. I came down here as a favor to you because you begged me to, so you could go to Europe, and now that I think about it, if you hadn't bought a new sports car every year since Mama died, you'd have more than enough money to go anywhere in the world," Jayden reminded her.

The door opened and all three of Jayden's girls rushed in out of the rain. They stopped dead in their tracks when they saw a strange woman sitting in their living area.

"We saw a car out front, and it looks like the one my mama drives," Tiffany said. "I thought maybe . . ." Her voice trailed off.

"This is my sister, Skyler." Jayden made introductions all around.

"So, y'all are the Daydreamers this summer! Are you ready to get back home where you can have your makeup and jewelry? I used to have little make-believe makeup parties with my girls. We'd use my makeup and have facials. Does Jayden do that with you?" Skyler came alive. All the tears dried up and her eyes sparkled.

"That would be against the rules," Tiffany said without so much as a tiny grin.

"Why did you make our Jayden cry?" Ashlyn asked.

Skyler's face turned red and she ignored the question. "I really must be going now." Skyler stood up, kicked her muddy clothes to the side, and headed for the door. "And, Jayden, thanks for the recommendation. Maybe someday I'll stop by again."

All three girls gave her the stink eye, but Skyler ignored it as she rushed out the door.

"I can't believe you were nice to her," Tiffany said and then blushed, "but then you were nice to all of us when we were hateful to you."

Jayden didn't feel like she'd been nice at all. She actually felt sorry for her older sister. The woman had some hard lessons ahead of her, and Jayden had no doubt that their paths would cross again the next time Skyler needed something. Most of the time, after Gramps died, she only came home to see Jayden and their mother when she wanted money for something, and Mama always gave it to her.

They all heard the sound of Skyler's engine starting and her vehicle driving away. "She's sure nothing like you. I'm glad we didn't get her for our counselor this year."

"Me too," Jayden said. "Because if you had, I never would have gotten to know you amazing girls, and I would have never gotten to make the decision to stay right here rather than going back to school."

The girls' whoops and hollers filled the whole cabin. When they finally settled down, Tiffany asked, "Can we tell everyone else? Does Elijah know?"

"Yes, and yes," Jayden answered. All was well in her life at the moment, and if any other problems arose, she would have Elijah to help get her through them.

Chapter Twenty-Three

*E*ach day for the next week more peace settled into Jayden's heart. By the last day in July she had already called a moving company to pack her things and bring all her belongings—and her truck—to Alpine. When Elijah flew her and the other counselors to North Texas, she would take the time to go to the school and clean out her room. Everything was planned and she was happier than she'd ever been.

Thank goodness it wasn't raining, because this was the day the girls would make their hike out to the foot of the mountain. Tomorrow, they would all be taken back to the airport, where they would depart for eight different towns or cities in the state of Texas. Jayden wouldn't think about saying goodbye. Every time she did, her eyes welled up with tears.

She vowed that she would simply dwell on today, the camping trip, and the fact that several of the girls had asked again if they could come "home" sometime during the Christmas holidays.

The siren blew that morning, but it was just to remind the girls that breakfast was ready. They didn't have to stand at attention, their toes on the edge of the sidewalk—and it would be the last time they would hear the noise. Their days of exercises every morning had ended the day before. As soon as breakfast was finished, Elijah would lead them out to the campsite that Jayden had helped him set up the day before. Bedrolls had been tossed in tents that made a circle around what would be their firepit, and everything was ready for the rest of the day and night.

The girls were too excited to eat much that morning, so Jayden made sure they had energy bars and an extra bottle of water in their backpacks before they left on the long hike out to the mountains. Novalene and Diana had gone to their cabins to get some last-minute packing done while she finished loading and starting the dishwasher.

"Hey!" Elijah poked his head in the door. "We're leaving in five minutes. The truck is loaded with the rest of the supplies. Everything is taken care of around here. Demon and Thunder have been put out to pasture for the next four weeks. Sam and Elvis have promised to keep the coyotes at bay so they don't bother our calves, and the hogs and chickens have plenty of food."

"Looks like you've got everything under control." She smiled.

He crossed the room and took her into his arms. "I'm looking forward to us having time for each other this next month," he whispered.

Like always, his warm breath sent delicious shivers down her spine. "Me too," she told him.

"See you in a couple of hours." He brushed one more kiss across her lips. "I've fallen in love with you, Jayden Bennett."

"I love you, too." She had thought that when they finally said those three magic words, there would be bells and whistles. Maybe they would say them after their first night together in bed, or the morning after. Today, there were no sparkles dancing around her, but instead a calmness in her world. What she and Elijah had, she realized, wasn't pretty fireworks that lasted only a few minutes and then faded. What they had was something that went so deep that it would last through eternity. She believed that with all her heart and soul.

She watched him all the way out the door and wondered how she'd ever gotten so lucky. If she hadn't agreed to let Skyler go to Europe, she would have spent the summer in her apartment, going about her normal routine, and would have never met her soul mate. Thank goodness she had agreed to come to Piney Wood, because now she had two new adult friends, eight little adopted sisters, and Elijah, the biggest prize of all.

She had removed her apron, hung it on a hook, and taken a few steps into the dining area when her phone rang. She saw that the call was from Skyler and almost hit the "Decline" button, but with a long sigh she answered it. "Hello from the beautiful Piney Wood Academy, where it's supposed to be hot and sunny today."

"I'd like to tell you not to be a smart-ass," Skyler said.

"So, why don't you?" Jayden asked.

"Because I didn't call to argue or to be . . . oh, hell, you told me to grow up, and I'm trying to do just that. It may be the hardest thing I've ever done," Skyler said. "I called to say that I'm sorry for everything, for being mean to you, for everything. Ray Don tells me that getting away from narcissism is like admitting you are an alcoholic. In either case, a person has to want to change before anything can get done."

"You are listening to Ray Don now?" Jayden asked.

"It's all part of that thing called growing up that you talked about. When Ray Don told me that's what I had, I argued with him and cried, but my tears didn't faze him. I went home and looked up the symptoms, and that's when your words came back to me," she said. "This thing has even more steps than alcoholism, and it's tough to change."

"Good for you for realizing you have a problem," Jayden said.

"Thank you. It'll be a long process, but Ray Don says I'm making progress already. He's my rock. I just didn't know how much until these past few weeks." She paused so long that Jayden held her phone out to be sure that she hadn't lost the connection.

"I didn't get the job at the private school or at the place where you taught, either one," Skyler finally spoke up again. "At the time, I whined to Ray Don, and he told me the same thing you did. He told me it was past time for me to grow up. I got mad and stormed out of his house. The next day, he came by with a pint of my favorite ice cream, and he gave me a 'come to Jesus' talk. He told me that you can kick any bush between here and New York City and find a dozen friends, but family can't be replaced, and that I needed to open my eyes and see what has always been right in front of me." She stopped and took another long breath. "He reminded me that I had thrown away the best sister ever, and I had taken him for granted. Then he gave me an ultimatum. Either be with him all the time right out in public, or it was over."

"Did you believe him?" Jayden asked.

"Yes, I did, and the thought of never being able to see him again terrified me. I realized right then that I'd been in love with him for sixteen years. I also know that the reason I've treated you so horrible is that I was jealous. You've always been what I wanted to be. Tall, confident, and you have such a big heart. I'm sorry about everything. If you'll let me have it, I'd like a second chance," Skyler said.

Did Novalene put liquor in Jayden's coffee that morning? Surely, she was hearing things. Skyler just paid her the first-ever compliment, and she wanted a second chance. Jayden frowned, and something the preacher had said the previous Sunday came to her mind: forgive your brother seventy times seven.

"I forgive you." Jayden realized in that moment that forgiving her sister had little to do with Skyler and everything to do with herself. Looking forward to the future depended on her letting go of the past—forgiving was part of that.

"Thank you," Skyler whimpered.

"Are you crying?" Jayden asked.

"I don't deserve to be your sister, but I'm glad you're going to let me be. I should also tell you that I'm not going to teach next year. I started to work here at Ray Don's construction company last Monday. His secretary plans to retire in a couple of years. She's training me to take her place, and . . ." Skyler hesitated.

Jayden sat down and waited.

"And what?" she finally asked.

"Ray Don has been here for me since high school. He's the one I run to for booty calls, and he's the one who offers a shoulder to cry on when I break up with a boyfriend. He held me while I cried my eyes out the night before I made the decision to take Mama off life support. The one I was always meant to be with right there before my eyes all this time, and I was too proud to see it," Skyler admitted. "The rest of the story is that we went to the courthouse yesterday and got married. I'm three months pregnant, and my baby needs her aunt Jayden to keep her feet on the ground when my DNA gets too strong."

"What does that mean?" Jayden still wasn't sure she wasn't dreaming. David would have been shocked at the surprise "preemie" born six months after the wedding. She couldn't begin to imagine Skyler pregnant or as a mother. Poor Ray Don had a hard row to hoe, as Gramps used to say.

"It means that this narcissism has been part of me my whole life. It won't go away in a day or even a few months. I pray that my child . . . our child . . . mine and Ray Don's . . . don't get our genes, like the spiteful ones or the bad boy ones we had when we were young, and that you'll be there for her like you've been for those girls at the camp," Skyler stammered through an explanation.

"What makes you think you're having a girl?" Jayden asked.

"If I don't, I'll have a boy, and he'll need his uncle Elijah and his aunt Jayden, and Ray Don will be in seventh heaven with a son." Skyler giggled.

Jayden was glad that she was sitting down. "Is the baby Ray Don's? And what makes you think he'll have an uncle Elijah?"

"Can't be anyone else's," Skyler answered. "I haven't been with anyone other than Ray Don in a year. And your eyes light up when Elijah's name is mentioned. I didn't realize it at the time, but that's the way I must look when I think about Ray Don."

"You said you didn't love him," Jayden reminded her.

"I know what I said, but I do, Jayden. I've always loved him, ever since high school. I just didn't want to admit it because he wasn't rich enough to suit me, but now I'm happy for the first time in my life. I was wondering if maybe we could come visit a little while over Christmas. Ray Don says he can take a few days off, and I'm going to work on my attitude even more," Skyler said.

"Of course, you can come visit anytime you want," Jayden answered. "I'd love to see you seven months pregnant."

"You are a much nicer person than I am, Jayden. I've always been jealous of that about you. People liked you for your personality and your sweet attitude. That was one of the things Ray Don brought to my attention. He said I should be more like you and my mother and less like my father," Skyler said. "Could I call you again next week?"

"Sure. How about we make a FaceTime date for Thursdays at seven?" Jayden would take it a week at a time, but Skyler was not going to threaten the peace and happiness she'd found in Alpine.

"Deal, and thank you, again, for being a bigger person than I am, and I'm not talking about height. See you next Thursday," Skyler said. "Have a good week."

"You too." Jayden ended the call, laid the phone down, and stared at it for a full minute. Had what just happened been real? She blinked a dozen times. She was awake. This was not a dream. Jayden would have believed that a snowstorm was hitting right there in South Texas on the last day of July before she would have ever thought she would hear kind words from her sister. Or an admission of a mistake, for that matter.

"Hey, we're ready if you are," Novalene called out from just inside the door. "Need me to help finish up with anything?"

"No, it's all under control," Jayden said. "I've just got to turn off the lights. Y'all already in the truck?"

"Hell, no!" Novalene laughed. "It's too hot to sit in that thing. We were kind of hoping you would already have it cooled down for us."

Jayden pushed her chair back, picked up her phone, and crossed the room. She switched off the lights and then followed Novalene outside to where the other two counselors were waiting beside the truck. "We'll mind the heat even more at the campsite if we all get cooled down with the truck's AC on the way out there, you know."

"Probably, but a little bit of cool might keep us from strangling one of those girls if they start whining about the heat tonight," Novalene replied. "This is my least favorite part of the whole session. A sixty-plus-year-old woman has no business sleeping on the ground."

"Or being zipped up in a bag like a burrito, after eating beans for dinner and supper," Diana added with a giggle.

"Our prissy little girls trying not to pass gas is always a hoot," Novalene said. "Let's get on out there and get this over with. I'm ready to go home and retire"—she glanced over toward Jayden—"and enjoy every drop of a bottle of good bourbon to celebrate."

"Best money I'll ever spend. I'll tell you about a phone call I just had from Skyler on the way out to the camp," Jayden said.

By the time they reached the tents, the women had fallen silent in disbelief. Finally, Novalene said, "Do you think the change will last, or is it a passing thing?"

"I know that Ray Don will probably be the best thing that ever happened to her, because he doesn't baby her. He tells her the truth, just like I did the last time she was here. Being pregnant, and then a mother, may also change her. Hopefully, we can find some common ground to build a sister relationship on," Jayden answered. "Here we are. Y'all got any last words of advice for me about this camping business?"

"Endure until the end, and then we'll all go home," Novalene said.

"Except for you," Diana said. "You are home."

"Yep, I am." Jayden nodded.

Elijah kept one eye on the path from the camp to the campsite, and his ears open to hear the first sounds of the old work truck rumbling his way. He was more excited to see the last day of a session than he'd ever been before, and that was all because Jayden had said she would be there. He would have time alone with her to explore all these new feelings he had.

"Please, God," he muttered, "let my bad luck streak be over."

"Hey, girls, we need sticks to build a fire," he yelled. "Tiffany, Bailey, Quinley, and Carmella go that way"—he pointed and then swung his finger around—"and the rest of you head out that way. We'll build a fire when you get back."

As they all headed off, he heard this distant rumble of a vehicle. He stood up and waited until Jayden parked; then he jogged over to the truck. Just seeing her throw her long legs out of the door set his pulse to racing. Tomorrow evening, he would finally have her all to himself, and he was downright antsy with anticipation.

"I was about to send up smoke signals." He dropped the tailgate down and hoisted a cooler full of steaks up on his shoulder.

"Skyler called me." Jayden slid another cooler toward the end of the truck bed and followed him over with it to the other side of the firepit. "I'll tell you about it later."

"Good or bad?" He hoped that woman hadn't upset Jayden.

"All is good," she told him.

"That's great." He stopped long enough to give her a chaste kiss on the cheek.

"PDA." Novalene pointed at them.

"Yep, and after y'all all get gone, there's going to be more of it." He grinned.

Diana brought over a paper bag filled with food. "I'm very happy for both of you."

"Thank you," Jayden said. "It's crazy how eight weeks have turned so many lives around."

"That's the gospel truth," Diana agreed. "I can't wait to get home and get on my new job. I'm so excited about it. If it hadn't been for all y'all and the long talks we've had, I would have never decided to do this."

"Wish you the best of luck, but I wouldn't mind it a bit if you sent along some suggestions for ladies to take your place for the summer session next year," Elijah told her.

"I'm already putting out feelers." Novalene set down a plastic bag of bananas. "A couple of my friends are retiring at the end of the year, and they're old dinosaurs like me who believe in discipline. They might be a good fit for this place."

"Thank you!" Elijah said. "Here come the girls with the sticks we need to build a fire."

"I thought that tow sack in the back of the truck was filled with firewood," Novalene said.

"It is," Elijah replied, "but they need to feel like they helped. Get ready to taste the best campfire beans in the whole world."

Diana pointed to a huge can of pinto beans sitting on top of one of the coolers. "You can fool all those hungry girls that walked three miles to get out here, but I see where they're coming from."

"But you don't know my extra ingredients," Elijah told her. "A little salsa, some barbecue sauce, and a touch of brown sugar and bacon. They'll be good with cowboy steak and potatoes rolled up in foil and tossed around the fire. It don't get no better than this." He slid a sly wink over toward Jayden. "Either food or company or girlfriend-wise."

"Is that right? What about when we get home tomorrow?" Jayden whispered just for his ears.

"That, darlin', is something altogether different than food," he murmured.

"What's different than food?" Tiffany asked as she dropped an armload of sticks into the firepit. "All right if I have one of those bananas? After that walk, I'm starving. Hey, Jayden, we picked wildflowers along the way and put them on Dynamite's grave. They'll be wilted in the morning, but we plan to put fresh ones on when we walk back. When we come at Christmas, we're going to bring some artificial ones. They'll last longer."

"That's great," Jayden said. "And yes, all of you can have a banana or an apple or both if you're really hungry. Dinner won't be for a couple of hours."

"You were pretty slick at avoiding that question," Elijah chuckled. He still had trouble believing that Jayden would be there with him after everyone had gone home.

They would have to make a trip up there later to move her things to Alpine, but they had a whole month to do that. He had cleared out his cabin and moved over into the house Henry and Mary had left behind, but he hoped that Jayden would just move in with him.

"Guidance counselors do have their little tricks." Jayden flashed a grin his way.

"Do tell," he flirted. "Is there more I'm going to find out after everyone is gone?"

"Patience, my darlin'," she told him with a wink. "Patience."

Elijah got a glimpse of the future in that moment. Forty years down the road, he saw himself and Jayden turning the place over to their children and retiring like Henry and Mary had done. No matter how much technology came and went, there would always be children who needed to spend eight weeks in a place like Piney Wood Academy, and the Thomas family would fill the need for them.

What makes you think any of your children will want to do this kind of work? Henry's voice was in his head so solid that he could see his uncle crossing his arms over his chest as he spoke.

We'll have enough that one of them will, Elijah answered.

I'd say that you'd better do some proposing to Jayden before you start planning forty years down the road.

Elijah smiled and muttered, "All in due time."

A four-person tent sounded pretty good until Jayden crawled inside it that night. She expected her girls to be snoring or at least sound asleep, but they were still whispering even though it was well past midnight.

"Now we can go to sleep." Ashlyn sighed.

Had they peeked through the window flap and seen Elijah give her that good-night kiss? Jayden wondered as she stretched out on top of her bedding. Even as cool as the night air was, after that long, hot kiss, there was no way she could zip herself into a down-filled sleeping bag.

"Are you going to marry Elijah?" Ashlyn asked.

"Can we come to the wedding?" Carmella asked.

Tiffany raised her hand. "Can I be a bridesmaid?"

"I have no idea if I'm going to marry Elijah," Jayden answered. "He hasn't asked me."

"When he does, can I be a bridesmaid?" Tiffany repeated her question.

"What makes you think he will?" Jayden answered her question with one of her own.

"Because he loves you, and y'all are so cute together, and he's so dreamy when he looks at you." Ashlyn sighed.

The drama of teenage girls had often irritated Jayden, but that night, it amused her. "Well, what do y'all think I should say if he ever does propose?"

"Yes!" they all said at the same time.

Jayden checked her phone. "It is now almost one o'clock. We get up at five, and y'all have to walk three miles back to camp, take a shower, and get dressed to go home. I think what we'd better all do is get some sleep."

"Going home is still scary," Tiffany said.

"Staying here is a little scary for me, too," Jayden told them. "But we are four strong women. We are the Daydream Cabin girls. Don't ever forget that."

"Yes, ma'am." Tiffany yawned.

Jayden stretched out on her back. Through the window flap she watched the clouds drift across the moon. She closed her eyes and gave thanks that she'd found Piney Wood and Elijah.

Chapter Twenty-Four

The two vans bringing the girls back to the airport parked next to the hangar. To Jayden, it seemed like they got out even slower than they had gotten into the vans eight weeks before. She looked out over the vehicles at three stretch limos, three Cadillacs, and two extra airplanes on Saturday morning, the first of August. Eight weeks before, the same vehicles had delivered the girls to Piney Wood, and now they were taking them home. The girls wore basically the same clothes that they'd arrived in, but somehow they all looked different in them that morning. They'd been given all their personal things back, but very few had put on makeup. Now they were all smiling and calm and far more interested in making sure they had the paper with everyone's phone numbers on it than anything else. Right up until their adult drivers began to stow the luggage.

Then the waterworks began.

Tiffany wrapped Jayden up in her arms and wept on her shoulder. "Thank you for not killing me that first day," she said between sobs.

"I want in on this." Ashlyn dropped her suitcase and purse on the ground and joined them.

"Me too." Carmella teared up. "I can't let y'all cry without me."

Expressions of shock spread across the faces of all the drivers and parents that morning as they waited beside whatever means of transportation they'd brought to Alpine. Jayden could understand the surprise. The counselors had witnessed the gradual growth in these kids. All these people had observed was the beginning and the end of the story. Those folks in their fancy clothes and expensive vehicles, knew nothing of the obstacles the girls had overcome during their stay at Piney Wood.

"It's time for you to go." Jayden took a step back and then gave each of her Daydream girls one last individual hug. "I can't tell you all how proud I am of you. You've got my phone number. Call me if you need anything and remember the words to 'The River.'"

"I have to try to reach my destination." Ashlyn didn't repeat the words verbatim, but Jayden got the message.

"I'm determined to sail my vessel through the rough waters," Carmella said.

"I'll choose to chance the rapids, and be my own self," Tiffany declared.

Jayden figured the girls would go straight to their own vehicles, but instead all eight of them gathered up in a huddle, not unlike a football group, whispered a few words, and then took a step back and yelled, "We love you all." Then they crawled into cars, slid into limos, or, in Ashlyn's and Tiffany's cases, went up the steps to small private planes.

The limousines were the first two vehicles to leave, and then the Cadillacs pulled out behind them to form a long parade. She closed her eyes and said a silent prayer that all the girls got home safely.

Tiffany's airplane taxied down the tarmac and was airborne just before Ashlyn's did the same. Jayden couldn't see that far, but she knew in her heart that they were waving goodbye from the skies.

Novalene pulled a small package of tissues from her purse and passed them around. "That's the best send-off we've ever had."

"It's been an extraordinary session," Elijah said as he led the way to his small plane. "You ladies sure you don't want to come back next summer?"

"Hey, we just ended on a fantastic note. We can't take a chance on ruining that." Novalene went up the stairs first.

"I can't believe they're gone. I wonder if this is the way a mother feels when her kids go off to college," Jayden said as she followed Novalene up the steps.

"This group will come back to see you," Novalene said. "The whole bunch of them really bonded with you. Someday, they might even offer to be counselors."

"Now wouldn't that be something?" Diana came in ahead of Elijah.

"Sit back and enjoy the ride. Skies are blue. No storms in sight," Elijah said as he took his seat. He taxied the plane down the runway, and only the two PWA vans were left sitting over by the hangar. If she hadn't needed to go back to Dallas and clean out her office, she wouldn't even be on the plane, but before dark, she and Elijah would be back home. She would drive one of those vans back to Piney Wood, and her new life would continue. It had actually begun eight weeks ago—she just hadn't known it at the time.

Elijah had checked the weather report twice that morning, and nothing had come up on the flight path north to Fort Worth. Once they landed, Diana called an Uber to share with Novalene. After a few more hugs and lots of promises to keep in touch, they left, leaving Elijah and Jayden alone.

"Well, what's next?" Elijah slipped an arm around her shoulders.

"I've ordered a car to take us to the school. I need to sign some papers, clean out my desk, and be sure everything is in order for the new teacher coming in to take my place. Shouldn't take more than an hour," she said. "Unless you want to see the sights of Dallas?"

"I like the view of them much better from up there in the air than on the ground." He smiled. "When you get finished with what you need to do at the school, maybe we could have our first official date, and I could take you out to dinner?"

"I'd like that," she told him. "We are talking about the noon meal, aren't we? I'd starve if we had to wait until evening."

"The noon meal is always dinner in my world. Supper is the evening meal. Think you can learn to live with that permanently?" he asked.

"Without a doubt," she answered.

Their car arrived, Jayden told the driver where to take them, and they settled into the wide back seat. Elijah put his arm around her and pulled her close to his side. "It's been years since anyone has driven me anywhere."

"Sit back and enjoy it," she said. "It'll take about forty-five minutes in this weekend traffic to get to my school."

Her phone rang, and her first thought was that one of her girls already needed her, but when she checked the ID, it was her principal.

"Hello." She put the phone on speaker.

"Hi, Jayden. This is Melanie, and I hope I haven't overstepped my boundaries, but I went ahead and packed up your room. The new guidance counselor arrived this morning, all gung ho to decorate it her way, so I just got three cardboard boxes and started shoving your things into them," she said.

"Thank you!" Jayden said. "Now all I'll have to do is pick them up. Are you going to be there the next half hour?"

"Nope," Melanie answered. "I'm on my way out. Got a last-minute meeting with a prospective science teacher, but the front door is open. The janitors are in here giving the place a good cleaning. Your boxes will be sitting beside your door."

"I'm glad you found someone so quickly," Jayden said, "and thank you again for packing up for me." She ended the call, shoved the phone into her purse, and turned to Elijah. "Think we might get our driver to go through a fast-food window for dinner? We can pick up my stuff, grab some takeout, go back to the plane, and have our first date in the hangar or on the plane. That way, we won't have to call another car."

"Another reason why I've fallen in love with you," he said.

"Because I'm a cheap date?" She laughed.

"No, because you are a planner, and you think of others all the time." He brought her knuckles to his lips and kissed each one. "And, honey, you didn't have to put the phone call on speaker."

"Yes, I did, or else I would have had to tell you what she said. Why waste what time we've got alone in this back seat repeating conversations? Except this one important conversation—I haven't told you about Skyler's last call. The short version is this." She told him all about Ray Don, the courthouse marriage, the pregnancy, and that they wanted to visit over Christmas. "You got a problem with that?"

"No, ma'am. Whatever makes you happy makes me happy. Now let's talk about us. I told you that you could have my cabin, but I would really like for you to move into the big house with me when we get back. If you're not comfortable doing that, I understand, but . . ."

She wrapped her arms around his neck and kissed him. "I thought you'd never ask. Let's get out of this big city and go home."

"Yes, ma'am." He grinned. "You've made me a very happy man, Jayden Bennett, by calling Piney Wood home. For the first time since getting out of the service, I'm at peace with the world and within my heart. It's a wonderful feeling and I have you to thank for it."

"Home isn't really a place." She laid her head on his shoulder. "It's a feeling, and as long as I'm with you, I'm home."

"We should write that down and frame it for our children to see," he told her.

"Oh, we're going to have children?" She raised her head and stared into his face.

"I thought four would be a good number," he answered.

"I always wanted six," she said. "Are we going to have these kids before or after we stand before the preacher and say our vows?"

"Are you proposing to me?" He grinned.

"Maybe." She leaned forward a few inches and kissed him on the cheek. "If I am, what would your answer be?"

"It would be 'Yes, ma'am, thank you. I love you. Just tell me where to be,'" he answered.

"Well, since I was raised not to be so brassy as to propose to a guy, you'll have to take care of that, but my answer would be 'Yes, I love you, and is Christmas too soon?'" She smiled.

"Not only do I love you, but I'm in love with you." He could see ahead forty years and the future looked beautiful.

Epilogue

December 18

*J*ayden was totally exhausted from having so much company for the past week, but she wouldn't have changed a single moment or memory for a million dollars.

All of her original girls had stayed in their old cabins for most of the week. Mary and Henry had arrived yesterday, and Novalene and Diana had flown in that morning for the weekend. Henry and Mary were going to hold down the place for Elijah and Jayden while they flew to Panama City Beach for a short three-day honeymoon after the wedding.

The girls had insisted that Jayden stay with them in Daydream Cabin the night before. After all, it was bad luck for the groom to see the bride on the day of the wedding.

The ceremony was to take place in the dining hall at two that afternoon, and the girls had done a fabulous job of decorating with poinsettias, holly, and even a few sprigs of mistletoe that they had hung from the ceiling. Jayden was helping Mary put the frosting on the three-tiered wedding cake when Tiffany got her by the hand.

"It's time for Ashlyn to do your makeup, and for us to get you ready," she said.

"Go on. These other girls can help me finish up here." Mary shooed her out of the building with a flick of her wrist.

"Come back even more beautiful," Novalene called out as the three girls ushered Jayden outside.

"We walked down to Dynamite's grave and put out poinsettias for him this morning," Carmella said. "I didn't see any bugs, but I did spot a pile of horse poop, and we all wondered where Lauren wound up. Remember how she got so mad when she stepped in it that last day she was here? We'd have googled her, but we couldn't remember her last name. I'm glad we stayed the whole time and got some help."

"Me too," Jayden said, "and before things get too crazy, let me say that I'm proud of every one of you and the way you have turned your lives around. I can see the pride you have in yourselves and that makes me happy."

"Thank you." Ashlyn dabbed her eyes. "But don't say anything else all sentimental or we'll all be crying and ruining our makeup."

"All right, changing the subject here." Tiffany opened the door and stood back to let the others go inside before her. "We're glad you saved our caps and we get to wear them to the ceremony."

"Well, I did do a little decorating on them." Jayden led them into the bedroom and pointed to their cots. The caps had been taken to the cleaners, and then she'd put a puff of illusion at the back and glittered the clouds on the front. "After all, my bridesmaids should have a little bling to go with their pretty velvet dresses."

When the girls finished with her makeup and hair and she was dressed, Jayden looked at her reflection in the floor-length mirror Mary had brought into the cabin, and gasped. "My Lord, I look . . ."

"Beautiful," Skyler said from the door.

"You made it!" Jayden squealed and hurried across the floor, then stopped dead and gasped again. "And sweet Jesus, girl. Are you having a baby or an elephant?"

"Twins," Skyler laughed. "Keeping that from you has been tough, but I wanted to surprise you. Looks like I did. Identical girls. Ray Don says he hopes they'll be more like you than me. He doesn't think he could handle three of me in the same house, but I'm a lot easier to live with now. Matter of fact, I even like the new me better."

"That's because you're happy." Jayden hugged her and then stepped back. "I felt a baby kick me."

"Which one? Harriet or Emma?" Skyler asked. "One's named for our grandmother, and one for Ray Don's granny."

"I don't know, but I'll love both of them, and"—she leaned down to whisper for Skyler's ears only—"they'll have a cousin next June."

"Does Elijah know?" Skyler asked.

"Of course, but so far, he's the only one," Jayden said.

Carmella poked her head inside the door. "Five minutes until the ceremony starts."

"I'm going to go on and get a seat," Skyler said. "I'll see you there."

"I'll be the one in the white dress, and Elijah will be the handsome one waiting for me," Jayden said.

Carmella held her head up high as she went into the building first. Ashlyn adjusted her cap just slightly and followed her inside. Tiffany handed Jayden a bouquet of poinsettias and baby's breath and gave her a peck on the cheek before she straightened her back and went inside the dining hall.

"This is it," Jayden muttered as she smoothed the front of her form-fitting white velvet dress and tightened her grip on the bouquet. She glanced over her shoulder at the Daydream Cabin, closed her eyes, and sent up a brief prayer of thanks for everything.

"Family, both biological and adopted, and friends and the man I love. Life don't get no better than this," she whispered as she opened her eyes and took her first step toward a beautiful future.

Dear Reader,

A year ago, my husband, Mr. B, our son, Lemar, and I took a road trip to Texas to research new books. This is the first of the three books that we all brainstormed and talked about. By the time we got back home, I could clearly see Piney Wood in my mind—and knew a little about Jayden and Elijah. However, it wasn't until I started writing the story that Jayden and Elijah began to confide in me about their insecurities, and I began to really get to know them. Sometimes they even popped into my dreams to tell me more of their stories. Now the story is told, the end is written, and I miss those ornery girls and the new friends I made with these characters.

As always, I have many folks to thank for helping me take this story from a rough idea to the book you are holding in your hands today. Hold your applause until the end, please, because the list is long: to my agent, Erin Niumata, and my agency, Folio Literary Management, thank you for taking a chance on a nobody author all those years ago and helping me build a career; to my Montlake editor, Alison Dasho, thank you for continuing to believe in me; to my developmental editor, Krista Stroever, bless your heart for drawing every emotion out of me and then pushing me for a little more; to all my team members at Montlake, from copyeditors and proofreaders to cover designers, know that you are appreciated and loved; to Mr. B, who is willing to do whatever is needed so I can continue to write, I love you with all my heart and soul; to my son, Lemar Brown, for all the brainstorming sessions; to all my readers and fans, y'all are the best in the whole universe, and your support means the world to me.

A very special thanks to Tiffany Samis, who won a contest and loaned me her grandparents' names for this book. I couldn't have written the book without Henry and Mary.

And now let me hear the applause all the way to Oklahoma!

As always, I hope all of you enjoy reading this story as much as I did writing it.

Until next time,
Carolyn Brown

About the Author

Photo © 2015 Charles Brown

Carolyn Brown is a *New York Times, USA Today, Publishers Weekly,* and *Wall Street Journal* bestselling author and a RITA finalist with more than one hundred published books to her name. They include women's fiction and historical, contemporary, cowboy, and country music romances. She and her husband live in the small town of Davis, Oklahoma, where everyone knows everyone else, including what they are doing and when—and they read the local newspaper on Wednesdays to see who got caught. They have three grown children and enough grandchildren and great-grandchildren to keep them young. For more information, visit www.carolynbrownbooks.com.